BLOOD
ON THE
Water

BLOOD
ON THE
Water

David Burton

By Light Unseen Media
Pepperell, Massachusetts

Blood on the Water

Original cover art, cover design and interior design by Vyrdolak, By Light Unseen Media.

This is a work of fiction. Names, characters, places and incidents are either the products of the author's imagination or are used fictitiously, and any resemblence to actual persons, living or dead, business establishments, events or locales is entirely coincidental.

Perfect Paperback Edition

ISBN-10: 1-935303-50-3
ISBN-13: 978-1-935303-50-3
LCCN: 2014947012

Published by
By Light Unseen Media
PO Box 1233
Pepperell, Massachusetts 01463-3233

Our Mission:
By Light Unseen Media presents the best of quality fiction and non-fiction on the theme of vampires and vampirism. We offer fictional works with original imagination and style, as well as non-fiction of academic calibre.

For additional information, visit:
http://bylightunseenmedia.com/

Printed in the United States of America

0 9 8 7 6 5 4 3 2 1

*As always, to Dee, who pushes
me to do better. Thanks.*

PROLOGUE

<u>*Bill Service's House*</u>

Justine Kroft sat cross-legged on the floor, staring at the naked man bound and gagged on a straight back chair in the middle of his living room. At sixty-two he kept in good shape—rode a bicycle to work when the weather turned nice, ran a couple miles once a week though he didn't like running much. He played a mean game of tennis with his wife or friends several times a month. "Mean" being the operative word as he was known to be a gracious winner, but a bad loser.

Bill Service was losing big time at the moment, and he was not happy about it.

Justine savored his anger. She almost hoped he would free himself and attack her. Clear provocation. Self-defense, she could tell herself after she sliced off his head with the slightly curved, two foot long sword resting across her knees.

Absently, she ran a finger along the smooth, razor sharp blade; thin, but with some heft to it, it was fashioned to cut through bone as well as flesh—a neck for instance. Simone carried its twin. She had given Justine the blade when they left California after the trouble there. For reasons she didn't need to explain, she thought Justine might have a use for it. Justine did.

Standing by thick carpeted steps rising to the second floor, Simone Gireaux cocked her head, listening. "Justine." A whisper barely heard by mortal ears.

Justine glanced over her shoulder. Simone shrugged. *Get on with it.*

Service knew what that slight movement meant. Yet, his redoubled efforts to free himself proved futile.

With no discernible effort, Justine rose to her feet. As she walked around him like a matador taking his time sizing up a bull, her sword tip left a thin red line around his neck. She raised his head with the blade under his chin and made him look into her eyes.

She didn't want self-defense; she wanted justice.

"Do you know who I am yet?"

Narrowed eyes studied her face.

She leaned over him. "If I remove the gag, do not cry out. Unless you want your wife to watch you die from the top of the stairs. I promise you, it is a good vantage point."

Wide eyes showed he understood very well who she was.

Justine ripped the tape off his mouth.

"You know why I'm here, don't you?"

"Yes." A slight catch revealed fear hidden under a thin veil of contempt.

"Twenty years of extra life, Mr. Service. You should thank me for that."

"You don't have the guts to do it. Your mother would have, not you."

Justine grinned. "Then I'll start small and work up." She placed the sword tip against his crotch.

He jerked his hips back against the chair.

"Like I said, start small." She lifted the sword straight up, jammed it down.

Service hissed, but refused to cry out.

Justine jabbed her blade down in quick little motions—jabjabjab. Service cried out. She clamped a hand over his mouth.

"Not something your wife, or daughter, should see, right?" She flicked his severed member off the chair. It landed with a liquid plop on the hardwood floor. "You won't need that anymore."

She yanked his head back, exposing his neck. In a barely audible whisper she asked Simone, "Do you want to feed on him?"

"He is your kill."

"I think his blood will be too bitter for me."

"Finish it then. We must go."

Justine let Service's head fall forward. A low moan escaped his lips. He struggled to hold his head up.

Avoiding the growing pool of blood, Justine stood in front of the man who had raped and murdered her mother twenty years earlier. Blade held with two hands she pressed the edge against his neck, lifting his head.

"Mr. Service." Justine made sure she held his attention. "I'm sorry." Was that a glimmer of hope in his eyes? "I'm sorry your death will not be as long and painful as I'd like it to be. If there is a Hell, I trust your torment will be appropriate."

With her eyes and mind she held his focus while pressing the blade against his flesh, one hand on the tip, one on the grip. Despite her strength she felt some resistance from the windpipe. It gave with a slight pop and a whoosh of air, cutting off his last attempt to cry out. Slowly, the blade cut through: windpipe, muscles, tendons, veins, carotid arteries, stopping against his spine.

As the blade sliced through Service's head fell forward, attempting to seal the cut. Blood sprayed to the side in unison with the last beats of his heart—PFFFT, Pfft, pfft. His body jerked once, twice, and relaxed into death.

Justine slid the sword out to the side and let the head settle back into place. She stepped back from the blood. Eyes closed, she let her sensitive ears listen to the blood drip from chair to floor like a hammer driving nails into a coffin. She smiled. Finally. Justice. Blood justice.

Silently, Simone appeared beside Justine. She gripped Justine's sword hand and raised up the bloody blade.

"You made the kill, you must taste. No matter the bitterness."

Justine eyed the blade, resisting the urge to slash the body into ribbons of flesh suitable only for rats and cockroaches. She might have done it if the man would have felt the least bit of pain she had felt at twelve as she witnessed her mother's murder and her father's slow decline to suicide. But Bill Service was past physical pain, past who knew what youthful psychic trauma, and past any ability to feel another person's emotional pain. It was done. She looked into her maker's eyes. Simone did not hold with unnecessary killing. To taste the blood was her symbolic way of acknowledging that you deliberately killed, like Native Americans who thank the rabbit or deer for providing food.

Though flush from visiting vengeance a week earlier on her daughter's killer, and now on her mother's killer, Justine was still a Young Blood. Despite Simone's casual demeanor, her 350 years of experience imbued her with an aura of strength which brooked no defiance should she choose to insist. Which she would.

Revenge is sweet, Justine told herself and ran her tongue along one side of the blade. The warm, thick liquid rolled into her mouth like a healing soup, mending, as best they could be, the years of loss. Though her head insisted it was bitter blood, her body responded with a shudder of delight. One crimson trail escaped from the corner of her generous lips.

"Is it bitter as you thought?" Simone asked, close now, eyes bright, voice soft.

"Taste for yourself."

Simone pressed closer. Her mouth captured the blood from Justine's chin, and lips, and tongue.

On the Road

On the road half an hour later, crossing the Mississippi River into Illinois, Teresa Diaz's sleepy voice came from the back seat of their full size SUV. She still carried a slight Hispanic accent from her childhood in Mexico. "What time is it?"

After a long expectant pause, Simone said from the driver's seat, "Almost midnight."

"How far to Boston?"

"About twelve hundred miles. You should sleep now."

Another long silence. "Did you…do it? *Es terminado?*"

Justine stared out the passenger seat window. "Yes."

"I will pray for him."

"Please don't. It's too late for him."

"Then I will pray for you."

"Too late for me, too."

"You're my friend. I'll pray anyway."

Justine reached her hand back through the gap between the front seats. Teresa took it.

"Thank you," Justine said. They held hands for a few minutes until Teresa drifted into sleep.

CHAPTER ONE

<u>Boston</u>

The three women cruised into Boston around eight at night under a clear, moonless sky. Justine drove, Simone navigated.

Teresa stretched in the back seat. "Are we there yet, *amigas*?"

"Boston, dead ahead," Justine said.

"No more dead because we're here, I hope."

"*Moi aussi*," Simone agreed, while perusing a city map.

"I thought you knew where we're going?"

"It has been forty years since I was last here," Simone said. "And I did not have much time to study the city then."

"Is there a crumbly arrest warrant waiting at the bottom of a drawer for you?" Teresa asked.

Simone turned a wounded expression to the back seat.

"Teresa, my mortal friend, you know I am as you say, one of the 'Good guys.' "

Teresa flashed her a scrunched up smile and patted into place her dark hair pulled back into a short chignon. "I can't believe I'm saying this, but I know you are."

Simone took Teresa's hand and held it against her thin lips.

Just for an instant, Teresa attempted to jerk her hand away from the vampire's gentle vise-like grip. "Sorry."

"I understand you still do not trust me," Simone said. "But I swear to you, Teresa, that I will never take your blood without your permission. *Ça va*?"

"I know that, too."

Simone kissed her mortal friend's hand and turned back to her map. "Exit here. Head for Cambridge."

Justine finally found a parking space a block down from Kendall Square. Only half joking Justine complained, "Couldn't we have pushed some of these cars together and made a space?"

"This is MIT. We'd return and find the vehicle in pieces," Simone said.

The three women exited and stretched in the glow of a streetlight.

Teresa twisted her solid mortal body. "Couldn't you have turned into bats and flown here while I flew first class?"

A rare chuckle came from Justine. "I wish." She rubbed Teresa's shoulders.

"Oh, that feels so good. I take back everything bad I ever said about your change."

"I hope you never have to take back your take back." Justine kissed her friend on the cheek and turned to Simone. Expression serious, she said, "Lead on."

Trees lined the street. Ivy covered much of the two and three story brick student apartment buildings. Justine and Simone wore long coats, loose trousers, and boots. With dark caps pulled low, one didn't need to know what they were to know they were dangerous. Teresa, the taller of the three, carried a few extra pounds. In sneakers and jeans, hands jammed into the pocket of a worn Cargill coat, she might be described as intimidating, but nothing more.

More than one person negotiating the nighttime streets glanced over their shoulders as the three strode down the sidewalk.

All four corners of the intersection consisted of small store fronts—Laundromat, 7-11, used records and CDs, printing, hole-in-the-wall restaurants. Around the corner, across the street was Kazza's Psychic Store.

Crossing the street, Simone whispered to the others, "Kazza is a friend. Her brother, Treen, and I did not part on good terms." She caught Justine's eye. "He has a temper." Justine nodded, and made sure the short sword hidden by her coat was loose in its scabbard. To Teresa, "It might be dang—."

"It's my daughter we're looking for. I'm going in." She squared her shoulders. "I won't stake anybody without your permission."

Simone shook her head, reaching for the door. "Stay alert."

Kazza's Psychic Store

Inside, they surveyed the narrow store. Glass cases filled with crystal balls, crystals, Tarot cards, ornate herb boxes and other psychic paraphernalia lined the right side. On the left, tables carried candles, incense and aromatic oils. Books lined the walls – New Age up front, running back to subjects closer to witchcraft, sorcery, vampires and other unsavory creatures. A counter with a well-worn wooden gate stretched across the back.

Spreading out, they approached the counter and waited.

Teresa looked around, searching. "I feel something. Like electricity in the air."

"Magic," Simone said. "No shoplifters here."

"Oh Dios. Brujeria? For real?"

Simone shrugged. *Yes.*

"Simone! You have returned." A chunky woman around forty trailing a voluminous tie-dyed gown with sewed on mystical signs burst through a door in the back. At a nod of her head the gate swung open as she came through, arms held wide for Simone. They embraced, kissing both cheeks. "Now you must go away."

"Treen? I told no one I was coming."

"Of course Treen. He felt you the minute you stepped out of your car. He will come for you."

Justine's hand went to the hilt of her sword. The woman arched an eyebrow.

Simone grinned. "Not yet, Justine. Only if he kills me." Justine removed her hand, but didn't relax. "Kazza, this is Justine Kroft."

Kazza held Justine's hand with both of hers while studying her up and down. Justine tried to avoid the woman's gaze, but couldn't turn away.

"You must be a special woman, Justine. Simone makes few Young Bloods." Over her shoulder she asked Simone, "I heard that the Master of the Sinakovs was destroyed. You?"

"Justine."

"See, special already."

Kazza turned to Teresa. "A mortal?"

"This is Teresa Diaz. Her daughter Antonia was taken by the Sinakov Family. We are in search of her."

Gripping both of Teresa's hands, Kazza stared deep into her dark eyes. Into her soul, Teresa thought, squirming under the scrutiny, feeling warm tendrils rummage about her brain and body. With a gasp Kazza stepped back, though she kept hold of Teresa's hand. "Simone, did you know?"

"I thought, maybe."

"Yes, how could you not? Does she suspect?"

"No."

Teresa looked from one to the other. "Suspect what?"

"You are hurting inside. Not only for your daughter. You have given up much to search for her."

"That doesn't matter." Teresa leaned forward, grasping Kazza's hands. "Do you know something? Is she alive?"

"Ah, yes, that would be helpful to know, wouldn't it?"

Kazza held still but for her head swinging with a slow bobbing motion. "I believe her body is alive."

"Her body? Is she...?"

"A vampire? I don't think so. She may be far away, or surrounded by...others."

"Where is she?"

"That I cannot tell you, dearie. But I might know where to find the one person who can. Which is why you are here, is it not?"

A door bell jangled annoyingly as the front door banged open. A tall man, slim, with fly-away dark hair, wearing sneakers, loose trousers tight at the ankles and a knee-length coat, stood framed in the door, looking like an escapee from a romance novel cover. Taking on a full swashbuckler stance, he proclaimed, "Simone. I knew you would come back."

In an instant he stood in front of her, sword point against her neck. In the next instant Justine pressed her blade against his neck.

"Treen, you have been thinking of me," Simone said.

"Oh yes, I have. Thinking I will kill you for what you did to me."

"So, I should have let her die?"

"No!" Treen tensed, ready to thrust the blade through her neck. "You should have died."

"Step back." Justine hissed, voice as sharp as her blade. "No one dies here tonight."

"Don't be so sure, Young Blood." Treen's sword flashed down, swung behind his left side and up, flicking Justine's sword away from his neck.

Simone's boot against his chest propelled him back. He somersaulted backward, landing on his feet.

Simone went after him. In seconds the clang of swords filled the small space as they fought around the tables.

"Don't you break anything," Kazza shouted at them. "Or you are both out of here." She gently restrained Justine from interfering. "Let them go. They've been waiting forty years for this."

"Will he really try and kill her?"

"Nah. He still loves her."

Teresa returned a round, sharpened stake to the three stake holster on her belt. "I've seen too many times when that didn't make any difference."

Kazza shrugged, accepting the point.

Leaning on the counter while Simone and Treen worked out their differences with swords and feet, slamming against bookshelves, rolling on the floor, Justine asked Kazza, "So what is it between them? She mentioned letting someone die."

Kazza winced as Simone snatched a figurine inches before it shattered. "Same old story," she said. "Girl meets boy. He thinks he's too cool for her and meets a mortal girl. First girl gets hurt. There's some trouble and she saves mortal girl's life, but reveals what boy is. Mortal girl freaks and leaves boy. Boy blames girl. Girl leaves town. Now girl has returned with a Young Blood and a mortal searching for a missing girl, and boy and girl are having the fight they should have had then."

"How long can they keep that up?" Teresa asked.

"To long." Kazza cringed as a delicate candle holder almost hit the floor. "Give them another ten minutes. Meanwhile, I don't have to be a psychic to know why you're here. I don't have the power to locate your daughter, but there is one who can, and you'll want to know where she is."

Without a word, Kazza passed through the gate and the back door. Justine heard the bolt shoot home.

"I used to have energy like that," Teresa said.

"Yeah, when we were six."

"That Kazza said Simone was here forty years ago. But she doesn't look much over thirty. Is she one of you?"

"No. I don't know what the hell she is. Something different."

"*Maravilloso.* I am still not accepting that vampires exist."

"Me either."

"What did she mean, 'Does she suspect?'"

"I haven't a clue. Maybe you're a werewolf."

"Aren't werewolves and vampires enemies?"

"Depends on which movie you watch."

Shoulder to shoulder they watched the two combatants for a few more minutes. Then, sword points at each other's throats, it was over. Neither would be the first to remove a sword, so Justine and Teresa pulled the blades away simultaneously.

"Are you going to kiss and be nice, now?" Justine asked.

"*Mais, oui.*" Simone held Treen's narrow face and planted a kiss on him to last another forty years.

With a quick shake to clear his head, Treen looked about. "Where is Kazza?"

"She's in back, locating somebody who can locate Antonia," Justine said.

"Antonia?"

"Teresa's daughter. The Sinakov Family took her."

"Ah. So she is not foo—?"

Justine's hand went to her sword. "As cliché as it sounds, don't even think about it."

Treen bowed an apology. "In that case, there is nourishment and," a nod to Teresa, "refreshments upstairs. Kazza may be some time doing whatever she does behind that door. Shall we?"

✎ ✎

A half hour later, ensconced in comfortable chairs, Treen finished telling an amusing story from the Civil War about how he and another Young Blood had become sick from the overabundance of blood after a major battle. Even Teresa laughed.

Kazza appeared at the top of the stairs and surveyed the group. "Been a long time since I heard laughter up here."

"Come, join us then." Simone patted the seat next to her. "And tell us where to find Grace."

"It cannot be spoken aloud."

Breaking an expectant pause, Justine said, "Can you write it down?"

Kazza added a smile to her you-know-it's-not-that-easy look. "Grace is a powerful witch with powerful enemies. Writing or speaking, it is too easy for her location to be discovered by the wrong people."

"If you ask her, I am not the wrong people," Simone said.

"No, you are not, but even the speaking or writing of the location has a very strong warding spell."

Justine asked, "What happens if you write or say it?"

Kazza shrugged. Fingers spread, her hands flew apart. "Puff?"

"Puff what? Puff who?"

"The speaker or writer."

"Even you?"

"I am not immune to her magic."

"So are you coming with us, then?"

"No need." Gaze focused on Teresa, Kazza said, "When the time comes, you'll know where to go."

"Why are you looking at me like that? Does this have anything to do with what I don't suspect?"

Kazza knelt before Teresa and took her hands. Smiling sympathetically, she said, "You have the power of magic in you. You are a *bruja*."

"Oh estupendo."

A bit later over mugs of warm blood for the vamps and hot chocolate for the others, Kazza asked Justine, "I understand why Teresa is searching for her daughter. Why are you?"

Justine stared into her mug of blood. "My daughter Brittany was murdered. I can never have her back. Antonia, Teresa's daughter, is still alive. She's my friend and I want to help her regain what I've lost."

"And revenge has nothing to do with it?"

Justine glanced at Teresa. Her lips formed a fragile smile. "That too."

Kazza's gaze locked on Justine. "And?"

"Don't you know all this already?"

"Vampires are hard to read." Her full lips curled up at the corners, but her gaze never wavered. "Not enough blood in the brain maybe."

Justine stared through the small panes of the window, not seeing the neon of a video rental store, but the past.

"When my daughter was killed, I died, too. Grief and rage consumed me; I didn't care what would happen afterward if I survived." She sighed deeply, dropping her gaze to the floor. "I couldn't save my Brittany, but now I have to help Teresa save her Antonia."

Kazza sat back and sipped her hot chocolate. "And the mortal? A detective? Harry, I think."

Justine's eyes widened. "I thought vampires were hard to read."

"Not when there's strong feelings attached."

Teresa caught her eye and nodded for her friend to continue.

A tiny smile made a brief appearance. "Detective Harry Frazer, San Diego Sheriff's Department. He helped me...us. He was injured, but in any case it was best he didn't come with us. He's too good and honest a man to look past anything we might have to do."

Expression straight as it was possible for him to keep it, Treen said, "Not to mention long days and nights on the road with three women would make him crazy as some vampires I know."

Simone flashed him an aren't-you-a-smartass smile.

Mood lightened, Treen asked, "And you, Simone. Helping a mortal and a Young Blood?"

Simone pressed her lips into a small moue. She glanced at Justine and Teresa. "They are *my* Young Blood and Mortal. I am only 'tagging along' as you say, to keep them out of trouble."

"You gave up much to 'tag along.' "

Simone flicked that idea away. "With the Sinakov Family *en desordre*, it is a good time to be out of town."

"As I recall, you also lost a child to vamps."

Simone locked eyes with Justine. *"Oui, c'est vrai."*

❧ ❧

An hour later Justine drove while Teresa navigated.

They headed north on Broadway in Chelsea, the direction Teresa, for no good reason, felt they should go. With no warning, Teresa screamed and grabbed her head. She rocked forward and back, body vibrating as if electrified. "Who, who, who. No, no, no, no. Nooooooo."

From the back seat Simone held her. "What's happening? Teresa, tell us."

Teresa jerked against Simone's hands. "Go back. Kazza. Trouble. Go back. Go back. Treen. *Dios. Dios.*" She slumped back. Her hands dropped to her lap. Sweat glistened on her brow. "It is too late, but go back."

Justine made a screeching u-turn and raced back toward Cambridge through light midnight traffic. All the way Teresa held herself tight and shivered. All she'd say was, *"Agusto."*

Justine screeched to a stop by a hydrant two stores past Kazza's Psychic Shop. On full alert, swords drawn and held down tight against legs, pistols on their hips, Justine and Simone pushed open the unlocked front door and stepped inside.

The store had a different feel to it, one of violence and death. Fresh blood scent filled the space like a thick mist. At the bottom of the stairs Treen lay slumped against the wall – bloody sword in hand, head three feet away, wide-open eyes staring dully at the beamed ceiling.

Simone made a small noise and dropped to her knees. Her fingers trembled as she closed his eyes.

"I'm sorry," Justine said from atop the stairs. "At least he took some with him."

One headless body sprawled midway up the steps. On the landing, another knelt in a darkening crimson pool, headless shoulders slumped, arms hanging slack. Justine inspected the shambles of the apartment, found more red smears and spatters, and broken furniture. "Kazza." She expected no answer and got none.

"Kazza is gone, isn't she?" Teresa said.

"Yeah."

"Vampires?"

"Yeah."

"Because of us?"

"Maybe," Simone said from the door. "The witch...Grace, has enemies. If they heard that Kazza knew how to find her..."

"They'd take her and make her tell them."

"*Mas, Dios*? A real witch? *Una bruja*?"

"Like you, apparently." Justine gripped Teresa's shoulder. "This is all new to me, too."

Simone slid her sword into its scabbard with a sharp snap. She stood in front of Teresa. "You obviously have a connection with Kazza. Can you locate her, hear her thoughts, see what she sees?"

Teresa inhaled a deep breath, let it out. "I don't know what I can do. I can try."

Justine righted a heavy wooden chair for Teresa. She sat and closed her eyes.

Except for Teresa's breathing the room was silent to the vampires. Justine leaned against the wall next to the kitchen door, waiting.

Tic.

Justine jerked away from the wall, cocked her head and listened. Instantly alert, hand on sword, Simone watched.

Silence.

Creak.

Simone joined her. Together they moved silently into the kitchen. They stepped over a leg severed above the knee. Listened. Sniffed. Simone pointed to a tall cupboard. A drop of blood leaked from one of the bottom doors and plopped softly on the wood plank floor.

Together, they yanked open the doors.

He had crammed himself into the bottom space. With one good hand he held the two parts of his severed forearm together against his chest. His severed leg seeped black blood. Dark eyes flicked from one vamp to the other; wary, uncertain.

Justine tapped his head with her sword tip and inclined her head toward the severed leg on the floor. "That your leg?"

"Yeah."

"Where's Kazza?"

"Who took her?" Simone demanded.

"And why?" Justine ticked his cut arm.

"You know I can't tell you that."

"You know how long it will take to reattach that leg? If you survive that long."

"Your friends left you here. You should show them the same loyalty."

"Tell us where she is, you can have your leg back."

"Why should I trust you?"

Justine grabbed his jacket and threw him sprawling on the floor. "Because if you don't tell, your head joins your leg. Simple."

Simone rested the edge of her blade on his neck.

A thump sounded in the living room. Justine rushed out.

The wounded vampire lay still on the floor. He appeared to take a breath, though he didn't need to breathe. "A house in Waltham. Summit Street. 56."

In the other room, Teresa had dropped to her knees. She held her head and nodded as if in pain. "*Si, si, si,*" she whispered through clenched teeth.

"Teresa, what is it?" Justine wrapped an arm around her shoulders. "Kazza?"

Big breaths. "Yes. A room, big warehouse by the docks. Filled with wooden crates."

"Do you know where? A street? A number?"

"Water. B Street?" She cried out and slumped into Justine's arms, gasping for breath. "Hurts."

Simone stood over them. "He told me where she is."

"Teresa connected with Kazza. A warehouse by the docks. B Street."

"That is opposite of where he told me."

"Great. Who do we trust?"

Simone, recognizing the rhetorical nature of the question, said, "Take Teresa downstairs. I'll be there in a minute."

"Right. The bodies?"

"There's a door to the roof on the landing. By ten o'clock they will be dust."

Justine helped Teresa to her feet while Simone drew her sword and, lips set in a grim frown, returned to the kitchen.

CHAPTER TWO

Boston Streets

"How will we find her?" Teresa asked. She had recovered her composure, but her face still occasionally wrinkled with confusion.

Driving, Justine said over her shoulder, "That's why you travel with vampires, for our superior senses, of smell for instance."

"You are full of yourself for a Young Blood," Teresa said.

"I have a good teacher, or maker, or whatever." Justine glanced at Simone who stared out the window instead of at the map on her lap. Though no tears stained her cheeks, a tight lipped frown and narrowed eyes were enough to show her thoughts were about Treen. Justine squeezed her arm sympathetically.

Simone's shoulders rose and fell with a silent sigh. "Stay left ahead. Windows down."

A few delivery trucks rumbling and spewing exhaust were the only traffic at one in the morning. Justine turned off of Dry Dock Avenue then cruised past a 700 foot concrete lined depression, an empty ship's dry dock. The aroma of saltwater hung thick in the cool night air, occasionally interrupted by the rank odor of a sour dumpster.

Justine drove slowly while she and Simone focused their sense of smell on detecting any trace of Kazza's scent. Teresa studied each building, large or small, warehouse or business, for movement or a shadow or anything out of place.

At the inland end, B Street curved right around the dry dock and continued straight back toward the water. They noticed nothing unusual along the row of relatively well maintained warehouses until a hundred yards before B Street turned into Canal Street. Justine stopped the SUV. They checked the wind direction. An abandoned warehouse hulked ahead.

"That building," Justine said.

"A bit cliché, but yes," Simone agreed. "Drive past. Next street up, we park."

Through a chain link gate they could see inside the building through tall, open rolling doors. With their superior eyesight they scanned the big empty space, stripped of all equipment, the only feature a rough, flat-roofed, plywood enclosure constructed against the far end with a single light over the door. Kazza's scent stayed strong.

With the SUV parked so the driver could watch the building, Justine and Simone geared up. They both wore short, slim bladed swords strapped to their backs under jackets, a .45 semi-auto on their hips, and a longer blade slung from the belt.

Simone handed Teresa a sawed-off shotgun and a pistol. "If you are attacked, shoot first and do not worry about the questions. *Ça va?*"

"I don't like it, but I get it."

"Self-defense, Teresa. Antonia will need her mother when we find her."

"I can live with that."

"That is the idea. *Vigilance, mon ami.*"

"You too."

Justine and Simone crossed the road and easily slipped over the fence. They waited a minute, senses wide open, searching for hidden sentries. None detected, they ran across an open paved area careful to avoid rusty metal, rotting wood, and concrete debris to the big sliding doors, the only way in.

A high catwalk ran along the far side of the interior with metal steps dropping down in front of a flat-topped, utilitarian building about fifty feet long. No light showed through the one window next to the only door.

On full alert, they moved silently along the wall under the catwalk up to the building. A crudely painted sign over the door said Office. Kazza's odor remained strong. They crept to the door and tried the knob. It was not locked. Still hanging on to the habit of breathing, Justine sucked in a deep breath and opened the door.

SUV

Teresa tried to relax in the driver's seat. She'd done her time in the seat on their trip from Oceanside, California to St. Louis.

She didn't want to think about what happened in St. Louis, but she did. Of course she did. When Justine began her quest to avenge

Brittany's murder Teresa told her friend that she would help her, but would not kill for her. That guy in St. Louis—she didn't want to even think his name lest he become real—probably deserved whatever might have happened to him. Teresa made the sign of the cross, a habit she was quickly losing, along with her faith in its meaning. Neither Justine nor Simone said what happened, and she did not ask. Plausible deniability—she could live with that. What was done was done. Justine had given up her life to seek justice for Brittany, Teresa could overlook something that may or may not have happened.

They'd traveled mostly at night, but there had been plenty of daylight driving with Justine and Simone under blankets in the back. Teresa's sleep cycle had been completely screwed up. Fortunately, now she was awake and alert, helped by a background hum, like listening to an empty telephone line—the connection she felt to Kazza's soul or chi or, as she didn't want to think of it, magic.

With the shotgun beside her, the pistol tucked between the door and the seat, and cell phone in her hand, Teresa nervously watched Justine and Simone make their way into the abandoned factory. Deep down she knew vampires were both impossible and an abomination. But, having recently lapsed somewhat from her forty years of traditional Catholic upbringing, she looked with awe, and occasional envy, at the attributes of vampires. She hated to admit it, but she felt safe with them. As a mere human without them close to her, she felt exposed and vulnerable sitting alone in the vehicle—shotgun, pistol and wooden stakes on her belt notwithstanding.

Once her two partners faded into the building, Teresa scanned the vicinity. Across the street, a vast area of darkness—water. Behind, streetlights, closed up businesses and newer warehouses. Ahead, a few Quonset huts in an otherwise empty lot. An inoperative streetlight occupied the far corner.

As she studied the huts and her eyes grew accustomed to the dark, the rear end of a black van hidden by the closest hut revealed itself. Teresa's brow wrinkled. The huts were old; weeds grew around them through cracks in the asphalt. The van was new.

She didn't notice the tiny spot of light until it blinked. Once noticed, it drew her attention. It blinked again, this time a slow blink from left to right. Almost as if someone had walked past it. Again the blink. And a change in the background hum in her head. *Fear, a warning, anger.*

At the far end of the nearest hut, movement—dark figures in darkness. Teresa opened the glove compartment door, wincing at the interior light, and drew out a pair of binoculars. Slumped in the seat, moving slowly—an unwanted idea had occurred to her—she scanned the area with the glasses. Her heart picked up its pace even as she held her breath.

Vampires! She'd recognize that flowing arrogant movement anywhere. She'd lived with it for weeks. The figures vanished, then reappeared on the other side of the hut. Four of them. One had the chin up, shoulders back swagger of a Master—the other three, his minions.

Teresa punched keys on her cell phone. *"I'm here!"* appeared in her head. She had no doubt it came from Kazza in the hut. *"One guard."*

"What?" Justine's voice low, guarded.

"The factory is a trap. Kazza is in the hut across the street. Four vamps are coming for you."

"We figured out the trap part. Can you get Kazza?"

"There's one guard. I will get her."

Metal weapons clashed in the background. "Good. Gotta go."

Teresa didn't allow herself time to think. She downed a slug of water, gathered up her weapons and gently exited the vehicle. The end of the chain link fence surrounding the lot left an eighteen inch wide gap to the building. Sucking in her stomach and chest—she was a "big-boned" woman with the figure to match—she slipped through and circled around to approach the hut from the rear.

Justine had told Teresa that if it was quiet enough, she could indeed hear a heart beating. Teresa had killed a vampire before, but that was a spur of the moment action to save Harry. Now, she was purposely, and she hoped not foolishly, putting herself in harm's way. No thoughts, memories or prayers, if she had still believed in their power, would prevent her heart from announcing her approach like a wild bass drum. So, heart thumping, armpits slick with nervous sweat, she crouched and peered through a one inch hole left by a long removed pipe.

What she saw took her breath away, like a punch to the stomach.

Warehouse

Empty!

The only illumination came from a bare bulb over the door. Their heightened vision saw that, except for a long slanted table covered with old blueprints, rat turds and dust, the only interesting thing inside was a metal folding chair surrounded by blood.

Simone sniffed the blood. "Kazza." She looked close at an object on the chair. *"Merde."* She picked it up, smelled it, set the severed finger down. "Kazza's."

"Too late," Justine said. Her eyes found Simone's. "Nobody here." She nodded toward the door and looked up.

Simone nodded. Loosening her gun in its holster, she moved to the door.

Justine peered out the window. She motioned for Simone to exit.

Simone stepped out and stopped at the bottom of the steps to the catwalk. She surveyed the empty building, while tapping her sword blade impatiently against her leg.

Less than thirty seconds passed before the young and impatient vampire crouching on the roof jumped.

Justine, waiting just inside the door, leaped to intercept him. Her timing was off a half second. His feet slammed Simone to the pavement as Justine hit him. They all tumbled to the floor. Justine rolled to her feet and she and the jumper went at it with flashing swords.

Simone took a few moments to rise up, as if her knees hurt. Before she could aid Justine a gunshot reverberated inside the larger empty building. Simone's leg kicked out and with a quick yelp of pain she went down again.

For a split second, the gunshot distracted the jumper. With one hand Justine grabbed his jacket and spun him around as a shield. With the other, she flung her sword at the new attacker, a stoutly built man about fifty when changed. Her blade glanced off his ribs. Though not a killing blow, it slowed him long enough for Justine to slam the jumper down next to Simone and rush to the new vamp. She jinked right to dodge a bullet then left to crash into him. Their collision drove him against a support column. With no hesitation Justine jammed her gun under his chin and pulled the trigger. She dropped the body and spun around.

With barely a glance at the first vamp and his now severed head, she helped Simone to her feet. "Do you want me to carry you?"

"I have been carrying myself for three hundred and fifty years, Young Blood. I can make it to the door." Nevertheless, she didn't pull away when Justine took her arm.

Justine's cell phone vibrated. "What?" Justine kept her voice guarded as she scanned for more surprises.

"The factory is a trap. Kazza is in the hut across the street. Four vamps are coming for you."

"We figured out the trap part. Can you get Kazza?"

Four vampires rushed out of the gloom.

"There's one guard. I'll get her."

The lead attacker clashed swords with Justine.

"Good. Gotta go."

Quonset Hut

Almost unrecognizable under the blood staining her face and neck, Kazza slumped in a wooden armchair in the middle of the otherwise bare hut. Blood dripped from the stub of a pinky finger. Alive or dead, it was impossible to tell.

A young vampire with short spiked hair and fingernails filed to points nudged Kazza's foot with a scuffed, steel-toed boot. He held a small cleaver by his leg.

Kazza started, glared at him through swollen eyes, managed a feeble attempt to spit at him, then dropped her head.

Mouth distended, fangs fully extended, Spiked Hair yanked her head back and licked blood from her cheek. "Tell me where that witch bitch is. I'll let you go. This will all be over and you can go back to your crystal ball and Ouija board. If you don't tell me," he caressed her neck with the cleaver's edge, "there will be nothing left of you." Then he ran his tongue across her lips, slurping blood.

Teresa saw her lips move, but could not hear what she said.

The vamp did. "Stupid bitch." He slapped her with the cleaver's flat face.

Fucking vampires, Teresa thought, then didn't think. Just acted.

She jammed the shotgun barrel into the hole, made sure it wasn't pointed at Kazza, and beat on the hut side. Through an open sliver of the hole she watched the curious vamp approach, blocking the light.

Boom! She yanked the barrel out and ran to the door, wrenched it open and charged in. She expected to see the young vampire writhing on the floor. He wasn't. He was nowhere. Only a splotch of blood marked the floor.

Teresa walked around Kazza, searching the shadows. "Where is he?" she asked, not expecting to hear an answer over the rush of blood in her ears.

"Up."

"Up?" Trembling, chest constricted, shoulders hunched, she whirled about in near panic. "Where?"

There! In the air. He slammed into her and slid off as they hit the floor. Filed fingernails ripped three gashes in her side. His outstretched hand landed inches from Kazza's foot. Kazza lifted her foot and stomped on his hand. This delayed him long enough for Teresa to roll, aim and shoot. With half his head gone, the vamp shuddered then lay still, out of it.

Teresa breathed deeply to catch her breath, then rolled onto her knees and puked. Unsteady on her feet, she stumbled to Kazza and cut her loose. "Can you walk? Never mind." She bound the mutilated hand with the dead vamp's shirt, then picked Kazza up. "Ahh. Fucking vampires." Her side burned like hell.

At the fence Teresa propped Kazza against the wall. "You have to stand up while I pull you through. Okay?" The wounded woman may or may not have nodded. Teresa slipped through then reached back and dragged Kazza after her.

Her nurse's instinct dictated that she tend Kazza's wounds. A quick inspection revealed that besides the missing finger, she'd been slashed, sliced and burned over her head and body. Fang marks showed on both sides of her neck. Her pulse was weak and erratic.

"We'll get you to a hospital as soon as Justine and Simone return."

"No."

Gunshots from the factory interrupted Teresa's reply.

"Shit." Teresa stared at the woman slowly bleeding to death in front of her, then at the factory. "Shit." Decision made, she strapped Kazza into the backseat. "I don't suppose you can tell me if any of us will be alive in five minutes?"

Putting aside any attempt at stealth, Teresa hit the gas and raced toward the factory gate.

Warehouse

Simone ignored the pain in her leg. No matter how careful a vampire was over a span of centuries, unless she spent all that time in a coffin six feet under, she was going to get hurt. Of necessity, Simone had not been careful and had not spent any time in a coffin, so she had learned about pain and how to use it.

Pain did not slow her down. The bullet had damaged her knee. Until it had time to heal, a half hour at least, she was at a disadvantage. *Turn the pain to power,* a soldier she had met soon after accidentally being turned into a vampire had told her.

Some years after they met in 1648, she and the soldier, Etienne, were on a mission for the King's Investigator when a man who did not want to be found shot Etienne. In great pain, shot in the leg with a musket ball that broke his leg, he used the power of pain to fight on and save them both.

Seeing her limp, a second vamp with broad shoulders and a shaved and tattooed head ran full speed at her. Simone sidestepped and swung at him as he passed. Missed. Shaved Head ran up the office wall, pushed off and came back swinging. He may have been impetuous, but he was no Young Blood. All the attackers were experienced. She could smell it on them, not the sharp acrid perfume of fresh blood, but the slight musty fragrance of just turned earth.

They fought, blades flashing in the dim glow of the office door. A third attacker, a grin on her gaunt forty-year-old face, circled, waiting.

Tito, the leader, six foot, broad shouldered, craggy faced from smallpox, watched them all with ice blue eyes. He would reserve his grin for when the two bitch vamps were dead or strapped helpless to a table. Preferably the latter.

Simone's opponent forced her toward Tito. She caught a whiff of his singular scent, two hundred years of musk, with an edge of disease and decay. Unpleasant, and somehow familiar. Shaved Head took advantage of her distraction, and struck for the neck. Too experienced to allow that, Simone ducked, spun around, swung up to slice his sword arm off, and back to sever his head.

"You old bitch!" the female vamp screamed. She rushed Simone. Simone hopped sideways, sticking out one foot that tripped the female and sent her sprawling.

Simone ran to Justine and stood beside her. Number One, an excellent swordsman, gave no ground against the two of them.

"We must leave now," Simone said.

"No shit," Justine said. "Tell him."

"You tell him. Now."

It was a bit unfair what they did next, but then four against two was also unfair. Simone moved left while Justine moved right until they had One in between and at a definite disadvantage. Simultaneously they impaled him from front and back, their swords snicking together as they protruded from opposite sides.

Number One coughed and clutched at his chest. Surprised, but not dead, his young face registered the unexpected pain, and perhaps for the first time in decades, fear.

His pain and disbelief did not last long. Blades quickly withdrew, swung about and, striking from opposite sides, decapitated him twice in an instant.

Tito roared. One moment an observer from the periphery, the next a furious dervish attacking with no mercy. His long blade flickered in the single light of the cavernous building. Overwhelmed, Justine and Simone gave way, backing toward the office building wall, suddenly fearful for their existence.

"Time to run?" Justine asked.

Simone's arm grew heavy. A vampire's energy was not inexhaustible. What must Justine's arms feel like? "Yes."

A loud snap-crash came from outside. Lights flashed. A horn blared. Their SUV blasted through the big doors, the engine wound up as the charging vehicle wove through the building's support columns.

Taken by surprise—as were Justine and Simone—Tito ceased his relentless onslaught. Without hesitation, the two women sprinted toward their ride.

Tito didn't chase them. He reared back and flung the sword with all his considerable strength and accuracy at Justine. With Tito's sword embedded in her back, Justine sprawled on the concrete floor, slamming against a column where she lay still.

Tito moved toward her.

Simone skidded to a stop and turned to confront him.

How cliché smashing through a locked chain link gate was didn't enter Teresa's thoughts until after she did it. She'd always thought it was fake when she saw it on TV. *Just like on TV,* she thought. Then she had other things to think about. She accelerated into the cavernous building with no idea what she'd find.

Headlights immediately picked out Justine and Simone battling the one she'd IDed as the obvious leader.

Teresa spied Justine falling. She headed for her friend, who was obviously in trouble.

The female vamp, jaws and fangs extended, eyes bulging with blood lust, intercepted the vehicle as Teresa wheeled toward Justine. She lunged through the open window and reached for Teresa's neck. Teresa, her own blood lust up, jammed the shotgun into the vamp's toothy mouth and yanked the trigger. Despite the back of her head being splattered across the concrete floor, she maintained her grip on the open window. Teresa swerved close to a column, neatly scraping off the dead-for-real vampire.

Teresa spared her an instant for regret and sympathy—*She was already dead. She was already dead*—and drove on.

Ahead, Simone knelt by Justine and without ceremony, wrenched the sword out of her. Justine rolled onto her back, drew out Simone's 9mm handgun and shot Tito eight times. With each impact he staggered back. After the last shot he sagged, like a sack of wheat opened at the bottom. As implacable as a rogue wave with a scar-marred grin, he pushed to his feet and moved toward Justine and Simone.

Teresa's experience with vampires was limited, but she knew a dangerous man when she saw one. Steering right for him, she stepped hard on the gas.

Justine struggled to her feet and staggered sideways, dead in front of the two-ton SUV. Teresa whipped the steering wheel left, just as Simone jerked Justine right. Teresa fought to keep control as the rear end broke away. She managed to miss the office corner with the front end, but the rear end took a chunk out, busting glass and ripping half the bumper off. Tires squealing, she made a smoky U-turn and slammed into the big vamp five feet from Justine.

He soared twenty feet and landed in a heap. Teresa clenched her teeth and ran over him. *He's already dead*, repeated in her mind as she cranked the wheel, circled through the columns and skidded to a stop by her two friends.

They didn't need to be invited in. Simone threw Justine into the rear seat beside Kazza, tore off the dangling bumper, and jumped in the front seat a second before Teresa hit the gas and left a screeching, tire smoking trail out of the building. A last glance in the rear view mirror showed the big vamp on his knees staring hard at them. Teresa shuddered as if she felt his rage projected right into her brain.

"Kazza needs a hospital," she said once they were headed north on the Expressway.

"*No.*"

"You are bleeding to death."

"*Yes.*" The word carried finality within it.

"Damn it, a hospital may save you."

Justine leaned forward from the back seat. "Who are you talking to? Don't go weird on us."

"Kazza. She doesn't want to go to a hospital." Teresa cocked her head, listening. "Call this number. Tell them what's happened."

"What? What the hell's going on?"

"Justine! Call the damn number."

CHAPTER THREE

Northway Motel

Too wound up to lie down on the king bed not occupied by Kazza, Justine paced the room which hadn't been updated, renovated, or too carefully cleaned in the twenty years since its grand opening. She wore only a sports bra and jeans, bandages stark against her forever tanned skin. Simone lounged without pants in a chair, bandaged leg propped up on the unoccupied bed. Teresa sat on the empty bed, head in hands. Three red-dotted lines stained one side of her T-shirt.

"Shouldn't you have stitches?" Justine had asked as she cleaned the wounds.

"Yes," she hissed through clenched teeth.

"You're going to have some heavy-duty scars."

"My brain already has heavy-duty scars. What do a few more matter?"

Justine had used a whole box of butterfly bandages from Teresa's extensive first aid kit to close the wounds.

"I don't suppose there's a question why this happened right after she was looking for your Grace?"

Simone said, "Grace has enemies with long memories."

"So somebody tweets somebody that Kazza knows where she is, and here we are. I assume she did not tell them, tell him, that big guy, where Grace is?"

A man and woman, unremarkable except for matching pale blue eyes that looked at the world with a sure serenity incapable of surprise, sat on either side of Kazza. They gently gripped her arms. At Justine's question they glanced at each other, frowns deepening. "She did not," the woman said.

"Tito is that man's name. Simone knows him."

"What?" Justine stopped pacing at Simone's feet. "You know that guy? An old boyfriend?"

Head laid back, eyes closed, Simone said, "Yes, no. Later."

Justine glared at Simone for fifteen seconds, then turned to Teresa.

Teresa shrugged, winced, and leaned forward, elbows on knees, studying the worn carpet as if trying to determine its original color.

"So how did they know?" Justine continued her pacing.

"One of us works with that man, Tito," the man said.

"One of us?"

He held up his hand to silence the questions sure to come. Releasing Kazza's arm, he turned to Teresa.

"It is time. Come. Hold her."

"Time?"

The finality of his expression was answer enough.

Tight-lipped, Justine nodded encouragement to her friend's glance as Teresa moved over and took Kazza's hand with both of her own. Teresa started once, then held still, eyes blank, for several minutes.

Kazza's eyes fluttered open. A half smile of contentment graced her ravaged face. She drew in a deep breath and let it out, saying one word, "Finally." She did not draw another.

Justine put an arm around Teresa. "I'm sorry. What was happening there? Something."

"I'm not sure." Brow furrowed, she looked up at the couple who stood together at the foot of the bed. "What did happen?"

"And what did she mean by 'finally?' " Justine asked, eyes narrowed mistrustfully. "It sounded like she was expecting…wanting to die."

"She was."

"*Aiee, merde.*" Simone jumped up and stared down at the bed.

Justine and Teresa also jumped back.

Kazza aged before their eyes. It seemed to Justine as if her muscles melted inside and her skin darkened and stretched tight over her bones. Lips pulled away from protruding teeth as her eyes shrunk into milky marbles.

"Eeww." Justine gripped Teresa's arm as if they were girls surprised by a yucky sight like a decomposing animal or a boy doing something he should be doing in private. "What are you people? How old was she?"

With gentle reverence, the couple folded a blanket over Kazza's desiccated body. That done, they leaned together against the wall.

"We are Oracles," he said. "And Kazza was…ageless."

Justine dropped onto the bed. For the first time in her short—was it only a month?—time as a vampire she felt fatigue. Her body hurt from her wounds. Her arm ached from the prolonged fighting. She had not had an extended sleep since they left California. She hadn't had time to process the killing of Bill Service, a long festering desire, suddenly possible. And she missed Harry. He'd be out of the hospital by now. Was he back at work? Did he miss her? Now this. What the fuck were Oracles? Not the old Greek legends. Here? Now? Shit.

"So you can tell the future?" Justine said.

"Not exactly. We are able to see parts of the future, to varying degrees. Kazza was one of the few who could see far into the future."

Weary, Justine said, "I'm sorry about Kazza. But I'm tired and need to sleep. Please elucidate, briefly."

"Of course. There are few of us, possibly five hundred around the world. We can see the future, as well as the past, as I said, to varying degrees. All can see backward. All can glimpse forward, though most only a few hours or days. Small snippets of somebody's time, disjointed images. We need no crystal balls or palms or cards. A simple touch will do."

"But Kazza could do more. Much more." Teresa rubbed her head as if searching for something.

"Yes. She could see years into the future and in more detail. She could see a person's death, whether in days or decades. But not all. None can see all."

"She thought it was a curse," Teresa said.

"Yes. Most with that great a power consider it so. To know of so much misery and pain to come, and not be able to change it, is a heavy burden to bear."

From her chair in the corner, Simone asked, "Surely they also saw joy and happiness ahead."

"Of course, but it seems that, regrettably, sadness and grief tend to linger, while joy is fleeting."

Justine stopped gently massaging Teresa's neck. "So you're saying that whatever she saw in the future, could not be changed no matter what?"

"Yes. They have tried for hundreds of years."

"In her shop, Kazza told Teresa that she would find Antonia. So..."

"However, it is unfortunate that she gave no details of what would happen before we found Antonia, or after." Simone rose and stretched. "I believe we must concentrate on the before, and deal with the after when it arrives. *N'est pas?*"

"But what did she do to me?" Teresa looked at them all, one at a time, her eyes sparkling with incipient tears. "In my head she said she would not give me the curse, but something that might help." She searched the floor for an answer. "She was very sad. Not about dying. A loss, a long time ago."

Eyes downcast, seeing who knew what past or future events, the woman spoke. "She, too, lost a child. Many years past. She knew it would happen, and was powerless to prevent it."

"Christ." Justine caught Simone's gaze. "No wonder she was ready to die. If I had known...?"

Her two friends, her only friends, stood close, comforting her with their presence.

Breaking the silence, the woman said, "That is one reason why she felt so connected to you. To you all."

Simone turned to the couple. "You said *one* reason they connected."

"Ah, yes." He held Teresa's eyes with his own. "Your friend has the latent ability to become a very powerful *bruja*, a sorceress. Kazza knew this and freed the power in you. But you are untrained. She reinforced your knowledge of the location of the person who can help you."

Teresa's brow wrinkled and her eyes jerked about as if searching for a memory lost at the edge of her mind.

"Yes, we know," Simone's eyes smiled. *"Une sorciere."*

Justine regarded Teresa with amused skepticism. "A witch."

"Her mother was born in Catemaco. A town with many *brujas*, some, such as her grandmother, for real."

"How did you know that?" Teresa asked.

"Kazza knew it."

"I didn't." Teresa's brow wrinkled with concentration as she shook her head. "I mean, I don't think I did."

"Just how powerful is she?" Justine slid her arm around her friend's shoulders. "Never mind. I think we all need a break here."

The couple reassured them that the motel was watched over. If they stayed until the next night they would be safe and undisturbed.

"Treen?" Simone said.

"The store has been taken care of. Treen and Kazza will be laid to rest together."

Left alone, weary as they all were, the three women sat apart quietly for a while, taking in the new developments.

Justine rubbed her tired eyes. Discovering vampires were real was hard enough. But Oracles? Witches? Christ, what other creatures were out there that shouldn't be in a normal ordered world? Eyebrows raised in question, she scowled at Simone. "Oracles? Really?"

Simone shrugged. "Fantasy. Do you blame them for their secrecy? If one was forced to tell what was going to happen in the Stock market in a week, a year? They would be targets for every greedy bastard out there. And what if the government got hold of one."

"What makes you think they haven't?"

"Politics wouldn't be near as fucked up as it is."

"What else weird is out there you didn't tell me about? Werewolves, fairies, trolls, leprechauns, lawn gnomes?"

"None that I know of." Simone shrugged, nodding at Teresa. "Aren't *brujas* enough?"

The two friends sat on the beds, knees almost touching. "Right." Justine gently gripped Teresa's knees, and she winced. "Your wounds are hurting. I suggest you prescribe yourself some pills and we all rest until dark. We know where we need to go, or at least you do. Tomorrow night we go there."

Diner

Teresa woke about four o'clock, a couple of hours before sunset. It was still a bit unnerving to see her vampire companions in the other bed, covered with blankets, and not detect even the faint movement of breathing. In the bathroom she showered and washed her hair for the first time in days, but didn't bother to shave her legs or armpits. Since she left Carlos and the kids who would care?

Her stomach felt like it was eating itself. She considered taking a gun with her, but decided on the big knife strapped to her belt. Was it a concealed weapon under a hoodie? She didn't care.

Outside their first floor room, the overcast sky added to that special chill that comes from being close to the water. The Northway sat back from the main route north to Salem. Clean and quiet, its peeling paint and weathered wood railings testified to twenty plus years of salt air and frosty winters. Half a block down a diner offered breakfast anytime and jumbo cheeseburgers.

With the low gray sky they could have left right then, but Teresa needed some alone time with real people, though she had no desire to speak to anyone.

As she began walking to the diner, hood up, hands jammed in pockets, the anger began to build. Chilly, a few trees struggling to show off their bright fall colors, a watery sun hanging close to the horizon, the day was not so gloomy as her disposition. A normal day like many others. Yet Kazza would not have a chance to experience it. By now she and Treen were probably ashes in an urn set on a mantelpiece somewhere. Teresa had connected with her. Like one sometimes does, when one person meets another and knows within seconds they are attuned to each other.

They had both lost a child, could there be a stronger reason for an instant bond? It's what brought her and Justine together. Simone, too, had lost a child. It had been more than that. Witchcraft? Kazza had been way older than the thirty-five she looked. Not immortal like a damn vampire; what else could keep her that young looking?

Fuck witchcraft. Fuck vampires, too. She'd had to kill two last night and try to kill another one. Didn't matter that they would have killed and eaten her in an instant, or that they were already dead. They didn't act dead. They were up and about with their own agendas, mostly doing evil it seemed. She told Justine she would help her avenge the murder of her daughter, but would not kill anybody, even the murderers. Now Justine was helping her find her daughter, Antonia, and in less than two weeks she'd killed two "beings." Though she wasn't there, she'd known what would happen to Bill Service, and had made no real effort to stop his death. For twenty years as an Emergency Room nurse saving lives had been her job, her life. Now look at her. God damn it, didn't she have a right to be pissed?

She considered the breakfast but decided on the jumbo cheeseburger, fries and a chocolate milkshake. Born in Mexico, she moved across the border at two and had lived the next forty six years in Southern California. Many times in the past she had not felt "American." It had been almost twenty years since she had a hamburger, but tearing her way through that cheeseburger, she thought, *Now I'm a real American, dude.*

Sated, yet still simmering with ill-defined anger, she slapped over the pages of the Boston *Globe* newspaper, searching for mention of Kazza's Psychic Shop. Her humor was not helped by a thick, scruffy man two booths down, wearing a plaid jacket and a Patriots hat that might have been on his head since their very first game. The reek of his alcohol fueled breath did not help, either.

He, too, seemed to have some anger issues. After he ripped off each bite he dropped what was left on the plate and stared at it like it was some slimy underground creature that crawled out of a floor drain in order to die on his plate. "Food not…shit. Ain't paying…this crap," he mumbled through his mouthfuls.

As he snuck a swig from a pint bottle, he noticed Teresa watching him. "What'er you lookin' at?" Squinting, he checked her out. She felt his bloodshot eyes assault her, lingering on her breasts then using booze-fueled x-ray vision to check her hips and legs and back up again. He broke out a smile that if he'd had a shower, shave, haircut, teeth cleaning, change of wardrobe, and a week to sober up, might have been attractive.

"You." Teresa was not in the mood to back down.

With a visible effort not to mangle his words, he said, "Then come on over, Honey. Get a real close look. Heh heh."

"No."

His jocularity dimmed for an instant, then bounced back with an unctuous, "Aw, come on, darlin', I'll be gentle with ya."

"No. Never."

With a quick glance of entreaty at Teresa, the waitress, a pretty, slip of a woman, probably a war hero's widow with two great freckle-faced kids and a lovely extended family, stepped between them. "Your check, sir."

He jerked back like she'd slapped him. His face scrunched up under startled eyes, so that Teresa thought he was going to spit at her. Instead he pushed his plate away with a quick bump of palms.

"I ain't payin' for this shit crap food. The fuckin' rats runnin' around this place wouldn't eat this God dammed puke shit slop. You should pay *me* to eat it."

"Sir, please, you should have returned it if it was not to your liking."

"I'll fucking return it." With a swipe of an arm he swept everything off the table. Speaking as much to himself as the waitress, he said, "There, purty li'le bitch, all returned."

At the other end of the diner the middle-aged Hispanic cook reached for the phone.

The drunk struggled to slide out of the booth and stand steady.

The hero's widow was ready to be a hero herself. "Sir, you have to pay for the meal, or we'll have to call the police."

"Fuck police. Fuck you too skinny nag. Had enough nag nag nag in my life don' need more from you."

Brave or foolish, she stood her ground. "Sir, please—"

"Shut up!" He backhanded her with a meaty hand, knocking her down. Kicking at her, he shouted, "Shut up damn naggin' slut. You don' tell *me* what to do anymore."

This was the excuse Teresa didn't know she was looking for. She slid out of the booth and with the waitress on the floor between their feet, she twisted back from the hip and slugged the guy with every trace of anger roiling inside her.

He staggered back, brought up short by a tall booth divider that kept him upright. Pure rage shot out of his eyes like flames from a dragon's mouth. Blood streamed from his nose. His jaw worked, emitting only a guttural snarl.

Teresa damn near snarled back. Her chest heaved, her fists clenched. If she could have stepped back and examined her feelings, she half wanted the drunk bastard to slip to the floor and pass out and half wanted him to attack. She got the latter wish.

He pushed off and launched a roundhouse at her that would have put her lights out if it had connected. But Teresa had learned some things in the ER. She'd dealt with drunks, nuts and pissed off patients worse than this guy.

She blocked up with her left arm barely changing the direction of his powerful punch. Knuckles smacked her temple, and kept going. Pain ricocheted inside her head. She didn't care. Reckless, and still not caring, Teresa reached over and punched his face, then stepped around and kicked the back of his knees. He went down with help from a shove on his chest. She bent his head back against a seat edge, and held him there with the edge of her knife.

His baggy jeans back pocket yielded a greasy wallet. She threw it on the table. To the waitress, now on her feet with the help of the cook, she said, "Take what he owes you. And give yourself a big tip." Nobody moved. "Take it."

The cook darted over, took out a twenty, and returned to the waitress.

It was over. Anger expended in a few punches, Teresa bowed her head and sucked in a few deep breaths. *Estupida! Idiota! Estupida pendeja!* What had she done? Nothing good would come of this. Get out. *Arriba,* damn it.

She stood up, pulled the hood over her head, dropped a twenty of her own, and hurried into the quickening night, the cook's quiet, *"Gracias,"* the only word said.

Blood from her bandaged wounds left a sticky trail down her side. Stupid. She deserved the sting. A siren wailed in the distance. Christ. If the police stopped her and saw the blood, they'd want to know what happened. If they found the dead vamps in the factory before they crumbled to dust, saw blood on the one in the hut and matched it to hers, they'd want to know what happened all the way back to California. The three of them needed to get out of town, now.

As soon as Teresa could she ducked down an alley to get off the main road. Careful not to expose herself to the street any more than necessary, she made her way through the graying dark to the motel, unaware that she was watched.

Northway Motel

Justine knew as soon as Teresa slipped quickly into the room that something was wrong. She smelled the acrid odor of fear and anger and blood on her. "Tee, what?"

"I fucked up. We have to go, now."

Justine pulled her jacket open to inspect her wounds. "We've been waiting. What'd you do?"

While Justine cleaned and bandaged her, and Simone alternated packing and peering through the window, Teresa explained.

"Jeez, Tee. That was fucked up, but I don't blame you a bit. Though the knife might have been a little much."

Simone stood over Teresa and gently stroked her hair. "Three and a half centuries, the anger and grief still come. *C'est la vie, mon amie.* And you are correct, we must leave."

Teresa nodded, let them help her up, and moved toward the door.

Justine stiffened, cocking her head. "Did you hear—?"

BAM! The door jamb splintered as the door slammed open.

Close to the door, Teresa yelped and jumped back.

The drunk from the diner stepped in like an ax murderer from a decades old B horror movie. He held a full size old-fashioned crowbar like a club.

Another man entered behind him. Stocky but gone to fat, maybe fifty something but looking sixty plus under lank hair and a week's worth of beard. All hyped up on booze and whatever, he bounced on the balls of his feet, twitching a bat in front of his face. They reeked of booze, two old men, codgers before their time, running on anger at the world for what it did or didn't do to their lives.

"That the bitch, Jimmy?" the stocky guy asked, his voice containing a permanent inciting snarl.

"That's her," Jimmy said, sounding like his tongue was swollen.

"Told ya I saw her when I was leaving the hardware. Go ahead, fuck her up."

"What about them?"

"They can watch and shut up, or get fucked. Or both."

"Yeah. I like that idea."

"Go ahead, do it, man. Whup her. She deserves it after what she did to you."

Jimmy hesitated a second, taking in Justine and Simone taking him in. His sneer of a grin told them what he thought he would do with two hot chicks after he showed the Mexi bitch what happens when you mess with him.

"Go on Jimmy, do it, do it. Ya can't let that wetback get away with fuckin' you up. What would the guys at the Revere House think?"

That was enough incentive for Jimmy. "You shouldn't ought ta mess with me God damn immigrant bitch."

Justine could tell the fire had gone out of Teresa. Anger spent, hurting, beating up on herself, she had no fight left in her. Until the man called her a wetback.

Jimmy swung the crowbar at her, a quick powerful swing with no warning. Teresa threw up an arm to block. The crack of a breaking bone sounded loud and clear. She uttered a short cry and punched his swollen nose before dropping to her knees.

Rage took him over. Jimmy raised the bar with the obvious intent of smashing the damn wetback immigrant job-stealing you're-the-one-not-me-who-fucked-up-my-life bitch's head into bloody mush.

Justine got to him first. She easily stopped the downward arc of the crowbar. For an instant, just long enough for his alcohol fogged brain to figure out that he should be very scared, she pushed her full vampire face inches from his. When his eyes signaled he understood his danger, Justine wrenched the bar from his hands, flipped it, and jammed it through his body until the curved end penetrated his chest.

Jimmy's mouth opened, exhaling a gush of fetid blood soaked air into Justine's face. Instantly Blood Hunger took over. As his knees buckled, she pushed his head sideways to expose his prickly neck.

The second man was brave or foolish enough not to run. With a curse, he raised his bat in one hand, jammed the other into his jacket pocket, and rushed Justine. A laudable but doomed gesture even as he brought out a snub-nosed revolver and aimed at Justine's head.

Simone intercepted, knocking him backward. The gun fired. The bullet smacked into Jimmy's head. Simone grabbed the bat, smashed his gun hand, then slammed his head. Influenced by Vampire instinct, she yanked his wrist to her distended mouth and bit.

"Dad! Look, they're making a movie."

Justine, Simone and Teresa snapped their attention to the door. Outlined in the open door stood a boy, towhead, glasses, a Celtic's hoodie, smiling, until the vamps raised their bloody muzzles and became way too real.

"What are you talking about, son?" Dad entered the frame, looking into the room. "Don't be looking into other people's..." Dad was quick on the uptake. He didn't know what it was, but he knew it was no movie.

"Justine, the boy." In a blink Simone grabbed the dad's head, held his eyes to hers. Using the full force of her glamour power on the man, she told him, *Take your family away. You saw nothing here. Take them away.*

The boy ran two steps before Justine caught him. Holding his head down so he couldn't see her fangs, she pressed her forehead to his. *You saw nothing here. Go with your father. You saw nothing scary.*

"Danny? Mitch? What's going on?" The mother, three doors down, pretty, young. Justine rose. Danny slumped to the sidewalk. Mom, already moving toward her boy, spied the blood on Justine's quickly normalizing face. "What have you done to Danny? Get away from him."

Justine seized her and grabbed her head. Mom flailed her fists. Justine said, "Your son and husband are all right. They are not hurt." The mother continued to struggle. "Listen to me!" Forced to stare deep into not quite human eyes, the intensity of the mother's rage gathered in her face. "You are safe." Knowing they had only seconds before someone else discovered them, Justine put all her concentration into the thoughts, *You are safe. Your family is safe. You saw no blood, no strangers, nothing strange. Sleep.*

"Let's go. Let's go." One handed, Teresa tossed the last bag into the SUV.

Justine gently lay the sleeping mom on the ground.

"You drive," Teresa said as she and Simone climbed in.

Within seconds the vehicle raced out of the parking lot onto the road heading north.

On the Road

Crossing the Pines River on the Salem Turnpike just north of Revere, Justine asked, "How the hell did that go so wrong?"

Teresa slammed her first aid kit shut. "My fault. Simone, you didn't happen to be a doctor at some point, did you?"

"No. But I can make the pain go away."

"Thank you. I still need to have this set by someone who knows what they're doing."

"Justine, can you stop for a minute or two?"

Justine slowed a little, but her attention was on the rearview mirror. "What?" Simone asked.

"Car came up fast. Now it's following us. God, I hope it's not police. I don't want to do anything to them."

Simone turned in her seat and stared through the back window. "Not police."

Teresa's head jerked up. "Friends. Pull over."

"Whoever they are, here they come."

The following car pulled up and matched speed. Gesturing for them to stop was the Oracle woman from the motel.

Once stopped, Justine went to meet the Oracles while Simone tended to Teresa.

"What the hell?" Justine didn't like stopping in the open, surrounded by wetlands. She wanted to get far away from the area as quick as possible. There was no place to run. She occasionally had to remind herself she was not a movie vampire. She wasn't about to bound above treetops, or leap a ten-story building, or run over water. She also wasn't sure she trusted, or liked, Oracles. That was a powerful ability, to see the future, too easy to misuse. Besides, she had no clue what she'd say if one of them asked if she wanted to know how she would end.

"One of the men survived, and your vehicle was seen at the motel," the man said.

"Take this one. We'll take care of yours. What happened?" the woman asked.

"Don't you know? Didn't you know?" Justine demanded. When the woman's face turned stony, she added, "Sorry, it's been an evening. How did you know where we'd be?"

Her voice was as brittle as her expression. "We don't know all and we don't see all, but we see some things."

"Sorry." She sketched out Teresa's little adventure.

"Seeing a doctor is not advisable. I believe Grace will be able to heal her arm."

"Then we should go." Justine turned away then turned back. "Thank you. We didn't mean to be such trouble."

"You should go quickly. They're looking for you."

"Right."

"What did you do to her?" Justine wanted know, once they had quickly transferred vehicles.

Simone, driving, glanced back at Teresa sleeping serenely in the back seat. "I *suggested* to her there was no pain. I put the bone in place and she wrapped it up. Then I told her to sleep."

"How long till the pain comes back?"

Simone frowned. "Until she wakes up."

"Then we'd better hurry up. That Oracle woman thought Grace could heal her."

"First we have to find her gatekeeper. Teresa is the only one who knows where he is."

❧ ❧

As they drove through Salem, Teresa woke up.

Justine said, "Don't worry Tee. We won't let them hang you."

"*Jesu*, I wish they would. A damn broken arm is not supposed to hurt this much. What did you do to me?" She reached for her first aid kit, fumbling for pain pills.

"I set the bone. There may have been some damage, and unfortunately, glamour does not last."

"*Mierda*. If you are immortal, and we're going to travel together, you both have to go to medical school. *Si?*"

"We'll sign up as soon as we find Antonia," Justine said. "But before you down all those pills in your hand, tell us where to go."

"That's a tempting thought." Teresa washed down three Vicodin.

"Tee, we can't go to a doctor or an Emergency Room. The police, and who knows who else, are looking for us. Grace can fix your arm, but we have to find the person to take us to her."

"Kazza told us you would know where to find him when the time came. Time's here, *mi Bruja*."

Teresa seemed to ignore Simone. Her body stiffened, then her eyes fluttered closed and she melted onto the seat. "Those pills work...faaast. Rockport, sorceress, Ian." And Teresa was out.

"Pills work faaast?"

"Maybe they had a little help. Why cannot these things be straight-forward? There's a town called Rockport ahead. Ian is probably who we are looking for. Sorceress? Not very subtle. I do hope this is not like the movies where we have to figure out clues to advance to the next destination."

"Rockport seems pretty straightforward."

Simone grunted, staring out the side window at the dark passing sea. "You Young Bloods, always so naive."

CHAPTER FOUR

<u>Rockport, MA</u>

Justine cruised into Rockport on Broadway, a two-lane street lined with hedges and picket fences and trees and two or three story white clapboard houses. It was ten o'clock at night and a light drizzle, remnants of a passing storm, coated the windows, dulling even vampire eyesight. Though they had the heater on, the two vampires felt the chill. They weren't in Southern California anymore.

"Couldn't we be searching for a tropical witch?"

Simone grunted for a reply, her attention on her phone. "There is no sorceress named Ian in this village. No business named sorceress. Perhaps we should wake Sleeping Beauty?"

"I'm parking first. Driving in this weather sucks."

Justine found a space between some restaurants overlooking the harbor. Seat tilted back a few notches, she lay back and stared through the rain blurred windshield at the lights around the harbor. She knew the view was picturesque as hell but wasn't in a mood to appreciate it.

"This is so fucked up. Are you sure this Grace is the only way to find Antonia?"

Simone had her feet on the dash, head lolling against the cool window. Justine hugged herself and turned away to stare into the black void of the ocean. Brittany had sat like that when she was alive. Seeing Simone in that same pose still brought a phantom tear to her eyes.

"You have the same information I do. Have you a better idea?"

"No. But let's do something. I don't want to be sitting here when the sun comes up."

Simone sighed and twisted around to kneel on the seat. She reached through the gap between the two front seats and shook Teresa.

She saw the headlights slowly approaching along the deserted street the same time Justine saw them in the rear view. They both scrunched down, hoping the car would shush right on by.

No such luck. The Rockport Police car stopped behind them, blocking them in.

"Shit."

"*Merde.*"

Teresa stirred.

Justine asked, "I don't suppose we can run on water?"

"No. But some think they do. Be nice. Maybe we are in a No Parking zone. Maybe they have not heard of our Boston adventure."

"I'm not killing a cop for any reason." Justine dug in her purse for her driver's license. "Just so you know."

Two cops wearing yellow rain jackets exited the police car and advanced with probing flashlight beams.

Justine had license and registration ready when the cop, one hand resting on his gun, asked for them with a no-nonsense tone. She wished she had a good fake ID like ones she had had at sixteen. A girlfriend's brother got them and they worked great because she was pretty and showed lots of cleavage. She had no doubt this stern-faced cop would not be impressed with any amount of cleavage, as he walked away with her real one.

Looking casual, though Justine knew her well enough to know she was quite concerned about the possible outcomes of this possible crisis, Simone said, "We could run."

"And leave Teresa?"

"Come back and get her."

"When they connect her to the motel that won't be so easy. Well, so easy to do quietly."

"If they take us to jail, how long until they figure out we're different and the *merde* hits the fan?"

"Fuck. How'd this get to be such a fuck up?"

"You guys should run," Teresa said. "Come back for me if you can. If not, will you still find Antonia?"

After a silent consultation with Simone, Justine said, as they put money and guns into the messenger bags that had become their purses, "Tee, we will not leave you behind. Besides, we need you to tell us how to find Grace."

A short silence passed. Teresa said as if repeating information she didn't understand, "Ian commands the sorceress. You *will* meet him." Quiet. "Did I say something? *Vaya! Vaya!*"

Justine reached for the door handle. Then looked into the rearview. "Well, we're about to meet somebody. Another car arrived. Six cops now, guns out."

Another quick eye consultation. With full vampire speed and force they tossed their guns out the window into the harbor.

"Maybe Ian will be in the next cell?"

An hour later Justine and Simone were held in separate cells, though in sight of each other, at the Rockport Police Department. Teresa had been taken to the hospital. They'd been fingerprinted and briefly interrogated. They knew nothing. Justine insisted on a phone call. She called Harry.

CHAPTER FIVE

Harry's Condo

A postcard night, Sheriff's Investigator Harry Frazer thought. Balmy breezes, a new moon floating over the Pacific allowing a few stars to poke through. White lines of relentless surf rolling up onto the Oceanside beach. He'd watched the late news and noticed the weather in New England was deteriorating fast with rain expected all over.

Ordinarily he didn't give a damn about New England weather, it being about as far away from Southern California as one can get. But Justine was there, somewhere. He'd had one voice mail from her as they passed New York City. They'd talked about going there, a city open twenty-four hours, perfect for a vampire and mortal on vacation.

Would he ever see her again? Or hear from her? Did he want to? Should he? He was an eighteen years on the job cop. She was a vampire. He still found it incredible there were such things, but when Teresa saved his life, he'd been forced to believe. Everything else since then just reinforced the belief. But still...

And she was a murderess. He was sure she'd murdered two men, had certainly been involved in a couple of other deaths. Not to mention the one that could have been put down to self defense, except he returned as a vamp and she killed him a second time. Not to mention Simone, her master or maker or whatever they were called, and her crimes. He didn't want to begin to think about the legal implications of prosecuting crimes done by a dead person.

So what? He wanted to see her, hold her, lend her his body warmth. When the phone rang, he knew it was her, and probably trouble. Cop instinct, or wishful thinking? He didn't know or care. He wanted to hear her voice.

"Harry Frazer."

"I miss you."

"I miss you, too. Where are you?"

Silence. "Can you save that for a couple minutes? Tell me how you are. Are you back to work? Catch any bad guys lately?"

Trouble all right. "Been back a week now. Arrested a bank robber this morning after he shot a hostage. They both survived."

She asked a few more inconsequential questions and he gave some inconsequential answers. That was fine, but she obviously had something to say and it was time to say it.

"Justine, what is it? Are Simone and Teresa okay?"

"We're all still…alive." In a rush she said. "Harry, I'm in over my head. Simone and I are in jail and I don't have time to explain and I don't know what to do and I don't think you can help, but I wanted to hear your voice."

Two vampires in jail. Yep, that could be big trouble for someone. "Christ. What happened? Maybe I can call somebody?"

"We have to find a guy called Ian who is master of the sorceress. How the hell do we do that?"

"Justine. Calm down. Why are you in jail? Where are you?"

"A guy attacked Teresa. Two guys. One's dead. The other might be. Shit. My time's up. I love you, Harry."

"Where are you? Don't say anything." She was gone. "God damn it!" Harry kicked the railing. "God damn it!" He kicked again. He wanted to kick the building, kick his cell phone into the ocean, kick Justine's ass. "You were supposed to be careful. Shit!"

"Harry, what are you doing?"

His neighbor, Bayley, and her partner Susan peered quizzically from their door. Attractive almost thirty somethings, they both owed Harry their lives. He could do no wrong in their eyes, but cussing and kicking at ten at night was not typical behavior for him. It might not be wrong, but they were going to question it, and help if possible.

Harry spun around to face them, his breathing heavy, face working to find an expression to match how he felt.

"And don't say 'nothing,' " Bayley added.

"Justine."

The two women knew *who* Justine was, though not *what* she was. They knew she was gone and that Harry had been moodier than usual ever since.

"She's in trouble three thousand…" his lips pressed tight as if to keep the word back, but it burst out anyway. "…fucking miles away and I can't help her."

Bayley went to him and put her hand on the fist holding the cell phone he'd been pounding the rail with.

Susan stayed by the door. She liked Harry, owed him big time, but was still a bit skittish around him. She didn't remember exactly what had happened, but enough of it had leaked through the fog of Darwin and Simone's glamour to scare her. And if nothing else the cast on her leg was a reminder of bad things.

"Harry!" Bayley said, holding down his fist. "Stop it. You won't help her by smashing your phone to itty-bitty pieces."

He breathed deep. Calm. Calm.

"What sort of trouble?"

Harry puffed out his cheeks. "I'm not really sure."

"Where is she?"

"I don't know."

Bayley's blonde eyebrows rose. "Oookay. You're a cop aren't you? Find out. What would you do if it was somebody you didn't know or care about?"

What *would* he do? Slowly his mind slipped into the logical, planning thought process of his short career in crime and his eighteen years as a cop. "I'd find her."

"I know you would. Can we help?"

"Thanks. You've done more than enough already."

Bayley smiled and pecked his cheek. "For what you've done for me, not nearly enough." She returned to Susan, threw an arm around her shoulders and said to Harry, "So?"

"Right." He spun on his heel and entered his condo. He had work to do.

It didn't take long to trace Justine's call to the Rockport Police, and find out what the women were to be charged with, and that Chief of Police Jackson Bingham would vigorously interrogate the prisoners in the morning, that the arrests were being kept under wraps for the moment, no, he could not speak with the prisoners, and that Teresa was being held overnight in Addison Gilbert Hospital about fifteen miles away in Gloucester.

A call to the hospital on "official business" finally got him through to Teresa. Left alone, except for a guard outside, she'd turned down the meds while she tried to contact an Oracle or the future or Justine or anybody. She was surprised more than groggy when the nurse said she had a phone call. Why hadn't she tried to call Harry?

"Harry, how did you know I was here? Did you talk to Justine?" She spoke low in case the guard was listening, though he seemed more bored than interested.

"I did, but she didn't have time to talk. Tell me exactly what happened." Teresa did. "Damn, Teresa, I don't blame you for what you did, though the knife to the neck is not good. And you can probably make self defense work, but it won't be easy."

"Justine and Simone can't be on trial. They'd be…"

"I know. I can't really help you from here. I know a guy in Boston I went to school with. Apparently his son is a hot shit lawyer. I'll try and contact him. Until you hear from him, do not say anything."

"All right. I'm scared. Not for me, for Justine."

"Me, too." He heard other voices come through the phone. "What's happening?"

"Someone wants to come in, the guard is saying no." The door banged open.

Harry whispered, "Don't hang up," then turned up the volume.

A male voice asked, "Are you Teresa Diaz?"

"Yes."

"My name is Ian Cadwaller. I am the Deputy Police Chief of Rockport. I have been looking for you."

Into the phone, Teresa whispered, "He said his name was Ian."

"I heard. Ask him for ID, then let me talk to him."

Hospital

Ian showed her his badge and ID. As a long time ER nurse she'd seen plenty of ID's from cops and patients, real and fake. His picture matched the man's broad weather-beaten face and unruly sun bleached hair. It looked real to her.

"You're the master of the sorceress?"

"No one is master of the sorceress you're looking for. I am, however, the captain of a lobster boat, the Sea Witch."

"*Mierda.*" She held out the phone. "You can trust this man." Her thoughts were growing fuzzy and she wasn't sure which man she meant. With hope, both.

The whisper of his voice lulled her. Teresa let her eyes droop closed. Now that Ian had been found all would be good. She could rest, and when she woke, they'd all be safe; no nasty vampires, no Oracles, no jail or interrogations. And Antonia would be safe and waiting for her mother to take her home.

Oh yes, all will be muy bueno, she thought, until she heard the words,

"She'll have to escape here, then help me get the other two."

Escape? Her? No, *por favor*, let me sleep.

"Teresa. Wake up." A hand shook her urgently. "Wake up. We have to get you out of here."

Escape, right. She forced her eyes open. Five minutes later she had pulled out the IV needle and dressed in a hospital robe.

"I can't just walk out dressed like this."

Ian stood an inch taller than Teresa, almost six feet. He had broad shoulders and a thick body, none of it fat as far as she could tell. It might have been the drugs still circulating, but he was damn handsome, in an Indiana Jones sort of way. She'd seen all the movies more than once. Nobody else knew how many times, even Justine.

His hands gripped her shoulders. Strong hands. Her eyes caught his icy green ones and for a few seconds she imagined what he could do to her with those hands. "Teresa. Are you with me?"

"Yes. Yes. How do we get out of here?"

"You're going to fly."

That got her attention. She watched, mouth open, as he swung open a window.

"Come here. Quick. Tito is probably on his way to Rockport. If he gets to your friends first, that's bad."

Wearing her hospital socks, she padded over to the window and looked out. "We're three stories up. Tito?"

"You stole Kazza from him yesterday."

"Oh. Him. We're three stories up."

"Not to worry."

Ian scooped her up in his arms, swung her legs out and set her down on the sill. Rain wet her legs. She glanced down three uninterrupted stories to the asphalt below. A quick stab of alarm struck her chest. She grabbed the edge of the window with both hands. Could she trust this guy? Was he too smooth to be trusted? Was he who he said he was, or an assassin sent to prevent her making any more trouble?

"Wait," she said. "This is *loco*." She sucked in a deep breath, ready to scream for help.

A hand clamped firmly over her mouth. He put his warm lips next to her ear. "Shhhh. Trust me." His scent calmed her; sweat, saltwater, after-shave, she couldn't quite remember but it had to be Old Spice, didn't it? The rugged seaman, captain of a sorceress.

He turned her head to face straight ahead into empty space. Forehead against her head, he began to intone words in a language she had never heard. She struggled for a moment, then froze as she rose up off the window ledge. What the hell? One of his hands was on her mouth, the other on her hand clutching to the window. Teresa couldn't have screamed if she wanted to.

Finger by finger he removed his hand from her face. Still sitting, she floated a couple of inches above the window sill. A gust of rain-filled wind spun her about like a wind vane. Ian peeled her hand from the sill, though he kept hold of it to control her spin.

Facing him, she managed an inarticulate, "How? What? How?"

He placed a finger to her lips. "Shhh." He turned on a mischievous grin and said, "One can't hang around a woman like Grace and not pick up a few tricks. Wait for me. I'll bring my pickup around."

He let her go. With both his hands palm down she slowly descended the side of the building. Too stunned to move, she looked up at him until her feet touched the ground. His hands turned vertical and the weightlessness vanished. The window closed. Teresa stood alone and wet in the dark and wondered what kind of drugs they used in that hospital. A few minutes later a crew cab pickup stopped. Without a word she got in, thankful for the heat.

As Ian raced around Blackburn Circle on the way back to Rockport, Teresa had warmed up, with the help of a down vest and wool cap from Ian, and put her magical descent in back of her brain with all the other weird occurrences of the last months. "I can understand why we don't want to meet this Tito again, but who is he? Why does he want to find Grace so bad?"

"I hate it on TV when they say, 'It's complicated,' but it is. And isn't."

"Give me the uncomplicated part."

"Tito works for a Russian billionaire Vampire called Rubicon. Back around the end of the Civil War his son, Josef, and Tito were slave hunters going after runaway slaves. Even then, Grace was known to have certain "Powers." They tracked her to a little town called Pepperell. Josef was a vamp and they caught her. But another vamp saved her and during the fight Grace killed Josef. Before Josef died he turned Tito and told him to go to his father for help seeking revenge."

"He and Justine should get along then. So this is all about revenge?"

"Not all. Rubicon wants to use her powers to his own ends."

"Which is what, world domination?"

"Nobody knows. But not good."

"I was sort of out of it when they took us, but your Police Chief looked scared and maybe surprised. Does he know anything?"

They came out of the trees onto Main Street. Ian didn't slow down.

"Nicky Travella is an ambitious man. I don't think he knows who he works for, but in exchange for allowing certain merchandise to be landed unseen, he gets monetary support for his ambitions and meets the movers and shakers who can make it happen."

"Drugs?"

"Some. No bombs, no girls. No more questions."

He slowed down as they approached the Police Station, a tall two story building with red siding and white trim. They glided into the dirt parking lot and Ian parked around back behind a thin stand of trees, facing out. A set of concrete steps at the back end of the building descended into the basement.

Ian whispered, "That black SUV is not usual, so we have to be quiet. Can you drive?"

"*Dios*, I should have got a chauffeur license. Yes, I can drive. What's your plan?"

Rockport Jail

Six cells ranked on one side of the narrow basement with a six-foot wide walkway connecting heavy steel doors with small wire-reinforced windows at each end. Concrete block partitions separated the cells, each cell fronted by steel bars and a steel bar door. Two small windows were set high in the walkway wall at ground level.

When they were first left alone Simone had pulled a heavy-duty bobbie pin from deep in her hair. She could barely reach the lock, but within minutes had it unlocked. Too much activity swirled about to escape undetected, so they waited. Justine, familiar with alarm systems from her years as a commercial real estate agent, was fairly sure the alarm by each door would sound after three wrong attempts to punch in the correct code. A frenzied, guns-blazing city, state and country wide chase was not what they wanted. To disappear quietly would be safer for all concerned.

When they were about to make their move almost an hour later, footsteps sounded through the steel door to the stairs.

Danny Travella strutted though the door, hands in his suit jacket pockets. A stout man just over six feet tall with a full head of dark hair over a round face, his arrogance preceded him like a bad odor.

Behind Travella, a uniformed officer slunk in, one hand on his gun, the other jangling keys. His name tag identified him as Kester. Thin, smug, with perfectly trimmed blond hair, he was no vampire under his pasty skin. Cruelty radiated from his close-set eyes and thin lipped sneer. Justine didn't need much imagination to have a good idea of what he'd like to do to her if he got her alone and strapped down. She figured fists were his weapon of choice against women.

Two vampires followed Kester. One wore a dark suit coat, the other a worn jean jacket. Of a type, around thirty when changed, tattooed tough guys. Wielding cut-off baseball bats whittled to a sharp point, they snickered at the two hot women in the cells. They might not have been so smug if they knew the door to Simone's cell was unlocked.

Travella inspected them up and down as if figuring their worth on his plantation.

"I know what you are. So don't go on about your rights. Dead people have no rights." Justine, leaning casually against the bars, glanced at the two vamps behind him. "Unless you're on my side," Travella added.

"And you are?"

"Rockport Chief of Police, Nicky Travella."

"Ah. Big time."

His smile looked like he had just enjoyed crushing a bug. "Big time, soon enough, Ms. Kroft, after you and your friends are dealt with."

"I bet Kester can't wait for that. He take care of all your women problems, Chief?"

Kester's eye's gleamed with anticipation. Fists clenched, he moved toward Justine's cell. "No, I don't, but you I will. I promise."

He was within three feet of the bars before Suit Coat stopped him. "Remember what she is, Kester. If she gets hold of you, you'll be dead before you can blink." Suit Coat shot Justine a look saying that'd be okay with him.

"Kester, go and check how long till he arrives," the Chief said. "You'll have your chance."

With a last glare meant to freeze Justine with terror, Kester swaggered up the stairs.

"As I was saying, what happens to you depends on how your interrogation goes. Unless you tell me right now where Grace is to be found."

Neither Justine nor Simone said a word. That they would gladly tear him apart if they got their hands on him was not lost in their stare. Involuntarily he stepped back, up against the two vamps. They grabbed his shoulders to stop him. Travella winced and quickly stepped away, spooked by the vampire power around him.

Backing toward the door, he said, "You will tell Mr. Tito what he wants to know. These men will make sure you're ready for him." He couldn't get out of there fast enough.

"Asshole," Jean Jacket said.

Casual, like talking to a neighbor across the fence, Justine asked, "So who's this Tito guy?"

The two vamps sniggered, nervously, she thought. "He's the one you had nightmares about when you was a kid," Suit Coat said.

"I'm not afraid of the nightmares I had as a kid anymore."

"You ought to be." He looked about, as if Tito might be listening in. "He's a badass son-of-a-bitch."

Jean Jacket shivered. "You'll tell what he wants to know, no matter how badass you think you are."

"What's he want with this Grace?"

"Huh. He wants to keep his own ass out of a sling," Suit Coat said. "Been lookin' for that witch for hundert and fifty years. His boss is gettin' antsy."

"So who's his boss?"

"Jeez, you are a Young Blood, ain't cha? Super rich Russian guy, been around a thousand years they say. Call him Rubicon."

"Don't be talking so much, man. I hear he doesn't like people mentioning his name around."

Lowering his voice as if Justine couldn't hear him, Suit Coat said, "Aw, don't worry about it. These vamps ain't goin' be around to tell anybody, 'cept Tito."

"I'm just saying."

"What's Rubicon want with Grace?" Justine asked, trying to keep them talking, maybe lure one of them close enough to grab.

Suit Coat laughed. "Ha. What everybody wants, Young Blood. Money, power and revenge. Not necessarily in that order. Ya know what I mean?"

Justine did.

The two vamps weren't the most intelligent undead, but they knew to keep their distance. After Jean Jacket's warning Suit Coat kept his mouth shut concerning Grace, Rubicon and Tito, but couldn't contain his volubility on any other subject.

Justine, in cell six, the farthest from the door to upstairs, had no trouble keeping him talking. Soon he was right across from her. The taciturn Jean Jacket kept his spot on the wall, while occasionally offering a few words to the conversation. If she could get him close enough to grab, Jean Jacket would come to his aid, allowing Simone time to exit and dispatch them both. That was the plan.

She had no idea when Tito would appear, but had to assume well before daylight. Jean jacket was so caught up in relating examples of how becoming a vampire helped his sex life, he had almost drifted within her reach.

A face appeared sideways in the high window opposite her. A man, not some kid. His eyes widened when he saw the two guardians. When he saw her notice him he placed a finger on his lips then pointed to the other vamps and drew a finger across his throat. His eyes posed the obvious question. Justine snuck in a bare nod. He then pointed at himself and the far door. Again, she barely nodded.

Who the hell was that? She had to assume a friend. Did Simone see him? She pressed her face to the bars and looked left. Simone's hands gripped the bars, one finger pointing to the window. Justine copied that action, then focused on Suit Coat encouraging him to continue with another of his bragging sex stories. Within five minutes the man glanced through the inside door window. About time, she was getting fed up, not to mention grossed out, by Suit Coat's supposed conquests.

In a conspiratorial stage whisper Justine said, "You think that was hot, let me tell you what Simone did."

Suit Jacket couldn't resist. He stepped right up to the bars, eager to hear. "Yeah? She's French ain't she?"

Jean jacket pushed off the wall, wary.

"Oh yes, she is. One time she met these two guys in a little club and..."

Justine grabbed Suit Coat's arm and yanked it through. His head smashed into the bars, stunning him.

Jean Jacket was there in a blink. He thrust his sharpened bat through the bars, penetrating a couple inches into Justine's side. Without missing a beat she spun away, grabbed the bat and flipped it through the bars to Simone, who caught it and rammed it through Jean Jacket's back into his heart.

Justine reached both arms through the same opening, took hold of Suit Coat's chin and the back of his head and jammed it through the bars, though his head was an inch or so too wide. Then she cranked it a hundred-eighty degrees. The crack of separating vertebrae echoed in the basement.

Ian was already through the door and sorting through keys. He unlocked cell six. "I'm Ian. There's a female vamp in the office being distracted by the duty officer, but she'll be here quick. Teresa is in the pickup out back."

Not waiting for proper introductions, he strode to the alarm pad by the outside door and punched in a code. The red light went out. He yanked open the door.

"Quietly."

Justine and Simone exchanged glances and ran toward the door.

"Stop!"

A pretty young woman vamp burst into the basement.

"Take him." Simone grabbed Ian and hustled him at full speed out the door. Justine followed, but jumped to the right just outside. Simone looked back. "Now!" With a bit of help from Justine, the woman impaled herself on the bat as she flew out the door. She tumbled across the ground and came up hard against a tree.

Justine jumped into the crew cab and Teresa drove with the lights off out of the parking lot and left onto a deserted Main Street. Lights on, the pickup raced toward the harbor.

"Tee, I didn't know when we'd see you again. Are you all right?"

"Under normal circumstances I'd be arrested for driving in my condition. But as the Deputy Police Chief is in the truck, I'm okay."

Simone reached over the seat and squeezed her shoulder. "Teresa, you continue to surprise me. Where are we going?"

Ian said over his shoulder, "Grace wants to see you."

"God, after all the crap we've had in trying to see her, I sure hope so."

The Sea Witch

Ian had Teresa park not far from where the police picked them up. Then he hustled them, and their weapons and papers that he had liberated earlier, down a short dock where he loaded them into a small outboard boat that smelled strongly of fish. Lights out, he wove quietly through the moored boats to a forty-two foot lobster boat. Even in the late morning darkness, the two vampires had no trouble reading the boat's name, *Sea Witch*. They shrugged and shook their heads.

Hurrying, but still keeping as low a profile as possible, Ian cranked the engine. Justine had some experience with boats so he sent her up to cast off the mooring. Quiet and inconspicuous, they slid from inner harbor to outer harbor and finally into the Atlantic Ocean. The storm had passed, leaving the sea surface calm, though the leftover swell could not be ignored.

"Why don't you just fly us?" Teresa asked from the small forward cabin. Ian had had them stay below out of sight until they cleared the jetty.

"Too much mojo for me. Come up. It's a beautiful night."

"You mean a beautiful very early morning." Nevertheless, with Simone's help she stood under the hard dodger that opened aft to the wide work area that took up about two-thirds of the boat's length.

It was a beautiful night. In open water Ian throttled up and they all huddled under the dodger by the steering station and took in the billion icy stars of a rain swept autumn night.

Ian told them they had a good hour before they arrived. Justine and Teresa went below to catch up.

Ian perched on the helmsman seat, his face ghostly in the red glow from the instrument panel. Simone steadied herself with the overhead grab rail, her body swaying sinuously with the *Sea Witch's* slow roll.

They traded information on the events of the last days. After a few minutes silence, Ian said, "Grace will be happy to see you. Do your friends know how you met?"

Pepperell, Massachusetts—1851

Simone felt it when another vampire entered the inn. She cracked open the door of her room to listen and smell. Much older than her own two hundred years, maybe double that, she thought. Like humans, every vampire had their own scent, and, like humans, some had a stronger enhanced sense of smell than other vampires. They made excellent trackers. Simone pursed her lips. Unfortunately there had been an incident in New Hampshire that might cause one to hire such a vampire to track her.

Simone had taken a small room on the north side of a charmless, though clean, inn called the Blind Man. There was a legend to go with the name, though mostly it signified that if enough money changed hands the proprietor turned a blind eye to what one did as long as they did it quietly and privately.

She had no intention of doing anything untoward in or out of the public eye. Just before sunrise, she'd left her carriage in the care of a sleepy groom with instructions to have it ready at sunset. The boy had the impudence to comment on a woman who would travel alone through the night, implying a question of morality. An extra dollar, a glimpse of a gun, and a deep look into his eyes convinced him it was a normal thing to do and not to mention it to anyone.

The innkeeper, a jowly man around forty, who hid his intelligence behind a scruffy exterior, promised she would not be disturbed until supper time. Simone guessed he had had guests like her before. Especially after he accepted an extra two dollars for his trouble by saying, "That is not necessary, Ma'am. But you will not be disturbed until the sun has set."

"Thank you, sir. That is very kind of you."

"This is a quiet town," he said, adding a warning, "we'd like to keep it that way." His eyes did not flinch as he said it.

Blind Man indeed. "As would I."

As good as his word, a knock woke her at dusk. In a few minutes, she dressed in boots, a simple, though stylish, black dress, and cape. A handbag big enough to carry the gun and other necessities, and a small traveling case completed her minimal travel accessories.

Ready to leave unseen by a back door, the arrival of another vampire, in that remote town, in that particular inn, gave her reason to pause.

Carrying her case and bag, Simone descended the narrow back stairs and turned left down a corridor that led to the public room. A quick scan easily picked out the vampire and his mortal companion. They sat on benches opposite each other at a long wooden table.

The mortal ate a generous portion of stew and bread, washed down with a tankard of ale. Around forty years old, though his face was pockmarked, he was a handsome man, in a rough, outdoors way, with his long dark hair pulled tightly back into a ponytail. His coat, breeches and boots were clean, suggesting a certain affluence and attention to detail. But his eyes were deep set and dark, hard and cruel, unrelenting in their survey of his surroundings. Despite her vampire power, Simone did not want to be at his mercy.

The vampire sat with his back to her. Smaller than the mortal, he nevertheless exuded authority, his back held straight, round head covered with close-cut blonde hair except for a small braided rattail. He held his head up and back in a way that suggested he was looking down his nose at everybody.

They both carried pistols and thin bladed sabers.

Concentrating, she sorted out his scent from the other patrons, many of whom hadn't bathed recently. Musty, with a strong accent of dirt and blood, recent blood being strongest. Hunters, she thought, but not for vampires, slaves. His first words confirmed it.

"That nigger bitch is close, John. I can feel her. I can smell her. She won't escape us again."

John grinned. "I can feel that two hundred dollar bounty in my pocket already."

Slave hunters. The people they chased had been kidnapped, sold like a cow or mule, treated cruelly, and had had the courage to escape to freedom. Hunters were paid to return them to beatings and humiliation, or to be sold again. It was a low way of making a living. Simone, having been herself a slave of sorts for a short time, felt that that type of work could not be permitted if she had a chance to prevent it.

For a month she had been chained in the basement of a chateau close to the Palace of Versailles. The chateau was owned by a Duke, a member of Louis XIV's court, with brutally voyeuristic tastes. It was one thing for a human to be enslaved, they were weak and fearful. But for a vampire the humiliation and degradation could only be banished by the ugly and painful death of the perpetrators. And so it had been.

Simone retreated down the corridor and out the back door. She missed the vampire becoming alert and cocking his head as if listening, or smelling, danger.

Grace

Grace knew that her invisibility spell would not hide her from Olaf Rubicon and his partner John Tito for long. He would not be able to see her, but the spell did not cover her scent and the Russian's powerful nose would find her. If they were both mortal, she could escape them, overpower them if necessary. Vampires were not immune to her spells though their strength to resist matched her power to create them.

She'd had to use the spell and others several times in the last weeks since Brett Greathouse discovered her true nature. Nye Wood had betrayed her, though he was a slave like thirty others on the Greathouse plantation outside of Franklin, Virginia. Word had spread quickly from the main house to the slave quarters. The house slaves had many ears and knew everything that happened in the mansion. Fortunately that day Grace had accompanied Mrs. Greathouse into town, a half hour carriage ride away.

Grace had foreseen the day coming when her efforts to alleviate the suffering of her people and her work to help other slaves escape might be discovered. Plans had been made along the Underground Railway for her own escape. With a speed that would have amazed Greathouse and his overseers, word of Wood's betrayal, to save himself from a minor punishment, made its way into Franklin and then to Grace.

Two men, one white, one black, approached Mrs. Greathouse as she prepared to mount her open carriage. The white man, James Delmonde, engaged the lady in a distracting conversation, while the black man, George, informed Grace it was time for her to join the Underground Railroad she had helped so many others to enter.

George took her arm to guide her to others who waited to spirit her away to freedom. Twenty feet away, she stopped and looked back over her shoulder. Mrs. Greathouse was a good and kind woman. A slave owner, yes, but she always treated them well and more than once had interceded on their behalf, sometimes lying to her husband. He would be furious with her for letting a suddenly very important slave escape.

At the same moment, Mrs. Greathouse, intelligent and perceptive as well as kind, glanced back over her shoulder. Their eyes met. With George's hand still on her arm, the fear frozen on his face, the lady immediately understood what was happening. If she raised an alarm, Grace would not escape. They all knew it. For a long moment that seemed to freeze time, they communicated with their eyes. Then Mrs. Greathouse's lips, that so often smiled, pressed tight. Her eyes glistened with both sadness and hope. She nodded once.

George immediately made to leave. Grace pulled her arm from his hand and strode to Mrs. Greathouse while reaching into her bag. She took the lady's hand and pressed a small patch of cloth tied with a white string into it, closing her fingers around it.

"Breath in the essence," Grace said, holding her own hand to her nose to illustrate. "Whatever you say next will be believed by your listener. Five times only." Then she walked quickly away, disappearing into the crowd with George.

A closed carriage took her to Suffolk where she rested a few hours in a safe house while others left a false trail into the Great Dismal Swamp. In the middle of the night another carriage conducted her to Norfolk, arriving just in time to board a frigate bound north to Boston with a cargo of cotton. For several days she kept out of sight, comforted by cotton that her own bruised fingers might have picked.

She spent a week in Boston in a house owned by a prominent businessman who was well known in the Underground Railroad as an ardent abolitionist. There she learned that Greathouse had put a bounty on her of five hundred dollars. An extreme amount, reflecting his knowledge of her power. Too much, Grace thought. Nye Wood had most likely exaggerated her abilities in his effort to avoid the lash.

Grace had known what she had within her since her mama began teaching her the craft at the age of ten. Now somewhere around thirty she felt the full extent of her abilities being revealed to her, though years were needed to gain full control.

The whites she came in contact with didn't know her power. They figured the high price on her head was because of her striking looks and strong body that would make her a good breeder. They were surprised to hear she had no children.

❧ ❦

Her mama told Gracey, as she was called back then, "Chil', don't you go having any children. You special. You have a youngen she will take you power, you strength."

"But Mama, you had me."

"Little Gracey, you was a glorious mistake. I fell in love with you father and any sense I had left me like a boss man's promise. He was sumpthin, you papa. Big and black and beautiful and hard as any man got right to be. Uh huh."

"Then I'm a love child then, Mama?"

"You were and you are, Baby. And you special in other ways, too. I didn't know it, being blinded by his smile I expect, until after they took him away that he had the Blood in him. Got it from his mama, a fool like me. So you got double blood in you."

Her mama had closed her eyes, remembering what it was like to be a fool in love. "I knowed it the minute you slid into this hateful world. You got double blood in you. Powerful blood. You be destined to be important somehow and you need all you strength to do it. So no babies for you. We all gon be babies to you. I seen it and I believe it."

There was no of lack of trying, by the slave handlers or those slave men eager to step up and try. Gracey was as fine a negra as there was at the time. Men fluttered around her like black bees wantin' to be king for a night, or even fifteen minutes if that's all they got. The man got

66

her with child would be cock of the walk, for a little while, anyways. Her mama had fixed it so that wouldn't happen, though Gracey didn't understand that until later.

Gracey was angry with her mama when she found out and for one summer and into fall she did her best to put the lie to what was done to her. It was a hot summer and Gracey tried and tried to get with child, but it wasn't to be. Wore out by fall, she finally accepted it. After a white woman in the next plantation and a young black girl who worked up at the main house died giving birth, she pushed the still eager men away and took up her mama's schooling with a vengeance.

She waited a week in Boston for arrangements to be made for her safe transit north. When word came that Rubicon and Tito were on her trail, the Railroad Conductors hastily found a carriage and guide. Within the hour she was on the road heading Northwest, bound for Pepperell, then New Hampshire and finally safety in Canada.

❧   ❦

Grace shivered under a hundred year old Oak tree, pulled her cloak tight and clutched her bag tighter. Her spell might make her invisible, but it did not make her warm. That afternoon the owner of the safe house, a Station Master, recognized John Tito from flyers sent out to identify well known slave hunters. With Tito in the area, Olaf Rubicon would be, too.

Once again quick alternative plans were made. Night fell and a local boy guided her to a spot by the Nashua River. As soon as her conductor could find a second man, they'd take a canoe down the river, which flowed North, to Nashua, New Hampshire.

Where was that man? She'd crouched by the tree for an hour, or so it seemed. She'd been raised on a plantation with little experience of woods and forests. Every rustle of leaves, every chirp of insect or animal sent her heart racing.

A faint snap off to the left jolted her. Was that the conductor with the other man, or…?

❧   ❦

Her carriage ready to go, Simone waited just inside the stable door where the horse odor might mask her scent. The slave hunters were on the trail of somebody; maybe she could be of assistance to the hunted. Nobody should be enslaved or hunted solely because they ran for freedom. Simone had been both. If she had a chance to help one slave stay free, it was worth a few minutes of her time.

67

Exiting the Inn, the hunters walked with purpose down the wide main street. Simone followed them to a large white house near the edge of the town, a two-story square with an attached one-story square on the left.

They knocked on the door. As it swung open they pushed in. Peering through a window, Simone watched and listened as the owner, a slender, gray-haired man, protested the outrageous invasion. While the mortal, Tito, bulled his way about the house, Olaf reminded the owner of the Fugitive Slave Act of 1850 which required him to assist in the capture of runaway slaves. The owner said there were no slaves in his house, he would not help and to get out. He backed that up with a pistol taken from a desk drawer.

The owner had a steady hand; it did not waver as Olaf approached. But his eyes said what they all knew, this was a standoff the vampire would win. Simone figuratively held her breath.

A female scream from upstairs drew all their attention. Simone tensed, gripping the short sword hidden in the folds of her dress. In a few long seconds Tito descended the stairs, hands up. A shotgun came into sight followed by a handsome woman wearing a robe, hair undone. She, too, had a steady hand.

"Out," she said. "There are no slaves here. If you do not remove yourselves, my husband will have to buy me a new rug to replace the one stained with your blood."

"You'll go to jail if you shoot me," Tito said.

"I doubt that. But if I do, you'll be watching me from your grave." Nobody in that room had any doubt she meant it.

The husband stepped back and pointed his pistol right between Olaf's eyes. A bullet in the brain was a serious wound to a vampire. There was no guarantee of recovery from a wound like that.

Olaf stepped back. "I believe that there are no slaves here, now. But there have been, many. You will be watched."

"From outside," the husband said.

The hunters left without a word.

Many slave hunters used dogs to track runaways. Olaf Rubicon's sense of smell was the equal of any dog's. Once out of the house he walked around it then followed a path into the woods. Simone caught the scent, too. Silently, she followed.

A couple hundred yards down the path the hunters stopped. Rubicon cut off into the trees. Tito waited a minute then moved forward.

All senses wide open, Simone also moved along the path. The slave was near, the trap closing. Calling a warning would be useless. Rubicon would run her down in seconds. Simone carefully drew her short sword. She saw only one way it could go.

Crouching by a bend in the path, Simone saw it unfold.

Snap. Tito stepped on a small twig.

Under a tree to the right—a sharp intake of breath.

A rustle of movement.

A yelp of surprise and pain.

There, beside a thick Birch tree, Olaf loomed behind the kneeling slave woman silhouetted against the white bark. One long hand gripped her right shoulder. The woman held her hands together. A flash of red escaped through her fingers. In a quick movement, she slapped her left hand onto Olaf's. Simone heard the sizzle of burning flesh.

Olaf cried out and yanked his hand away.

The woman ran to the path. She had to pass between Tito and another tree.

Tito spun.

She threw something at his feet.

His feet stuck to the ground. He fell as he reached for her. She stumbled. At the limit of his reach, Tito caught her ankle. She screamed and sprawled on the ground.

In a second, Olaf lifted her off the ground by the back of her dress, holding her up like a squirming puppy.

"Gotch ya, damn nigger."

"Not yet, damn hunter."

He whirled around at the new voice.

Simone jammed a wood stake into him right below the breast bone up into his heart. Olaf froze, face a mask of astonishment. He dropped Grace, then his legs buckled in stages. He fell to his knees, sat back on his feet, dropped his head, and pitched forward.

Grace struggled to untangle herself from some bushes, but again, Tito, free of the binding spell, grabbed her leg and dragged her to her feet, a knife pressed against her throat.

"Who are you?" he demanded of Simone.

"A friend."

"None of mine. Step aside. She is worth some dead, also."

Silence shrouded the woods. Even the river's flow muted.

"To me, you are worth nothing, alive or dead."

Tito had no chance to reply. One second, ten feet separated them, the next, Simone's sword scraped past Grace's ear and impaled his neck.

Unfortunately for his future century and a half of victims, it missed the artery and spine. Simone wrenched the knife away and let it drop. She withdrew the sword and held the black woman up.

"Come. I will get you to safety."

A gunshot slashed the silence.

Grace jerked. "Oh."

Simone kicked the gun and kicked Tito. Bone cracked. With Grace in her arms, she headed for the river.

Boom. Pain ripped through her body. Simone stumbled, dropping her burden. A few seconds to assimilate the pain. She turned. Tito should be dead. Now she would make sure.

Tito crawled toward Olaf's body, unmoving in the middle of the path. A moonlit silhouette, Simone lurched toward him. He rolled over and shot her again. The bullet tore through her leg above her knee.

Flash of pain. Falling sideways. Another shot to her arm. Now a flash of fear with the pain. Unable to move. If he removed the stake from Olaf before she recovered…

Grace tugged at her. "We must run, Miss. I fear we cannot stop them."

Tito had gained his partner. Pausing to cough blood, he rolled him over. He coughed again and grabbed the stake.

Her handbag with the gun lay under her. "My sword," Simone said. "Take his head. Quick."

Tito yanked out the stake. Olaf shuddered and cried out.

Grace crawled to the sword and snatched it up.

"Quick, or we are finished."

Olaf sat up, a spring released, and shook his head. Beside him, Tito choked on his own blood. Olaf looked into his dying partner's eyes. "My friend, there is only one way to save you, if you want it."

Tito choked an unintelligible answer.

Olaf's mouth opened wide. Fangs glinted in the moonlight and dug into Tito's neck.

"Now," Simone urged. "Now."

Grace raised the sword, gasped at a throb of pain and swung.

Warned by her sound, Olaf raised his head, blood dripping from thick fangs. The blade sliced into his back and shoulder at the same time as he struck out with a knife, slicing deep into her side.

Determined to finish it before dying, Grace struck again, the blade cutting only a few inches into the back of his neck. She staggered back, taking a few seconds to gather her strength.

Losing the ability to move, Olaf leaned over Tito. "Go to my father."

Once again he lowered his extended mouth to his partner's neck. That's where the blade found him.

A few minutes later the sound of men running reached Simone. Sufficiently recovered, Simone tossed the bodies into the brush, and carried Grace to the river's edge.

Grace was dying.

"I will save you," Simone told her though unsure if the woman could hear. "If you do not like the life I give you, I will take it back."

Aware of the approaching men, she extended her fangs and sucked in witch's blood. Imagination told her she tasted the magic power in it, then she returned a small portion of the blood. Enough to change Grace's life for a very long time. She would not have to fear slave hunters ever again.

One man found them there and guided two men in a large canoe to their position.

"We have to go now," Simone told them. "The hunters are close." The men balked at taking Simone. Was she a hunter also? "Your Grace will recover, but she will need guidance only I can give her. We go together, or we go our own way."

Simone cradled the ex-slave's head as the men silently paddled the canoe down the dark river.

CHAPTER SIX

Grace's House

The Sea Witch made its way north through calm seas around Cape Ann then west toward lights lining the shore ten miles away.

Justine and Teresa traded information for a few minutes until Teresa fell asleep.

Curled up in a corner watching her friend sleep, Justine wondered if it was going to be worth all this trouble to find Antonia. What were the chances of Antonia still being alive? She'd been kidnapped right off the street and sold to the highest bidder to use as they desired; a slave, a sex slave, a plaything, or an object on which to work out a living or dead person's most violent and fantastical fantasies and then be discarded.

Teresa saw her daughter as a delicate flower, a girly girl, feminine and innocent, and a little spoiled. Justine knew Antonia away from her mother. Feminine, yes, innocent maybe not so much. She'd heard her speak when she thought no adult was listening. A virgin, yes, otherwise not worth taking. As virginity became rarer and rarer, its worth to those who desired to defile it rose. The girl had a stubborn streak, but also more sense than her mother gave her credit for. Under pressure, she might survive.

Whatever Teresa knew or did not know about her child, she had one thing Justine did not. Hope. Justine's daughter Brittany was dead. Killed twice, once by Justine's own hand. She had no hope that her child, her life, would someday be found alive. Since she killed the vampire Stephan Sinakov, she had closure, revenge in full measure. When she saw the hope in Teresa's face, she clung to that satisfaction. But Justine had no hope. And for that she envied Teresa.

Rancho Santa Fe, CA

Moonlight shadows illuminated The Girl as she crept through the boulders that hid the cave entrance. She didn't need the light to find her way, she knew it by heart, though hers had not beat in many years.

Sirens broke the silence of the exclusive neighborhood. They were on their way to a car accident about a mile away from the cave. The Girl figured nobody would miss a couple liters of blood from the bodies in the car.

Inside, lit by the remnants of several candles, the dirt floor had been brushed clean. There were no cooking or eating utensils, no furniture except a pallet made of blanket covered leaves. Any small animal carcasses had been removed.

On the bed lay a whip thin man. Muscles stood out under pale skin drawn tight as did the bones of his gaunt face. He lay still, not breathing. A thick scar encircled his neck.

The Girl set down the two water bottles filled with still warm blood and shook the man. "Master?"

Stephan Sinakov sat up in one quick motion. The Girl knelt beside him. He attacked her. Hands on her throat, he jumped on her and threw her to the dirt. He straddled her and shook her.

"Dee!" He tried to yell, but his voice came out as a harsh whisper. "Dee. Feed this girl to the dogs."

He heard no answer. Sinakov scanned the cave, dark to a mortal's eyes, bright to his. No one else was there.

"Who are you? How did you enter my room without being detected? Are you a ghost, come to haunt me?"

"Yes, I am a ghost. But I am here to help you, Master. "

Sinakov, hands tight on her neck, pulled her face close and inspected it with eyes and nose. "My...ghost. Yes?"

She held his eyes with hers. "Forever."

Tension drained from him like sand. His hands released her neck. He stared at her for a moment, then rolled off her to sit stiffly cross-legged on the pallet. He gave her no acknowledgment, as it should be. She was his servant, meant to be anonymous and inconspicuous, yet always there. The Girl was a good servant.

She wasted no time thinking about the attack. Since he had regained consciousness after the first week, his actions had been unpredictable.

For the next two weeks she had helped him regain control of his body. Even for a vampire, decapitation was a traumatic injury that took time to heal. He was prone to sudden irrational outbursts and just as sudden calms. The last week the outbursts and calms had mostly come together in a sort of uneasy equilibrium.

The Girl handed him a bottle of blood. Slowly he took it. "Thank you," he said. She flushed with happiness to be thanked for her service.

"It is time to leave here." His voice came out smoother with the soothing effect of the warm blood.

"Yes," the Girl agreed. "Where shall we go? The Families will not be pleased with your return."

"Families." He figuratively spit on them. "I don't need the Families anymore. I'll be my own Family."

To question her Master was not her way, but the Girl couldn't stop herself from blurting out, "Are you sure, Sir? A Vampire without a Family is vulnerable."

Like a switch flipped, he went into full vamp mode, snarling through fully extended fangs, "You dare question me? I am the Master. Do you want to be thrown to the dogs, girl?"

The Girl didn't flinch. In a few seconds Sinakov settled down and drank his blood.

"Where will we go, sir? Nobody will help us."

"There is one. He has no love for the Families. He will help me destroy them."

"Destroy the...?" Turning away, she glanced up at the ceiling and shook her head at that idea. "What of the one who...injured you?"

"He will help me destroy her!"

The Girl sighed, a mortal action she had recently used often. She thought she knew the answer to her question before she asked it. "Who will help us, sir?"

"Rubicon. We were allies once. We will go to him now."

She said nothing. Rubicon was more likely to cut off Sinakov's head or stake him out in the sun than help him.

"Do you know where he is, sir?"

"He travels the world. But I know who can find him. We must go to Florida. Now."

She had her doubts about contacting Rubicon, but they needed to get out of the cave. Slinging a messenger bag over her shoulder and picking up a gym bag with clothes for her Master, she said, "Shall we go, sir. I have a car."

Outside she led him through the dark woods. They passed within sight of a large open area surrounded by grass. The debris from the fire that destroyed the mansion had been removed. All that remained was the blackened concrete foundation.

"I hope the owner had insurance," Sinakov said.

"I believe he did, sir. This way."

Grace's House

A band of gray lightened the Eastern sky by the time the Sea Witch entered a narrow rocky channel. All were on deck, the two vampires glancing uneasily at the pale horizon.

"Plenty of time," Ian said. "We're almost there."

As the boat turned left into an open water area two hundred yards in diameter, a floating dock appeared as from a thick mist. Tied to one side of the dock was a forty foot speedboat that looked like it was going fifty knots standing still. From the beach, wood steps searched their way up an easy slope of rock to a rambling weathered-gray, two-story beach house.

Ian expertly backed his boat to the dock. Two men, mortals by their absence of anxiety over the coming sunrise, wearing boat shoes, khakis, and blue hoodies, stood by.

"Ladies, it's been interesting meeting you all. These men will help you." Ian scanned the eastern sky. "I think you have time to avoid a nasty sunburn. And please try and stay out of trouble. They will be looking for you, and there is only so much I can do without having to sneak off and hide in some secluded little beach town in Mexico. Which during the winter always sounds like an excellent idea."

The men helped Teresa onto the dock. She said to Ian, *"Muchas gracias.* I see a long and happy future for you. Well, I'm sure I would if I could see that far. I hope so, anyway."

Ian nodded. "And you. All of you."

"Keep your feet on the ground," Teresa said.

A muscular, dark-skinned man with a shaved head and caring eyes took her arm. "I am Pablo. You are welcome here."

"I'm Teresa." Despite her pain and fatigue she tried to pat her hair into place, then gave it up. She allowed him to help her up the steps while the other man carried her gear.

Before they reached the house, the Sea Witch had turned the corner out of sight. The sun broke the horizon as an African-American woman wrapped tightly in a plush terrycloth robe opened the sea-green front door for them.

Dark curtains in an otherwise bright living room covered the east-facing windows. The three took in their new surroundings filled with African and Caribbean motifs—exotic woods, white wicker furniture with brilliant tropical cushions, African artifacts. They turned to face their hostess. Teresa leaned on Pablo more than she needed to. Justine smiled to herself.

"I am Grace," the woman said. "I have been waiting."

"We had a little excitement on the way," Justine said, not sure how to treat this supposedly most powerful witch. "This is Teresa. She's injured. Can you help her?"

From what little Justine knew of Grace she had expected an imposing woman, projecting power and strength. At first look she was average height and weight, with long dark hair flowing back in a loose braid from a narrow forehead. Gleaming black skin with a hint of mahogany stretched over high cheekbones. A beautiful woman.

Justine had never quite got the *eyes are the windows of the soul* reference, until then. Staring into her eyes was like staring into wormholes to a past of pain and anguish. Horrific suffering had happened in there that made the lenses glitter like ice cold crystal, hard and strong and unforgiving. Yet, they reflected kindness and gentleness, too. As the woman studied her in return, Justine understood the warning: *I can be your friend, but if you cross me, I will be your worst enemy.*

"I am aware of your journey. You are safe here." She stood face to face with Teresa who only kept her feet because of Pablo's strong arm around her body. Grace put her hands on Teresa's hips and casually regarded her. Teresa's eyes fluttered, closed, then popped open. "I have taken away your pain for awhile," Grace said. "We will fix you in a few minutes."

Grace's eyes turned warm and inviting when they met Simone's steady gaze. She bowed her head in deference. "Welcome...Mistress."

Simone stepped forward and favored Grace with a genuine smile. "Did I not tell you once that you never need to call anyone Mistress or Master again? Including me."

Grace took Simone's hands in hers. "Yes, I believe you did. However, in this one instance, I want to."

They hugged for long moments, saying nothing, communicating everything.

Simone held the other's face in her hands. "You have done well here, yet you still have enemies."

She gripped Simone's hands, nodding. "They have long memories. As do I. But you are safe here. There are rooms for you all. Perhaps over dinner you can tell me what you wish of me that you have come so far with so much trouble." She pointed behind them. "Kerry will show you where. If you need anything, please ask."

Kerry, a pretty, dark-haired woman maybe nineteen years old when changed, had that shoulders back, slightly arrogant stance of a vampire. Justine looked at Kerry then at the two mortal men.

Grace stood shoulder to shoulder with Justine. "I do not turn anyone without their permission, and never that young. She did a great selfless kindness for a friend some years ago. It would have cost her life. When recovered, she could choose to end it if she wished. A choice I, too, had to make. It was hard for her. She loved the outdoors."

Justine remembered her own choice. With nothing left to live for, it had not been hard. She'd been dead inside already. She might as well have been dead outside, also.

"Can you really help Teresa? Glamour, and Pablo, can only do so much, and I don't want to have to turn her."

"Of course. Go. Rest. We will talk later."

Grace signaled to the other man, Nigel. He joined them as she said a few unintelligible words and touched Teresa's forehead. Teresa slumped, and the two men carried her away, the vampire witch following close behind.

At Grace's Table

Teresa set down her knife and fork, leaned back and savored the last bite of the biggest filet mignon she'd ever seen. With her previously broken arm she downed the last taste of a wonderful Burgundy. A small burp completed the meal. She'd never felt better—she'd woken with no broken bones, no cuts or bruises.

The others at the table, Justine, Simone, and Grace, smiled at her obvious satisfaction.

Grace said, "I hope the steak was a suitable substitute for anything resembling Mexican food. That is not often on the menu here."

"I had so-called Mexican food last week. I've never had a steak like that. It was perfect." She breathed out a deep sigh of contentment. "I still can't believe I can say this, but I hope your blood was satisfactory."

Justine lifted her crystal glass and studied the remains. "It was blood of exceptional quality."

Simone wafted her glass under her nose. "Extraordinary bouquet."

"Very clean taste. A vegetarian, I'd say."

"Free range, also. No more than twenty-one or twenty-two years old. Very fresh."

"But hearty."

"Yes, but not too much so. Thick on the tongue, easy going down."

"And with its beautiful, deep burgundy color, an exquisite vintage. My compliments to Grace and the provider of this exceptional elixir."

They raised their glasses to their hostess, then with a flourish, drank off the remainder.

Suppressing a smile, Teresa said, "You could have just said it was pretty good."

They all burst into laughter which took a while to calm.

Kerry cleared the table, brought coffee for Teresa and Simone and wine for Justine and Grace. They grew serious.

Keeping the conversation as light as possible considering the subject, the guests told their story of how they came to be together. Justine let the others tell most of it. At first the events they described seemed like they took place decades, centuries ago. Until she spoke of Brittany. Then it seemed as if it was happening right then. She had to stop and close her eyes. Beating or not, a broken heart hurts.

She felt Teresa's fingers intertwine with hers. The unrestricted sympathy of a friend; there was no better cure for grief than that.

Finally, Simone told Grace what they wanted.

"We had no idea this would cause so much trouble," Justine added. "We apologize for—"

Grace waved away the apology. "Kazza knew how it would end, but she didn't know they watched for people looking for me. You didn't either. It was mighty good of you to go after her."

"She was a friend. As was Treen." Simone stared into her coffee cup.

"Still." Grace glanced at Teresa. "Maybe not such a good idea to humiliate a man in public like that." Teresa gave a little shrug of agreement. "Though I understand and applaud you. As for Tito, it is inevitable that he will find a way to find me. He is patient and relentless."

Justine said, "I understand Tito's desire for revenge. Especially since you and he tangled several times after that first meeting. But what about this Rubicon? Have you met him? Is he driving Tito, patiently waiting for his revenge through him? Or is Tito on his own mission?"

"I have not met him personally, however I have seen him." She flashed a smile at their puzzled looks. "There are other ways to spy on someone besides security cameras and satellites. But even for a vampire, night has its limitations."

"Christ. The CIA would love to get their hands on you," Teresa said, absently inspecting her healed arm.

"I'm sure they would, if they knew where I was."

Justine leaned forward. "I still want to know about Rubicon, but this house seems awfully exposed, even though the trees block sight of the road. Especially considering the patience of your pursuers."

"When I first met Simone I was still learning the limits of my power."

"You have limits?" Simone asked, all innocent.

"I haven't turned you human yet, have I?"

"Thank the Gods."

"No, thank me." She wasn't joking. "After a hundred years I knew a thing or two. Several permanent warding spells limit visibility from all directions. The driveway is invisible from the road."

"We saw it from the water."

"You were with Ian."

Justine slumped back in her chair. "Jeez. Vampires, Oracles, and now witches. Zombies?"

Grace hesitated a couple of seconds. "Not like you're thinking."

Justine threw up a hand, giving up on the subject. "Rubicon?" Before Grace could speak, "Werewolves?"

A slight shrug from their host.

"Teresa, why didn't you talk me out of all this before?"

"I did try. You weren't listening."

"That's no excuse. Rubicon. And if he's a troll or a fairy I don't want to know."

"Only a vampire."

"Thank God for that."

"He is very rich, very powerful, and still very much wants to cut off my head. Tito is his man."

"Great."

Teresa brought up the real question. "Can you find my daughter?"

Grace sighed and nodded. "I can. Much depends on her location. Also, I am not the only witch there is. If she is shielded, it will be difficult."

"If she's dead?" Teresa's eyes glistened.

"Difficult. Eventually."

"How much...What do you want for...?"

Grace laid fingertips on Teresa's arm, and moved her head slightly side to side. "However, if you get a chance to stop Tito from coming after me..."

North of Thatcher Island

Rosalie, a small thirty foot sportfisher idled through the calm early-morning water a quarter mile north of Thatcher Island. The two fishermen aboard, Clint and George, lifelong fishing buddies, had lines out for bluefish. They'd been east of the island and as the sun rose had turned west.

Clint manned the helm from the flying bridge while George tended the lines. With high-powered binoculars Clint scanned the shoreline, as he always did. "Looking for naked women," he said, though he never saw any. Really, he was looking at the houses built at the edge of the rocky shore.

Rich folks' houses. Clint wanted to live in one of them. Working on the state road maintenance crew and a few bucks from fishing would never move him into one, unless he won the lottery or had a rich uncle he didn't know about. He knew that, and was mostly okay with it. Though he'd love to move his wife, Rosalie, and two kids out of the forty-year-old cottage they lived in.

He'd scanned the shore up and down a couple of times when a lobster boat appeared close to shore heading out. Strange. Where had it come from? There were no bays, harbors or anchorages in that area. A good size swell was running, but nothing that would hide a white, forty-something-foot boat.

The powerful glasses didn't reveal the identity of the skipper. He knew a couple lobstermen, but not the boats.

"Hey, George. You know that boat?"

George scanned it with a smaller pair of binoculars. "Seen it in Rockport, I think. Why?"

"It just sorta appeared real close to shore. Weird."

"Another mystery of the sea. Why doncha steer this sinker to some fish instead of wonder'n about a damn lobster boat?"

Clint steered south, keeping an eye on the boat until it slid behind the island. Strange. But that was the sea for ya.

Scotty's Fish Shack Bar

Scotty's was one of the best—some years The Best when he bothered to hustle votes—restaurants in Rockport. It was also one of the oldest, and Scotty went to great lengths to preserve that old-timey ambiance, mostly by contrived neglect. Netting and manila lines hung from the ceiling while old photos and moldy mounted fish decked the walls. A full size carving of a mermaid graced the men's room with her breasts rubbed bare for luck.

Clint and George held down stools in the bar as they had for all the years since they turned twenty-one. They no longer noticed the ambiance. They were on their second beer when Jack Kester slid onto a stool next to them.

"Better watch out, Clint," George said. "The law's here to arrest you for peeping in those houses on Penzance Road."

"So how many naked women you seen," Jack asked.

"Too many to count."

"Yeah, right."

They laughed and drank.

"I did see a ghost boat, though."

"Shit, are you still on that?"

"I'm telling ya. It came out of nowhere."

"You need to tell Clint to wear a hat out in the sun."

"I told him I thought I'd seen the boat in the harbor."

"So tell me about this ghost boat. Should I call Mulder and Scully?"

Ten minutes later Kester said, "I gotta go. Dad'll need his supper. If you see the boat again, get a name. The law will track it down."

Jack Kester's House

Jack Kester liked the kitchen in his house. More properly it was his father's house, though Jack lived there and paid his share of expenses, including the mortgage which would be paid off in fourteen months.

The kitchen had been remodeled ten years ago with new cabinets and counter tops. None of the appliances was more than five years old. He liked the breakfast table by the bay window that looked out on the large, treed backyard.

What he hated was having to cook in it. More specifically, having to cook his father's meals. He loved and respected his father. Even after the old man's heart attack, he was there for Jack, supporting him, keeping him strong, even as he grew weaker.

His dad, Nicholas—never Nick or Nicky—was on a strict low sodium, low fat diet that he wouldn't, sometimes couldn't, make for himself. Jack dutifully made the meals his mother should have been making. His efforts seemed to be working. Nicholas held his own and might yet survive to get the heart transplant he needed. Then Nicholas's lying, cheating, cowardly bitch of a wife would be sorry she ran out when they needed her most. Just like all the other lying cunts who made promises with their bodies and mouths they never kept. You can't trust a single one of them, his father told him, and he was right.

"Here ya go, Dad." Jack slid a plate of tasteless mashed potatoes, white meat turkey, and carrots in front of him.

Shaking his unkempt head, Nicholas stared at the food. Poked at it. "Same healthy shit?"

"Same healthy shit. You have to eat it, Dad. You're close to the top of the list. You have to be healthy when a heart becomes available."

The old man stared at his son with a sarcastic smile.

"You know what I mean."

Jack related his day, ending with, "Had a beer with Clint and George. Clint said he saw a ghost lobster boat down off Penzance Road. Just appeared from nowhere he said. Right off the rocks."

"Yeah? Saw a car disappear there ta other day."

"Oh yeah?"

"Yep, John Bartholomew took me to the doctor down Gloucester two days ago. He had to drop something off on Penzance Road. There was a car ahead. It goes around that corner where there's no house, ya know. Goes out of sight, five seconds later we come around, and the Goddamn car is gone. Ain't no driveways there. No place to go. But it's gone. Poof. We noticed it, some foreign piece of shit. Poof."

Jack stared at his plate. "That's about where Clint saw his ghost boat."

"Well, now you got a ghost car, too. Oooo."

"Always wondered why nobody ever built there. What do ya think of the Patriots this year?"

Grace's House

After dinner Justine and Teresa wandered onto an open flagstone terrace laid on the cliff edge. North, East and South opened to magnificent ocean vistas with the lighthouse on Thatcher Island at their center.

They lay on lounge chairs under the stars and talked about California—that seemed so long ago. About Harry. "Did you talk to him?"

"Only for a few minutes. He had a case and had to go. He knows I'm safe. And you, too."

About what they'd done, what they might have to do. There was no going back, only forward. They were on their path and determined to follow it. They had no choice, and no regrets strong enough to stop them.

About Antonia. Though she may have been a little spoiled and fragile, she had a stubborn streak that might get her in trouble, or help her survive. They had no illusions as to what she was abducted and sold for. If she was still alive—and Teresa insisted she was because she'd know if she was not—and they found her, would she be the Antonia they searched for? Or only a shell, or something worse? Could Teresa do what Justine had done to Brittany if it came to it? Teresa said yes, but neither one believed it. Justine wiped away her friend's tears and reassured her that everything would be all right. They had doubts about that, too.

Simone and Grace joined them, sitting on the low stone wall defining the patio's edge.

"Tomorrow night we will search for your daughter. There are preparations to make. Because she could be anywhere in the world the search will have to be done in two parts. Locate the general area, then a more specific spot. That is when I will know if she is alive."

"She is alive." Teresa thumped her chest.

"Let us hope. Do you have any other items of hers? Things she had for a long time?"

"I have her favorite sweater. A stuffed turtle she had since she was five. A picture of us."

Justine asked, "You said 'other items?' "

The witch studied Teresa. "Those things you brought will help, but *you* are her closest connection. I will use you to focus the energy. It will not be easy. You must be strong and patient. Can you be that?"

Teresa received a nod from Justine.

"If any mortal can be strong enough..." Sporting a crooked grin, Simone pointed at Teresa. "Patient...?"

"I'll do whatever I have to."

"I know you will, my dear. Pablo will provide whatever you need."

Grace rose up, every inch the powerful vampire witch. She nodded at her guests and left them, her movement so smooth she could have been floating.

Pablo waited by the door, eyes on Teresa.

Teresa met his gaze as she sorted through what she might need. Her thoughts kept returning to one thing, and it wasn't a glass of hot milk.

Penzance Drive

Kester parked his police cruiser on the narrow shoulder of Penzance Road. Behind him was the corner his dad mentioned. Ahead, the road curved gently for at least a quarter of a mile. Trees grew close to the road. He walked the edge between the trees and narrow shoulder a hundred yards up to the first dirt driveway, seeing no tire tracks up to the chain across the road.

Walking back he spotted the tire tracks. They showed up in the dirt for about two feet, then stopped as if cut. He saw no sign in the trees or brush that a vehicle had passed through. Following the angle of the tracks, Kester stepped into the trees.

Past the tire track cutoff line he felt...something, then entered the trees. Five feet in he felt something else. Everything looked the same, smelled the same. The temperature rose a few degrees. Curious, because the temperature usually decreased under the thick canopy, especially that early in the morning. It was as if the air pressure had increased a point or two. Not unpleasant, only different.

Kester pushed on through the thick underbrush. Ten more feet and his heart raced. To his surprise, he found his hand on his sidearm. He jerked his head around, looking for...what? He took a couple more steps. His heart was really pounding now—sweat on his brow, breathing quick and shallow. His gun was in his hand.

Two more steps. No farther. Danger lurked. Danger watched. He spun about searching for whatever evil stalked him. One more step and he'd have gone too far. He'd never make it out of the stygian wood. Panic churned in his chest. Where was it? He spun around. There? There?

Kester backed up, gun swinging wide, ready for the evil hidden behind every tree and bush. Watching him. Waiting for him.

Back at his cruiser, Kester downed half a bottle of water and caught his breath. What the fuck was that? Jeeesus. Nothing he was going to tell anyone about, that's for damn sure. Still, as he drove away he couldn't help wondering, ghost boat, ghost car and now a...ghost? Was that why nobody had built a house on that property? Something to look into-after he went home and changed his sweat soaked shirt.

Police Chief's Office—Rockport, MA

Danny Travella lounged in his leather desk chair, feet on his heavy wooden desk, a glass of whiskey on his stomach. On a wine colored couch across the room, Tito stretched out, boots on the thick upholstered arm.

A slender man, about six feet tall, slumped in a simpler chair usually reserved for the more common visitors the Chief had invited or who had invited themselves. Casually dressed in khakis and a black chamois shirt, his neck length amber hair flowed fashionably unruly, the picture of a wealthy tourist. But he was no summer visitor stayed too long. He was in Rockport to find Grace and destroy her, thus setting himself up to be the most powerful sorcerer.

Oakes did not share his ambition with the others. Ostensibly he was there to locate Grace and the two vampires and mortal who had humiliated Tito. Oakes thought it was about time somebody took the vamp down a notch. Tito was an arrogant, cruel son-of-a-bitch and if one of those vamps sent his head rolling, Oakes would count that as a satisfactory side benefit of any operation.

Tito said, "Grace has to be in this area. Those three, which you had in custody and let escape, disappeared too quickly. We know they came here looking for her. So where are they? Oakes, can't you do your witchery and find them?"

Oakes had too much experience to let a vamp bait him. "Grace is as powerful as me. She will be prepared for my *sorcery*. Her place will have multiple wards, probably one for invisibility, at least two to scare the mortals away. A warning spell, a few defensive ones. Wards are meant to not be detectable. If you can find a place you think she could be, then I can determine if there are warding spells in place. I can work with that. Often it's a spot where small, out of the ordinary things happen."

Jack Kester only half listened. He sat by the door, meant to be more an observer than a participant. Clenched fists lay in his lap. He picked absently at a couple of tiny scabs on his left knuckles, thinking how they had felt against that woman's face.

Gloucester

Jack didn't like being scared. It made him feel insignificant and unwanted like when his mother left. Sure his dad had been there for him, but his mother didn't want him. She was the best mother ever, beautiful and caring, he thought she loved him. Then she left, without a word or explanation. And if your mother didn't want you, what other woman would?

When he finally understood she wasn't coming back he became angry. Why would she make him feel like that? He was fifteen at the time. A girl he liked turned him down for a date. Just like his mother, she didn't want him. He hit her—a right to her cheek. That was the only part he remembered. That solid smack of his fist against her cheek. He got in trouble of course, but nothing was broken, and they understood his anger. Even after a sincere apology, which he did feel at the time, he would never have a chance with her again. After a short suspension from school and some perfunctory therapy, he was cool.

But he remembered how it felt, that satisfying jolt through his arm into his chest. He took up boxing for a brief time, but he wasn't very good and when he did connect, it wasn't the same hitting a guy as the feeling of his bare fist against the softness of a woman's flesh.

Occasionally over the years when he'd been scared or his dad got drunk and went off on a rant about his chicken shit whore of a mother, he'd find a woman and get his calmness back.

He'd seen the woman in Gloucester a month ago while delivering a suspect to the city jail. At first he thought his mother had come back to him, but she hadn't. He took her license number. A couple evenings he went by her house. He saw her husband who owned a hotel, and their young daughter. *Someday I'll do you a favor, kid. She's beautiful and pretends to love you, but one day she'll run off, leaving you alone and* unwanted. If she's not beautiful anymore she won't leave you. She'll stay forever.

After a quick shower to wash away his fear, Kester dressed in civilian clothes and drove his father's car to Gloucester, parking a few blocks from the woman's house.

Most of the houses were two-story, wood sided, in good repair with plenty of trees and fences around large yards. A dirt alley ran behind all the houses for trash and service trucks. He walked down the alley and slipped through the gate. Crouching behind a thick spruce he watched the windows. When he saw her in an upstairs window, he raced to the back door. Christ, not even locked. Don't we keep telling people they can't leave their doors unlocked anymore?

He grabbed her in the kitchen, one gloved hand covering her mouth and nose. By the time she regained consciousness he had her tied to a chair and blindfolded.

Still with gloves on, Kester held her head with one hand on top. Mouth close to her ear, he said, "Don't scream, Mom. You don't get to scream."

Then he hit her.

"Ohhhhh." Warmth grew in his fist. Yes, yes, that's what he needed. That warmth to grow and travel up his arm into his chest and warm him like a hug, all arms and breasts and that scent, only hers, so that he'd know her even in the dark when she rescued him from his nightmares.

Smack! Left hand. Same glow, same heat. Yes, balance, a full two arm hug, warm and safe, no reason to be afraid.

Right. Left. Right. Left. Each blow brought him closer to that safe place free of anger and fear.

Right. Left. Blood spattered now, on her clothes, on the bed, on him. Good thing he was naked, but for the gloves.

Warmth spread up his arms. But he still hadn't touched her flesh to flesh. It was important to protect his hands. "What would you do without your hands?" she had always asked him. You have such nice big hands, so soft. She would hold them to her face and kiss the palms. Take care of your hands.

But you aren't here anymore to care, are you? I can do what I want with my hands—and you don't CARE. He slipped the gloves off and laid them on her blood soaked lap. Cradling her face, he lifted her head and removed the blindfold. It wasn't needed now, her eyes were swollen shut. Open palms formed fists, pressed against her ruined cheeks. Oh yes. There it was, hot skin to hot skin. The warmth surged into his shoulders. Almost there. Almost there.

Smack.

Smack.

Smack.

Smack.

Ahhh. The calming heat splattered his arms and face and chest. Fists to his own temples. Pressing hard.

Calm.

Calm.

Calm.

Calm.

Nothing to be scared of now. Fear gone. Nothing to worry about. But look at his hands, dirty. He should take care of his hands.

At peace, Jack walked into the bathroom and turned on the shower.

<u>*Police Chief's Office—Rockport, MA*</u>

"I can work with that. Often it's a spot where small, out of the ordinary things happen."

It took a few seconds for Oakes' words to break Kester's focus on his fists. It had been a relaxing drive back from Gloucester. Another storm was supposed to come in, but the afternoon had been sunny and warm. "What do you mean out of the ordinary things happen?"

The police chief, the sorcerer, and the vampire turned their attention to the officer they'd forgotten was there.

Oakes said, "Seeing things that aren't there, a strange smell or noise that doesn't belong. An unusual feeling when you pass a particular place."

"What about things appearing and disappearing?"

Oakes scootched around in his seat, his stare unwavering. "Like what?"

Kester spread sweaty palms on his uniform trousers. "Well, my dad told me..."

Grace's House

Sundown. Justine, Simone and Teresa lounged on the stone patio. A thin corrugated cloud layer glowed pink for a brief time before it faded to gray. A three-quarters moon hung like a milky, lopsided ball. Holding hands, Justine and Teresa sat cross-legged on plush bamboo armchairs with matching ottomans. Justine felt the quiver in her friend's hand.

"Are you ready, Tee? It may not be good news."

"I just want to know."

"Teresa," Simone said from a lounge chair on the opposite side. "I hope Antonia is alive, but if she isn't, what will you do?"

"Do you think she's...*muerte?*"

"After this amount of time, I think I will be more surprised that she is alive than if she is not."

"Then let us surprise you." Grace stood behind them. None had witnessed her entrance. She wore a flowing, full length dress of many colors. The patterns did not seem to be fixed, though no movement was obvious. Bracelets adorned her arms, black on the right, silver on the left.

Grace lay a hand on Teresa's shoulder. "Are you ready?"

Teresa sighed. "Yes. I want to know. I want to know whether to keep hoping, or to..."

"Then come. Let us find out."

Grace led them to a wing of the house they had not been allowed into. They all felt it when they passed through the heavy, iron bound door—a prickly feeling of power, like the electric anticipation of a thunderstorm times ten.

The last door of three on the right was also a heavy iron door. Inside, Kerry and Pablo waited. Teresa and Pablo shared a glance before he closed the door with a solid thunk.

The light walls of the thirty by thirty foot room had no decoration or finish, strictly bare wood. In each corner an ebony column rose to a foot below the high ceiling, topped by a ball of white stone carved with two circles of runes at right angles to each other.

Dark stone made up the floor with a twenty foot circle of golden stone in the center, and where there was a smaller circle about three feet in diameter.

"No hexagrams?" questioned Justine.

Grace laughed. "Hexagrams are for Black Magic. I do not participate in Black Magic here." The little yeah-right smiles of Kerry and Pablo suggested otherwise. "White Magic encompasses all while the other is done in secret."

Justine didn't question Grace about that. They had other business that night. She looked up to the fifteen foot high ceiling and made a small surprised sound. A ten foot circle opened to the night. Inside the opening, copper formed an upside down funnel, the wide bottom end three feet in diameter, ending in a broad curled lip.

"Do you need all this to find one person?"

"If we had some small area to search, such as a city or even a state, no. To search Earth for one person, yes. It takes much more power. Shall we begin?"

Kerry, dressed similarly to Grace, placed Justine and Simone opposite each other between the columns. Nigel entered, and he and Pablo took positions on the remaining walls. Grace led Teresa, who held Antonia's turtle to her breast with both hands, to the center of the circles.

"Once it has begun, you must not move. You will grow weak. Magic takes power. Each of us has only so much. Do not waver. Whatever you see, do not move from this circle." Grace flashed an encouraging smile. "We will find your Antonia."

Kerry brought Grace an oversized wand, a three foot length of polished wood tipped with silver and what looked to Justine like an ivory handle. Kerry retrieved a similar, though smaller wand and they faced each other, wands held out with both hands.

Danger! Danger! Justine tensed, ready to run, ready to fight. Her body quivered with dread as if it had been injected into her chest and spread quickly, infecting her. Yet, she could not move. Across the room she saw that Simone felt the same.

Grace and Kerry moved to opposite corners. Wands raised with both hands they quietly recited words not of any language Justine had ever heard. "Haf!" both women cried out. The dread in Justine vanished with such speed she slumped against the wall, as did Simone. Their wide open eyes had a *what-the-Hell?* look to them. Teresa's apprehensive expression almost made them laugh.

The women performed the same ritual at the other corners. Now the atmosphere in the room was of power held in check, waiting to be unleashed. Grace stood just inside the larger circle. Both hands on the ivory handle, she aimed the wand above Teresa's head. Again she murmured strange words. An indistinct line of shimmery air shot out of all the white balls, meeting above Teresa.

Still murmuring, still pointing, Grace strode around the circle. A tiny ball of white light materialized where the shimmers met. Spinning slowly, it grew quickly as Grace made two more circuits. Colors appeared as random smears. The light took on definition. At about ten feet in diameter it slowed and resolved into a detailed globe of the Earth, with blue oceans, green continents and white polar caps, all rotating slowly.

Teresa gaped upward, expression a mixture of awe and fear. Justine felt the same.

Grace approached Teresa and touched the wand to her chest.

Teresa stiffened. A golden aura seeped out of her, enveloped her body, then flowed upward, covering the floating Earth.

"Haf!"

From the top of the Earth the aura leaped up into the copper funnel which guided it through the roof's opening, where it dispersed into the night.

Minutes went by. The aura continued to flow. Grace and Kerry strode around the globe seeking a sign.

Kerry spotted it first. "There. Oh my God. Does that mean...?"

Grace joined her. "I don't know."

Justine wanted to cry out, "What? Where is she?" Afraid to break the spell, she said nothing, only waited impatiently for the globe to turn.

Finally, she saw a spot of golden light, in the middle of the Atlantic Ocean. That can't be good.

Grace stuck her wand into the light. The Earth stopped turning. The gold aura traveled down the wand to coat Grace with its haze. After half a minute, she removed the wand.

"FAH!"

The aura faded from her, the globe, and finally Teresa. Pablo rushed to ease her to the floor. Above them the globe contracted and faded away.

Justine and Simone joined the others around Teresa. All looked expectantly at Grace.

"I believe she is alive." She held up a hand. "But I cannot promise it. She is moving to the west. Too slow for an airplane."

"A boat," Justine said. "Probably headed for the Caribbean. It's that time of year."

Simone and Pablo lifted Teresa to her feet.

Justine asked, "Is it possible to get more detail now that you know where she is?"

"I believe the boat has warding charms. Strong ones. I must be careful or they will know I am interested in them."

Teresa shook off her helpers. "Can we do it now? I'm ready."

"You are not ready. You must rest. As I must." Grace rubbed a hand over her forehead. "Magic takes a heavy toll on the body. Like working out in a gym, one gets stronger the more you use your power. But you must rest."

Pablo caught Teresa in his arms as she fell. "I will make sure she rests." He carried her through the heavy door.

"Rest means rest," Justine called after them. "Those two are like rabbits." She smiled. "A good thing for her."

Simone asked, "What do you do now?"

"And do you really think Antonia is alive?"

"I believe so, but the signs are weak. It may be that she is weak, or it may be the warding. I will have to be very careful with the scrying. Midnight, we will try."

"Will you be able to identify the boat, its course or position?"

"Doubtful. Midnight." Kerry and Nigel unobtrusively escorted her from the room.

❧   ❧

Justine lay on the bed in her cozy guestroom. Pastels reminiscent of the Bahamas predominated. A mural at the end of the room showed a Caribbean beach view through a window.

Simone lounged in an armchair, feet up, a glass of red in her hand. "What do you think?" Simone asked. "You are *le navigateur* here."

"Right. Me and my vast experience. We're dealing with rich people here. Rich people have yachts. My guess she's on a large yacht probably headed for the Caribbean. At least as a first stop."

"If Grace cannot identify the boat it will be hard to find."

"Not for the police." Justine held up her cell phone. Smiling, she gave Simone a raised eyebrow look.

Simone downed her wine and, emitting a theatrical groan, rose to her feet. "I get it. A private love chat with the mortal. Don't worry about me. I'll be doing…something. Maybe Nigel wants to play."

"We'll find Antonia, won't we?"

"*Oui, ma cher.* We will find her. Tell Harry I am taking very good care of you."

93

The Sundowner

Harry sat in his usual seat next to the wall at one end of the Sundowner's U-shaped bar. It was Happy Hour, though a subdued one, even for the middle of the week. Darwin wasn't there. Too early for him and he was busy lately dealing behind the scenes with the fallout of Stephan Sinakov's death. He should say Henri Gireaux's death.

He nursed his beer and thought about that death—same as he'd been doing for the last hour. He hadn't mentioned anything to Darwin, with numerous factions of the Sinakov Family in the area attempting with little success, so far, to decide who would become Master Vampire of the Family. Bad enough the previous Master was dead, he had been a fake, murdering the real Stephan Sinakov hundreds of years ago and usurping his place.

The Sinakov Family plied their main trade—transporting people, whether they wanted to be transported or not—worldwide. Why did they have to come to northern San Diego county to sort out their differences? There had been incidents. Through Darwin, Harry had warned them that if anybody went missing, especially young women, vampires or not, law enforcement was coming down on them like a ton of bricks. That many bricks would give even the strongest vampire a hell of a headache.

Harry didn't have anywhere near that kind of juice, but somebody had taken the warning seriously. A fourteen year old girl had gone missing. Within twelve hours the girl was found unharmed. Such could not be said of the man who abducted her. He died hard. Another murder where Harry knew who did it, but couldn't say anything. The whole vampire thing was best left in the closet—not that anybody was looking too hard.

But two other suspicious deaths had him thinking and making phone calls outside his jurisdiction. He had to be sure before passing his suspicions along. What a shit storm if he was right.

He signaled Bayley for another beer at the same time his cell chirped.

"Hi."

"Hi. Catch any bad guys lately?"

"Haven't been any bad guys around since you all left."

"That's because they're all over here."

"Trouble?"

Justine brought him up to date.

"So Antonia may be alive?"

"We may find out at midnight. The witching hour, you know."

"I'm still finding it hard to believe all this is real."

"Apparently it is."

The silence stretched.

"How's Teresa holding up?"

"She totally healed and getting some personal relaxation therapy from a hunk called Pablo."

"Ah. So she's adapting well to the road. What happens if you find Antonia?"

"I imagine they'll go home."

"And you?"

"We have leads on a few other missing girls."

"Will you come…here first?"

"If you still—"

"Yes."

"Then yes."

It was totally crazy, him and Justine, he'd known that from the start. But the thought of actually seeing her again brought a smile to his face and joy to his heart, to use a clichéd sappy phrase. A bunch of squabbling vampires didn't seem so important at that moment. Harry was tempted to tell her of his concerns, but he had to be sure before he unloaded that bombshell on her.

"Harry? You still there?"

"Always. So, midnight."

"Yep. The thing is that she may not be able to identify the boat because of warding spells or some such mumbo-jumbo. I think we'll be able to get some coordinates. Is there any way you can do something with that? Otherwise, we have no way of knowing what boat to look for or where it's going."

"So you just love me for my satellites."

"Among other things."

Drawing it out to have time to think, Harry said, "Well, without a compelling open case here I can't go through official channels. But I do know a guy I went to school with who works for NASA Search and Rescue. Maybe he can help, warding spells or not."

"Thank you, Harry. This is all way more complicated than I ever thought it would be."

"And you think usurping government satellites is going to make it less complicated?"

"No comment. Sounds like you're at the Sundowner. Say hi to Bayley. And Darwin?"

"He's busy." He hadn't told her much about the Sinakov doings. She had enough to worry about.

They talked of inconsequential things for a few minutes, said they missed each other and hung up.

Bayley leaned on the bar opposite him. "Justine?"

"She says hi."

"Hi back. I know that look on your face. You've had it for weeks. Trouble of some kind. What have you got yourself into, Harry?"

What indeed? All he could do was shrug and shake his head. "How about, nothing another beer can't fix, and leave it at that?"

Bayley gently touched his hand. "One day you have to tell me what the hell's going on."

Penzance Road

Full night approached quickly. Tito and Kester leaned against a large SUV parked on the edge of Penzance Road and watched Oakes move toward them.

"He looks like he just saw the Widow Teeker taking a bath down at Callahan Falls."

"Widow Teeker?" Being this close to Tito scared Kester. His fists clenched and relaxed, though Kester felt he had every right to be scared of him. What mortal shouldn't be scared of Tito? And he'd probably have vampire buddies here soon, all of them as tough, unsympathetic to mortals, and at times incomprehensible as him. Some of the things he said were from another world. The Widow Teeker? Come on.

"She was the finest woman I ever saw. Killed the man who killed her man and swore she'd never marry again. And never did, though many asked." His expression softened in the fading light. "On a fine day she would bathe in a small waterfall behind her house. Some of the boys, and the men too, would sneak up to watch. I think she knew it, but didn't care. A fine woman was the Widow Teeker. Kind and generous she was."

"Shit. She's lucky she didn't get raped."

"More'n one tried. She weren't scared of nothing and could defend herself. We looked out for her, too. Didn't nobody not like her."

"This is it," Oakes said. "This is it." Already in his head he could hear one of the few real sorcerers or witches say, "That Oakes is the most powerful sorcerer on Earth."

"You are sure?" Tito asked. Oakes liked to be called Sorcerer when he was working. Tito never did. The man could probably make him burst into flame or turn him into a toad, but he was too full of himself and Tito wasn't about to give him the satisfaction. Besides, the arrogant bastard was in it for the glory, to best Grace, not for the money. And Tito didn't trust anybody who wasn't interested in the money.

Sure, he wanted to get Grace for killing Olaf, but if Olaf's father wasn't offering a huge bonus for her capture, he wouldn't be so keen to confront her.

"How long to break through the spells?"

"Hard to say. Couple hours at least. I have to be very careful. There are sure to be many ward layers. The invisibility, a couple repulsive layers like your man Kester here experienced, a warning layer, defensive layers. Any mistake, and she could be gone no matter what I do. I need to work uninterrupted."

Oakes picked up a small, worn suitcase and with his leather bag embossed with arcane symbols on his shoulder, marched to the first invisible barrier just inside the tree line.

Tito said to Kester, "Better call your boss, tell him what's what. It'll take a couple hours to get my men here. Don't care what that witch man says, that Grace ain't going down easy. Keep an eye on him."

❧ ❧

Oakes worked carefully. He studied each ward to be sure there were no hidden spells or warnings. He channeled the power from an amulet he wore around his neck—a gold oval, rune inscribed, with dark blue sapphires at each end. All people of magic had one, all different. They came when both were ready to be joined. It was a defining moment in a magical person's life, when he or she could truly be called Witch or Sorcerer.

He sent the power over the ward, read its color, watched the patterns as the energy gently spread, gently probed the ward shell.

The invisible shell was benign, no tricks included. The two repulsive shells were less so. He could understand why Kester backed off; deep into the first layer the anxiety level rose quickly, an emotional boundary no normal mortal would pass. Oakes had to raise the strength of his own protective aura to quell his urge to run. The second layer was even more effective. It raised the degree of fright to a high level: physical illness caused by the expectation of imminent death by an unknown terror manufactured by a person's own imagination. Both, however with no alarm triggers. Curious.

Then he found it, inches from setting it off himself. Oakes froze, then backed off into a tunnel of power he'd formed inside of which the ward effects were nullified. Damn it! Too close. If he blew this chance he may never get another one. He wiped sweat from his forehead and gently moved forward. The warning was like a thin coating on the inside of the second fear layer. Virtually undetectable, except to a sorcerer with his skill and power.

Carefully, with the lightest touch, Oakes constructed a hole through the ward with a magic reflecting surface on the outside that caused the ward to believe it was still intact. It took him half an hour of complete focus. After a few minutes to settle down and congratulate himself, he stepped through.

He'd been too concentrated to notice before, but the landscape looked the same. This was the place. It had Grace's signature all over it. Where was the house? Surely she wasn't living underground in a cave. Mindful of alarms, he cast out a delicate tendril of his power. Not twenty feet away he detected another invisibility ward. Of course. A secondary screen and, as he quickly discovered, an alarm layer and a defensive one.

Working in his own sphere of light undetectable five feet away, Oakes took an hour to crack the first two wards and get one spell away from breaching the last defensive one. The house was similar to others in the area, a sprawling single story with a garden and trees between him and the building. Bare rock ran up to a deck overlooking the ocean. Lights were on; an occasional shadow passed the windows.

A huge grin broke out on Oakes' face. He had broken through all Grace's defenses. Nobody can deny that, not even Frederica in Durban with that stick up her ass about following rules. Wait until she hears.

Once more he probed the layers. Clean. He had extended his tunnel all the way through from the road. Once Tito's men arrived he'd breach the last defense and Grace would be knocked down from the pedestal the others put her on and discredited, ultimately stripped of her power, banished and forgotten.

Oakes retreated and carefully made his way back to the road. Kester jumped in the seat of his cruiser when Oakes materialized a few feet from his car. Oakes sucked in deep breaths of the cool salt air. What a beautiful night.

He opened the passenger door and slid in. "Tell your boss I'm ready."

Grace's House

Midnight. They gathered in a room lined with shelves and glass-fronted cabinets, and counter tops covered with jars, canisters, boxes and bags filled with unidentifiable powders, pills and gross-looking objects, the smell at once heady and repellent. Lights from under and over the cabinets illuminated the room. Suspended from the ceiling was a white ball similar to the ones in the big room. A tiny spotlight lit a rectangular table. Flat on the table lay a large chart of the North Atlantic ocean.

Kerry entered carrying a foot square mahogany box which she set down beside the chart.

Justine and Teresa stood shoulder to shoulder opposite Grace. Teresa jammed hands in the pockets of her jeans to keep from fidgeting.

At a nod from Grace, Kerry raised the lid of the box. The three guests ogled at what lay inside. By a silk string Grace picked up a five inch long crystal that tapered down to a point. All colors of light glittered from its surface.

"*Un diamant?*" Leave it to Simone to only be impressed by a huge diamond, Justine thought. As was she.

Grace, casual now, said, "This is much simpler than before. I will hold the stone. Teresa, you will put your hand on mine and we will press against the ball. Think of what Antonia looks like.

The stone will circle the chart and set itself on the position of the boat. Once it does that, withdraw your hand. Then I will attempt to 'see' the boat, and possibly those on board."

"Will you be able to tell if she is alive? She must be. Why would they have her body on board?"

Grace and Simone exchanged looks. "These people are very wealthy. They do not think like normal mortals or vampires. There is no telling what they might do."

"*Oh Dios.* Maybe they have made her a vampire. *Dios, Dios,* I did not mean...I mean that's not a..."

Justine hugged her friend to her. "We know what you mean, Tee. No offense."

Simone asked, "Will you be able to distinguish between one of us and a dead mortal?"

"All depends on how close I can get. Shall we start?"

Thunder rolled and rain scratched at the two small curtain covered windows.

Justine noticed Teresa frown at the sound. She caught her friend's eye and raised a questioning eyebrow. Teresa forced a quick smile and shrugged. Teresa's connection with Kazza had been strong, and she was supposedly a *bruja* of some sort, and things had become so much weirder than Justine had ever imagined. She was not convinced Teresa wasn't sensing something, if not bad, then not good. If they were going to work together they might need to figure out what she could do and what she thought she could do. All superpowers on the table. Definitely weird.

By the silk string, Grace lifted the scrying diamond with both hands, pressing Teresa's hand against the white ball. Head down, eyes closed, she murmured the appropriate magic words, then, "Haf!"

The two women tensed as a thin gold aura enveloped their hands and traveled down the silk string to illuminate the diamond. The stone circled the map, each circumference smaller until it strained to point at a spot midway in the Atlantic Ocean between Africa and the Caribbean Islands. Grace let the string slip until the point rested against the map. Kerry leaned forward and marked the spot.

Justine noted the latitude and longitude as Kerry gently removed Teresa's hand. Grace released the string and diamond pointer. They remained in place. She made a circle of thumb and index finger around the string then lowered her hands to the map. Eyes closed, she did not move.

Penzance Road

Kester had put up Road Closed signs a hundred yards on either side of where they were gathered— including Tito and six men just like him, all dressed in black, carrying swords and knives, like a Ninja Swat team. Oakes had put up his own invisibility spell. Only Kester and Tito carried guns. Wards did not mask gunshots.

Oakes addressed them. "I have created a narrow passageway through the wards. You must not touch it. She will notice if you do. So watch those swords. I will need about five minutes to breach the last layer. After that you must locate Grace quickly and get me there. You cannot defeat her alone. I can. She must be taken alive."

"How many others?" one man asked.

"I don't know. Within seconds I will."

Tito said, "Let's go. Don't touch the walls. Kester, your boss wants you to arrest Grace."

Great. "On what charge?"

"Harboring fugitives and anything else you want."

Oakes led them through the tunnel marked by its crystal shimmer. At the end, he breathed in deeply, ready for his big moment. His lips murmured, his hands made intricate movements, palms finishing against the last barrier.

"Now!"

Two vamps rushed past before Oakes realized he'd made a big mistake. "Stop! Stop! Come back!" The next two were a few yards in. "Stop!" They all stopped and looked back. "Come back," Oakes shouted. "Come."

As ingoing met outgoing, confusion slowed Oakes' panicked push to reenter his glittery tunnel.

A reddish glow filled the magical dome over the house. Confused, the first two vamps looked up. Red terror washed over their faces. Then, too late and too slow, they ran.

Grace's House

Grace jerked her head up. "They are here. Tito and Oakes." Eyes closed, she concentrated for a few seconds. "The others have been warned. Nigel, get the boat ready. You three, get your belongings. Kerry, Pablo, time to put your training to use."

"I am sorry we brought this trouble to you."

"Simone, dear mistress, do not blame yourself. This was coming, now or another time."

"The least we can do is fight for you," Justine said.

"Not much of a fight, but if you wish." Grace grabbed Teresa's arm. "Antonia is alive. You have the location of the boat. Yes? Be careful, *Bruja*. Go to the boat."

They separated then, Grace joined by Kerry. Teresa caught a quick kiss and caress from Pablo. Justine and Simone ran to their rooms to grab bags already packed.

On the outside deck overlooking the dock, Justine said, "Meet you at the boat, Tee," and she and Simone, swords drawn, vanished around the house.

Teresa ran to the end of the deck. She started at the sight of a dome shaped ball of flame where before there was only grass and rock. Lit by the fire, four men in black appeared, vampires, she had no doubt. Then a fifth, and familiar one. Tito. Shit. Behind him stalked a fair-haired man in a knee-length coat with a leather bag over his shoulder. Then a uniformed cop, wide-eyed, head jerking about. Like Teresa, he was mesmerized by the closing attack.

Grace's Compound

Flame spilled down the dome walls to the ground. It seemed to gather its breath and with a WHOOSH that didn't quite drown out the screams of the two trapped vampires, filled the dome.

Oakes, knocked down in the confusion, barely snapped shut the breach he had opened seconds before.

His shimmery tunnel had vanished. They lay in the open next to the fire. Less than a hundred yards away, illuminated by the flickering flames, was a real house, not a fake like the one he'd tried to attack. Fury pinched his chest so he could barely breath. She tricked me. That damned fucking low witch tricked me. Humiliation squeezed tears from his eyes. He wanted his hands around her neck choking the life out of those black eyes. That thought took hold and nothing less than death would ever be enough.

A hand grabbed his jacket and hauled him up. "What the pissing hell happened, magic man."

Magic Man wiped tears as if wiping dust from his eyes. "A trick. A trap. Time still matters. That's the house."

Tito raised a thick, skeptical eyebrow. "You still think you can best this bitch?"

Oakes grabbed up his magic bag. "Fuck, yes."

They ran toward the house. Oakes conjured up power balls in his palms as he strode over the grass. When Grace showed herself, if she was brave enough to face him, he intended no mercy. His heart pounded and the blood rushed as he built up his power. Where is she? Where is she? Balls of flame popped in his hands.

Ahead of Oakes, three of Grace's defenders clashed with the four attacking vamps. The defenders moved quickly, spreading out. One, barefoot in jeans and an unbuttoned shirt took on two black attackers in a virtuoso display of swordsmanship.

Another bested his opponent. Wound up with rage, Oakes flicked a ball of flame and knocked the defender back on his ass. The attacker moved in for the kill. He froze with his blade raised high and crumpled with a crossbow bolt in his heart. Oakes didn't give the dead vamp a second thought. Grace had appeared from the other side of the house.

❧

Pablo cocked his crossbow and inserted a new bolt, but not fast enough. One of the attackers broke off and with vampire speed and accuracy flung a long throwing knife. The blade buried itself deep in Pablo's chest.

"No!" Teresa dropped the bags and ran to Pablo in time to break his fall. "Pablo. Sweet man, hang on. Grace will heal you."

Blood already leaked from his lips. "Too late, Tee." He coughed blood. "She's busy."

Past the house Grace blocked Oakes' fire balls while sending some of her own as well as shimmering lines of power. Their hands flew as they drew magic to themselves. Lips moved, speaking spells.

"I don't care about her. I'm told I have magic of my own. Maybe I can—"

"Tee." Pablo raised a shaky finger to point at the vamp who'd tossed the knife coming to take it back.

Teresa would have taken the vampire on barehanded if she had to. Instead she grabbed up the crossbow and fired a bolt into his chest. He kept coming until he dropped to his knees, shook, and fell over. Filled with anger, she couldn't help but pick up his sword and whack his head off.

"Nice...form," Pablo said between raspy breaths. "Find...your... Antonia." With a bit of his old cheeky grin on his lips, Pablo died.

"Oh Pablo. You sweet *hombre*. I am so sorry." She kissed his forehead, held him a last time and laid him on the ground. Then she got back some of the hardened ER nurse she used to be, picked up the sword and went to kick some vampire ass.

❧ ❦

Justine heard the crossbow bolt whiz past, and saw the vampire attacker go down. Only four invaders, including Tito? Didn't seem like much of an attack, though those fireballs popping out of the mortal's hand were impressive.

Intent on taking on Tito, she almost missed the new vampires emerging from nothing next to the already fading dome-shaped flames. She lost track at four as the first one, a lanky big nosed guy about fifty when changed, engaged her within seconds.

There was little swordplay in their fight. She had him on his ass quickly. But before she could congratulate herself, he kicked her feet out and she was on her ass. In seconds it turned into a short-lived martial arts brawl. Back on her feet, she had to take on a second attacker as well.

While she fought, she kept track of the others.

Simone had marked Tito several times, as he had her. She, too, had to mix it up as the fight evolved into a free-for-all of flashing swords, fists and feet all at vampire speed. One of the original defenders had lost his head as had three of the attackers.

Ahead of Grace, Kerry entered the fray wielding a wooden bo-staff with one pointed end. She definitely knew how to use it, knocking feet out from under, blocking swords, impaling hearts. An impaled vampire is out of it, frozen and unconscious, until the stake is removed. They'll recover, but not quick enough to prevent someone from taking their head—like Teresa. Kerry impaled them and flung the bodies in Teresa's direction where she decapitated them with evident glee.

All the fighting moved to one side as Grace and Oakes fought their own battle. Fire and power balls flew, aimed high and low. Shields were erected, penetrated, reconfigured. Holes appeared in the ground, walked over as if they were covered with glass. Objects flew. Oakes sent a spinning sword toward Grace. She stopped it in midair, inches from her neck. The combatants also flew. One, or both, would leap in the air and take long seconds to come down.

The flow of battle forced Kerry to the far edge of the fighting, close to Kester, who had basically been an observer, no match for a vampire.

One of Oakes' fireballs ricocheted off one of the magical shields Grace put up and knocked Kerry off her feet, slamming her against a boulder. She lay still. Kester saw his chance.

He should have grabbed up her bo-staff, rammed it through her heart, and let her be. But he was wired. The power generated by the sorcerers scared him. The speed and force of the vampires scared him. The tunnel scared him. The fire scared him. Then he saw a defenseless woman on the ground and could not have done anything but clench his fists and work out his fear on her face.

Justine spied Kester straddling Kerry, his fists rising and falling. Vampire attack or no, Justine could not let that stand. In seconds she left the fray. She caught Kester's fist as he drove it down, twisted it and sent him sprawling, though she kept hold of his hand.

"That woman is a friend of mine, Officer."

Justine smashed his fist against a boulder. The crack and snap of crushed bones sounded loud despite the screams and clash of swords.

"You like beating up women, don't you?"

Kester curled on the ground, cradling his ruined hand. "No," he managed.

"Yes you do. I saw it on your face." Bloody and bruised, Kerry wavered over him. "How many women have you devastated with your fists?"

"Don't know." His words came out as a sob.

"Why do you do it?"

He attempted to squirm away from her. Justine blocked him.

"Scared. I was scared."

"But not too scared to terrorize innocent women."

Tears rolled across his face. Pain nearly paralyzed his mouth. "She wasn't innocent. She left," came as a whisper Kerry didn't hear.

"No more, you bastard. No more."

Kerry stomped his unharmed hand against the hard ground.

Kester's scream drew the attention of all remaining combatants. Fighting stopped, all eyes on the mortal curled around his bloody hands. A mortal's scream was like a siren call to Vampires.

Oakes didn't flinch. What did a mortal's pain matter to him now that he was about to become the most powerful sorcerer in the world?

Grace did flinch. She understood the pain of others. She had cowered in her mother's arms to block out the screams of whipped slaves. She'd attended with her mother to the beaten, whipped and raped. She had her own scars from when the screams were hers. She knew nothing of Kester, only of pain. Whether from Black or White, mortal or not, cries of pain went to her heart and she responded.

Oakes, having no such feeling, took advantage. Floating ten feet over the ground, with a twist of a hand he sent a swirl of crackling energy that hit Grace from the side and slammed her to earth next to the stone facade of the house. A twist of his other hand and a fiery column bounced off the stone wall and pinned her down.

Kerry froze a few seconds, taking in Grace's danger. Without a word she snatched up her bo-staff and ran to within twenty feet of Grace. Feet together she twirled the staff in front of her. Faster it spun, faster than normal vampire speed could account for, until it formed a moaning, whirring shield. Kerry braced with one foot back.

Under a fast shrinking dome of personal protection, Grace set an energy-filled ball rolling across the ground toward Oakes. He cocked his head as he watched the ball tumble steadily toward him, though obviously it would miss. A satisfied grin creased his face as the ball continued past him. He knew he had won.

Grace flipped a hand up and the ball rose slowly to hover over Oakes and flatten into a swirling disc. While the disc held his attention, Grace flung a ball of blue flame at Kerry. The ball hit the spinning staff which launched it straight to the disc.

Too late, Oakes understood. He spun around, hands up to defend himself, face twisted with anger and fear.

The blue ball ricocheted off the disc and slammed Oakes down.

Grace rolled from under the column of power which hit the ground in a splash of flame that dissipated in a shower of sparks. A wave of her hand swept away all of Oakes' defensive energy. Another wave settled an amorphous blob of blue energy on top of him.

Oakes heard the scream, saw Grace falter and knew he had her. Only after he had her pinned down did he allow himself to admit that he had had doubts about his success. Grace had been stronger than he anticipated, quicker to respond, more inventive. But he met her every move and he knew he surprised her with some of his own. Now he had her pinned on her own territory. She couldn't even attack him. Her last attempt, a feeble ball, barely left the ground. Then it rose up and flattened into a disc, and he knew!

A heavy weight dropped on him. Pressed to the rock, he watched helpless as Grace waved a hand. His defensive spells were ripped away as if torn from his gut. A blue weight settled on him. He could see and hear, but not move.

Grace knelt beside him. "If you had spent more time developing your craft and less time trying to prove how good you were, you might be as good as you think you are. You work for Rubicon. What does he want with me?"

Oakes found he could speak. "You killed his son."

"And?"

"He wants to use your power to make himself the most powerful being on Earth."

Grace snorted. "He's a thousand-year old vampire with billions of dollars."

"He wants more."

"He wants too much. Like you."

Grace reached through the shimmer that held him motionless and grasped his amulet.

His expression opened up with horror. "No. You can't take that. It's my power. My life. It isn't done."

"You're too dangerous, Oakes. And it is done. You know it is. You've taken several as you pushed your way almost to the top." She yanked the amulet off, leaving the chain intact.

He felt weakness settle into his body. Not in muscles and bones, but in his psyche. He ran through a few spells in his head. No tingle of power swelled in his chest. His fingertips warmed slightly indicating he still had his original power that had led him to search for his amulet. That power was considerable. He'd learned much during his years as a sorcerer. He could come back from this, stronger and without the need of an amulet. He'd pretend defeat, then come back at her alone. Not with these loser vampires.

He felt his natural magical force begin to subtly flow. His hands warmed. It had been a long time since he called upon only his natural magic. He almost didn't recognize it.

Oakes gazed up into Grace's eyes, ready to play the defeated. He didn't like what he saw. No victorious smirk on her lips. No gleeful glimmer in her eyes. She placed a hand on his chest. The hand warmed and emitted a dark red aura.

No. No. No! She couldn't do that. She wouldn't do that. My God was she powerful enough to do it?

Her hand sunk into his chest. His hands and feet turned cold. Oakes screamed.

Teresa let her head rest on Justine's shoulder. Justine pressed her lips to her friend's hair while holding her tight. Simone gently caressed Teresa's back to let her know she was there.

"I'm so sorry, Tee. He seemed like a good guy," Justine said.

Teresa nodded and wiped tears from her cheeks.

"I, too, am sorry," Simone said. "He made you happy. A thing none of us should take for granted. In a few days or weeks you will be able to look back and take some satisfaction that you were able to end the one who took him from you. Some wait years for their chance." Justine and Simone made eye contact for a moment. "Some never get it."

Twenty feet away Grace removed her hand from inside Oakes' chest.

"Did you kill him?" Teresa asked.

Grace stared at the throbbing pink glow in her hand. "It might have been kinder if I had." She leaned back on her knees, held up the glow, then pressed it into her own chest. Her body quivered. Simone knelt down to support her. "Ahhahahah." Deep breaths settled her.

With an arm around her friend, Simone asked, "Did you do what I think you did?"

Grace nodded. "I took most of his natural magic. Though he may wish I had taken his life. I left some in him. Enough to give him an advantage. To be stripped of the magic you were born with is a harsh punishment and a difficult adjustment." Grace rose up and looked down on the unconscious Oakes. "But he shouldn't have fucked with me."

Grace scanned around: the dead vampires, Kester moaning against a boulder, a long look at Pablo. "Where's Tito?"

Kerry leaned on her bo-staff, her face temporarily swollen and bruised. "He ran away."

"To Travella. Rubicon won't be happy about this." Grace smiled, no humor on her thin lips. She nodded toward Kester, curled against a rock, keening with pain. "He deserve that?"

Justine and Kerry said, "Yes."

Grace motioned with her hand. Kester slumped. "I'll take care of him later."

Hesitant, she trudged around the battlefield, staying a moment by each of her dead defenders. She came to Pablo. She knelt beside him and yanked the knife from his chest. Tears ran unheeded on smooth cheeks. Teresa stood beside her.

"Can you...?"

Grace touched his face, his chest. "No. Even I cannot mend a ruined heart."

Nigel and Kerry hugged, gently sobbing.

With a kiss to Pablo's forehead, Grace rose.

"I'm so sorry," Teresa said. "He was a good man and—"

Grace wiped Teresa's tears away with her thumbs. "I know. You all must leave now. You have your daughter to find. I have a mess to clean up."

Simone asked, "What about Tito? He knows where you are."

"Not now. A forget spell was triggered when he broke the defense ward. I'll deal with him and Travella. And your officer there. Nigel will take you in the boat. Go now. Complete your quest."

On the Water

Nigel led them to the boat, though Simone stayed a few minutes for a private word with Grace. All aboard, Nigel guided the speedboat, it's three huge diesel engines rumbling impatiently, away from the dock.

"Grace said Tito might have people watching from the water. Keep an eye out," Simone said.

Entering the calm early morning open water, Nigel pushed the throttles forward. The sleek boat jumped up onto plane and raced into the fading night.

They'd reached fifty miles per hour when Justine spotted the other boat. It had been hiding behind Thatcher Island. It showed no running lights, but Justine's vampire vision easily picked it out as it raced after them.

"Grace was right."

Nigel told Justine, "Take the wheel."

"Me?"

"Just keep straight. Don't hit anything."

He grabbed a large pair of binoculars and left the wheel. Sporting an egad-what-do-I-do-now? face, Justine grabbed it. She'd never steered a fast, powerful boat like that. It was exciting and terrifying at the same time. Afraid to do anything, she stared ahead hoping nothing got in their way.

Nigel had his sea legs. While the others held on, he swayed unsupported as he studied the pursuing boat.

"Can we outrun them?" Teresa asked.

"No." Nigel reached around Justine and pulled back a little on the throttles. "Steady on."

"But they'll catch us now," Justine said.

"No. Get them directly astern of us." To Simone he said, "I must concentrate. Can I lean on you?"

Nigel faced their pursuers. Simone stood behind him, hands on his back. Justine steered the boat to be directly ahead of them.

Nigel raised his hands, palms facing aft. He spoke indecipherable words, raising and lowering his hands with a flowing motion, each wave slightly longer than the last.

"HAF!" Arms stretched up, he brought them down with a fast push outward. They all felt the spell, like a burst of static, their hair wanting to stand on end. Simone had to push back hard to keep Nigel upright.

Behind them, directly in front of the pursuing boat, a trough opened in the water, a hundred yards long, fifty wide. If the men in the boat saw it, there was nothing they could do. Launched off a wave their boat flew almost over the gap. At the last twenty feet, the bow dipped and dug into the wall of the trough, flipping the boat end over end, spewing men and equipment like a disintegrating pinwheel before landing bottom up.

"Holy shit," Teresa said. "You're a witch, too?"

Simone helped Nigel sit down to regain his composure. "No. Grace taught me a few things. Just in case."

"So, Moses, where are we going?"

Justine pushed the throttles up and the boat roared into the night.

CHAPTER SEVEN

Truck Stop—Albuquerque, NM

"Hi. You want to have some fun?"

Jimmy Schaffer jumped. Where the hell had that girl come from? Though on second thought she looked like a girl, but she had some experience on her. Eighteen at least, he told himself.

"Where'd you come from?"

She waved a slender hand at somewhere behind her. "What do you think? Won't cost much."

She came close to him and looked up into his eyes. She was pretty, though awful pale. Course the truck stop lights weren't meant to be flattering that far out in the parking lot. Her eyes held his. There was promise in them of pleasure he had never imagined. He had to have this girl. His need grew in his mind as well as in his pants. He had been on the road a long time, and he wasn't married, and this was a rest stop.

She touched him where he was already hard. God damn he wanted that girl. Had never wanted, no, needed a woman so bad. Not even that bitch Charlene when they first met, before she turned into a cheat'n slut.

"Come on." He unlocked the cab door and scrambled up. The girl followed him, shut the door and was in his bunk in an instant.

"Lay down," she said.

He did.

She yanked off his boots, socks and pants. Shit she was strong. Then she was out of her clothes, climbing on top of him. She gripped his pulsing erection and lowered herself onto it.

Her eyes found his. He couldn't look away. A wave of bliss flowed over him with each rise and fall. Oh God Oh God Oh God. He wanted to explode. Impossibly, her stare held him back. Shit, what was she doing to him? Too much. Too good. How could he last this long?

The girl raised her head. Her body vibrated as she let out a long shuddering sigh.

Jimmy finally let go. He thrashed about as if having a seizure. As long as he lived he would never experience an orgasm as intense. When he opened his eyes she was still there on top of him. But somebody else was there, too. A gaunt man with the same old eyes as the girl.

He tried to move. She held him down. "What the fuck? Who's that?"

"It doesn't matter now, Mr. Schaffer," the girl said with formality. Then her mouth stretched unbelievably wide.

On the Road

Harry had put it together the day after he talked with Justine. She'd called him back around midnight his time to give him the coordinates of the boat they were interested in, and to tell him the three of them were back in Boston and probably headed south, depending on what his friend found out.

The possibility had been on his mind since a couple had disappeared from the Rancho Santa Fe area where the Sinakov Family's mansion had burned down, and their blood drained bodies had been found at a truck stop in Needles. A truck had disappeared from that same stop, the driver's bloodless body found beside the road in the Arizona desert.

Sinakov. Regular vampires—how easy that rolled off the tongue now—did not need to hijack trucks. He had asked Darwin if any vamps were missing or gone rogue. Darwin assured him all vampires were on their best behavior.

Not that long ago the crimes wouldn't have been on his radar and he'd assume it was a serial killer on the move, out of his jurisdiction.

Sinakov. Harry didn't know it as a fact, but he knew it. Somehow, the dead bastard was alive, and heading somewhere. East, as Justine was headed South. Coincidence or a plan? If Law Enforcement became involved some, maybe many, would die. If he said nothing, other innocent travelers would die—if he was right.

He'd asked to be notified of missing travelers throughout the West. When he heard about one Jimmy Schaffer going missing from Albuquerque, Harry knew what he had to do. Within hours he arranged to take vacation time and for Bayley to take care of his mail, and was on the road, traveling fast, heading East.

CHAPTER EIGHT

South of the Border

"Tee."

"*Que?*"

"Stay out of trouble."

"Lunch and shopping. What could go wrong?"

Teresa shut the door and wandered out into the kitschiest tourist stop ever. The South of the Border complex south of the North Carolina line on Interstate 95 contained over 125 acres of ersatz Mexican culture.

Ten hours before, cutting it close to sunrise, they'd driven in, all testy and tired from the nonstop road trip from Boston. They'd taken a suite with two queen sized four poster beds.

Teresa was exhausted by the trip and the emotional beating of the last few days, not the least of which was Pablo's death. She'd liked the younger man, but had no illusions of a long term relationship. The time they spent together, mostly in bed, had done much to ease her anxiety level from the violence and danger of the few days before. And he was mortal.

She loved Justine as her best friend, and had grown to like Simone despite her superior attitude, however well-earned after three hundred and fifty something years of survival on her own. But they were vampires, with, she had to admit, an inherent deserved arrogance for their physical powers. Even Justine, still a Young Blood, had acquired a tendency to haughtiness when dealing with mortals. Teresa used to let it go, but not anymore. As Teresa saw it, best friends aside, she had proved herself a part of the team and next time she'd call Justine or Simone on it. Somebody had to stand up for the weakling mortals.

Though famished, Teresa took some time to stroll around South of the Border, taking in the kitschy Mexican atmosphere where all the employees were called Pedro. Thank God they weren't called Pablo. That would have been too much to take. For a little while she could pretend to be a normal person—just a tourist on the way south with no knowledge of vampires or Oracles or witches, and nobody after her, police or supernatural. At least not immediately.

She strolled through the Reptile Lagoon. Without sadness she thought of how much Antonia would have enjoyed it. Inexplicably her daughter had no fear of lizards, snakes or alligators. She'd wanted a baby alligator for a pet. Teresa and her husband Miguel had vetoed that idea. Baby alligators grow up to be hungry adult alligators. Then she wanted a Boa constrictor. They had settled on a small anole, a pretty, green, benign lizard that ate bugs and topped out around eight inches in length. It didn't take long before Teresa was doing the feeding and cleaning. Anything that ate spiders deserved to be taken care of.

From the top of the two hundred foot tall Sombrero Tower she gazed into the sunset and wondered where the hell the quest she was on would end up.

In the Sombrero Restaurant she skipped the Mexican food, not wanting to be disappointed. Instead she ordered a steak cooked medium, instead of her usual medium-well. When she began ordering it rare, she'd know she'd been hanging out with vamps too long.

About the time she started in on a fudge brownie chocolate sundae, she got a weird feeling in her head.

∾ ∾

Justine's cell phone chirped at her just as she was realizing that dozing in bed after waking up was as enjoyable as a vampire as it had been for a workaholic real estate agent. Her phone chirped. Harry. Even so, she took her time answering.

"Hi Harry."

"Hi sleepyhead. You sound sexy."

"If you can get here in ten minutes you can see for yourself."

"How about fifteen?"

"Sorry. Ten minutes and I'm a bloodthirsty vamp again."

"I'll call earlier next time. I heard from my friend at NASA. He stepped out of bounds for this, so we owe him. Though I got the impression this is not the first time this sort of thing has been done. Your boat's name is *Night Watch*. It's a two hundred and sixty foot private yacht, registered in Switzerland to an Olaf Corporation. Basically a private holding company."

Justine lay back and closed her eyes. "The one lead we have is that a Russian bought Antonia. Do you know where they're headed?"

"It's not like flying where you have to file a flight plan. If the boat stays on its present course he thinks the Virgin Islands area. Though there are plenty of other islands around. He estimates maybe three, four days. That help?"

"Yes. At least we know what boat we're looking for. Thank you. Thank your friend. What are you doing?"

"Nothing much. Following leads on a missing couple case."

"Like us. We could use your help."

"I'm sure I could use yours. Your company anyway."

They chatted a few minutes about nothing in particular, enjoying each other's voice with no drama to interfere. Then a thump and a scream cut short came to Justine's sensitive hearing from the room next door.

"Hold on a sec, Harry." Justine focused on the wall.

She heard, "Liar!" and a sharp smack.

A woman's voice pleaded, "Steve, I love you. I wouldn't see anybody but you."

"Lying bitch! I saw you with him. You know I hate to punish you, but you have to learn to behave. Come here."

"No. Please. I'll be good. Please don't."

Justine's face tightened, eyes blazing. "I'll call you back, Harry." She rolled out of bed and in seconds pulled on jeans and a T-shirt.

Simone sat up in the other bed. "It's not your business, Justine."

Justine shot her a withering you-know-you-don't-mean-that look that would have cowed a lesser vamp and headed for the door.

"I'll start packing," Simone said.

Justine yanked open their door and strode down the outside walk to the next door. Concentrating, she heard a slap, and, "I'm sorry. I'm sorry. Please." Slap. Thump.

A snap kick beside the knob popped the door open. Justine rushed in, ready to break Steve into tiny pieces. She found them by the bathroom door. A young woman on her knees, head bowed, disheveled hair revealing a glimpse of red on her face.

Fists clenched, a beefy man stood over her. His expression was as tight as his fists, except for strangely cool eyes that showed no emotion.

"Help me," the woman pleaded. "Help me." On hands and knees she scrambled across the carpet to Justine.

"Shit!" Something wasn't right. Vampires were in the room. The man was a vamp. One, no, two, more. Not the woman. Where?

Reaching Justine, the woman wrapped arms around her legs and yanked, twisting her legs as she fell back so she landed on her stomach.

One second to take in what had happened was too long. Vampires fell on her. She struggled. Three of them were too much and inside of twenty seconds they had her bound, legs, arms and wrists. "Simone!" A hand clamped over her mouth. More hands dragged her into the bathroom.

Seconds later Simone raced into the room, sword ready. The woman lay immobile on the floor. Simone stopped next to her, ready for anything—except for the woman to grab her legs. Three male vamps came at her. Simone managed to slice the neck of one as she went down. Not enough. All her experience and training weren't enough to overcome a surprise attack by two burly men and an unexpectedly strong woman.

Justine watched Simone's losing struggle. She had no doubt who the attackers were. But how the hell did they find them and what was their plan?

❧ ❧

Teresa's unease increased despite her efforts to ignore it with spoonfuls of chocolate. They were safe here. Anonymous, three women driving south on vacation.

DANGER.

Her spoon clattered into the dish. Palms pressed to the table, she "listened" to a warning with no words but clear enough meaning. Teresa dropped money on the table and hurried out of the restaurant. Full dark had fallen. The only sound was a distant laugh and the swoosh of cars on the Interstate.

One hand on the gun in her purse, the other holding a cell phone, she wound her way back toward the room. Justine didn't answer her cell. The danger feeling grew stronger as she approached the room.

A quick survey from the corner showed their car still parked in the carport. She walked casually to her room's door, then past it when she saw the door to the adjacent room had a splintered jamb.

At the corner she turned around and moved to her own door, listened, and quietly entered. The suitcases were on the beds, partially packed. Justine's shoes were on the floor, her cell on the bed. Angry, heart racing, Teresa tried to use some of her supposed magical powers to look into the next room. She saw and felt nothing, but she really didn't know how to work magic, so it meant nothing.

She peered out her door. Nobody was around. She slipped out, and with the gun at her side she moved to the broken door, listened, and peered in. Seeing blood on the carpet, she pushed the door open enough to sidestep through.

Nobody. Except for the blood the room showed no sign of having been occupied. She checked the closets, under the bed, nothing. She could sense the vampire presence, smell the musty scent. A mortal, too. Female by the unfamiliar perfume.

Teresa stepped outside and pulled the door closed. She made herself calm down and think. Obviously they'd been tracked and Justine and Simone taken. She didn't feel Tito's presence, so they'd probably take them north to him.

There had been a van parked next to the room. Brown, she thought. She'd been gone about an hour and a half. The feeling of danger began about twenty minutes ago. Maybe she could catch them?

"Hi. You from Massachusetts?"

Teresa started, and looked up at a balding man and his pregnant wife. "Excuse me?"

"Ah, we saw the van with the Massachusetts plates. We're from Boston, but live in Pennsylvania now. Pittsburgh. It's nice, but we miss Boston. Thought maybe you were from there."

"No. Sorry. But I was supposed to meet them and I'm late. Did you see when they left?"

The wife said, "No. But the van was there fifteen minutes ago."

"Fifteen minutes. That's great. I can still catch up to them for dinner. I have to go."

"Okay. Maybe we can see them tomorrow."

"Sure. I'll tell them."

Teresa ducked into her room, finished the packing, checked that the Pittsburghers were gone, loaded the car and sped north on the Interstate.

On the Road

Teresa caught up with the van just south of Lumberton, North Carolina. She approached close enough to identify the Massachusetts license plates and see that there were no rear or side windows. Vampires were in the van. She knew it. No time for second-guessing or wondering how. *I'm here*, she thought to Justine.

It was a weekday night with light traffic. Dropping back she waited. Swords or machetes wouldn't help here. Fortunately they had a few firearms stashed in the car. She had a 12 gauge pump shotgun on the seat, a .45 semi-auto in a jacket pocket and a smaller pistol in her purse. And just in case, a sword close at hand.

A pickup passed. No lights showed behind. A thin line of trees partly screened the southbound traffic. The van stuck to the speed limit and the right-hand lane. Teresa gathered her courage, prayed they weren't friendly vampires chauffeuring a group of Girl Scouts, and hit the gas.

She passed the van on the left, then jogged right and took her foot off the gas. With an angry horn blast, the van jerked left passing Teresa. She matched their speed.

A male vamp glared down at her. His eyes snapped wide open when he spied the shotgun barrel sticking out the window. Instinctively, his mouth dropped open. Fangs slid out.

Teresa fired. Glass shattered. The vampire's face disintegrated. She let go of the wheel, pumped a shell into the chamber and shot out the front tire. Hitting the brakes, she shot the back tire, then slammed on her brakes hard.

Barely under control, the van slewed back and forth, ending at a dangerous angle on the right shoulder.

Simultaneously, the sliding side door and the driver's door popped open. Gun in hand, the driver slid out. Teresa hit the gas. Steering within inches of the van's left side, she caught the vamp between the vehicles, rolling him screaming against the van. She slammed into the door, snapping it off. Leaving the crushed vamp sprawled on the ground, Teresa skidded to a stop just beyond the van.

A second vamp from the sliding door ran up to the sedan's passenger side ready to blow away the crazy-ass bastard who almost wrecked them. BOOM! He flew back ten feet, a ragged hole in his gut.

Teresa slid out of the car and laid the shotgun on the roof. She wasn't sure if there were any vamps left. There had been a mortal. Where was she?

She noticed movement in the van, then three shots from the left side creased the sedan's roof. Something stung her neck. Shit. *You're not an immortal fucking vampire,* she reminded herself. With a scream, a woman flew out of the van and tumbled down a short embankment. Shotgun ready, sword dangling from her left hand, Teresa moved toward the woman. She saw the dark outline of a gun swing in her direction. BOOM. A scream. A moan. Covering the van, Teresa kicked the gun from the woman's hand.

"God damn bitch. You killed my husband."

"You kidnapped my friends." Still on alert, Teresa approached the van. After a quick look, she reached in and removed the gag from Simone's mouth. "You can't get rid of me that easy."

The sword cut Simone's hands free.

A bullet thumped into the van inches from Teresa's head. She ducked, spun, and searched for the shooter. Easy to see in the moonlight, it was the vamp with a hole in his gut, struggling up. Still wired, Teresa dropped him with the shotgun. Teresa stalked across a carpet of pine needles. Two strikes with the sword and he was finished. She strode to the crushed vamp, struggling to make his broken body work, dragged him down the embankment and finished him.

Simone had Justine free.

"Christ, Tee. How the hell did you find us?"

"We should leave here before someone sees…this."

Her hands shook. Justine and Simone traded glances and gently took her weapons.

"What about the woman?" Justine asked her.

"I.…She's a mortal. I can't."

Simone turned Teresa toward the sedan. "Go back to the car. We'll take care of…this."

Teresa nodded. "You should turn the headlights off."

Her kidnappers knew what they were doing. Her bonds were of heavy braided line with no stretch. A woman and one male vamp rode in back so she and Simone had no chance to help one another. The body of the vamp she'd taken out lay between them. They were helpless and knew it.

Where was Teresa? Did they get her? Justine didn't think so. They'd asked where she was. Simone had said she was dead, wounded at the fight. She'd died on the boat so they buried her at sea. They'd looked skeptical, but hadn't pushed it. Teresa would have been a bonus.

When the shooting started, Justine had no idea who it might be. For a moment she thought it might be Harry. Despite the gag, she smiled for a second, thinking of Harry riding in guns blazing to rescue the damsels in distress. But he was in California being a good cop. Though she was supposedly immortal, she did wonder if she'd ever see him again.

Her thoughts on the shooter changed when the vamp in the passenger seat said, "What the fuck's that bitch doing," just before half his head spattered the roof.

After they jolted to a stop Justine and Simone ended up face to face. "Tee," Justine said behind the gag. Simone nodded. Her eyes smiled.

While they, and the kidnappers, followed the action, Simone

managed to squirm around behind the woman. When she started cussing and shooting after the shotgun blast, Simone wound herself up then uncoiled like a spring let loose and kicked the woman out to roll down a small slope.

Christ, was that Teresa coming out of the dark like a B-movie avenger? When the bullet hit inches from her head, she barely flinched. They watched as she impassively dispatched the two vampires. What had happened to the sweet, tough woman who'd vowed to help her, but not kill for her. "She's a mortal. I can't." There she was. And Justine was glad of it.

"She's right," Simone said. "We need to distance ourselves from this."

Justine agreed. Quickly they carried the dead vampires into the trees a couple hundred feet in either direction, laying them out where the sunrise would turn them to dust.

The woman's blood scent dispelled any discussion about what to do with her. They buried her bloodless body in a shallow ditch. Careful not to leave any fingerprints or other evidence of their presence, Justine drove the van to the next exit and left it beside a gas station.

∾ ∿

They'd left South of the Border well behind before anybody said anything. Simone turned around and faced Teresa in the back seat. Her tears glistened in the headlights of the occasional passing car.

"Teresa, thank you for rescuing us. I'd like to think we would have freed ourselves. But the truth is we were, as you Americans like to say, 'Totally fucked.' I have no doubt we owe our existence, and any future we might have, to you. Also we are, if you will excuse the expression, dying to know how you found us. And how *they* found us."

Teresa told them what happened. "I think I know how they found us," she said. "We forgot they have an Oracle working for them."

"*Merde.*"

"Shit," out of a big sigh from Justine. "You obviously have some mojo now, Tee. Can you block that sort of thing?"

Teresa laughed. "Huh. I don't know how I'm doing whatever it is I am doing."

"Call Grace," Simone said.

"We need a new car," Teresa said.

"Christ. If they can see into the fricking future what difference does it make? They'll be waiting wherever we go."

"But they cannot see all the time, *n'est pas*? Only sometime, I think. Unless...?"

"Unless their tame Oracle can see whenever he wants. Tee, call Grace. This is a problem."

"I agree," Simone added. "Even if we keep moving all the time they can go two or three days ahead and wait. There must be a way to hide from this Oracle person."

"What we need," Justine glanced over her shoulder at Teresa, "is our own Oracle who can tell us where and when they will waiting. I can see the movie now, *The Oracle Wars*."

"I'll call Grace." Simone pulled out her cell phone. "Perhaps she can put one of those domes over us."

Through the rear view mirror Justine caught Teresa's eye. "You did good, Tee. And you know all this Oracle crap is not your fault, right?"

Teresa managed a smile. "I know. I never thought this would be so complicated."

"Me neither. This is fucked up."

"Grace. This is Simone. We have a problem."

CHAPTER NINE

The Breeze Motel

The Breeze Motel didn't have any. Humid, breathless air suffused with the rotting-vegetation aroma of the anonymous swamp which began fifty feet away smothered the motel. Amongst trees dripping with Spanish Moss, fifteen units stretched out in an L-shape from an office fronted by an ancient wood porch and entered by a creaky screen door. Justine was being born the last time the place had been painted.

A pale band of morning light showed in the eastern sky as Simone entered the cramped office and tapped the bell. A grizzled old man with slicked back gray hair, a blue dress shirt buttoned to the neck, and a steaming cup of coffee appeared in a door behind a counter that showed scars of a long hard life. A name tag announced him as Rodney. He gave her an appreciative once-over.

"What can I do ya for, darling?"

"Need a room. Two rooms. Adjoining. If you have anything like that?"

Rodney looked out at Justine relaxing behind the wheel. Teresa slept in the back seat. "You ladies plannin' to set up shop?"

Simone turned on her sexy smile. "Depends on how management treats us."

"I'll treat you right, darlin'. If you treat me right." His eyes went back to Justine, who wiggled a finger wave at him.

Simone touched a finger to his chin and brought his eyes to hers. They widened and brightened and stared deep into him with the full force of her glamour. "To start with, Mr. Manager, we have been on the road all night. We would appreciate no interruptions until tonight. No room service. No maid service." She placed a hundred dollar bill on the counter. "And if anybody asks, you haven't seen us. Can you do that for me, Rodney?"

"Why yes, Ma'am. I can."

❧   ❧

Most of the furniture was original equipment from well back into the last century. Still serviceable and with a comfortable and quiet bed it wasn't a place most people usually stayed for more than an hour. The pull down shades and dusty curtains were designed for privacy.

They said little once in the rooms. Turned out The Breeze did have two adjoining rooms at the corner of the L. Teresa automatically took one room, leaving her vampire companions the darkest room for their daytime sleeping pleasure.

Teresa knew they sometimes shared a bed. She didn't mind. Raised as a good Catholic girl, her long stint as an ER nurse had opened her mind. Discovering that vampires were real had blown it wide open. Two consenting adults of the same sex seeking comfort and pleasure together was hardly a big deal compared to all the other nastiness roaming the world.

She lay a loaded shotgun on her bed. In the ER she'd learned from many prostitutes how they disassociated themselves from what was being done to them. That's how she felt about the gun. Already dead or not, blowing someone's head to mush was not something she wanted to think of herself as doing.

Pistol in hand, Teresa wandered into the other room. Justine and Simone had guns and swords handy, too.

"I don't feel safe here," she said.

Justine racked a round into her handgun. "Does it look like I do? If they know where we are, we might as well have gone to the Ritz. They'd have better security than Rodney."

Simone stretched out on the bed, hands behind her head. "This is where Grace told us to come. The man we are to meet will help us." She looked on Teresa not with arrogance or condensation, but real warmth. "By teaching our resident witch a trick or two."

"I can barely remember my name, let alone learn a witch thing or two."

"And until we meet this guy tonight?" Justine asked.

"We're on our own."

First watch went to Teresa as she'd slept for a couple of hours in the car. She started reading a vampire novel but quickly grew bored. Fictional vamps weren't nearly as exciting as real life ones. With a handgun stuck in her waistband she walked around back of the motel. A shadowy path wound through a narrow stand of Cypress trees, leading her to a rickety wood dock surrounded by lily pads that threatened to choke a narrow, clear channel, both ends disappearing into Cypress and pine woods.

Miguel and the kids would go nuts over the trees. She thought for a moment of what she'd lost: a husband and two good kids, a good job, nice house. But only for a moment. Truth was she'd lost them months ago when they moved on from Antonia's disappearance and she didn't. The house had ceased to be a home without her oldest daughter in it. The job lost much of its appeal with the death of Justine's Brittany. She didn't feel sorry for herself. Scared, yes. Sorry no.

She did feel a little sorry for Justine and Simone. Justine had lost the only person, besides Teresa, who she cared for or who cared for her. She hadn't expected to live past serving blood justice to Stephan Sinakov. Now she was dedicated to finding Antonia. But what after that?

Simone, over three hundred and fifty years old, seemed to have many acquaintances but no real friends. She'd lived a solitary life back in Carlsbad. When her house burned down, she'd never looked back.

A Sand Hill crane took flight downstream. A fish wiggled in its beak. If only life were so simple. Catch a fish, take it home, eat it.

At four o'clock Teresa opened the adjoining door to wake Justine. Her friend was already awake with a gun pointed at her. "Wake up Sleeping Beauty."

"Everything okay?"

"Sure. Especially in number seven. A couple took a long lunch and you couldn't help but hear what a good time they were having."

A few minutes later Teresa lay on her bed, trying to relax.

Justine peered out the window. "No premonitions, or visions, or danger feelings?"

"Only the sense of danger I've had for the last few days, or weeks, or months."

Justine sat beside Teresa. "I know. I've had that feeling of dread in my stomach since we got to Boston." She gazed through the wall to the outside. "I expect Tito and a dozen vamps to burst through the door any second. And I'm getting tired of it. I hope this guy can bring out the inner witch in you."

"I don't feel very magical."

"You're always magical to me, darlin'. You've been so strong through all this. I'm so proud of you."

They held hands until Teresa closed her eyes and slowly relaxed. "I still think we need a new car. Maybe Rodney knows somebody. If you treat him right...darlin'."

❧　❦

After a few minutes Justine slipped out the door. Keeping to the shadows she cautiously made her way to the office. As the sun vanished into the swamp to the west she felt her body energy and confidence rising. Her senses ramped up. She smelled the decaying peat from the swamp, the odor of sex from number seven. She noticed the evening sounds of crickets and frogs, the swish of bird wings. Her enhanced vision searched the trees and bushes, cars and windows for enemies.

She heard the distinct pop of a beer can as she pulled open the office screen door. Rodney had his muddy sneakers on the desk.

"There ya are, darlin'." He gave her a wiggling finger wave. "What can I do for ya ya can't do for yourself?"

"We need a car. Legal and reliable. Big sedan or SUV. We'll pay cash."

"Ya ain't goin' nowhere are ya? Ya got, ahhh, friends already lookin' for ya."

It took a moment for her to comprehend what Rodney meant. "Already looking for us? Who?"

"Couple tourists. Fishermen, probably. Though one was awful pale. They knew you'd been here, but I told 'em to come back after dark." He pointed outside. "That's about now, darlin'. Better get yerself fixed up."

"Right. Guess I'd better."

The door slammed behind Justine as Rodney asked, "What about the car, darlin'?"

"Wake up. They're coming," Justine said.

"Damn it! You sure?"

"Two tourists from up north." She grabbed a messenger bag and stuffed clothes into it. "One, too pale to be a fisherman. They're coming back after dark. Which is now."

Dressed, packed and armed, Simone entered Teresa's room. "You're not really surprised, are you?"

Teresa pulled on a pair of stout walking shoes. "I suppose not." She grabbed her shotgun.

Simone peeked through the curtains. "They're here. Two SUVs and a pickup truck."

"Not taking any chances on Dirty Tee this time. Bathroom window."

Justine threw up the sash of the old fashioned window. Simone, the slenderest of the three, dove through. Though she'd somehow lost weight in the past few weeks and was thinner than she'd been in years, Teresa was a full-sized woman and she didn't slip through as easily as the others. Simone kept her from breaking her neck. Justine tumbled through and closed the window. It might slow the vamps for a few seconds.

"There's a trail into the swamp," Teresa said.

"Oh wonderful. You first."

"Not a swamp rat, Simone?" Justine asked as they ran down the path.

"You know, *deja vu*, yes?"

"I get it."

Justine took the lead as the pines gave way to Cypress that blocked out any light. Shouts came from the motel. The vamps had discovered the trail.

They ran as fast as Teresa could, which they all knew meant their pursuers would catch up quickly. Above the soft ground Cypress roots created an almost invisible obstacle course that slowed them further.

"I'm slowing you down," Teresa panted. "Maybe...I can...take a few out."

"We're not—ahhh!"

Justine, then Teresa ran out of trail into lily pad covered water two feet deep.

Simone stopped in time. "Teresa, keep going through the water. Land is fifty feet. We will find you. Justine, we might slow them down a little. Yes?"

"Yes."

While Teresa waded through the water, Justine and Simone drew swords and took up staggered stations behind old Cypress trees on either side of the trail. Within seconds the first pursuers approached at speed.

Justine let the leader pass. Her blade caught the second vamp under the chin and sliced off his head. A similar fate ended the first vamp.

Shouts came through the trees. They answered them with random bullets. Silence. Justine crouched down and cast out with all her senses. Any noises she heard were unidentifiable—birds, insects, animals, wind, or vamps.

A shout startled her. Teresa. "They're surrounding you!"

Justine didn't doubt her for a second. Being surrounded would not be good. They had a small army this time and she had no illusions about the outcome if they all attacked at once. Neither did Simone. They leaped half the distance to more or less solid ground and pushed through the shallow water the rest of the way.

They raced through heavy brush, zig-zagging around Cypress trees' buttress-like roots, following Teresa's scent. They found her hunkered down behind a fallen Cypress, and almost got a face full of buckshot.

"How the hell did you know they were surrounding us?"

"I don't *know*. I just did."

"We must go, *maintenant*. Now," Simone said.

"*Christos*. When will we stop running?" Teresa started to get up, then froze. She'd heard that sound live before, with Miguel and the kids in the mountains, but not within two feet of her. Simone had moved past her. Justine concentrated on the darkness behind them.

"Tee, come on, let's go."

"Rattlesnake. On my right."

"What? Shit."

"Ahhhh!" A vamp burst through brush on Teresa's left.

Teresa jumped.

The rattler struck.

Justine leaped. Grabbing the snake mid-strike, she rolled and flung the writhing serpent at the attacking vamp.

Mortal or immortal, a rattlesnake in your face is a distraction. He swatted at the buzzing reptile.

Justine rolled to her knees, swung her shotgun around over Teresa's back and blew the snake in two and half the vamp's head off.

"Two for one. Tee. We have to go."

"What? Can't hear you."

Simone and Justine lifted her and dragged her into the woods.

"Sorry. Next time I'll let him cut your head off."

"That I heard."

The three women slogged on through the swamp, collecting bug bites, scratches and close encounters with reptiles, poisonous and toothy. Vamps still followed, but kept their distance. Though game, Teresa lagged. A deep scratch on her neck from a broken branch hurt like hell and after a hard slog through lily pad choked water, she had to rest. All three stopped and listened.

Simone whispered, "This is strange. Now they do not attack. They wait also."

"They've lost a lot of men," Justine said.

"There are at least five. If they were smart, they could have us." Simone continued to stare back across the water.

"Is Tito one of them?" Teresa asked.

"Yes."

"Where are we going, anyway? We can't just keep running. Lost in a swamp is okay for you guys, but I've had enough bugs and snakes and alligator filled water and killer vampires for today."

"Me, too." Justine slapped her neck. "Do mosquitoes become

immortal if they drink vamp blood?"

"We could hunt them instead of running," Teresa offered, not really wanting to do that.

"Yes, a possibility. For now, you two go ahead. I want to watch and listen a little more."

Justine thought a moment. "I get it. But I agree with Tee."

"Yes, I agree, also. I will catch you up. Then we will decide."

Justine took Teresa's arm. "Come on, Tee. Let's get more lost."

"I think I know where to go," Teresa said.

"I'm not even going to ask. After you."

Teresa stood still for a few seconds before setting off. Justine and Simone touched fingers. "Careful."

"Toujours."

Justine let her friend lead, since she seemed to know which way to go, while she scanned to the side and back. Their pursuers were out there, pacing them as if waiting for a signal to attack.

They'd only been moving for ten minutes when Justine smelled someone ahead. She grabbed Teresa and pulled her close to a tree, whispering, "Somebody ahead. A mortal."

"He works with Messer, the man we came to see."

"You're sure of this? Who's giving you all this information?"

Teresa leaned against the tree and bowed her head. "I don't know. It feels right, though. And has been, so far."

"I'm not wild about it, but let's go see what this guy has to say. You may trust him. I don't."

"Simone?"

"She'll catch up."

On full alert, Justine led. They came to an open watery grassland. A moonlit path glinted on the shallow water. A couple hundred feet ahead, Justine made out a small outboard boat alongside a lopsided wooden dock. The silhouette of a man stood on shore. He turned to face them when they emerged from the trees, otherwise he did not move.

Sticking close to the trees, they approached.

"My name is John Redbone, though everybody just calls me Redbone," the man said, voice rough and slow, his accent native Southern. "I work with Messer. Come with me, ladies. You all will be safe with us."

"How do we know that?"

"You are Justine. This is Miss Teresa, the one Grace sent, who has come to learn certain things about them Oracles. That right?"

"Yes."

"I think there's a third lady?"

Justine focused on the dense brush. "She's coming."

"We should shove off soon, Ma'am. Them bad guys are still out there."

Justine spun about, gun up. Teresa followed suit. Both aimed at a dark form gliding quickly along the edge of the underbrush.

"Simone," Justine said, not relaxing one little bit.

Simone stopped in front of Justine and pushed the gun away from her stomach. "They're coming." Simone flicked her gaze to Redbone, back to connect with Justine.

Justine could tell Simone had something else on her mind but now wasn't the time. She shrugged. "Then let's go."

The boat was an ancient Boston Whaler with a square bow and wood plank seats peeling varnish. Simone stepped to the bow and, facing ahead, took the forward seat. She gripped Teresa's arm and had her sit beside her. Justine straddled the center seat with a shotgun on her lap while Redbone sat by the engine. He yanked the starter cord and pushed off.

Ten feet from the dock a cry came from shore. A black form ran from the trees, thumped on the dock and launched himself high in the air toward the retreating boat. Justine had plenty of time to swing up the shotgun and shoot the flying vamp like a live action clay pigeon. The body hung in mid-air, then tumbled into the water, like an Olympic high dive gone very wrong.

Redbone twisted the throttle and they motored off along a narrow moonlit channel. In the bow of the boat Simone and Teresa huddled together over a cell phone.

On the Road

Harry kept himself awake with Mountain Dew and coffee. He had pushed his Mustang across Arizona and New Mexico to Albuquerque. He had no idea where Sinakov was heading. He could have gone north or south on I-25, or continued east on I-40. He figured that if they had wanted to go north or south they would have taken I-15 or I-10. Plus, the truck stop was east of Albuquerque. So he had continued east.

Approaching Oklahoma City he had to make another decision. He checked his alerts on his computer back in California. The truck missing from New Mexico had been found east of Dallas. Okay. It had just been found and hadn't been there more than an hour. So they had an hour head start. He glanced at the radio clock. Christ, 4:15 in the morning. So about three hours to the truck stop. That gave them a four hour lead, but they'd have to stop at sunrise.

Harry figured Sinakov had acquired a new vehicle, but it had to be one he could sleep in. If not a truck with a bunk, a van would be his best bet. He'd probably stop at a freeway rest stop or an anonymous truck stop.

Harry was wide awake; he was catching up. If he checked out all trucks and vans stopped during the day maybe he could spot Sinakov and stop him.

There were a hundred holes in his plan. Would Sinakov stop someplace public and not go off the main road? Where was he heading? At Shreveport he might continue east or go south toward New Orleans. Maybe he was forcing a driver to drive during the day?

What else could he do? Harry cranked up the radio—the only stations coming in clear were country, for Christ's sake—tried not to contemplate for the hundredth time whether not telling law enforcement about Sinakov and his strengths was saving lives or not, and turned south toward Dallas, foot to the floor.

East of Shreveport, LA

Harry spent the morning checking out truck stops and rest areas, all the while trying to convince himself it wasn't a crazy waste of time. He had no clue if he was on the right road, what type of vehicle he was looking for, or what he would do if he did find Sinakov. And what if he had a mortal driving him—someone working with him either voluntarily or involuntarily? They could be anywhere while Harry spun his wheels going nowhere.

Around two o'clock in the afternoon just east of Shreveport, he fell asleep at the wheel. Grassy ground bounced him around enough to jolt him awake before he hit the trees that lined the interstate. Driving slow, window open, shaking his head to keep awake, he made it to the next rest stop and parked at the far end. He woke up a bit once out of the car; he was able to stretch, walk over to the bathrooms, pee, splash water on his face and amble back to his car. He surveyed the few parked vehicles but saw nothing suspicious. Then he happened to glance over to the street paralleling the freeway. A couple hundred feet down he saw a parish roadside park by a pretty pond. In the parking lot he saw a van—brown, no windows, only a flowery logo with Garcia Landscape underneath. Oklahoma license plates.

Shit.

What were the chances Sinakov slept inside? A hundred per cent or zero. There was one way to find out. Fatigue forgotten, but not gone, he considered walking to the van. A low post and rail fence separated the rest area from the park—easy to cross, but not carrying a shotgun which he thought might be useful, if a bit conspicuous. Instead he drove to the next exit and navigated his way back to the park, positioning the Mustang on the dirt parking lot so that the van was between him and the street.

On the other side of the pond a woman worked in a garden and an old man repaired a fence. Setting the shotgun on the front seat, Harry donned a light jacket to cover the 9mm tucked into the back of his jean's waistband and the .45 tucked in at the front. When the woman went inside, Harry quietly closed his door and warily approached the van on a strip of grass to muffle his footsteps.

Through the windshield he saw a blanket separating the back compartment from the front. He circled the van. No movement, no sound. He stood by the sliding door considering whether to knock or just barge in. A cop would have to knock, a civilian wouldn't. Which was he?

He didn't have time to decide. The door slid open, Sinakov grabbed him and yanked him inside. The door slammed shut.

Harry bounced off wooden slats lining the sides and landed in a heap in the middle of the floor. He stayed conscious enough to recognize the Girl from the Sinakov Family mansion as she took the .45 from him.

Sinakov sat cross-legged against a blanket hung on one side. He wore only black martial arts pants, tight at the waist and ankles. His ribs were as gaunt as his face. A thick red scar circled his neck.

"The detective," the twice dead vampire said, voice struggling through the neck scar. "I thought you were dead."

"I thought *you* were dead."

"A faithful servant is a rare thing." He waved a thin hand at the Girl crouching beside him, a small delighted smile on her ingenuous face, her gun aimed at Harry's crotch. "How did you find me?"

Harry struggled to sit up against the rear doors. "You should clean up after yourself better." He dropped hands to the floor and shifted an inch over. "Where are you going anyway? Maybe we could car pool, save on gas."

Sinakov's voice leaped from polite to raging as he said, "You and your bitch Young Blood girlfriend took everything away from me, and I am going to get it all back and take everything away from her and," he leaped at Harry, landing in a crouch between his legs like some mad simian mimic, "take back the Sinakov Family and all the families and *I* will be the Master Vampire." He slapped Harry. It felt like getting hit with a brick. Harry tasted blood.

Sinakov grabbed his head and tilted it back to the neck's limit. He licked the blood from Harry's face. "And I'll take you first." His mouth opened wide, wider.

Harry got his first close-up look of a full-on vampire face. The primal fear of being eaten alive trumped any ideas he had of handling Sinakov quietly—which, if he had bothered to think about it, were totally unrealistic. Eyes fixed on protruding canines, he reached behind him, grasped the 9mm from his belt, jammed it against the vamp's belly and pulled the trigger.

Sinakov jerked back. Harry got both hands on his chest and shoved him, a lightweight now that he was stunned for a few moments, at the Girl.

She fired the .45. Pain ripped along Harry's thigh. He snapped a shot at her, lucked out and hit her gun arm.

He reached up and yanked the rear door handle. The door swung open and Harry tumbled out, picked himself up, fired blind into the van and ran to his car.

Door open, he stretched for the shotgun. His wound rubbed on the door post, sending a spark of pain up his body. His knees slipped off the seat as he twisted away, sitting hard on the seat edge.

"Sir. No!" the Girl cried from the van.

Sinakov came out the rear doors with the .45 in one hand. A trickle of blood seeped between the fingers held over his stomach. A mortal would be bleeding out about then. Wounded fucking vampire walking with a big gun. No wonder they were arrogant bastards. But even arrogant bastards couldn't survive a shotgun blast to the head. Or too long in the sun.

Sinakov seemed confused. He squinted up at the sun then looked about him with a wrinkled brow like he didn't know where he was.

Harry reached back to drag the shotgun around. Fuck inconspicuous. The guy would be dust before the cops arrived.

He heard a gunshot. Something tugged at his sleeve. From the van's side door the Girl aimed her pistol at him. She fired again, hitting the door. And again.

Shit. She had another gun. Of course she did. Probably took it from one of the truckers. Good thing it's small caliber. If it was the .45…?

Boom. A louder gunshot. The slug ripped through the door and embedded in the seatback. Sinakov had come back from wherever he'd been. Boom. Harry scrambled back into the car, keeping low. He finally got the shotgun pointed the right way. He laid the barrel on top of the door and aimed in the general direction of Sinakov. BOOM.

A cry.

Harry peeked over the door sill. One of Sinakov's arms hung useless. Unfortunately not the one with the gun. The vamp fired.

Harry ducked.

The slug thunked into the vehicle somewhere.

Harry peeked.

Boom. His shot went wild.

It seemed to Harry he pumped a round into the chamber in slow motion. He sat up to blow that crazy ass vampire's head off.

The Girl's shot creased the leather steering wheel. Hot leather burned his face. Harry fired blind.

Sinakov still fired. A .45 slug pierced the door and stung Harry's leg again. He looked up. Sinakov stood there, looking down at him—weapon aimed at Harry's head. But the muzzle of Harry's shotgun was a foot from his chest.

"Master, do you think we should leave now?" The Girl, ever the subservient servant. The van engine started up.

Sinakov squinted, ignoring his devoted servant who seemed to have herself together more than he did. Red blisters turning black popped up on the pale skin of his face and hands. Christ, the vamp was crazy to be out in the sun. Shoot him. Harry jerked the trigger.

Click.

Sinakov had the same idea. Click.

Shit.

The 9mm. He still had it.

An engine roared. Rear doors swinging, the van appeared behind Sinakov. It skidded to a stop, kicking up a dust cloud.

Harry reached back for the 9mm and snatched it off the seat. A head shot to the vamp. Easy. Scramble his brains, almost as good as, and as satisfying as, swinging a sword. But he was too late.

The Girl grabbed her master, unceremoniously pushed him into the van, slammed the door, and shot Harry.

On the Water

Redbone slipped the boat into a space between two Cypress trees that should not have had room for it. He had navigated for twenty minutes without a light or any markers Justine could make out. He was not a vampire. "You seem to know where you're going," she said.

He grinned. "I do, ma'am. I was born and raised here. Been fishin' and explorin' since I was a pollywog."

"I'm partial to the ocean, but from what little I've seen it has its beauty."

"It surely does, ma'am. Maybe I'll get a chance to show you some things most folks don't get to see."

"I'd like that. How long have you worked for Messer?"

"Gator got my daddy when I was 'bout fifteen. Messer took me in. Been 'bout ten year now."

"Seriously? An alligator ate your father?"

"Mostly. My daddy was huntin' gators for forty some years. One of 'em finally got him back."

"You're bullshitting me."

"No ma'am. Me and Messer found him. What was left, anyways."

"So is this Messer the real deal? Can he be trusted?"

"I trust him with my life," Redbone said.

"Hmmm." He hadn't actually answered her question, but he was practically his kid, so what else would he say?

Redbone had eased the boat through a narrow channel in a tall grass filled open water area. Ahead, Justine could make out a dock with a pram tied up.

"Here we are, ladies. Safe and sound."

"We'll see," Simone muttered. What was it about sorcerers and witches that they had to hide? Grace hid from the world and look how that turned out.

Messer's House

Pine and Cypress surrounded the house. Two story, covered in unfinished wood paneling, it blended in but was obviously an anomaly. A single story wing swept back into the trees. Steep shingled roofs curled in at the eaves giving the house an otherworldly look. One might expect Hobbits to amble by.

A wood deck supported by gnarled wood posts extended over the water. Messer stood on the deck. A burly white man, his wild white hair and goatee stood out in the moonlight. He wore a loose white shirt, black pants and no shoes. A fairytale sorcerer and his fairytale house. He held up a hand in greeting.

From fifty feet away Simone focused on his eyes. She saw no welcome there. She gave Teresa a squeeze of support as Redbone helped her onto the dock. On the dock, Simone looked deep into Redbone's eyes. There, she saw no guile.

"Welcome," Messer said, enunciation perfect, like a practiced showman. "Please come into my house. It is invisible to the outside world, but warding spells over water are uncertain things."

If the outside could be mistaken for a slightly melted family vacation cabin in the woods, the interior could be mistaken for any upscale suburban tract home. Open, eggshell white walls, stylish leather furniture, plenty of electronics and original paintings on the wall.

Messer led them into a wood paneled den and stood back to allow his visitors to admire his taste and style.

"Nice digs for a cabin in the middle of a swamp," Justine offered.

"Thank you. It is quite comfortable. Though your location is a bit off. There is a four lane highway a half a mile away and a shopping center within two miles."

"Sorcery pays well," Simone said.

Messer poured himself a glass of wine from a well stocked bar. "Just because one knows a bit of magic does not mean one has to live in a hovel deep in a forest."

Teresa settled into an armchair that looked as comfortable as a cloud while Justine and Simone questioned Messer.

Justine said, "This is certainly no hovel, as anyone can see. Including those who are chasing us."

"Ah, fear not. This house is invisible to all outside its boundaries."

"We've heard that before. Can they detect us?"

"No siree. This house itself is shielded. And the rooms in back are especially secure."

"What about the Oracles?" Simone asked. "Won't they know we're here?"

She and Justine stood facing him as he leaned casually against the bar sipping his wine. They still shouldered their messenger bags, pants and shoes wet, clothes ripped, hair a tangle. She thought he was trying very hard to appear casual, even as he snuck glances at a cell phone lying on the bar counter. He had not offered them anything. So much for Southern hospitality.

Messer leaned back against the bar, elbows on the counter. "As far as the not-quite-all-seeing Oracles are concerned you ladies do not exist now. As long as you are in my house, you are safe from all threats."

Justine said, "We appreciate that. It's when we leave that concerns us."

"Hmm." Messer glanced at the phone. One finger unconsciously tapped his wine glass.

Simone exchanged a glance with Justine. She had noticed it, too. He really wanted that phone to ring.

"I deduce that now we are arriving at the reason for your visit. Grace was not particularly specific when she…<u>asked</u> me to extend you ladies my hospitality. Which of course I am most pleased to offer." He glanced down at his wine glass and stilled his finger. "And in that, I have been most remiss. May I offer you refreshment? Wine, beer, orange juice? I have an excellent Bourbon, smooth as a magician's cape."

"Wine will be good," Simone said.

"An ice cold beer would be *muy bien*," Teresa said from the armchair. "I might not be able to get out of this chair afterward, but…" She waved away the possibility.

Their host selected a bottle of Chablis from a small wine cooler. Plying a corkscrew, he asked, "So what assistance may I provide you?"

"We would like you to teach Teresa how to block the Oracles from being able to see where we are going."

"While we are going there," Simone added.

Eyebrows raised, he gave Teresa a skeptical once over. "She is a… sorceress?"

"So we are told."

Teresa rolled her head to look at the three by the bar. "You're talking about me, aren't you?"

"All good things, Tee."

"I'm sure." She raised her hands and wiggled her fingers at them. "Poof." She smiled and closed her eyes.

Justine shrugged. "See. Sorceress."

Messer pulled the cork with a pop. As if the pop was a signal, his cell phone rang with a section of "The Sorcerer's Apprentice" to which Mickey Mouse made the mops dance in *Fantasia*. Messer started, nearly dropping the bottle.

"I have to take that. The supernatural never sleeps." He snatched up the phone and strode across the room to a corner window. Once there he spun a finger over his head causing a rippling cone of energy to cover him, blocking out all sound.

"He seems a bit uptight," Justine said as she took a beer from a refrigerator and handed it to Teresa.

Simone poured two glasses of wine. "Think we can trust him?"

Justine sipped the wine. "Grace sent us here."

Simone caught Teresa's eye. She gave a tiny shrug.

Justine noticed. "What?" Another look passed between vamp and *bruja*. "What was that phone call on the boat about?"

Simone downed half her wine and said, "Grace gave Teresa a spell of some sort in case we get in a tight situation. Like if Tito is going to catch us."

"It is a last resort. Panic time. It will be rough on me." Teresa sipped her beer and laid her head back.

"That means she will be unconscious afterward."

"And on Grace. It takes power from her, also."

"What does this panic spell do?"

"Transports us, if we are physically connected, to someplace else."

"Even from here with its wards and whatnot?"

"Especially from here," Simone said, downing the last of her wine.

"So Grace doesn't trust this guy."

"Paranoia is part of the job description of anyone who is the most powerful anything." Simone topped off Justine's glass and her own. "Where I imagine this guy thinks he is."

"Ladies, I apologize for the interruption. An important call I had to take. Now, if, Simone, isn't it? will pour me a glass of that excellent wine, I will tell you the problems with your request."

"But it can be done?" Justine asked.

"Of course, I can teach you how. But there are still problems."

Simone handed him his glass. "Of course there are. Please explain."

"If possible so us poor muggles can understand?" Justine said.

Simone shot her a squinty-eyed quizzical look. "Muggles?"

"Harry Potter, boy wizard?"

"Ah," Simone replied as if she understood, though she didn't.

Teresa and Justine exchanged a rolling-eye glance. A muggle indeed.

Messer assumed a lecturial pose. "To simplify, Oracles tap into a person's life force, or *qui*, some say their soul, in order to "see" them in the future. Without that connection, they can see nothing. You do not exist. Now, in this house, you are shielded. They can see nothing of you, neither past nor future."

"So they don't know where we will be in a week or a month?"

"Correct, Teresa. Unless they have already seen it."

"Then they might know where we will be if they happened to see something before we entered here."

"Is there a possibility to change what they have already seen?" Simone asked.

"I am sorry, but no." He raised a finger to make his point. "However, you may change how you came to that place. And, unless they see a clock and a calendar, their timing is not precise."

"Well, that's something. But how does Teresa shield us once we leave?"

"It's called a shield cloud. Fairly easy to construct when still. However, difficult while moving. It is a different, more complicated spell. It takes power and concentration to maintain." He kept his gaze fixed on Teresa. "Also, very dangerous for one who does not have true ability, and power."

"Teresa has both."

"So you say. And Grace, too. Will you give me a demonstration?"

All eyes turned to Teresa. Finally she said, "No. I can't. It's not something I can demonstrate. I can do your spell."

Messer frowned. "Not good enough." He pulled a leather cushioned straight-back chair away from a carved table with an inlaid chess board and set it in an open space. "Sit."

Justine stepped in front of Teresa. "Why?"

"Because I will not help you if she does not. Saying you have the power of magic does not mean you do. I must be sure. Sit, or Redbone will show you out."

Justine helped Teresa out of the comfortable chair. "It's okay. I would like to know, too."

Teresa sat down.

Messer stood behind her, eyes closed, breathing deep for half a minute. He placed his hands where her neck joined her shoulders. For a full minute only his lips moved, mumble-whispering unintelligible words. Suddenly he shouted, "Haf!"

Teresa cried out and sprang from the chair as if launched. Messer flew backward ten feet to fetch up hard against a bookcase filled with ancient-looking leather-bound texts.

Justine jumped to steady her friend.

Simone helped Messer to his feet. "What the hell just happened?"

Breathing hard, one hand on Simone's shoulder to steady himself, he frowned at Teresa. "We will rest. We must be awake and aware. And I must read up on the proper procedure. It is almost dawn. Dinner will be at eight o'clock tonight. After, I will teach you what you want to know."

He shivered, as if shaking off a deep coldness, and regained his composure. With a long pensive glance at Teresa he turned on his heel and strutted out of the room. Over his shoulder he said, "Redbone will show you to your rooms."

The three women turned to Redbone who waited uncomfortably, perhaps a bit embarrassed, by the door.

Simone said, "I'll ask again, what the hell just happened?"

Redbone did a good imitation of a schoolboy addressed by the pretty teacher he had a crush on. Simone took his arm, flashed him a soft, feminine smile, and led him to the bar where Teresa handed him a cold beer.

"That was a test, right?" Teresa asked.

Redbone was obviously not used to three attractive women wanting to know what he thought. He cleared his throat, downed a long slug of beer, cleared his throat a couple times more and said, "Yes. It was a test. And he was surprised at what he found. Shocked, actually."

"So she has magic fingers?" Justine asked.

Simone felt a surge of tension in the man. Fear, if her senses were any judge.

He avoided Teresa's eyes. "More than fingers, I think. Much more."

❧　☙

Messer Chanaut had a lot to think about when he closed and locked his bedroom door. He stopped in the middle of the room and stared at the rug covered bamboo wood floor. After a minute he surveyed the room as if fixing it in memory because he might never see it again. Which, he realized, was a possibility.

He took in the corner desk, the file cabinets, the walk-in closet, a heavy king-sized bed, built-in bookshelves, all crafted with local woods—pecan, pine, oak. It was a good room, comfortable and solid. He stood in front of the bookshelf and ran a hand over the spines. Finally he stopped on one particular volume.

It wasn't a remarkable looking book: rough brown leather, thin, about the size of a million other forgotten self-help books or novels. On the spine and front cover it had one gold embossed word—*Magicum*.

He pulled it out and held it in his hands. It could have been printed yesterday. No stains, no dried and cracked areas, no worn spots, pristine, though it was "published" thousands of years ago.

Being born with the power of magic meant nothing without training, instruction, study and practice. Messer had been trained as a magician by his father until it became obvious that he had something more than a talent for card tricks. His uncle took over his training and when he passed away he left his nephew *Magicum*.

This was no instruction manual on sleight of hand, misdirection or illusion. It dealt with deeper, darker magics—the harsh magic of survival in a primitive age, including how to hide from the Oracles.

Harsh magic relied more on hand movements than spoken spells. It developed in a time when language was new and learning a spell quickly was most often a matter of life or death. But the power within the user made the spells and wards work. That woman Teresa had the power, at least as much as him. In Grace's league. But so untrained. That's why he had a decision to make. Oh what he could do with her. With proper training he could revive his magic act with her as a partner. He gazed at the posters and photos on the wall—*An Evening with Messer the Magician*. God he missed the stage. Let those other wizards and witches live in seclusion, he needed the spotlight and applause. But he'd learned the hard way that as soon as you think you've got it handled, under control, that's when it can go bad real fast. A woman, booze and arrogance took him down. Despite his power, he hadn't been able to get himself together again. So there wasn't nearly as much money as there used to be.

Messer dropped into an elegant armchair and opened the book to the page with the Oracle blocking spell. Instead of studying it, he laid his head back and closed his eyes.

When Grace called and asked him to help the three women he'd readily agreed. The problem came when that vampire Tito called and offered him a great amount of money to hold the three for him. More than enough to get back on his feet. But was it enough to survive Grace's ire? Maybe not on his own. But if Teresa had the magic in her he thought she had, the two of them could stand up to anybody.

Apparently these women were on a mission to find Teresa's daughter. Not something she could easily be persuaded to give up. Though hypnotism had been a part of his act, boosted with a skosh of magic he was confident her mind could be changed. Perhaps he could make a deal with Tito…a lesser bounty for just the two vampires, and maybe a word to the powers that be that the mortal died in the swamp.

The anticipated thrill of a standing ovation quickly faded. This time, he promised, he would not make the same mistakes. This time, this woman would adore him as she should.

A risky strategy, to be sure. But he could hear the applause already.

Redbone showed the women to their temporary quarters. Teresa's room was comfortable with plenty of light wood and windows and colorful curtains and linens.

Teresa poked her head in the bathroom. "And a real bathroom, with a tub and a shower and no mildew smell. Perhaps I died in the swamp and this is my Heavenly reward."

Justine said to Redbone, "If you're going to stick us in a basement with guest coffins it better have a bathroom like this."

He laughed. "The only coffin here is a prop from Messer's act."

Justine perused the framed posters and photographs of Messer with various celebrities on the wall. "I had tickets to see his show once. Maybe three years ago. I gave them up to make a half-million dollar sale. I wonder if it was worth it. I heard he put on a good show. Why did he quit?"

Redbone glanced at the door to check if his escape route was open then stared at the floor.

"A woman involved, yes?" Simone said.

The others shook their heads and shrugged. Of course there was a woman.

Justine gently patted his shoulder. "Go ahead, dish."

He sighed. "There's not much to tell. He had two women assistants. He was mad in love with one of them. Carol Ann, she was sure pretty, and in love with him, too. For awhile, anyway." He cast another glance at the door.

"You can't stop now. Don't make me have Simone force the rest out of you."

"Okay. He thought Carol Ann was running around on him. She wasn't, but he tried to, you know, restrict her and she wasn't going for that and they fought. Then one night during a performance he was so mad he put her in the disappearing box thing and...really made her disappear. He tried everything, but never found where she went."

"*Mon Dieu*, he used real magic in front of an audience?"

"Yep."

"I vaguely remember that," Teresa said. "Didn't they want to charge him with murder, but couldn't find a body?"

"Yep."

"Tee, don't piss him off when he's teaching you that spell."

"Best behavior, I promise."

☙ ❧

Redbone led them down the hall then to the end of a short intersecting corridor. White painted walls and natural finished wood trim greeted them. The furniture was simple but comfortable. One wall had a large fake window with a view of the swamp at dawn painted on it. High up on an adjacent wall heavy blackout curtains covered a row of long, narrow windows. Two queen size beds were set underneath.

"The window with the view faces west. The high windows face north. You will be safe here." Redbone opened a plain door. "A bathroom, should you need it."

"Does it have a shower?" Justine asked.

"Yes, Ma'am."

"Dibs on first shower."

But Simone was already at the door, grinning.

"Great. What do you think, Redbone? That shower big enough for two?"

"Ah...Yes, Ma'am."

Justine threw an arm around Simone. They both let loose their most invitingly seductive looks. "Big enough for three?"

Redbone did a perfect imitation of a dazed deer in the headlights, as his face filled with red like someone had opened the top of his head and poured in bright red paint. "What? Oh. OH. Um...I'm not sure, Ma'am." He backed out the door. "Dinner at eight."

"*J'espere qu'ils ont de l'eau fraiche ici.*"

"Me too. We've been in too much hot water lately."

In the shower Simone's soapy hands gently washed Justine's back. "Do you trust this Messer?"

Justine hunched her back with pleasure. "Grace trusts him."

"But do you?"

"Not really. I'd like to know about that phone call he was waiting for."

"*Moi aussi*. I think it may be a simple task to find out."

"How?"

Simone's hands wandered lower and for a long while Justine forgot about any phone calls.

East of Shreveport, LA

For a few seconds, maybe fifteen, Harry thought he was dying. Then he figured he wasn't. Then the pain started and he wished he would—quickly.

Shouts came from somewhere. For once they're probably doing what they're supposed to do. Calling 911. Christ, what a fuck up. How the hell was he going to explain what he was doing here?

"Ah shit." Harry sat up. A wave of vertigo swept over him and he almost tumbled out the door to the ground. Behind the wheel, he started the engine while trying to breath deep, but a stab of pain stopped him.

Blurry people ran across the park toward him.

Harry reversed the car, jammed it in drive and raced out of the parking lot onto the side road and out of sight.

Where was he going to go? Where was Sinakov going? It was daylight, too dangerous for them to drive around. They'd need a place to hole up until dark. And they'd need some time to heal.

Sirens approached. Harry caught sight of blue flashing lights. He passed through a residential area of older, well tended houses on larger lots. He ducked into a driveway with a detached garage. Foot off the brake to keep the lights off, he waited for two police cars to pass, then backed out and drove away.

A few blocks away he parked on the street in line with several other cars. The Girl's bullet had hit just below his left shoulder, in and out of the fleshy part. After downing Tylenol and Advil, he cleaned the blood as best he could and slapped on some inadequate bandages from a shoulder bag that held a change of clothes and other necessities like toothpaste, ammunition and wooden stakes.

While reloading, he considered what he would do if he was Sinakov.

Many of the houses in the area had fences with drive through gates between the house and a detached garage. A perfect place to duck in out of sight from the street. Harry couldn't drive around the neighborhood and stop at every house to peek over the fence. His Mustang was not inconspicuous. But he remembered a 7-Eleven down toward the Interstate exit.

Fifteen minutes later he walked along the treed streets. He wore a dark T-shirt and dark windbreaker to hide the blood seeping from various inconvenient places. A gun tucked in his waistband and stakes in his pockets were his only weapons.

He found the empty van behind the fifth house he checked. They had to be inside. Who else was in there he couldn't tell. An inexpensive compact car parked in the garage yielded evidence of two people. He missed Justine and wished she was there with him. Or Simone, or Teresa, or somebody who had a clue what to do next. He wished he had the shotgun with him. But walking around the neighborhood with a shotgun while he poked into backyards probably would not have gone well.

Hung on the wall or stacked in corners was the usual garage stuff. Lawn and garden tools, old paint cans and stiff brushes, boxes and totes that hadn't been opened in years, judging by the dust layer, filled the limited space. A small workbench took up one corner. Woodworking tools hung from a pegboard, also not used in years. A rack held scrap wood, plywood strips, a few two by fours, miscellaneous trim, some pieces of one by twos.

Using a rusty but still sharp hand plane, he quickly shaped a three and a four foot stake. It was no shotgun, but somehow he felt better having them.

He had to go in now. His own wounds were getting worse while theirs were getting better. Sunset loomed. Possibly any mortal inside was still alive. If he thought about it too long he might lose his nerve. One thing to do first, just in case.

Justine's cell went right to voice mail. Shit. "Hi. It's me. I was going to say I have good news and bad news, but there isn't any good news. Sinakov is alive, so to speak. That strange girl put his head back on and is with him. They've killed four people that I know of. We're in a small town east of Shreveport. I sure wish you and Simone and Teresa were here. Stay out of trouble. I love you. I'll call you later." *I hope.*

Harry turned off his phone and slipped out of the garage side door into the back yard. Lawn furniture, barbeque, a couple old oak trees, one with a swing from a massive branch. Americana. He could as well be in a California backyard. He wished he was as he approached the back of the house.

He peeked through a closed screen door into a kitchen. Old, but clean and homey. Christ, a teddy bear cookie jar. A sliding screen door opened to a family room with a felt topped card table, a Foosball table and a deep couch in front of a flat screen TV.

Harry gently slid open the screen door and slipped through. He felt like he was watching the pretty teenage girl start down the steps to the haunted house basement. Inside, a door led to a more formal living room.

All the curtains had been drawn and the lights turned out. Enough of the fading daylight leaked in to reveal a woman, around thirty-five with short dark hair, wearing a blue nurse's uniform, strapped to a chair in the middle of the room with tie down straps. Blood leaked from her neck, yet she struggled against her bonds.

Another woman, older, lay on the floor behind her, not moving.

Harry crept in, slowly, cautiously, long stake in each hand. The woman's eyes bulged when she saw him. She shook her head with quick little movements. He froze, crouched at the end of a sofa.

Little three inch blade pocket knife in hand—too bad it wasn't a three foot sword—he crawled to the woman. She vibrated with tension. Careful not to let the heavy ratchet end fall, and wake up every vampire in the neighborhood with their damn super ears, he cut the first strap.

She made a tiny little sound in her throat. Harry looked up with a finger to his lips. She kept tilting her head back, pointing with her chin, wide eyes questioning, like, *Look, dummy.*

He looked.

Shit.

Sinakov lay on the couch, arms crossed over his chest like a desiccated corpse.

One eye on the vampire and one on what he was doing, Harry cut the straps.

As he cut the last one, her face opened up and she sucked in a deep breath. She was going to scream, he knew it. Quickly he pressed his hand over her mouth. Then he looked.

Shit.

Sinakov stood behind him, head swiveling, gaunt face bunched as if trying to figure out where he was. He wasn't paying Harry any mind.

Harry knew he'd never have an opportunity like that again. He grabbed one of his stakes and jumped up, drawing back to ram the stake into the dead heart.

The scream waiting to come out, did. She cut it short, perhaps under the illusion that Sinakov's Girl, standing at the bottom of the stairs, wouldn't notice her.

The Girl rushed him at vampire speed. Sinakov's body must have blocked the stake in Harry's hand from her sight. With only an instant to defend himself, he swung the stake a few inches to the right.

Even with vamp reflexes, she couldn't stop. She impaled herself on the stake, right through the heart. Her momentum so great she slammed into Harry. They tumbled across the floor to fetch up against a bookcase filled with tiny ceramic figurines of angels which rained down on them with sharp edges and pain instead of blessings.

Harry felt like his shoulder had been ripped open. A moan rose from deep in his chest as he attempted to breathe. Broken angels clinked to the floor. "Go," he said to the woman now kneeling beside the other fallen mortal.

"She's still alive."

Though Harry saw two of him, Sinakov still seemed a bit bewildered. Christ, could it be this easy? His servant lay on her side, hands gripping the stake that pierced her ninety pound frame.

"Take her. Slowly."

Able to focus again, he searched for his other long stake. It lay at Sinakov's feet. He remembered the ten inch one in his pocket. Okay. If he could stand, and if the twice dead vampire stayed confused, maybe he could take him out right now. If he could stand.

Harry blinked. Sinakov was gone. Harry heard a quick scream. There he was, holding the nurse from behind, her head stretched sideways to expose the neck. Fascinated and horrified, he watched as Sinakov's jaw opened in fits and starts as if it hadn't been worked in a long while. She struggled against him, but it was futile. He might have looked like a skeleton with a thin coating of skin, but he still had vampire strength.

Harry reached for his gun. Shit. Lost in the tumble with the Girl. A quick scan located it under a chair on the other side of the vampire.

Sinakov bent his head back to strike. After what he did to the others since his resurrection, there was no reason to think he'd be gentle about it. His eyes narrowed for a moment, like he was wondering why he was holding that woman. But only for a moment. He struck.

"Henri. Stop!" The sound of his real name, given to him more than three hundred and fifty years ago, cut through Sinakov's Hunger. He raised his head and regarded Harry with his head cocked to one side, like a ghoulish bird.

Harry held the Girl's head in his lap, knife in his fist ready to rip into her throat.

"If you hurt her, I'll cut her head off. You need this Girl. She gave you your so called Life back."

A second and Sinakov seemed to appear, standing over Harry, a focused malevolence in his eyes. Behind him the woman dropped to the ground with a thump. "Do not harm her, mortal. I will most happily kill all the mortals in this neighborhood if you do."

"Where are you going?" Harry asked. He couldn't stop being a cop.

Like a switch had been flipped, all the malice in Sinakov's stare vanished. "To see a friend in Miami, Florida. I think."

"Who?"

He had to think about it. Looking at his minion, he said, "Ketch?"

She didn't answer. She had a stake through her heart. To Harry's understanding that meant dead, but not gone. If the stake was pulled out, she'd recover.

"Why do you want to see Ketch?" Still the cop.

This seemed to confuse the vampire. Harry thought he might faint the way he swayed on his feet. "Rubicon." His body spasmed, and the evil mask returned. "She is only a servant. You can watch her recover as I feed on you."

Behind Sinakov's back, the nurse had dragged the unconscious woman out of the room. She appeared in the door, fresh red blotches staining the front of her uniform.

Sinakov spun around as the scent reached him. "And you."

The nurse wasn't having any of it. Without a word she raised Harry's gun and shot Sinakov six times.

She could handle a gun. Five of six slugs smacked into his torso. If he'd been a mortal, any of the five would have killed him. Unfortunately, all they did was drive him backward until he tripped over his Girl's legs. He stumbled against the stake protruding from her chest, inadvertently using it as a lever to wrench her from Harry's grasp on his way to collapsing in a corner.

Harry tried to hold her, but the wound in his shoulder felt like someone had jammed two hands into it and ripped him apart. Small keening sounds came from his lips as his body quivered.

"What the fuck is goin' on?" the nurse asked, still pointing the gun in Sinakov's direction. "Is he dead? He must be dead."

"Yes. But not for long," Harry gasped. He rolled to his knees, but could not quite stand up.

The nurse helped him. "What does that mean?"

"We have to leave here, now."

"This is my house, Mister. Nobody tells me to leave it."

Harry leaned on her shoulder. "You stay, you'll probably be dead in five minutes. Go now." He stumbled to the door.

"But they're dead." She looked over her shoulder at the two vampires lying still as death. Sinakov raised his head and glared at her with pure malice. "Holy shit."

She caught up with him at the screen door and helped him to the fence.

"Your car."

With the other woman in her arms she led Harry to the car. "Mister, you'd better tell me that what I think is happening here, isn't."

"Just go."

In thirty seconds the car rushed down the street. "The hospital is on the other side of town."

"No." Harry could barely keep his eyes open. A dull ache throbbed through his body. He wanted to cry with relief. Words a bare whisper, he said, "Off the street. Private. Hide car. No hospital. No police."

"Buddy, you wanted by the cops?"

"Am cop."

For some reason he thought that was worth a laugh, just before darkness took him.

Teresa

"Get some rest," Simone told Teresa, with a companionable squeeze of her arm.

"But keep one eye open," Justine added, giving her a good, strong hug, the kind Teresa thought of as her vamp hug. A nice tight squeeze where Justine wasn't holding back, afraid to hurt her, instead of a human hug, careful, tentative, as if hugging someone you're not sure you know well enough to get that close to. Teresa preferred the former, though sometimes she felt her joints pop and bones crack.

Teresa stood in the middle of the room for a minute after the heavy door thumped closed, too tired to move or decide whether to take a long shower or flop on the bed as is.

One good whiff of herself and a glance in a full length mirror made the decision easy. Her shoes were soaked, her legs had multiple scratches mingled with rings of dried swamp water, her arms were also scratched, there were twigs in her hair, the deep scratch on her neck seeped crimson, and she stunk. How her two vampire friends, another phrase she would never have thought of not so long ago, could stand to be around her she couldn't fathom.

Leaning her hands against the wall under the shower, Teresa thought about Justine and Simone. She'd never seen Justine have any interest in other women, even as friends. It had taken the heartbreak of Antonia's kidnapping to bring them together as more than office colleagues. Now she seemed to be with Simone. Were they in the shower now, washing each other's backs, quietly discussing the day's events?

Suddenly, a deep, wrenching sob escaped her. Then another and another. It felt like her body had something toxic inside that it had to get out to function properly.

She and Miguel used to shower together early on. They laughed, washed each other, talked about the day or nothing in particular. Sometimes they had sex, sometimes not. That wasn't the intimacy that counted. The memories of that time had to go. And her subconscious had decided that there, alone in the shower, coming from trouble, most likely going to trouble, was the time to purge those memories of another time and place.

Teresa had a different life now. Except for Antonia, any memories that happened before vampires came into her life were baggage, best left in lost luggage.

She was a *bruja, a hechicera*. Focus on that. Focus on finding Antonia.

It took some time before the blood, tears and memories swirled down the drain. Between the shower and the bed she wore nothing and thought of nothing, well aware she was being watched. She may need training, but she had learned a trick or two.

Morpheus quickly took her, though he had no dreams of import for her that night.

Justine

Justine's eyes popped open, instantly awake from a deep daytime sleep. Beside her Simone lay on her back, propped up by pillows, covered by a sheet to the waist. Justine smiled, wondering if she'd look as good at three and a half centuries old.

Though her eyes were closed and Justine hadn't moved, Simone said, "You're awake."

"No. You know how it is with us Young Bloods, we need our beauty sleep."

Simone chuffed and ran the back of her fingers lightly over Justine's cheek. "You won't need any beauty sleep until at least a hundred. Then I will have to find a younger *amant*."

"You'll be back to men by then."

Simone let her head roll to gaze fondly at her *enfant*. "And you also? Harry will be gone by then. Unless…"

Justine rolled onto her back and stared at the ceiling. "Is it dinner time yet?"

Shaking her head, Simone swung legs off the bed and stretched her back and arms. "Do you think Messer will serve us alligator blood? I do not believe I have ever tried it."

"I'm sure it's a delicacy." Justine didn't want to talk or even think about making Harry a vampire. Her new vampire thinking and senses allowed her to enjoy sleeping with Simone. She was her maker, friend, partner and bedmate, but Harry was her love. As heartbreaking as it would be she wouldn't change him without his truly wanting it. Still thinking like a mortal, Simone would have said. Well, on that subject she didn't want to think at all.

They'd found time to wash out their clothes before sleeping and they were mostly dry as they dressed.

"Eight o'clock," Justine said. "Let's go see what our *bruja* friend can learn. And then get out of here. Nice as it is, this place gives me the creeps."

"Yes, I agree. It feels like a tomb."

"Of which you have experience, I'm sure."

"Too many."

Simone grabbed the door lever, pushed down and pulled. The door didn't open. She tried again—up, down, push, pull, check for locks—nothing.

"What's the matter, didn't they teach you how to open a door in France?"

Simone stood aside, inviting Justine to try. She did, with the same results. Their eyes made contact.

"Merde."

Teresa and Messer

Teresa stood naked in front of the full length mirror, inspecting the scars on her dusky skin. Her memories skipped through the events that led to them—killing her first vampire, her kidnapping and betrayal of Justine, the fire, the fight in Boston, Grace's compound, South of the Border, and the race through the swamp. Christ. At least as an ER head nurse you got to go home occasionally. And now a *bruja*? She snorted a laugh. Christ probably had nothing to do with *that*.

She checked her watch. Time to go learn how to hide from Oracles and get the hell on the road. The house was a nice refuge, but that Messer gave her the creeps.

Her clothes had been washed while she slept. She wondered if Redbone had snuck a peek. She didn't care, she concluded. He seemed like a good guy, and she did look good naked. How far she'd come, beginning to think like a vamp.

Dressed in clean jeans, a dark T-shirt and blue blouse, the most elegant any of them had dressed for dinner in a long time, she sat on the bed, elbows on knees, head down, going over in her mind what she had learned from Grace. A fair amount, actually. There was a knock on the door. She opened it to Redbone, ready to escort her to dinner.

Messer sat at the head of a long dining table set for two.

She hesitated when Messer pulled out a chair for her. "Only two?"

"I don't think our dinner tonight is bloody enough for them." He pushed in the chair and she had no choice but to sit. "Besides..." She could hear the "Dear lady," in there, though he didn't say it. "It's you I need to teach and it helps to know you a little better. Wine?"

Teresa hadn't spent her years in the ER dealing with druggies and scammers not to suspect within minutes she was being played.

The wine was wonderful, the soup delicious, though she didn't care for killing turtles for soup. She didn't ask what the main course was, but she was pretty sure she'd rather be eating it than have it eating her.

She gave him the basics of her life—married, nurse, daughter abducted, separated, no time for a divorce, searching for Antonia, now a *bruja*. Smooth as he was, he didn't seem to care much about her past. He was more interested in his.

He told her amusing stories about his stage magician days. The applause, the money, the characters and the famous people, the rush of perfecting a new illusion and performing it on stage for the first time.

How important the "lovely assistants" were and the closeness of a team, a family really, working together. How perfect they, she, would be on the stage.

All the time he talked she felt the subtle push in her head to like the idea. It was similar to a vampire's glamour. Justine and Simone had shown her what it felt like, and a few ways to resist it. She also felt a tension coming from him separate from the tension of his attempt to persuade her to join him.

He was wasting time. It all did sound interesting and glamorous, but not now. And where were her companions? They would have at least showed up and teased her about eating swamp rat or some such thing.

When Redbone served a pecan pie to die for, a phrase she did not use lightly these days, she said, "That all sounds great, but I need to learn that spell."

"Ah, yes, yes, I do get carried away sometimes. As I said, it's old magic. Hand gestures are very important."

Justine and Simone

"That bastard sold us out to Tito." Justine punctuated her statement of the obvious with a punch to the door, hurting nothing but her hand.

Simone pounded on the door. "Redbone, let us out. We will be late for dinner." Forehead pressed to the solid steel door, she went quiet, casting out her glamour. For a full minute she held still.

Justine searched the room. A chest of drawers and a small bathroom cabinet were made of cheap particle board, useless as weapons against vampires. The bed turned out to be a welded steel frame bolted to the concrete floor and covered with cheap veneer. The narrow high windows were thick reinforced glass, hard to get to and impossible to break without heavy tools.

"I can sense him," Simone said. "But he's too far away to be reached. Weapons?"

"This was built as a vampire cell. Nothing useful."

They spent a few minutes wandering about the room, inspecting, searching, finding nothing useful, until across the room Justine watched Simone peering into a full length mirror on the bathroom door. "Is that glass?"

Simone rapped on it. She turned and grinned.

❧   ❦

Teresa had the basics of the Oracle shielding spell down. It wasn't that hard, a short invocation sounding like ugh, oot, and oog, and a few hand movements similar to cramps in her fingers. It didn't work inside the already shielded house, though Messer said she had it right. The trick would be keeping it focused once outside and moving.

Messer touched her hand. His eyes found hers. His voice was smooth, inviting and sincere as his words insinuated themselves into her thoughts. "Are you sure you want to leave here, Teresa? Stay here with me. Become a part of a new and wonderful Magical Show. With our power joined we can create a show like no one has ever seen before. We will be celebrated, adored around the world. Stay with me. The world is a dangerous place and you were not doing anything else important with your life. You are so tired of being alone."

A soothing warmth spread from her head into her body. It *was* dangerous out there. She *wasn't* doing anything important. A magic show sounded wonderful. And she did not want to be alone anymore. Why wouldn't she want to stay here with him?

"Teresa, you *want* to stay here. You *want* to be safe in this house with me. You *want* me to protect you because nobody else will keep you safe. Swear to me that you will stay with me."

The warmth relaxed her bones, brought a feeling of languor to her body and mind. She wanted to stay, to be safe because…nobody…else…? Was that right? It seemed there were others who cared for her, kept her safe. Two others? Questions—triggered a surge of…something that cooled the heat suffusing her thoughts. Questions—Brought a warning, from Grace, words to say. She said them in her head. Awareness. Clarity of what was being done to her. And something else. Faint, hardly there. *Two others. Prisoners.*

All this happened in seconds. Teresa remained relaxed in her chair, eyes half open, mind wide open.

"Swear to me, Teresa, you will stay with me as long as I want you. Swear on this book." He slid a book with a tattered leather cover in front of her.

She remembered warning words from Grace, "Swear to nothing for no one. *"Teresa. We are prisoners. Help us.*

Redbone, one eye visible from a doorway, was staring, his head moving side to side with minute movements.

And more. Danger. Awareness of approaching peril.

Vampires at the door.

Redbone, with a final glare and grimace at Teresa, opened the door. Tito, wearing light boots, dark pants, and a tight T-shirt that showed off his muscles stood impatiently under a dim yellow porch light. None of what he wore had run through a swamp lately.

After a few seconds he growled at Redbone, "Well?"

"Oh. Sorry. You may enter."

Which Tito did, followed by six vampires armed with machetes, some with sidearms.

When Messer heard the knock on the door he glanced quickly over his shoulder, grabbed her hand and held it to the book. "Swear," he ordered, sending a heavy wave of magical persuasion up her arm and throughout her body. "Swear, now, Teresa."

Teresa let the warmth flow for a few seconds. It would be so easy to let it take control of her mind. No thinking, no fighting, no vampires. But that was not what she was about. Thoughts still fuzzy, she repeated the phrase Grace gave her to block attempts on her mind. She repeated Justine and Simone's defense against glamour. Awareness jolted her, bringing clarity. She knew exactly what Messer was trying to do and was not going to let him hijack her search for Antonia or leave her friends.

Eyes wide open, Teresa sat up in her chair and caught Messer's own wide-eyed fervent gaze. Before she could tell Messer, "No. I will not swear," Tito strode up behind him and said, "I know this one. We will take her, too."

Messer jumped up and faced the vampire. "No. We have a deal. She's mine."

"This one killed some of my people. So we have a new deal. I take the three and let you live."

"I will not let you have her."

"*You* will keep her from *me*?" Tito's arm shot out, grabbed the sorcerer by the neck and lifted him up. "I get what I want, sorcerer." The word an insult.

Messer's voice came out raspy but strong. "Not in this house, vampire." Palm up, fingers holding an invisible ball, Messer jammed his hand underneath Tito's arm. He uttered a guttural intonation. Smoke floated from Tito's arm, bringing the odor of burning flesh.

He cried out and dropped Messer. "Now I will take everything."

Tito drew out a machete with a blade curved from years of sharpening.

Messer did a finger wagging move and the blade rose straight up taking Tito with it. Tito lashed out with a foot, knocking Messer to the floor. He dropped to his feet. Messer swiped a hand and Tito's legs flew out from under him.

Messer sprang up. Tito followed, feinted with his blade, snatched the Sorcerer with his free hand and had a hand on his chin and the blade to his neck in an instant.

Teresa had no intention of going with either man. While they fought over her, she slid off the chair and slipped around the table, making for the door.

Tito spied her. He threw Messer across the room and in half a blink caught her. He held her face inches from his own and threw the full force of his glamour at her. She barely had time to repeat Grace's phrase. Even so, she felt herself losing control, wanting to sit and wait until he came for her.

From across the room, Messer shouted, "You will not have her!" A sizzling ball of pure energy smacked Tito, slamming him against a wall. But he did not let go of Teresa. He shook off the blast. He held up his machete. "I was going to kill her anyway, sorcerer. Now is as good a time as any."

"No!" Palm to palm, thumbs overlapping, Messer pointed his fingers at her.

Teresa felt as if she'd grabbed a high power line. Her body vibrated. A dark smoky globe encircled her, slowly shutting out the light. Pure dark. Falling, falling, falling. A flash of bright light, pain…then nothing.

Side by side Justine and Simone pressed hands and foreheads against the door, all senses wide open.

"He is here," Simone said.

"Yes. How many with him?"

"*Je ne sait pas.* More than one or two."

"I can sense Teresa. Angry?"

"Yes. Redbone is scared."

"I don't blame him."

A minute of silent concentration, then, they tensed and jumped back.

"*Merde!*"

"Shit!"

"They're fighting."

Ears pressed to the door they heard a cry, a shout, a thud.

"Christ, Tee. Teresa! Teresa!"

Straining to hear or feel through the damned door, they held totally still, not a breath or a heartbeat to disturb their intensity.

Simone said it. "She's...gone."

"Where? How? Did she run out?"

"I do not think so. Redbone is very shocked."

Justine pounded the door. "Tee!"

"Shh. They are coming. Are you ready?"

"Fuck, yeah."

Quickly they took their places. They had removed the box spring from the queen bed and set it on edge against the wall next to the door. Simone leaped on top, ready to pounce. Justine stood by the bed to draw the attention of anyone who entered. For weapons, each had several pieces of broken mirror with handles of wrapped towels secured by ripped lengths of torn sheets.

Justine had to force herself to focus on what happened when the door opened. Getting herself truly dead would not help Teresa.

Simone held up five fingers, then one. Six vamps. Most likely all with more experience than her at this sort of thing. Great.

The outside bolts shot back with a solid snap. The door swung open.

Limbo

Black.

"Hey. Wake up. You all right?"

An unfamiliar voice. Pain. She made a quick survey of her body. It seemed to be intact.

"Wake up, will you?"

Her eyes opened. She saw long blonde hair hanging around a woman's face—big lips, lots of makeup, pretty.

Teresa managed, *"Que'...? Quien...? Donde estoy?"* Where am I? What a cliché, she thought. Though appropriate.

"That's what I want to know."

"You speak Spanish?" Teresa worked through her body again, stretching, flexing.

"Enough to know you're wondering what happened and where the hell you are. That's what I asked."

The blonde woman helped her sit up and lean against a white wall.

All the walls, and the ceiling and floor were translucent white. It felt solid against her back, but didn't look solid, sort of fuzzy.

"And...?"

Her new companion sat next to her. "Don't know."

Teresa surveyed the room again. It was about twenty by twenty by twenty feet of white. That was all there was. "I do not see a door."

"Nope."

"Dios."

"Doubt it."

"How long have you been here?"

"Don't know. No day or night. Not hungry, not thirsty, haven't had to pee. I figure I'm dead."

"What's your name?"

"Nadia."

"Teresa."

They sat quiet awhile.

Nadia rested her head back, eyes closed. She'd been through the first minutes or hours already. Didn't seem to be in any hurry.

Teresa thought about searching for a door, or something, but figured it would be a waste of time—if that meant anything there. She took notice of Nadia's clothes: black high-waisted pants, shimmering white blouse under a black and red vest, black stockings and no shoes.

"What happened to your shoes?"

"Red stilettos. As comfortable as they looked. Took 'em off, turned around and they were gone. If you want to keep it, don't set it down."

Eventually, Teresa asked, "So where were you before you were here?"

"Huh." Her red lips curled into a smile with little humor. "I was on stage in Denver. I walked into a little box where I was supposed to disappear and reappear in another little box. Instead I appeared in this big box."

"Oh mierda. Messer?"

For the first time Nadia showed surprise. She shifted around to face Teresa. Mouth and eyes wide open, she scrutinized her new box mate. "What the hell?"

"What year is it do you think?"

"Last I knew, December 12, 2009."

"Dios," Teresa muttered. "Last I knew, it was September, 2014."

Nadia's mouth worked but no words came out. Finally, "I've been here almost five fucking years? I don't believe it."

"Si." As much to herself as to Nadia, she added, "Six months ago I

wouldn't have believed it either. But now…"

"So why are you here. Was that bastard Messer pissed at you, too?"

"Actually he was trying to save me. Probably did. By the way, he didn't send you here on purpose. He pretty much fell apart afterward."

Nadia leaned back against the wall. They sat together with legs drawn up and arms on knees.

"Why didn't he bring me back?"

"He tried for years. Didn't know where you were."

"Does he know where you are?"

"I don't know."

"Fucking magic." A minute, hour, day, week later Nadia said, "So what's your story? I think we have time for the long version."

Messer's House

Tito came in first, ancient machete in a scabbard hanging from his waist, all sure of himself. Those two women weren't getting away from him this time.

Two more tough guy vamps with sawed off shotguns entered close behind. Two more with machetes in hand, though loosely held, came next. Their attention was on Justine who stood by the bed, her hand inches from a pillow fluffed up at the foot of it.

Tito said, "Justine, you have no place to go but with me. Why make me angry by fighting a losing battle?"

Justine shouted, "I'm not going with you, Tito, you asshole. I'm taking you down, right now."

From behind the pillow she drew a glass shard about a foot long, and raised it up as if to stab down. She had everyone's attention.

Simone struck.

She leaped down from atop of the mattress. Swinging a machete-size piece of glass with a hook at the end, she ripped the throat of vamp 3 through to the spine. A second later she crashed into number 4. As they tumbled down, Simone snatched the blade from his hand, spun, and took his head off. Continuing that strike, she swept the blade down and severed the hand of vamp 2 as he spun around with his shotgun. She grabbed the gun before it hit the floor and swung it up to blow off vamp 1's head.

The quick carnage used up her two second advantage. Vamp 5,

a muscular no nonsense sort, snatched the gun from her hands and punched her head with a blow that would have killed a mortal.

During second two, Tito glanced over his shoulder at Simone flying through the air. Justine struck, missing his neck, leaving the glass knife embedded in his shoulder. That distracted him for half a second. From under the pillow she drew out a larger piece, a long thin triangle. Grasping the padded small end, she swung for his neck.

Tito was no Young Blood. He had experience, strength, and speed. No piece of glass embedded in his shoulder was going to slow him down. His reliable blade shattered Justine's glass in a glittery explosion. His swing followed through the cloud of silver splinters. As he drew back around he nailed Justine with his elbow, sending her sprawling back on the bed.

Justine thought her head had exploded. For the first time since becoming acclimated to the change she felt like throwing up. For a moment she saw two Titos standing over her, machete raised to split her aching head open.

Justine threw the pillow at him. It erupted in a feathery swirl against his blade as she rolled out from under. Better a cloud of feathers than one of brains.

Simone knew that to stay still was to die. Even she could not outrun a shotgun blast. She hit the floor rolling while taking out a glass knife tucked into the back of her waistband. She flung it at vamp 5 like skipping a stone. The edge sliced his eye just as he pulled the shotgun trigger. Buckshot ripped the air an inch from her ear.

With 5 momentarily distracted, Simone scooped up a stray machete, ducked around him, wound up like a softball pitcher, and hurled it underhand at vamp 1, slicing into his thigh. His shotgun fired wild. She slammed into him with a solid knee in his groin, driving him into a corner. He doubled over as he emitted a groan any man alive or dead would relate to.

"Macho that, bitch," Simone spat.

A hand clamped the back of her neck, lifted her up and slammed her down on the hard floor. Before she could move, Vamp 5 stomped a boot on her chest and aimed a shotgun at her head. "Macho, this, bitch."

Tito stood between Justine and everything. Grinning, knowing he had the upper hand, Tito shifted the machete to his left hand. With barely a wince he yanked the glass out of his shoulder. Moving as if to toss it away to his left, he suddenly flipped it backhanded.

It struck Justine between the ribs. Startled by the move and unexpected shock of pain, she staggered back into the corner.

Tito's grin widened to a sneer. "I hope you will join us, Justine. Such a shame to kill a smart, strong woman. Though there would be some pleasure in the killing, for me."

Slowly, as if performing some secret martial arts snake charming ritual, he waved his weapon back and forth, extending his reach to show her she had no chance of escape.

Justine had just as much belief in herself as Tito did. What she didn't have was the experience and training and strength he did. She did not believe she would be caught or killed there. Hadn't they all survived so far? She just wasn't quite sure how they would escape this.

"Simone, get up off your lazy ass and help me, will you?"

"She's going to have a headache if she tries," Vamp 5 said.

"Beck," Tito said to vamp 6 who had been standing in the doorway watching the action. "Call the others. We have them."

"Yes, sir."

Simone caught Justine's eye. She shrugged as best she could. Justine shrugged and cocked her head. Not much they could do but be ready to move.

Justine had a view of the whole room. She watched Beck speaking on the radio. Then, from out of sight, a baseball bat smashed into his head with a mushy crunch.

Redbone, she thought. Maybe Messer. Beck slumped to the floor. Justine's eyes popped wide.

Teresa stepped over Beck like a dark avenger and stalked up behind vamp 5. She swung with everything she had. He had that one vampire fraction of a second to react enough to slightly deflect the blow. But it was enough to disorient him and make him stagger back to drop to his knees.

Simone jumped to her feet and turned to help Justine.

"Tee, look out!" Justine shouted.

Simone glanced over her shoulder and saw vamp 1 lift his gun to Teresa. Leaving Justine, Simone raced back to Teresa, grabbed her around the waist and carried her full speed out the door.

Number 1's shot passed through the now empty space and grazed Tito's back, leaving a ragged hole in his shirt.

Justine took advantage by yanking the glass from her ribs, jamming it in Tito's body, and racing out the door.

Simone slammed the door shut. Teresa shot the heavy bolts home.

"Lazy ass?" Simone said.

"Sorry. You were laying down. Tee, what the hell?"

"Later. More are coming."

Ignoring the pain of their various wounds, they followed Teresa through the house, leaving behind the thumps and curses coming through the door. She led them out the front door and down to the dock.

Redbone stood on the dock next to a strangely dressed blonde woman. Messer sat in the boat, hunched over, wrapped in a blanket.

The woman grabbed Teresa's hand. "The Oracle Block spell? Is it working?"

Teresa closed her eyes and held still. "*Si.* Yes. It's still holding." She wasted no time. "Nadia, this is Justine and Simone."

"Hello," Nadia said. "Teresa has told me so much about you. But you have to go."

Redbone handed Teresa some keys. "Car's a couple hundred feet up that path. When you hit pavement hang a left to get to the Interstate. Go right then left to use the back roads. There's a map."

"Thank you, Redbone. You'll be okay?"

"I have a huntin' shack farther in. It's warded. We be okay. You go."

Teresa and Nadia exchanged a tight, quick hug.

"Thank you." Nadia said, as sincerely as those words were ever said. "I hope you find Antonia."

"See you on stage," Teresa replied. "Come on, we have to go. More vamps are coming."

Slightly bewildered, Justine and Simone followed.

Cypress trees gave way to white pine as the path rose to solid ground, leading them to a three year old Jeep Grand Cherokee. Teresa jumped into the driver's seat and had the motor running and in gear before the others had closed their doors. She left a spray of dirt and pine needles as she floored it and raced down a narrow dirt road.

"Freeway or back roads?" Teresa asked.

"We are shielded from the Oracles?" Simone asked.

"Yes."

"Freeway," Justine said. "Let's get the hell away from here as fast as we can."

At the end of the dirt road Teresa barely slowed as she turned left onto a two lane paved road.

Justine laid a hand on her friend's arm. "Tee, I'm all for speed, but let's not crash or get the cops after us. Neither one will do us any good."

Teresa breathed deeply, in, out, flexed hands on the wheel and let off the gas a little. She took a few more deep breaths. She reached over and grasped Justine's hand.

"For a while, I thought I might never see you again." A tear left a shiny track on her cheek.

Simone reached from the back seat and gripped her arm. "We are happy that you did. What do you mean by 'a while?' "

"Something else has happened with you. Who was that woman? What happened to Messer?" Justine reached over and wiped the tear away.

More deep breaths. "She's—"

Simone interrupted. "Do you hear that?" She stared intently behind them. "*Merde. Gerdarmes,* coming fast."

The road curved. Ahead, more flashing lights and cars blocking the road. Teresa brought the Jeep to a skidding halt.

"Tito. His people would be able to do this," Simone said.

"We can't let them take us. It would be much too complicated. I don't want to fight them. Run?"

Teresa unbuckled her seat belt and turned in her seat. "No running. I have a better way."

The pursuing cars had stopped, doors opened. Men with guns approached from both directions.

Simone said, "Grace's spell."

"Yes."

"You know how to use it?"

Teresa turned her back to them. "Hold on to my shoulders. Don't let go."

Teresa formed some quick, sharp hand motions while uttering indecipherable words. She clapped her hands three times. "Haf!" A bright light enveloped them.

Claire's House

Harry woke with a start and threw up an arm to ward off the circle of vampires attacking him. He gasped as fire consumed his shoulder, then froze, afraid to move. A hand wrapped around his wrist. He cried out as he attempted to pull away.

"Easy, Harry. Relax. Move slow."

"Justine?" His eyes blinked open, focusing on the woman beside him.

"Sorry, not Justine. Claire."

The woman from the house. The nurse. He let the tenseness flow out of him. He didn't have the strength to keep it up, anyway. The fire lessened as Claire lowered his arm.

"You're alive."

"Thanks to you most likely."

Moving nothing but his eyes, he studied her face. Paler than he remembered, with circles under bloodshot eyes. Her dirty blonde hair hadn't felt a brush in some time.

"Have you slept?"

"No."

"How long?"

"Couple days."

Harry closed his eyes and let the memories rush back. Shit shit shit. And deep in it. Two days head start.

"The other woman with you?"

Claire leaned forward, elbows on knees, fingers massaging her tired eyes. "My cousin. She's in the hospital. Attacked by unknown assailants."

"Us?"

"A friend's house. They're on vacation for another week."

"Police?"

"You tell me."

Harry weakly gripped her arm. "Please, it's important."

"I bet, Detective Harry Frazer, of the San Diego, California Sheriff's Department. On leave of duty while recovering from an injury."

They made eye contact, she waiting to hear what he had to say, he wondering what to say.

"Those two people have murdered at least five victims in the last week or so."

"People?"

Jesus. Harry stared at the ceiling. "Can we just leave it at that for now. I'll tell you what you need to know later."

"Way to avoid the issue, Detective. I'll want to know more than I *need* to know. Your shoulder hurt?"

"Only when I breathe."

She gave him a couple pills then inspected his wound. One of the stitches had torn loose. While she restitched and rebandaged him, she told him what had happened.

A neighbor reported a van leaving the area fast. The police found the van. They searched the area, but no other vehicles were reported stolen and nobody saw anyone suspicious. She left Harry at the house and took her cousin to the hospital. She'd been afraid the "people" would find her and had kept watch for two nights and a day.

Harry relaxed a little. It sounded like all was good. Then he started. "Sorry, you're going to be sore for a while."

"My car. If they find it..."

"It's in the garage. Nice wheels."

"How?"

"My cousin's father is a cop. I wanted to be Dana Scully, but decided I'd rather fix the victims than shoot the perps. And I read a lot of mysteries. Figured you didn't walk here from California."

Harry felt the pills starting to work. He had to get up. Sinakov had two days head start. "I need to get on the road."

Claire pushed him back down on the couch. "You need to, but you can't. You wouldn't make it out the door. Where are the 'people?' "

He couldn't keep his eyes open. "Gone. There are probably some bodies in a house close to where they found the van. Their car will be gone. Probably be found in Mississippi. Maybe Alabama."

"Where are they going?"

"To see Ketch." Harry let the warm and fuzzy take him.

When he woke, it was dark in the house. Dusk outside. A light in the kitchen illuminated the living room he lay in. Recliners along with the couch he was on faced a big screen TV surrounded by a large compliment of electronic boxes. Family pictures covered a large area of the white walls. On a sturdy pine coffee table he spied a large note. *Do not leave. Will be back by 6. Do not leave.*

The next thing he noticed was that the catheter had been removed, because he had to piss like that proverbial horse. Moving carefully, he managed to take care of that chore, then rummaged around the kitchen. He wiped up the last bit of gravy from a TV dinner as headlights flashed across the windows.

Claire found him sitting at the well-used oak kitchen table. "I could have fixed you something better than that."

"Hard to beat microwaved Salisbury steak and mashed potatoes. This brownie makes it all worthwhile."

"No more drugs for you."

"How's your cousin?"

Claire sat down across from him with a Budweiser and a couple cheeseburgers and fries. She pushed one to him.

"Those 'people' beat her up and she lost a lot of blood, but she'll be okay. Physically anyway. She's a bit high-strung." They ate in silence until she said, "This is when you tell me those 'people' weren't what I think they were."

Harry wished he could tell her that Sinakov and his Girl weren't vampires. He could see no good coming from telling Claire the truth. The less people who knew, the better. Including him if he could turn back the clock. A deep sigh escaped him. He could use some advice from Justine and Simone about what to say. Maybe they could glamour Claire into believing some plausible lie.

On the other hand she took a big risk for him. He owed her something. She seemed to be well-grounded, not likely to freak out, able to keep a secret. She probably won't believe him anyway. He'd tell her the truth, as little as he could get away with.

"I can't tell you that."

She stared at him, cheeseburger halfway to her mouth. "Ho-ly shit." Harry kept his expression neutral. "You're not bullshitting me, are you?"

"You wanted to be Scully."

Claire chewed on her meal for awhile. Then she said. "I'm a realist. I know what I saw. Tell me what's going on. I can keep a secret."

Harry meant to give her a barebones account. They killed somebody in his jurisdiction and he was trailing them. But somehow most of the rest of the story came out, and with it a great relief. He'd been keeping the Truth About Vampires to himself, unable to talk about it with any other mortals. Bayley, his friend, neighbor, and bartender suspected something, but she and her partner had experienced enough trauma. Darwin, who he'd thought was mortal, was actually a vampire. It wasn't quite the same.

Two beers later they sat at the table not looking at each other. Harry was drained, and a little nervous to have said so much. He hoped she could keep a secret. Though who would believe her?

She glanced at him occasionally, probably trying to figure out if he was trustworthy or just plain crazy. After a big sigh and a last glance she drained her beer, set it down loudly on the table, and left the room.

She returned with the small messenger bag which served as her purse. She pulled out a notebook, opened it, and hands and elbows on the table said, "I have no choice but to believe you. I saw what I saw. Even Scully had to believe what she saw. So, they're headed East. You mentioned *Transporte Francaise.* I googled them. Not much about them, but I did see a mention of KVS Shipping, which is apparently related to *Transporte Francaise.* Not much on them either, but the CEO is Bernard Ketch."

Harry hadn't been paying much attention to her. The beer, injury and pills wanted him to sleep. It took him a few seconds to understand what she said, and a few more seconds to say something. "You're sure they're connected?"

"I'm no expert at this, but unless you're looking for seafood restaurants, seems like our best bet."

That he got. "Our?"

"Look Harry, I know you want to get on the road after these guys. But trust me as your nurse, you're in no shape to be driving yourself to Miami, Fort Lauderdale actually, which is where KVS is."

"No no no. This isn't some movie or TV show where you hook up with the cop and become his indispensable sidekick. These people play for keeps."

"You're right, no TV or movie badass, tough guy heroes. You're tough, but if you try and drive yourself there you will not make it. Period. So, my cousin gets out of the hospital tomorrow. We have family in Florida, Delray Beach, a bit north of Miami. The three of us drive your car there. Then you're on your own. You have no choice here. Deal?"

CHAPTER TEN

<u>*Jasmine's House, Fort Myers, FL*</u>

"Jesus, what the fuck was that?" Justine lay on cool grass, gazing up at random points of blurry light that slowly coalesced into stars in a light polluted night sky. Her immediate thought was *Danger!* but she couldn't quite summon up the energy to move. Teresa? Simone? Where were they?

A screen door slammed and footsteps shushed through the grass. Tito! She struggled to gain her feet. She felt like her mortal self after a brutal ten mile run.

"Relax, Hon," a female voice said. "You all are safe here."

A face blacker than the starry night sky peered down at her, white eyes wary, but showing no fear. Justine's gaze shifted to the shotgun the woman held pointing to the ground inches from her body.

"Not to worry, Girl. This ain't for you. But one's got to be careful these days. Don't know who's gonna show up in your backyard in the middle of the night." She stepped back and called out, "Lenny, come give these ladies a hand. Looks like they had a rough time of it lately."

A brawny, barefoot young man in jeans and T-shirt appeared.

The woman reached a hand out to help Justine. "I'm Jasmine, this my boy Lenny, we've been expecting you."

On her feet, Justine surveyed the area. They were in a large backyard surrounded by a high wood fence. A huge Banyan tree sheltered the far end, with a swing set, sandbox and blowup pool off to the side.

"Momma, this one is pretty whacked out. I'm going to take her in."

Simone helped support Teresa. She looked quizzically at Justine. Justine shrugged and nodded.

"I'll help," Simone said.

Not that Lenny needed help. He easily lifted Teresa, who had never in her life been close to being anorexic, and carried her into the house. Simone opened the door for him.

Justine studied Jasmine. A couple inches shorter than her, maybe five foot six, long black hair in a loose braid, well built, confident and attractive. She stood easy, shotgun held casually across her body.

Justine looked around again. "Where are we?"

Jasmine laughed. "You are just outside the city limits of Fort Myers, Florida."

Justine raised her face to the sky. "Damn. Did Teresa do this?"

"If she's the one Lenny carried in, I expect so. Takes a lot out of a body doing what she did. Where'd you come from?"

"Georgia. You said we were expected?"

"Grace gave me a heads up. Guess she figured you'd need a quick exit at some point. Guess she was right."

"Oh shit. The Oracles. They're tracking us."

"We're shielded here. You safe."

"Yeah? Well. I've heard that before."

"Well, it's true here. Come on inside. Be daylight soon and you three need time to heal."

Justine followed Jasmine into the two-story stucco house. "I'm Justine," she said.

∾ ∾

All three slept straight through to supper that night. While Teresa, barely able to keep her eyes open, downed the best fried chicken she'd ever had, and Justine and Simone sipped blood from wine glasses, origin unknown and unasked, they caught up on the latest events with Jasmine and Lenny listening and shaking their heads.

Jasmine said to Teresa, "You performed that spell twice in an hour, with one person and two people? Lord, woman, no wonder you're so whacked out. You need at least another ten—twelve hours of rest."

"And she saved our *derrières,* once again," Simone added. "Please remind me to never return to Georgia."

Justine asked, "How long did you think you were in this limbo?"

Teresa stared at her empty plate. Finally she hunched her shoulders and said, "Days, weeks, months. I tried to get a sense of time passing, but there was nothing. No light change, no noise, no sleeping, never hungry, hair didn't grow, never had to pee. We talked forever, became friends, had arguments over nothing, made up. Nadia was there for almost four *years.* How she didn't go crazy, I don't know."

"I assume you used Grace's escape spell to finally get out," Simone said.

"I feel *estupida* for not trying it sooner. Nadia knows some magic tricks, but she didn't have any cards or coins so she was showing me how they would work if she did have some. Watching her hands reminded me of the spell."

"But how did you come back at the same time you left?" Though her posture and voice were casual, Simone's eyes held severe interest.

Teresa slouched back in her chair and stared at her beer bottle as she rotated it with her strong fingers. "You have to focus on where you want to go. I didn't think going into the house was a good idea, I focused on the dock at the time I was zapped."

Jasmine and Lenny traded wide-eyed holy-shit glances.

"I'll bet Messer was surprised to see Nadia."

"He loved her, loves her, terribly. We should all be so lucky to be loved like that."

Silence followed as they all considered past or future loves. Justine and Teresa held hands. They knew each other's history in that area.

Before dinner Justine and Teresa had a few minutes alone together. Side by side they leaned against the fence by the Banyan tree.

"When we figured out we were prisoners I was so worried about you, Tee. I know you can take care of yourself, but...we were worried."

"We?"

"I think Simone is coming to like you."

With a smile Teresa said, "She's growing on me, too. In limbo, or wherever we were, I was afraid I'd never see either of you again. You can't cry in there, either. It makes a difference."

"I remember."

"Oh, shit." Teresa shifted until they touched shoulder to shoulder. "I forgot."

"It's okay. Just having you back in the land of the living...so to speak, is enough."

Teresa rubbed her arm against her friend's. Grinning, she said, "I'm glad we're in the tropics now. This is as warm as you've been in months."

"I have to admit it's the warmest I've felt in a long time."

"Except when you speak with Harry. Have you talked with him?"

"I don't even remember the last time. I'm going to call after dinner if I can. All our cell phones are gone."

At the table Simone said, "Do we know where the boat is, and how do we get there?"

"Getting you all there we have covered. Inquiries and arrangements are being made. It will be best if you stay with us until tomorrow night and we can transport you to Fort Lauderdale. It will not harm any of you to rest another day."

"I do not object to that," Simone said. "Do you have any more wine?"

❧ ❦

"Bayley, this is Justine. I can't get hold of Harry. Have you seen him?"

"Justine, hi. Harry is out of town. He left about a week ago, driving. Didn't say where he was going."

"Was it for Sheriff's Department business?"

"I asked him that, too. He just said it's everybody's business. Especially if I fail. I don't know what that means, but he was real uptight, like he needed to get going right now. He asked us to water his plants twice a week. Like he was going to be gone awhile."

"And you haven't heard from him?"

"Nope."

"Okay. I'm going to give you a phone number. I'll be here until tomorrow night. If he calls, please have him call me as soon as possible. And you can call, too, if you hear anything. Or Darwin. Please."

She gave her the number.

"Got it. How are you? You sound a little stressed yourself."

"I'm surviving, so far. Worrying about Harry isn't helping."

Bayley said carefully, "You know I owe Harry. Whatever he needs, I'm there. But I also know there's something else going on with him, and you, and Darwin. Something dangerous, and you're protecting me and Susan. Some time I hope you'll trust me enough to tell me…whatever."

"Bayley, I can't promise anything, it's really Harry's call, but if anybody deserves to know, it's you. Though you might wish you didn't."

"Okay. Be careful. And one more thing. Before he left, Harry said to tell you he loved you. He said it like he wasn't sure if he'd have a chance to tell you himself."

"Thank you. Please tell him I love him, too, forever."

❧ ❦

"Harry?" Simone asked. The three of them relaxed on the patio outside while Jasmine and Lenny cleaned up inside. Jasmine had strongly encouraged Teresa to go back to bed, but she strongly resisted, saying she needed some time with her homies. Jasmine relented after extracting a promise to go back in half an hour.

"He left Oceanside a week ago. Bayley said he was uptight and in a hurry. Acted like he might not be back. No idea where he was going or why. Darwin?"

"He hasn't heard from him either. He's busy monitoring the Families. The Sinakov Family is divided over who will be Master, the ones faithful to Stephan or the ones with a more modern outlook. And the Sulwaytup Family is trying to take over all their business. There have been casualties. Darwin is keeping it all under the mortal radar, but it could all explode in a heartbeat."

A phone chirped inside and was quickly answered.

Teresa laid back on a lounge chair, staring up at the half moon. "I don't have anybody to call, so no updates."

"Miguel?"

"No. I'll call when I have found Antonia. Not before."

The others traded a look. "*Ça va.* So we go to Rubicon's yacht and find Antonia. Do we know where it is?"

The screen door to the patio slid open and shut. Jasmine appeared and dropped into a chair beside them. The three turned to her with expectant looks.

"The *Night Watch* is docked at Freeport in the Bahamas. Our original plan was to wait for sunset tomorrow, and Lenny would drive you to Fort Lauderdale where you'd board a yacht to take you there. Now, we think they are preparing to depart any time. Even though you all need to rest, it's best you leave here early in the morning. You will board and the captain will leave in time to get you there at sunset. Questions?"

"What kind of yacht is it?" Justine asked.

"A hundred and fifty foot motor yacht. It's been tastefully modified for travelers such as yourselves. You'll like it."

Delray Beach, FL

"Bayley, it's Harry. Is Darwin there?"

"Jesus, Harry, where are you? I've been getting worried."

"Road trip. I really need to speak with Darwin. Is he there?"

"Haven't been seeing much of him, either. But he's here tonight. Hang on."

Harry waited impatiently. He sat on a bench above the beach at Delray Beach, Florida. The last vestige of the sun had disappeared behind him and the dark over the water quickly climbed the sky. The slow lap of the waves did not soothe him at all. It smelled different and felt different from a California beach. Humidity was not something he was used to.

"Harry, where are you?" Darwin's familiar Italian accent brought a quick attempt at a smile to Harry's lips.

"*Buonasera*, Darwin. I'm in Florida. With bad news."

"Of course, Harry. Why should there be anything but bad news. Are you all right?"

Harry chuffed. "All right enough. Stephan Sinakov is alive. He's here in Florida."

Darwin didn't reply for long seconds. "That is not possible. Your Justine, and Simone, decapitated him."

"Yes they did. He had a girl, a servant, with him in his house and she is with him now. Somehow she saved him, reattached his head."

"You are mistaken. You must be mistaken."

"He tried to kill me before the fire, he tried to kill me a few days ago. It's him. He's not quite right in the head. Sometimes he doesn't seem to know where he is or what's happening. The Girl takes care of him. I think they're going to see a man called Bernard Ketch. Do you know of him?"

"No."

"He owns KVS Shipping. They are associated with *Transporte Francaise*."

"Yes, the Sinakov Family business. Why is he going to Bernard Ketch?"

"I don't know. Does Rubicon mean anything to you?"

Harry heard his friend's sharp intake of breath, though the man had had no need to breathe for a couple of centuries. "*Mio Dio*, Rubicon." The name came out as a curse, with a sense of awe.

"You know of him."

"*Si…Si*. He is a vampire. Perhaps one thousand years old. No one knows. Very rich, billions I believe, very powerful. It is said he started as a fish merchant. And has always owned boats. Shipping is one of his major businesses. He lives on a grand yacht and cruises the world."

"Sinakov knows him?"

"Yes, they have done business for many years."

"Do you know where this Rubicon is now?"

"No. But it would seem that your man Ketch might know." The clink of glasses, boisterous greetings and shrill laughter came through the phone loud and clear—Happy Hour in full swing. Harry allowed the sounds to surround him, take him in. He should be there with Darwin and Bayley, sipping beer with nothing much on his mind but finding the latest kidnapper or killer on a nine to five schedule. Sinakov was vampire business, not his. At least not if you discounted the trail of dead mortals he and the Girl left behind.

Of course that was why he was sitting on a bench by a strange beach talking to a two hundred year old vampire two thousand miles away to ask for help tracking a partly insane vampire who was beheaded by his five month old vampire girlfriend. Dead mortals, whose cases he knew law enforcement had no chance to ever solve. So here he was, a modern day Van Helsing on the trail of a demented killer vampire and his faithful servant.

"I think so, too. But I don't know the area and frankly don't really know much about hunting vampires. Do you know anybody in the Miami/Fort Lauderdale area who can help me out? Someone I can trust. I'm not exactly at a hundred per cent at the moment, either."

"Give me your number. I will call you in return. And Harry, please, tell no one of this. There is a strong faction in the Sinakov family who are still loyal to him. If they find out he is alive, they will do anything to find him. Also the negotiations will devolve into chaos."

"Thanks. Let me speak with Bayley again."

Bayley said, "I don't suppose you're going to tell me what's going on now, are you?"

"Someday. I promise. Have you heard from Justine lately?"

"Yes I have."

"Christ, where is she?"

"You think I know? I'm just the secretary. She left you a number."

He wrote down the number. "Where is that area code from?"

"I don't *know*, Harry. You're the detective. Look, I gotta go. She did leave you a message besides call her. She said she loves you, too. Take care of yourself."

Harry stared out at the water. A cruise ship, lit up like a small city, vanished over the horizon. She loved him, still. He had begun to wonder. He punched in the numbers.

"Hello." Not Justine.

"I'm calling for Justine."

"Who is this?"

"Harry."

"Harry who?"

Keep calm. "Frazer. Detective Harry Frazer. Is Justine there?"

"Does she have anyone traveling with her?"

"Simone and Teresa. Who are you?"

"Harry, I'm sorry but Justine is not here. She left earlier than planned. I don't have a new number for her at this time. If you'll leave your number I will pass it on when I can."

"Is she all right? Where did she go?"

"You know, hon, it don't take a woman like Justine long to be all right no matter what happens. She's fine. And I can't tell you where she went. She'll have to tell you that herself."

"Do you know when you'll hear from her?"

"Tomorrow, maybe. Don't worry, hon. Those girls can take care of themselves. And she wants to talk with you as bad as you want to talk with her."

Harry let out a deep sigh. He wasn't going to get any more information out of this woman. All he could do was wait for Justine's call and move on with his own task. He gave the woman his new cell number, then asked, "Do they have a lead on Antonia?"

"They lookin', hon. They lookin'."

A few minutes later, Darwin called and gave him a name and number. He called the number, and made some arrangements. He winced as he stood up to walk carefully down Seaspray Street to Claire's grandparents' house. No, definitely not a hundred per cent.

Mover

Justine nudged Teresa awake as Lenny brought the big sedan to a stop. "You ladies must be special," he'd said as they climbed in. "You get the VIP car instead of the old van." Teresa had slept the few hour drive from Fort Myers to Fort Lauderdale, her head on Justine's lap.

She started awake. "Are we home yet, Papa?"

"With any luck we're on the homestretch," Justine said. "You ready for a boat ride?"

They stood on a rather bare dock by an empty lot on the southeast side of the Seventeenth Street drawbridge. Across the Intercoastal Waterway a huge cruise ship hogged the view. In front of them a narrow gangplank spanned the gap between concrete and teak decks. At a hundred and fifty feet the *Mover* was tiny compared to the cruise ship. There was a small swim platform off the aft end from which some steps rose to a small open deck. More steps rose to a covered deck. The yacht had been designed more for interior space than outdoor use.

A band of gray shading to blue filled the horizon as the three women looked over the *Mover*. Their attention was drawn to a man striding up the gangplank. About fifty, he wore tan pants and an untucked dark blue polo shirt on his athletic six foot two frame. As he passed under a docklight his *café au lait* skin shone. Square jawed, dark haired, and bright eyed, he was gorgeous. Flashing a genuine welcoming smile, he surveyed each woman in turn. Teresa drew the most interest.

"Oh, *hombre*," she whispered, suddenly wide awake.

Teresa stood between Justine and Simone. Grinning at their friend's quiet exclamation, they took a small step back and surreptitiously pushed her forward.

"I am Captain César Perez," the man announced in an accent that pleasantly mixed British English, French, and the Caribbean islands. "If I had known my passengers were three such beautiful women, I would have worn shoes."

Three sets of eyes followed his long legs to his wide, brown feet. Bare feet fit him perfectly.

"We are quite informal on *Mover*, so please call me César, and let me welcome you aboard. The sun, sadly, waits for no woman." To Lenny he said, "Thank you, Lenny, for delivering these lovely ladies, I trust they *are* ladies, to my humble vessel. Please tell Jasmine I will take good care of them."

Simone poked Teresa and whispered, "That means you, *chérie*."

Teresa slapped Simone's hand away while attempting to suppress a grin. She took César's arm and strolled down the gangplank.

Fort Lauderdale, FL

"That's it, over there." Claire pointed to the right as Harry drove slowly down a street close to the Intercoastal.

They were looking at a plain two-story building with one glass-fronted door by the left corner and one window next to it. From the street, KVS Shipping was barely visible on the door. A narrow parking lot held six cars. An automatic chain-link gate led to a truck yard in back.

"Not exactly looking for walk-in customers," Harry said.

"So what do we do now?"

"We drop you off at your friend's house."

"Harry, they almost killed me and my cousin, and you. I want to help."

"You saved my life and you got me here. You've helped plenty."

"But…"

"No. This is not TV. I'll drop you off and you don't tell anyone about all this and get on with your life. That's the best way to help."

Claire slumped in her seat, arms tight across her chest. "At the end of that street is where you're supposed to meet that guy."

"Thanks."

They remained silent for the ten minute drive to a flower surrounded house on a canal offshoot of the Intercoastal Waterway. Neither spoke for an uncomfortable minute.

"Okay, I'll go if you promise me two things," Claire said, looking out the window.

"Like what?"

"If you really do need some help you won't be afraid to call me. I've had experience patching people up."

"I can vouch for that. And?"

"You'll tell me what happened when it's all over. Oh, and I'd like to meet Justine."

"I can't promise you'll meet Justine, but if I can, I'll tell you the whole story. If, you don't do anything…not smart."

"Agreed." She got out of the car then looked in through the window. "Who decides what's not smart? Good luck, Harry."

Harry nodded and drove away.

❧ ❧

Harry parked his Mustang down the street from the Hilton just north of the bridge. He walked to where the street ended at the water, then strolled down the seawall past multi-million dollar yachts moored to the narrow dock.

At the end of the dock a black man around forty stood with hands in pockets, staring into the water. Wearing sneakers, dark pants and a thin windbreaker over a white buttoned shirt, he could be any anonymous businessman taking a break. The only feature about him that might give one pause was a thick, five inch scar front to rear on his shaved head.

As Harry came close the man glanced at him then returned his gaze to the water. "Fish, you'd think they had it made, just swimming around, living their lives, not a care in the world."

"Except something is always trying to eat them," Harry said.

"Same with…mortals."

"So I'm finding out."

They watched a small school of fish darting in random directions under the swim step of a fifty foot sportfisher.

"We spoke last night," Harry said.

"About?"

"Help finding a couple of vampires. I'm Harry."

"Blair. Let's walk."

They strolled together back the way Harry had come.

"I'd heard of your man Ketch, but didn't know much about him. He's a mortal, not a vamp, keeps under the radar. On the outside, he runs a legitimate shipping business and is an agent for *Transporte Francaise*. Inside, not so much. People mostly, I hear. A nasty business, immigrants and bad guys in, girls and bad guys out. Well protected. I hope you have a good reason for going after him."

They stopped in the shadow of the bridge. It was four in the afternoon. The sun was behind them and the breeze was losing some of its heat. A cruise ship let go a long blast of its horn.

"Have you heard of the Sinakov Vampire family?"

"Sure. Wasn't their master killed a while ago. A big deal goin' on out in California."

"It'll be a bigger deal if they find out Stephan Sinakov is alive."

"I imagine that will complicate things. What's that have to do with Ketch?"

"I believe that through Ketch, Sinakov and his servant, a vamp girl, are trying to connect with Rubicon."

"Rubicon? Damn, man. You playin' with the big boys. What's all this to you?"

Harry gazed across the water to a large yacht leaving the dock and heading south toward the jetty leading out to the ocean.

"Want to see my scars?"

Harry continued to stare at the departing yacht. Beautiful women on fancy yachts was an everyday occurrence in Southern Florida. He wondered how normal it was to have three, one with raven hair, one brunette, and one blonde.

"Why don't you buy me an early dinner and tell me all about it," Blair said.

"Right. Okay."

Blair stuck his hands in his jacket pockets and walked away.

Harry looked after the yacht then followed. Probably a requirement on large yachts to have three women aboard—raven, brunette, blonde. And what kind of name for a boat was *Mover?"*

KV's Office

Around eight o'clock, Harry parked his Mustang facing toward the main street. He got out, looked around, stuffed a 9mm in his waistband, slid a couple sharpened wood dowels into his front pocket, and held a sharp machete against his arm. He checked for nonexistent traffic and crossed the street to a five year old Toyota Corolla last washed the day it drove off the lot. He opened the rear door and slipped in the back seat.

"He still in there?" he asked.

"Yes, sir," Blair said, his eyes on a laptop screen showing the rear of the building. He cocked his head to the woman in the driver's seat. "This is Paula, my assistant."

"Partner," Paula said. Her pudgy fingers worked a smart phone jumping from security camera to security camera. "Don't see any vamps of your description anyplace around here now, or since sunset. You sure he hasn't already been and gone?"

"No."

Paula looked over her shoulder at him. "Oh, that's a big help."

He felt her unflinching stare bore into him. His head felt like a fiery pinball had been let loose inside. She was a vampire!

"Yes, I'm a vamp. Not all of us can be tall, thin and beautiful." She turned back to her phone.

I guess not, Harry thought. Paula was maybe five feet tall and could only charitably be called plump. A bowl of blonde hair, button nose, thin lips and pale eyes surrounded by dark makeup all added up to, at best, Goth plain.

"But none of them is smarter than you, babe," Blair said, slapping closed the laptop.

"*Si vrai, si e vero, so wahr, tan cierto.* Are we ready?" She tapped her cell a couple times, turned it off, stuffed it in a pocket of her Capri pants, and opened the door. "Local surveillance is offline. Who knows, maybe he'll talk and we'll be in and out in two minutes. Easy peasy."

Harry and Blair moved together toward the front door while Paula, in an eye blink, appeared at the automatic gate. Not hindered in the least by heavy boots, she jumped the six foot fence.

"That's some partner you have," Harry observed.

"Yeah, she's got an attitude, but you would, too, if you had to live your immortal life on the fluffy side. On the other hand, she has five bachelor degrees, two masters, and is writing a doctoral thesis on *The Electrical, Magnetic, and Spectrographic Aspects of the Paranormality of Modern Supernatural Occurrences and Myths.* She'll kill it."

Blair tested the door with a gloved hand. Locked. "You're not wearing your badge, are you?"

While Blair picked the lock, Harry nervously loosened the short machete strapped to his left arm and covered by a thin jacket.

Done with the locks, Blair gripped the door handle, holding his own machete against his leg. "She also writes a comic book which she thinks I don't know about. It's called *Fluffy's Adventures.* Guess who the heroine looks like."

One small light illuminated the office which was obviously not meant to impress rich clients. Five worn desks covered with in and out trays, papers and computers seemed to be randomly placed behind a high counter.

Harry had had ambitions to be a master thief, back in the day—a dream cut short when a friend was killed in prison. This could have been his life, sneaking into dark places. He got the same adrenaline rush as a cop, to start with. Until he became involved with Justine that rush had became more of a plod.

That familiar rush returned as he moved past the gate toward a door in the back with light showing underneath. He and Blair nodded at each other and Harry opened the door, ready for anything, or nothing.

Spacious and plain, the cheap wood paneled walls were covered with several large scheduling calendars and other papers. A door with a window in it led to the warehouse. An open door showed a small storage closet.

Ketch bent over an old wood desk, sleeves rolled up, tie loosened, pen in hand. He looked up and started slightly when he saw Blair's machete and Harry's gun. He had a narrow, angular face with a blade of a nose and close-set eyes. Wary, he said, "Is no money here. You make a mistake." He had some sort of Eastern European accent.

Blair stepped aside and nodded to Harry. It was his show.

"Do you know Stephan Sinakov?"

"No."

"Master of the Sinakov Vampire Family. *Transporte Francaise.* You do business with them."

Ketch slumped back in his plush desk chair. He pushed out his thin lips while he studied his two visitors.

Blair casually moved around behind him and tapped the chair with his big blade.

Ketch shrugged. "I hear rumor he is dead."

"When was the last time you heard from him?"

Another shrug. "Six, seven, maybe eight months ago."

"You sure?"

Blair pressed the flat of his blade against his arm.

"Yes. Sure. Why do you want know?" Ketch didn't like the blade touching him, though he didn't seem intimidated at all. The guy was mortal with no help in sight. Why wasn't he at least a little bit nervous?

"You know Rubicon, yes?" Harry asked.

Ketch tensed at the name. "No. I do not know this Rubicon. Who are you? What do you want?"

"Where is he?"

Blair grabbed Ketch's sharp chin from behind and pressed the blade to his stretched tight neck. "You're no use to us if you don't answer."

Now he was nervous. "I do not know. But if I do, I will not tell you. So shoot me. I do not care."

Shit. Harry thought he understood. "No, Bernard, I won't shoot you. I'll have him cut off your head and dump it in the water." To Blair he said, "Go ahead, take it off. He knows nothing."

Blair shot him a quizzical look, his thoughts churning, searching for the angle. Harry backed up against a wall, his eyes twitching, searching, expecting.

"Sorry friend." Blair raised the machete to strike.

"Wait! I tell you. He is…"

The rear door banged open as Sinakov's Girl rushed Blair at vampire speed. She grabbed for his machete.

Blair had spotted Harry fix his attention on the door to the warehouse, and seen his eyes go wide.

The Girl had to jump up to reach the weapon, but Blair had already tossed it to his other hand. She grabbed his arm and yanked it to pull him down to her level. He was already swinging the blade at her neck. Smaller than he'd figured, she easily ducked under. He jerked his arm loose and kept spinning with the momentum of the machete. She punched his body a glancing blow as he spun.

Blair dropped lower as he spun full circle for another try at her neck. She was ready, grabbing his wrist with both hands. Despite her vampire strength, she didn't have the size to stop his mass. She fell back on her ass.

Seeing his opportunity, Blair spun the blade up and sliced down. But in the blink of an eye the Girl wrapped her thin arms around his ankles and yanked his feet out from under. He went down hard on his face, the machete taking a slice out of the thin carpet. She jumped on his back, took hold of his head and slammed it on the floor.

As she raised it for another blow a cry came from the warehouse and a black and white streak came through the door and crashed into the Girl, sending her and Paula tumbling against a wall, shattering the panels.

Harry tried to follow the action, hoping for a clear shot. Movement in the corner of his eye drew his attention.

Sinakov stood an arm's length away.

"Bon soir, Detective Harry. I thought you were dead."

Harry stepped back and swung his gun to aim at Sinakov's head. "And I thought you were dead."

"Apparently, we are both wrong. Why are you looking for my friend Rubicon?"

"I'm not, now." Jesus, shoot him, don't talk. That's why you're here. But somehow the gaunt vampire held his gaze. Somehow the will to pull the trigger faded. The rictus of Sinakov's grin struck a nerve. Harry forced his eyes to break their connection and get his will back.

With Harry having to take a few seconds to clear his thinking, Sinakov snatched his gun. He raked the muzzle across Harry's face and pressed it against his forehead.

"Where is Justine Kroft? Where is…my…?" Sinakov's eyes lost focus and his head cocked a little as he tried to find the thread of a lost thought.

On the other side of the office Paula and the Girl fought, Paula's strength and bulk against the Girl's speed. Paula finally managed a side kick to the Girl's chest that smashed her against a row of file cabinets. She dropped to the floor and lay still.

The noise woke up Sinakov. His eyes bulged and the hand on the gun trembled. "…where is Simone Gireaux?"

"I don't know." But he did know. He hadn't really thought the women on that yacht were Justine, Simone and Teresa. It was them, though, he was sure of it. The yacht in the middle of the Atlantic, Rubicon, Ketch, Sinakov, all here. They must be sure Antonia was on that big boat and were going after it.

"Tell me or die. I will find them whatever you say."

"I can't—"

A thick phone book flew between them, knocking the gun away from his head. Bam! A bullet nicked Harry's ear. The pressure and noise of the discharge hurt more than the tiny wound.

Pretty sure he was about to die, Harry's thoughts ran lean and fast, focused on his options: Tell what he thought he knew and probably die. Don't tell and die. Jam one of the wooden stakes in Sinakov's heart and maybe live.

Harry took advantage of his one second opportunity, drew out a stake and plunged it with all his adrenaline fueled human strength into Sinakov's chest.

The gun fired next to his ear again.

Sinakov froze, mouth an O of disbelief.

Ketch had been crouching by his desk. Seeing Sinakov staked, he ran around his desk and into the main office.

Blair yelled from the floor, "Paula, get him."

Paula left a blur of color behind.

Harry grabbed the gun as Sinakov staggered back and slowly slid down the wall. He stuffed the weapon butt end first into his pocket and grabbed the handle of his machete. This time he'd make sure the head couldn't be reattached.

"Master!"

Shit! The Girl was on her feet, eyes wide with horror at the sight of her master on his knees. Harry fumbled for the gun. If he could get in a headshot and slow her down he had one more stake in his pocket.

Even at his best, Harry was too slow. Her little hands slammed against his chest and he flew through the air to land in a painful tangle inside the storage closet. Blair got off one shot that left a long crease high on her back before she scooped up Sinakov and vanished into the warehouse.

"I'll get 'em," Paula said a few seconds later, dumping a semi-conscious Ketch in a corner and racing after the two vampires.

Five minutes later Paula returned at mortal speed. "Lost them in the tank fields. Got to give it up to that little runt of the litter bitch. She's got some moxie."

Blair sat in a straight back chair holding a wad of bloody paper towels to his head. Harry leaned on the desk beside Ketch who slumped in his own chair. He held his left arm gently against his body. Something was broken. It hurt like hell now the excitement was over. The back of his hand seeped blood. Half of Blair's head glistened with it. Even Harry could smell it.

Paula could too. Harry knew that intense look, the flaring nostrils, the twitching lips.

"Can you make it stop hurting?" Harry asked Paula, offering up his arm.

"You really okay with it?"

"I know how cranky you guys can get when you're hungry."

"This isn't *True Blood,* you know. I can't heal it."

Harry had to shut his eyes and force himself to breathe as the pain ramped up another notch. "I know."

Their eyes connected. "Don't worry, I won't change you. I'm too young for progeny. Though having someone call me Master for real sounds sort of cool."

The pain just sort of floated away as he gazed into the strangely enticing dark swirl of her eyes. He felt her lips on the back of his hand like a kiss, then two sharp pricks on his wrist. He knew what was happening, but didn't care.

"Paula! Enough," Blair said, bringing Harry out of his blissful daze. "Let's get this over with. All we need is Rubicon's location. Right, Mister new blood vamp hunter?"

"Right." Harry nudged Ketch with his foot. "Where's Rubicon?"

"I do not know. Go ahead and shoot me."

"You'd like that wouldn't you? Got your insurance paid up, don't you?"

"Can we just do this the less messy way?" Paula strode over to Ketch, lifted him by the head and sat him up straight.

He struggled, but had no chance when Blair took hold of his arms from behind and held him immobile.

Paula put thumbs over his eyes and forced them open. She stared hard into his head. In a few seconds he ceased struggling.

"Yeah, he's been bit, all right. Just waitin' to die and become an automatic vamp. Too chicken shit to do it himself. Ketch, where is Rubicon?"

Harry could feel the overflow of her glamour. Christ, he'd tell her if he knew.

Ketch tensed, fighting it, but really had no choice but to answer. "Freeport," he said in a gush.

"Freeport in the Bahamas?"

"Yes," through clenched teeth.

"What boat?"

"Ahh. *Night Watch*."

"Anything else you want to know?" she asked Harry.

"Is Sinakov going there, and how."

"Answer the man, Bernie, and this will all be over. We can go drink some Black Dahlias and party."

Fight gone out of him, Ketch said, "Yes. Helicopter."

❧　❧

Outside they stood in a loose group beside Paula's Toyota. She had put a hard glamour on Ketch and left him unconscious. When he woke he wouldn't remember a thing.

"So how far is Freeport?" Harry asked.

"'Bout fifty miles across the Gulf Stream."

"What's the best way to get there?"

"Helicopter," Paula offered with a smirk. "You probably missed it."

"Won't be any regular flights till tomorrow." Blair said. "I know you're a tough guy California cop, but you need to have that arm looked at. Glamour doesn't last forever."

Thinking hard, wanting to be on the way, now, Harry looked in an Easterly direction, toward the Bahamas. Blair was right, he knew that. But Justine was so close, and she needed to know about Sinakov. He found himself breathing hard, his vision a blur as things began to spin around him.

He woke, laying on the backseat of the Toyota, feet against the door, legs bent to fit. He groaned, feeling wetness around his gunshot wound.

Blair noticed Harry was stirring. "You forgot to tell me you got shot, there, Detective. You are either the hard-boiled detective of legend, or a fool on a mission."

"Both?"

"Huh. I doubt that."

"Where are we going?"

"To see an angel of mercy. I know it might slow you down for five minutes, but you need some fixin'. Me too. Don't worry, the San Diego County Sheriff's Department doesn't need to know their pride and joy got shot and beat up by a girl."

Christ, the Department didn't even need to know he was out of state, let alone what happened during the last week. "Do you know a big power boat called *Mover*?"

"Damn, man. How'd you know about that? It's a transport vessel, specializing in vampires. Lightproof staterooms, blood warmers, the whole bit."

"And don't make any snide comments about sunny tropical paradises and vampires. Tropical nights are the sexy part."

Justine was on that boat. So close. He felt his chest close in on itself. He missed her, and feared for her.

"Guess I missed that boat, too."

Mover

"I have big engines in her and enough fuel for a cruising range of fifteen hundred miles at a steady eighteen knots. Top speed of about twenty-five knots. I have all the electronic, entertainment and safety gadgets known to man or vampire. All the life rafts have full canopies. Besides me, there's four crew, two mortals, two vamps. Six passenger staterooms, three small and one large lightproof, and one small and one large with portlights and deck hatches. Any questions?" César asked Teresa, though Justine and Simone were listening, too.

"A hundred," she said. "Later."

"Of course." He nodded to a well built black man and a handsome Asian woman, both in their forties. "Lucian and Luney will show you to your quarters." They bowed slightly to their new guests. "Her parents thought she would be a werewolf so they named her Lunetta after some Roman goddess of the moon. They were so disappointed when she took another road."

Luney shook her head with an exasperated roll of brown eyes. "César, don't you think that lame joke has worn itself out?"

"No," he said with a mischievous rise of his eyebrows and a grin. "Marshall and Harriet, our day-time crew, aren't up yet. We'll leave about four this afternoon. That should get us to Freeport about sunset."

Lucian and Luney showed Simone and Justine to their lightproof stateroom.

Justine inspected the door and the locks. "Don't you dare lock this door, or we'll be leaving a trail of splinters."

Lucian started to protest. Observing the don't-fuck-with-us stares from his new guests, he thought better of it.

César had personally shown Teresa to the large mortal friendly stateroom. Teresa was well aware of the flirtatious and handsome captain. She was attracted, no doubt. Also she was caught between her excitement of finally being close to Antonia and a deep fatigue. In limbo, she'd never really slept. She'd laid down and closed her eyes, but never felt like she had truly fallen asleep. Sometimes she felt that she would never get over being tired. Doing those escape spells had exhausted her like Grace had said it would.

It must have been the water and the barely detectable motion of the boat, because she slept solidly until woken by the rumble of the twin diesel engines.

∂⊱　⊰∂

They were all in the main bridge of the yacht, a smart wood paneled and trimmed space high on the forward end of the superstructure. A state-of-the-art dashboard filled with dials, gauges, electronic displays, buttons, switches and levers stretched the full ten foot width of the bridge. Justine lounged and Simone sat cross-legged on a plush bench seat inset in the rear bulkhead. Teresa sat beside César on a matching captain's chair.

They had just cast off from the dock and entered the main channel. César said, "You had questions?"

"Wine?" Simone said immediately.

"Cerveza?"

"Wine, too."

Lucian, who'd been on the starboard bridge wing assisting with their departure, said, "On their way, ladies," and silently descended the stairway. César turned *Mover* to port and headed straight out the entrance to Port Everglades as Lucian returned with two beers and two glasses of wine and left the bridge. César asked Teresa, "Did Lucian give you his seasickness cure?"

"You mean did he somehow convince me to let him look into my eyes and do something inside my head?"

"That's what I mean. Unless you've spent a lot of time on the water and have your sea-legs, you'll thank him. Crossing the stream can be rough."

"Simone offered to do the same thing, but Lucian said he had the touch."

"Lucian has been on the water his whole life. Nobody he's treated has ever puked because of seasickness. Overindulgence, yeah man, but not the smooth motion of my boat."

Teresa thought about Simone and how she became an accidental vampire, and Justine who begged to be changed. She knew at some point it was an option for her, that her two friends would stay the same as she aged and died. The thought of it saddened her, and scared her. She took little solace in knowing Harry faced the same decision. That there were so many vampires was an incredible idea. How many of them wanted to be what they became?

"How did he become...what he is?"

"He was a fisherman down in the islands. He'd had a good catch, made some money and wanted to spend it on his girlfriend. There is nothing better to spend money on than a woman, is that not so?"

Teresa humphed. "No comment."

"He planned on asking her to marry him. Not the best way to spend your money."

She shot him a raised-eyebrow look and watched the port entrance pass astern.

"He asked, she broke his heart. So he did what any broken-hearted man would do, got drunk, money well spent, and got into a fight with three men who didn't know when to stop. Luney saved his ass, they fell in love, got married. On their wedding night, she gave him immortality. Twenty-fifth anniversary next month."

"What about you?" Teresa asked, gazing straight ahead at the open ocean. "Die and live forever, or just die?"

His amusement vanished and he, too, stared ahead, trying to see farther than the horizon. He hunched his shoulders, let them fall, shook his head.

Once they got their wine, Simone and Justine quietly left the bridge for the main salon. A generous open area, the main salon contained four distinct spaces: A ten foot bar along the starboard side; a more formal area with luxurious upholstered couches and armchairs all set around a 72 inch flat screen, and a cabinet full of electronic entertainment which took up the forward three quarters of the space; a dining area equipped to seat ten on the aft starboard side; and an intimate conversation area in the aft portside corner with a loveseat and matching armchair.

Simone curled up in the armchair while Justine reclined on the loveseat. Suitably dark curtains had been drawn over the aft window to keep out the setting sun.

Justine said, "Do you think Antonia is on this Rubicon's boat?"

"We know she was. We have to believe she still is."

"But what will she be when we find her? Not a virgin, I expect."

"Will Teresa care?"

"She'll be happy just to find her alive."

"Which brings the problem of how we get onboard to find her."

"I don't suppose we can just sneak aboard and poke around?"

Simone patted Justine's leg. "Are you drunk already, *cher*? This guy has Oracles and sorcerers and vampires like Tito working for him. We are not ghosts, they will know when we are close."

"Shit. I forgot the damned Oracles. Do you think Tee is still shielding us?"

"*Maintenant*, I think she must shield herself from César's hands."

"I'm not sure she wants to."

"No, I think not. For me, she deserves to take her pleasure when she finds it."

"You have become friends," Justine said with a fond smile.

"*Oui, oui*." Simone gazed forward where occasional laughter floated down from the bridge. "She has proved to be a good partner...and friend."

"Yes she has." Justine finished her wine and swung her feet to the thick carpet. "However, I think we need to check on the shield spell. If they know we're coming, we'll never get aboard."

She pulled back a dark curtain and peeked through a side window. *Mover* was doing about twenty knots through a choppy sea. Thousands of small breaking waves gleamed in the late afternoon sun. Ahead was a distinct line where the lighter blue/green water changed to the deep blue of the Gulf Stream.

Justine mentally sighed. She wanted to be out in the wind and weather, watching the water and clouds and birds without any barrier between her and nature. Surely a hat and jacket would protect her for ten minutes.

"I'll go check on Tee," she said.

"Justine."

Justine turned back to Simone.

"What will she do if we find Antonia alive and well?"

Justine's lips pressed tight in a crooked line. "She'll go home." More sadness than joy tinged her words.

Teresa assured her that she still maintained the shield. "But in the last few days, I've been so tired and when we jumped from the car to Jasmine's I don't know what happened."

Justine assured her that all was well, then donned a hat and jacket and stood in the bow holding her face to the wind. Five minutes later Teresa joined her. They linked arms and didn't speak. A few minutes later, Simone joined them as well. Arm in arm they stood together, facing the darkening horizon.

∾ ∾

"Anything?" Simone asked.

"Just normal, mortal vampire luxury super yacht activities," Justine said. "Looks like they're taking on supplies."

Simone rested a hand on Teresa's shoulder, feeling the tension consuming her. "I feel your Antonia is there. But they would not want to expose her."

"How will we get onboard to find out?"

The two vampires traded looks.

"Tee, we were thinking just the two of us would go onboard. There are quite a few vamps and we could blend in better than a mortal, and have a better chance to get out." Justine winced as she spoke because she wasn't at all sure any of what she said was true.

Teresa put down her binoculars and glared at them. "Do you really think I can't handle myself? Onboard, I can find her, and get her away. You know that."

Justine sighed. "We do know that. But, we're dealing with much more powerful..." she threw up her hands, "...beings on that boat. Probably some super Oracle, and super sorcerer, and that thousand year-old vampire, Rubicon. If being that old doesn't make him stronger it surely makes him smarter and more experienced. And maybe that bastard, Tito, too."

"Do you think you two are better to go against them than me?"

Justine and Simone locked eyes for a second.

Simone said, "Yes, we do. We are better able to keep our emotions out of it. We are better able to fight if necessary." Teresa, not liking what she was hearing, opened her mouth to speak. Simone held up a hand for silence. "We know you are *una bruja muy fuerte*. But you are new, with maybe two weeks of experience, going against decades, maybe centuries of experience. As you say in America, 'Do not get cocky.' "

Teresa sat still, the rigidity of her body and face reflecting her turmoil, knowing Simone was right and desperately wanting her to be wrong.

A cell phone's trill broke the uneasy silence. Justine looked around for the source.

"That's you." Simone said.

Justine patted her pockets to find it, then stared at the screen. It was an inexpensive prepaid phone with no bells and whistles. She stared at an unfamiliar number, then answered. Listening intently, her eyes and smile grew wide.

"Harry? Oh my God. Where the hell are you? Where the hell have you been? I've tried to call you."

"I know. I've tried to call you, too. But that's not important right now. What is important is that Stephan Sinakov is alive."

Justine's head jerked back as if she'd been punched.

"Harry, this is no time for—"

"Yes it is time," Harry interrupted in a rush. "Him and that girl of his, the one Simone called a ghost. Somehow she rescued him and reattached his Goddamned head. They left a trail of bodies across the country. I've been tracking them. They've tried to kill me twice. He's on his way to meet with a vampire called Rubicon in Freeport. Which I'm pretty sure is where *Mover*, the yacht you're on, is headed."

Justine dropped onto a seat, mouth open, but not a word to say.

Simone stared at the phone. With her enhanced hearing she'd heard every word. "That cannot be."

Justine twitched. Her thoughts were racing. She put the cell phone on speaker. "Harry, Simone and Teresa are with me, you're on speaker. How do you know where we are? Where *are* you? Are you close?" The last question sounded desperate. She didn't care. Knowing he had to be close let loose the yearning for him she'd been suppressing.

"I'm in Delray Beach, up the coast from Ft. Lauderdale. Myself and two others had a run in with Sinakov and his girl a few hours ago. We think they're taking a helicopter to Rubicon's boat. Can you see it?"

"Yes. It has a landing pad, but no helicopter. I killed him, Harry. I don't understand how he can be here."

"He's not *all* there. Sometimes he seems to check out, doesn't know where or who he is. Lucky for me. The Girl seems to be the brains now. Be very careful if you run into her."

César walked through the main salon. It was obvious on the stunned faces peering at him that something had happened. He disliked bringing more bad news. "*Night Watch* has started her main engines. I think they are preparing to sail."

"No. They cannot." Teresa pressed her face against the window. In the glare of the dock lights exhaust smoke could be seen emitting from the smokestack. "My Antonia is aboard. We can't let them leave."

"We can't stop them," Justine said.

On deck outside, Simone scanned the night sky. "Helicopter coming."

"If that's Sinakov, they will probably leave as soon as it lands."

"But Antonia is onboard."

"I know, Tee. But there's nothing we can do right now. We'll have to follow them."

"Can we call the police? Can we hit them with this boat to make them stop?"

"No, Teresa, we cannot ram them," César said reasonably. "Like Justine said, we can follow them until a better opportunity comes."

Across the port channel a helicopter landed on the pad extending aft from the smokestack. As soon as it landed figures swarmed around it. Through the binoculars Simone watched two people escorted across the pad to vanish through sliding glass doors. Even as the aircraft was secured, the dock lines were let go and the *Night Watch* separated from the quay and headed for open water.

Simone said, "Two were taken into the boat. I could not see their faces, but I am sure it was Henri...Sinakov and his Girl."

Justine squeezed Simone's arm in understanding. His birth name was Henri Gireaux, Simone's son who she thought dead three and a half centuries ago.

"They can't leave. Antonia!" Teresa cried. "Antonia!" She tried to gain the deck. "Antonia, I am here."

As gently as they could Justine and Simone held her back.

"Quiet, Tee." Simone insisted. "They will hear you. If they know you are close it will not go well for her."

Teresa ceased struggling and forced her mouth closed. "Okay. Okay." She shrugged off their hands.

"Justine! What's happening there?"

"A helicopter just landed on the boat. They're heading out to sea."

"Are you going to follow them?"

"Yes. But we don't know where they're headed. Can you get to me. Meet the boat somewhere, soon. I miss you."

"I miss you, too. To tell the truth, I'm not really in any shape to travel at the moment. My meetings with Sinakov have been a bit rough."

"Christ, Harry, I should have been with you. You should have called me."

"I wasn't sure it was him at first. When I was sure...well, it was a little late. And you didn't answer."

"I guess we've had a few rough spots, too. Been out of touch. Thank goodness for Bayley. Please tell me what you've been through. It's so good to hear your voice."

Justine turned off the speaker and for a couple minutes they were aware only of each other.

"*Merde*! Teresa, *qu'est ca tout fait*. What are you doing?"

Simone's outburst caught Justine's attention. She ran out to the side deck. Looking forward she spied Teresa where she had an unobstructed view of *Night Watch* clearing the harbor entrance. She had a machete strapped to her leg and a long knife on her belt. Her free hands were making familiar movements.

"Tee, don't!" Justine shouted. Too late.

Teresa vanished.

"*Merde.*"

"Yeah, shit for sure."

Simone scanned the departing yacht with the binoculars. "I think she appeared on the pad. I don't see her now."

"Well…fuck," was all Justine could think to say. That was a stupid thing for Teresa to do, yet Justine understood. If that was Brittany on that boat, she would have done the same. Being so close, then having to watch your daughter sail away like that, not knowing where they were taking her or what they were doing to her, was not something a mother could let go. Justine would have done the same.

"Justine. Justine." Harry's insistent voice from the cell phone still gripped in her hand broke into her mixed thoughts about what Teresa did.

"Yes, I'm here."

"What the hell happened?"

"I need a drink. Then I'll tell you everything. You think me becoming a vampire was bizarre?"

CHAPTER ELEVEN

Night Watch

Night Watch's landing pad lurched just as Teresa appeared on the aft end. Her feet shifted six inches. She stumbled and sprawled face down on the pad, an arm and a leg hanging over a twenty foot drop to the next deck.

Still dizzy, she slowly drew in her overhanging limbs. She scanned the pad. The chopper had been secured and the crew dispersed, landing lights turned off. Carefully she looked back. She could barely pick out *Mover* among the harbor lights.

What have I done? quickly became *What do I do now?* Her body made sure she knew how much making that emergency only jump had taken. A lethargy spread through her. It took great effort just to keep her eyes open.

Voices from below spurred her into a crouching run across the pad. She ducked through the unlocked—*gracias Dios*—sliding doors into a gallery. On the right she saw a small glass enclosed conference room with a long wood and glass table and chairs. Straight forward at the end of a long passage she caught a glimpse of the bridge. Low business-like voices drifted back to her.

On each side, just forward of doors opening to an outside deck, stairways led down and up. She trudged up to a U-shaped observation area, surrounded by windows. Leather seats followed the curve of the forward windows. Teresa found a private space to hide behind a wide support at one end of the seats where she drew up her legs and rested, head on knees.

Alone. All her life it seemed that someone had been around her: family, school, nursing school, a busy ER, Miguel, her kids, Justine when Antonia went missing, Justine when her Brittany died, then Simone. Always someone needing help or to help her or to talk to. Now, she was alone. Nobody to help or lean on, except herself.

Antonia was close, she felt it. Not as a *bruja*, as a mother. Then she felt something else—or didn't feel it. Her magic. Ever since she discovered her power and Grace helped bring it out there'd been that slight tingle along her spine, a reserve available to be called upon. She tried a few simple practice spells Grace had taught her. Nothing.

She hadn't really thought about how they'd get off the boat when she found Antonia. Somewhere in the back of her mind was the idea of using the emergency exit spell. Simone was right. Her magic wouldn't work here. She tried her cell. No service. Just as well. She didn't really want to hear Justine tell her what a dumb move this had been. Another thought struck her. If her magic didn't work, then her Oracle shielding spell for Justine and Simone didn't work, either. Shit.

Teresa spent a few minutes feeling sorry for herself, then she had an idea.

"Fuck it." Standing, she took some deep breaths, then twisted and stretched to loosen up. The machete came off her belt and disappeared up the left hand sleeve of her jacket. Unconsciously she'd dressed similar to the ship's uniform, tan pants or shorts, black—what else?—T-shirt. Maybe she could pass.

Teresa crept down the steps and slipped out the port side door. Down a tight spiral staircase she came to what she assumed was the main deck. Going by the layout of *Mover*, she also assumed the crew quarters would be forward. That's where Antonia would be.

She had always assumed Antonia would be held in a cell like a prisoner. That was a fantasy. After almost a year, why would they? She didn't even want to consider what might have been done to her.

The yacht was quiet after the departure. Besides the occasional slap of a wave against the hull, the steady faint rumble of the engine only seemed to enhance the silence.

She moved forward.

Through a partially covered window she gazed at a huge main salon, with a small stage and dance floor forward, two bars, and several seating configurations. Stark, modern, clean, lush.

Moving forward, straining to hear any approaching voices, Teresa peeked through a narrow gap in dark curtains into a small room the exact opposite of the modern main salon. This was an old-world drawing room, which was modern two centuries ago. It was dim with dark stained solid wood paneling and furniture, hand carved trim surrounding bookcases filled with old books.

"Oh." She gasped and ducked back, holding her breath, but could not look away. She had to press hands against her chest to hold in her racing heart.

It was true. Sinakov had been resurrected. There he was sitting in one of four brocade covered wingback chairs next to his Girl. Next to him sat Rubicon.

She knew it was him. Even through her narrow viewpoint and the thick glass she could feel his…age. She'd thought a thousand year old vampire would somehow *look* like a thousand year old vampire—not like a stoutly-built forty year-old real estate salesman who'd made good. Maybe six feet tall, he had a round head covered with fashionably long, dirty-blond hair, a round nose, and thin lips that naturally settled into a frown when listening. He was good-looking, but no model for a supernatural romance novel cover. A man you wouldn't look at twice on the street.

A fourth man came into view. He filled Rubicon's glass from an open wine bottle, then sat in the fourth chair. No less than six feet tall with reddish brown skin like a polished piece of mahogany, and a shaved head, he sat easily in the chair, crossing his bare legs. He wore white shorts and a black and gold shirt. Speaking with Sinakov, he showed an expansive smile that didn't reach his flat, deep set eyes. He wore a heavy cord around his thick neck, but she could not see what it held.

Footsteps came from the aft staircase. Totally exposed, Teresa ran forward. At a slight indentation in the cabin side she found a door with a glass window. A quick glance revealed a wide corridor that spanned the width of the boat. With no other choice, she slipped inside.

Paneled with lightly stained wood, two narrower passages ran forward from the cross corridor. A short one with doors on each side led aft to the main salon. One of the doors would open into the study where Sinakov relaxed, not a care in the world. Teresa wanted to burst into the room and take all their heads off and toss them into the ocean. She had herself together enough to know she'd probably die herself before she collected any heads. But it was tempting.

The latch on the outside door clicked. Teresa dashed into the far narrow passage leading forward, found the first door unlocked and slipped in. She eased the deadbolt lock closed and held her breath. Two men, speaking what sounded like Russian, walked past.

She surveyed the room. An office, with file cabinets, a built in desk, computers and on the wall, photographs, plans and cross sections of the yacht. Teresa found a sweater draped over a desk chair and used it to cover the gap between door and floor. She switched on a light and studied the plans.

The labels and notations were in French. She stifled a pang as she wished Simone was with her to translate and lean on. After ten minutes she determined that the crew quarters were forward, one deck down. A deck below that, next to the massive engine room, were more cabins, but they were probably for the engineers.

Teresa stood still for five minutes, listening, gathering herself. But for the faint thrum of the engines, all was quiet. She took a deep breath. She replaced the sweater, listened again and eased open the door.

Three doors down the narrow passage, a central set of steps led down to the next deck. Now what? Forward, another corridor, five doors a side, numbers, but no names. Aft, six more doors.

She moved aft. Should she knock on doors? Call out? A young woman, mortal, if the light in her eyes meant anything, came down the forward corridor. Heart pounding, Teresa squared her shoulders as she used to do when facing a recalcitrant patient.

"Where is the girl, Antonia?"

The woman gave Teresa a quick up and down assessment. She tried to stare Teresa down, and failed.

"The girl, Antonia? Where is she kept?"

"Why do you want her?"

"I don't. He does." Teresa waved a casual hand indicating the upper deck.

The woman seemed to shrink a bit, shaking her head. "Again?" The sympathy in her voice seemed genuine. She pointed aft. "Number four." She quickly ascended the steps.

Teresa huffed a few times. Almost there. In front of number four, in the middle, she listened intently. No sound from inside. Light under the door, though.

Suddenly she was terrified of what she would find inside. She wanted her daughter to be exactly the same as the day she was taken, but knew she wouldn't, couldn't, be. Teresa brushed aside the beginning of a notion that this quest for Antonia would not be worth the lives lost on the way.

She tapped lightly on the door of number four. "Antonia?"

A hand grabbed her neck and slammed her back against the bulkhead. Over Tito's shoulder the door opened an inch. One wide eye peered out. Then he reached behind him and yanked the door closed.

"Teresa, how very good of you to come to me. Where is your new, and I must admit, strong, *bruja* power now? How does it feel to be only a mortal?" He let off the pressure on her neck.

"All I want is Antonia. Let me take her and you'll never see me again."

Tito chuckled. "But I have already taken her, several times. So I do not think she wants to go with her mama."

"She did not want to visit her grandmother in Mexico, either. But she went."

Tito didn't notice her reaching for the knife on her belt until she jammed it to the hilt in his belly. The third time she stuck him he let go and staggered back, more from surprise than because of the brief intense pain.

"*Cabrón.*" Teresa shoved him against the bulkhead, and kneed him in the crotch. She stepped back, drew the machete from her sleeve, and raised up the blade to take his head off. Before she could strike, a blur of motion slammed into her, sending her rolling down the passage toward the stairway.

Somehow she kept hold of her weapons. Without the surprise element, she didn't have a chance. But her daughter was there. "Antonia, *yo estoy aqui!*" She ran up the steps. At the top of the steps she made a wrong turn and burst into the galley.

Three crew members froze as Teresa scanned the gleaming, stainless steel space. Spying another door, she raced through it into a short, narrow passage with several locked doors. At the end was a small, formal dining room. Through that she came to the main cross corridor. Two men came through the door at the other end. Another blocked the passage from the main salon. No other choice. She slammed out the door to the deck, and ran into a very large vampire, like hitting a brick wall.

She attempted to duck under his arms. But he was in full vampire speed mode. He grabbed her under her arms with massive hands and lifted her two feet off the deck. She fought, twisting and kicking, while cussing at him in Spanish, English, and few words she'd picked up from Simone.

He smiled, then pulled her close and head butted her.

She vaguely felt herself falling to the deck. There was motion and voices and pain then someone looked hard in her eye and things became fuzzy and blurry and floaty. She floated here and there, down and through until she landed on a hard metal floor. A metallic clang jolted her awake for a moment, long enough to curl up and drift into silent darkness.

Mover

*M*over had no choice but to shadow *Night Watch* as it cruised south through the Bahamas, anchoring occasionally for the night, but leaving no opening for Justine and Simone to sneak aboard.

During the four days it took to travel almost seven hundred miles they didn't sit around and drink wine while watching the lovely shallow green or deep blue sea pass by. Justine and Harry talked often. His NASA friend kept track of the two yachts. Simone spoke several times with Darwin, and connected with other sources of information.

On the third day Harry flew in to Spring Point Airport on Acklins Island at the south end of the Bahamas. Justine watched from the shade of the main salon as Marshall and Harriet tied up the launch. She didn't know what to do with her hands. She gripped the door frame, fingers tapping as nervously as any woman waiting for the man she loved after a long absence, wondering if he was still that man.

Simone stood beside her, hands in pockets. They bumped shoulders. "He would not be here if he did not still love you."

"He's after Sinakov."

"He's after you, *cher*. Be gentle with him. I do not think he needs more broken bones."

Harry stepped off the small boat onto the aft landing platform. Spying Justine, he held up his uninjured hand in a hesitant fashion, as if unsure of his reception.

Justine's wave matched his. Then he grinned, and she grinned and waved like a love sick school girl. Ignoring the dangers of the bright Bahamian sun, she ran to him, hugged him, kissed him, and ran back to the upper deck shade.

Pleasantly stunned, Harry quickly mounted the steps into her arms. A minute later, beaming, he held her at arm's length and looked her up and down. *"Bon jour,* Simone. I see you have taken good care of her."

With a sly smile Simone glanced at Justine. "Mostly. Better than you have taken care of yourself."

"He went up against Sinakov, twice, and is still alive. I'd say he was doing a good job of looking after himself."

Simone's expression softened. "With some surprise, I agree." She kissed his cheeks and said, "Welcome, Harry. It is good that you are here."

A few hours later, Justine and Harry lounged on the open aft deck having taken some time to get reacquainted in private. Simone had discreetly moved to her own cabin. *Mover* anchored for the night after receiving a report from Harry's NASA friend that *Night Watch* had dropped anchor. With a calm sea, a warm breeze, and the last rays of the setting sun tinting the clouds pink, they relaxed in the pristine tropical evening. César sat with them, while the four crew relaxed around a table on the other side of the deck. They all had full wine glasses, bellies and smiles.

Harry sipped his wine and said, "Bayley knows something strange is going on. We have to tell her something. She's been a big help."

Justine lay her head back and gazed at the emerging half moon. "I like Bayley. Do you think it would be a favor to tell her about...everything? I was perfectly happy not knowing, until..." Lips twisted, eyes firmly shut, she braced herself until a wave of grief for her daughter passed.

Harry squeezed her hand until she opened her eyes. "We have to survive first. Then tell her something."

"We'll survive. It's Teresa I'm worried about. No sign or word of her for three days. That can't be good."

"You said that Grace thought she was alive."

"That's encouraging, but the boat is warded and shielded and spelled like a million dollar real estate listing. I want to see her for myself. If we ever get anywhere. César, do you have any idea where the hell we're headed?"

"I do," Simone said, dropping into a chair beside her. "I just spoke with a friend in Paris. Rubicon is not on a random pleasure cruise." She sipped her wine, looked at a paper in her hand, then tossed it on the table. "They are going to Hawke's Nest anchorage on Grand Turk Island for a business meeting."

"I assume it's an offshore business meeting that never happened," Justine said. "I've had one or two of those myself. Who with?"

"He only knew there's supposed to be three other yachts. The *Dragon*, from Taiwan, *Zerelda*, from Mumbai, and *Atlas Flight*, from New York."

"Is that Atlas Mining? They have mining interests all over the world."

Simone shrugged. "Whatever it's about, they probably do not want it made public."

"How far is Grand Turk?" César calculated a few seconds. "Leave here in the morning, be there for cocktails."

"Did you say *Atlas Flight*?" Marshall asked from the other table.

"Yes, I did. Why?"

"I know the captain, Dave Perkins. He's an old family friend. Used to date my sister."

For long seconds Simone and Justine looked at each other, eyebrows raised quizzically like they were considering the same question.

Justine turned to him and asked, "Do you think he would let us visit his boat?"

Marshall studied each vamp in turn before saying a tentative, "Sure."

Simone said to César, "Tell us about this Hawk's Nest Anchorage."

Night Watch

Teresa woke up with a sore head. It didn't take long to inspect her new accommodations, an eight foot by six foot metal box painted white. She had a welded metal bunk with a thin mattress and a sheet, blanket and pillow. A plain stainless steel toilet and sink occupied one corner. Welded to the bulkhead at the foot of the bunk a small table held a plastic glass of water and a bottle of Tylenol.

She sniffed the water, inspected the Tylenol, then downed a few. Inspection of the cell took a minute. The door, locked, had a narrow slot and a welded shelf under it. The toilet flushed. The sink had water. Of course they left her no weapons.

Lying on the bunk, hands behind her head, she sorted through her anger at everything and everyone. Especially herself. It had been a totally rash action to jump from one ship to another. She knew it as she did it, watching from outside, unable to stop herself. Antonia had been so close and they were just watching, doing nothing. When the *Night Watch* left she had to *do* something, foolish or not, or go *loco*.

Now, here she was, waiting for Sinakov or his Girl or Rubicon or Tito to come and suck her dry. Her only defenses were her magic or her wits, neither of which seemed to be working. Though the Tylenol was.

Food came through the door slot. Breakfast, lunch, dinner. The engines stopped, for hours, started again. Breakfast, lunch. The door opened.

The black man from the drawing room entered. Smiling, he shut the door.

Teresa caught a glimpse of at least one guard. She sat propped up on the bunk, arms crossed over her chest. Her earlier anger had tamped down to *I don't give a damn what happens as long as* something *happens.*

"I am Jang," he said with a deep mellifluous voice. He could have said he was God and you'd have to believe him.

Teresa said nothing. She took in his broad shoulders and tight body under a brown T-shirt. And his hips and ass and long legs and…Damn it, what kind of spell was he working on her? She could feel his energy as warm prickles on her skin—a not unpleasant sensation.

She'd tried all her magic in the last day and a half, with no results. She tried again thinking she could steal some of Jang's power.

"Your magic will not work here, Teresa."

"What magic?"

Jang leaned a shoulder against the bulkhead at the foot of the bunk, arms crossed. He looked down on her with a superior, if charming, damn it, smile. "You are a *bruja*, a witch, a sorceress, with the potential of great power, so I'm told. Messer was quite taken with you. As was Grace." His mouth twisted with hostility as he spoke her name. "She stole Oakes' magic. A most cruel act."

"He was the second most powerful sorcerer in the world. She was defending herself."

"Second most powerful? Oakes? He was strong, but not that strong."

"So you think you are."

Jang shrugged and favored her with a half smile. "Perhaps you are."

"Let me take Antonia and leave. Then you won't have to worry about that. You can be number fifty or number one. I don't care."

"So you will forget you have any magical power and go back to being a housewife?"

"Forget, yes. Housewife, no."

"Ah Teresa, ignore the power lurking within you? Yes, it's possible." He pushed off the bulkhead and sat on the bed beside her. She put a hand on his chest to push him away. It was like pushing against a rock wall. His black—or were they brown or red—eyes caught hers. "But you will never forget it's there, hiding in the back of your brain, sleeping behind your heart. Growing stronger and stronger until you cannot help but use it. And then it will consume you because you will not have the training or experience to control it. I have seen it many times before, Teresa. It-will-not-end-well."

Teresa didn't care. "*Bueno*, I'll do magic tricks at birthday parties. I want to see Antonia."

"I'm sure you do. But first…" He stood and waved a hand at the door. It clicked open. "Let us discover how powerful you really are." The friendly smile vanished, replaced by a warning frown.

She glanced at the open door.

Jang shook his head—Don't even think about it.

"After my test, I will see Antonia."

Jang swept his hand toward the door, smile now enigmatic at best.

Teresa followed Jang up to the exit door to the landing platform. An alert, vaguely Asian looking vampire escort followed her, holding a Samurai sword with one hand on the scabbard and one on the handle as if expecting her to attack at any second. On the starboard side, Jang opened a door and ushered her through. Jang and the guard followed.

Teresa knew little about culture based interior design, but had no trouble recognizing the mix of African and Asian design of the open room. Fantastic African carvings, bamboo, primitive weapons along with exquisite Samurai and Chinese swords. The guard closed the door then moved—more like glided—to the center of the end wall, and leaned against it, waiting.

A slight thrill of exhilaration passed through her, front to back, as she entered the room—a tiny hit of adrenaline that made her breath catch and her fingers tingle. The feeling of magic.

The only furniture in the thirty by fifteen foot room was a heavy wood chair set in the middle of an eight foot square of dark wood at one end. Teresa immediately thought of the chair in Messer's house and decided she did not want to sit in it.

Hand firmly against her back, Jang guided her to the middle of the room, then backed away to stand between her and the door. "You feel it, don't you? The magic."

Teresa flexed her fingers as she surveyed the room, eyes lingering an extra second on the exit.

"You can try it," Jang said. "But Tet has orders not to let you out. Unless I am unconscious or dead."

Her eyes narrowed and her head cocked quizzically to the side.

Grinning, Jang said. "I am sure you realize that your magic works in this room, Teresa. You can't use your little exit spell to leave the ship. However, if you can make it out the door, you can take your Antonia and do as you will." He gently waved a hand in her direction. His generous lips moved in silent incantation.

Though nothing changed that she could see, Teresa felt an invisible force gently press on her. She staggered, then pushed back. It was like walking against water. No matter how much magic "power" she had, she had no idea how to use it to push against Jang. She was still in Magic 101 kindergarten. But something he said gave her an idea. Surely this counted as an emergency.

Back turned against Jang's force, Teresa's hands made the movements, her lips said the words. She vanished. She slammed hard against the bulkhead across from cabin number four. After a few seconds to think how clever she was and recover her equilibrium, Teresa knocked on the door. Without waiting for an invitation, she entered.

"*Mi hija*, I've come to take you home."

"Mama, it really is you."

Antonia swung her legs off the single bunk, and wide-eyed, looked up, mouth searching for more words. She gripped the mattress edge.

"Yes it is. Come with me. We have only a few seconds before they find me."

"I can't go."

"Yes you can. Come. I'll get you off this boat."

"They won't let me leave."

"That's why it's called kidnapping." Teresa grabbed Antonia's arm and yanked her up off the bunk. "Come. Now."

She glanced out the door, saw nobody and dragged her daughter down the corridor and up the steps.

"Mama, what are you doing?"

"Getting us off this boat."

She knew where she was going now. Down the passage to the main cross corridor, then through the main salon, heading for the aft deck.

At the aft exit from the main salon leading to open air, Antonia jerked loose from Teresa's grasp. "I can't go out there," she cried.

Teresa spun to face her. "Why not? Yes you can."

"The sun."

"The sun? What the hell?" She grabbed Antonia by the shoulders and looked deep into her eyes. They were the same soft brown that they should be, yet despite her anxiety, flat, reflecting defeat and hopelessness. Teresa had seen enough undead eyes to know that they were not vampire eyes. *Gracias Dios.*

Shouts came from many forward directions.

"You are not a goddamn vampire. *Vamos!*" She dragged her cringing daughter into the sunlight.

Almost there. Down a short set of steps to a narrow sport deck and over the transom to a built-in swim deck and into the water. There she hoped to be out of the dome of Jang's wards and spells. Some words, some hand motions and they'd be back on *Mover*.

In a blur Tet seemed to materialize in front of them, blocking the transom door, sword held ready in both hands. Tight lipped, he moved his head slightly side to side, as if pleading with her not to make him use it. More feet pounded the deck. Other crew approached from behind.

Escape blocked fore and aft, Teresa went sideways. She grabbed Antonia and threw her over the side. Before the water stifled Antonia's scream, Teresa rolled over the side after her into the warm Caribbean water.

Teresa wasn't a great swimmer, but the adrenaline surging through her made up for her lack of experience.

"Mama, are you crazy? You can't swim away from them. You're going to drown us."

Teresa pushed her away from the yacht. At least fifteen people watched them from various decks. "Move Antonia. Don't you want to go home?"

Ten feet away she felt her power return like a ripple of warm water.

"Hold on to me." Antonia hesitated, then shook her head. "Hold on to me," Teresa ordered in her don't-give-me-any-shit mother's voice.

Antonia grasped her mother's arm. "Mom, you don't understand."

Her mother wasn't listening. Teresa held hands out of the water, again making the movements and muttering the words. She felt the surge of power within her, then…it vanished, like a lost orgasm.

"Ahhh." Teresa spun in the water. Immediately Jang caught her eye. He stood on the deck, hands outstretched. He had extended the no-magic-but-his zone. She was powerless. Helpless. She didn't bother to struggle as two crew lifted her into their launch.

Sitting beside Antonia during the minute trip back to the yacht, Teresa asked, "What do you mean I don't understand?" Hanging her head so hair hid her face, Antonia held herself tight. "Don't you want to come home?"

A jerky nod and a tight shrug indicated an unconvincing yes. A fear that had nothing to do with vampires or magic gripped Teresa's throat. She chose not to accept Antonia's slight jerk when she put an arm around her shoulders as an unwelcome sign. "*Mi hija*, talk to me."

All the answer she got was her daughter turning away. Hands roughly lifted her onto the yacht and pushed her up to the shaded deck outside the main salon. At the first step she pushed back, swinging at the hands. "Let go of me, *cabron*. I want to talk with my daughter."

Two crew held her in iron grips and forced her to turn and look at Antonia. The same big crewman who stopped her before held a long knife at her throat.

One of the crewmen said, "It would be best to cooperate, or her head goes into the water."

"Biggs likes that sort of thing," the other guard said with distaste.

Antonia looked like she might like that, too, rather than have to explain to her mother.

As soon as she reached the deck, Jang used his magic to slam her against the cabin side. He had an audience—Rubicon, Sinakov, his Girl, Tito. In the background was a raven haired woman who might have been a model until she got the half-circle scar that ran from the middle of her forehead through her left eye to the middle of her chin.

Jang stood in front of her. Hand a foot away from her chest, the pressure of his power was such that she had to fight for each breath. The sneer on his lips and the intensity of his glare were clear indicators that he was not happy.

"Rubicon admires your cleverness, Teresa. I do not." His sneer turned to an arrogant grin. "I will still determine your magic power. I hope you survive."

Teresa fought for a deep breath and let it out by asking, "What have you done to Antonia?"

Jang grinned. "Best me in the trial room and I will tell you."

Standing behind the rest, Tito flashed her a knowing smile.

Sinakov had no smiles. He pushed Jang away and put his gaunt face inches from Teresa. "Where is Justine Kroft?" He had to reach up to tilt her head so he could catch her eyes with his.

She felt the power of his glamour chipping away her will to resist. She had a couple of tricks to beat glamour. Simone had told her to focus on a far distance. Teresa focused on Antonia as she was escorted away, head hanging, face obscured by tangled hair. In her years in the ER she'd spoken with many prostitutes. When their customers were doing their thing, in their mind they'd go to a "Happy" place, whether a time in the past before it all went to shit, or an imaginary future that was clean, with good food, nice clothes, and real friends, and it was never too cold, and they weren't doing drugs and nobody beat them up.

Teresa tried to think back to her dream job as an ER nurse, insane hours, cleaning up vomit and shit, psycho patients. Or time with the family which she now saw without the rose-colored glasses. Her husband, Miguel, angry she had a daughter without his permission, pulling away, virtually ignoring Antonia, but embracing the two later kids. Mother-daughter time with her willful, self-centered, manipulative daughter. Miguel's weird tree religion. Surprisingly, her thoughts turned to time with Justine. Simone. Vampires. She glossed over her shame of betraying Justine to Sinakov. The road trip East. Grace.

Escaping Limbo. She'd fixed the consequences of violence every day in the ER. Now it seemed like it was her time to cause the violence.

"Don't worry about it, Stephan. She'll find you."

He didn't seem to hear. He brought his full vampire strength to bear on her head. His finger distorted her face, nails cut into her flesh. Her mouth opened, but she didn't have the breath to cry out. "Justine... Justine killed me. Me. But I can't be killed. You see. I'm alive. I'm..."

His Girl was there. "Master, please do not kill her now." She easily removed his hands.

Sinakov stepped back and looked around, his brow wrinkled in confusion. He seemed to notice Teresa for the first time. "Teresa, I hope you enjoyed our dinner together. I know I did."

Jang released his magic hold on Teresa. Gasping, head burning from the pressure, face stinging from Sinakov's fingernails, hands bloody from several small cuts, Teresa slid down the wall.

The Girl leaned toward Teresa. "Justine Kroft made him this way. She will pay."

"She will probably kill him again, and you, too."

The Girl flashed her a pitying look, nodded an apology to Rubicon, and guided her master into the main salon.

Rubicon offered Teresa his hand. Without hesitation, she took it. After Antonia's strange attitude, she was close to not giving a damn what happened to anybody, including herself. With his index finger he wiped a trail of blood from her cheek. Holding her gaze with his, no glamour, he savored her blood with his tongue.

Teresa had readied to fight his glamour, but he needed none to hold her attention. His great age was like an aura that reached out and enveloped her, his eyes held extraordinary secrets, and licking her blood from his finger was way more sexy than it should have been.

"Most vampires think that all human blood tastes the same," Rubicon said, eyes fluttering with pleasure. "Some of us are fortunate enough to be able to distinguish the subtle differences. Your blood is quite delightful. Magic adds its own tang. Tomorrow, I have an important meeting. After, we will talk, and drink." Suddenly, his hand covered her mouth and nose.

Unable to breathe, Teresa gripped his arm, but did not struggle—it was a waste of energy.

He thrust his face within six inches of hers. Still no glamour. He didn't need it to emphasize his warning. "I trust you will behave until then."

She stared back into his deep, deep, dark eyes, terrifying and alluring together.

Rubicon pulled back, smiling, pleased with himself, wiping another trickle of blood with his thumb as he removed his hand.

As he placed thumb to lips, Teresa said, "Antonia?"

"Ah, Antonia. Yes we will talk of her, also." Savoring his thumb, he turned away as Tet and a female vamp crewmember moved in.

"And Sinakov?"

He hesitated, studied her for five long seconds, then entered the salon, thumb still against his lips.

On deck, while a young woman tended her wounds from Sinakov, Teresa noticed the woman with the crescent scar watching from the shadows just inside the main salon. In white blouse and jeans, her dusky skin was Arabic maybe. Long dark hair hung loose over her shoulders. She held a strand in both hands. Forty, fifty, hard to tell, her eyes were deep pits with an occasional flash of white. *Christo*, who the hell was this? The woman stood back and followed with her eyes as Tet escorted Teresa through the salon on the way to her cell next to the gleaming white engine room.

Mover

Weak sunlight peeked around the blackout curtain in Justine's stateroom. Morning light brought out a vampire's natural—unnatural as Justine still thought of it—inclination to sleep during the day. Her eyelids hung heavy, she wanted to sleep; in the evening, if things went right, she'd need to be at the top of her game.

But she worried about Teresa. Where was she? What had happened to her? And Antonia, too.

What she really wanted to do was lie with Harry spooned behind her. She held his good arm to her chest taking pleasure in his warmth. Not that they hadn't shared heat throughout the night. But this was different, sharing the morning quiet together.

Testing her vampire liberation, she and Simone had been lovers since leaving California. Now that they were reunited, he was the one she wanted. Coming to terms with the real ages of vampires, two hundred, three hundred fifty, Rubicon possibly a thousand years old, had filled her with an urgency to spend time with Harry, a mortal. She just didn't think about how that might turn out. She loved Harry and could not conceive of changing him without his permission. His will to live would never allow him to give it. It would be suicide, in his mind. If one has somebody to live for how could they allow it? But what did Justine know? She'd had nothing but revenge to live for and so had begged for the change.

Engines rumbled to life. Harry sighed, kissed her neck, and settled into sleep again. Justine would have cried if she could with the sheer joy that small kiss brought her. For a moment it counteracted the anxiety the start of the engine brought. That night it could all be over, one way or another, but for now, she let her eyes close and enjoyed the small intimate moment.

Later, as *Mover* cruised south toward Grand Turk Island, Justine, hands in the pockets of her khaki pants—no more shorts—leaned in a corner looking out a window at the boat deck where the two main small boats were kept. Outside in the afternoon sun, Harry talked with Marshall by the larger launch, an eighteen foot inboard with a tiny cabin in the bow. They were discussing something to do with their tentative plan.

Harry came inside and stood next to her, hands in the pockets of his blue shorts. "Man, California sun has nothing on this place."

"I'll take your word for it."

"Oh, sorry." He lightly touched shoulders.

Justine kept the contact, enjoying his touch while she could. For a minute they watched the northern tip of the Caicos Islands come into view.

When she had changed into a vampire she hadn't cared about missing the sun. Avenging the murder of her daughter was her sole motivation. What happened after, she didn't give a damn about. Now, finding Teresa and Antonia had become her focus, but removing Sinakov's head again, permanently, was a very close second. If she saw him, she'd take his head without hesitation and to hell with them all.

"Think you'll have to fight tonight?"

"Probably."

"Vamps and mortals?"

"Probably."

Harry's lips twisted with disapproval.

"I don't like it either." She shrugged. "Self-defense."

He gave her a raised-eyebrow-really? look and a big sigh. "I know, not my jurisdiction."

❦   ❧

By mid-afternoon *Mover* rounded the southern tip of Grand Turk and motored slowly up the leeward side. *Night Watch* had already anchored at the south end of the open anchorage about a quarter mile south of the cruise ship dock. *Zerelda*, at two hundred feet, was also there, with *Atlas Flight*, a hundred-eighty feet, approaching from the southwest. César said his radar put *Dragon* an hour away.

A few smaller yachts, fishing boats and sailboats were anchored closer to a white sand beach by a small boat dock. César dropped anchor far enough north of *Zerelda* for *Atlas Flight* to fit in between. It was also far enough away from *Night Watch* not to seem like they were stalking it.

As soon as the sun flamed out into the sea *Mover's* larger launch headed for *Atlas Flight* with Justine, Simone and Marshall on board. Luney drove, expertly guiding the launch to the stern of *Atlas Flight* where two crew secured the boat.

Captain Perkins met them. A solidly built man about five foot eight, with a hairless bullet head, he greeted Marshall with a broad grin and a quick man hug.

"Marshall, good to see you, man. I heard you were crewing on a boat out of Fort Lauderdale."

"Yeah, been on it about eighteen months. This is Justine and Simone. They want to see what a real yacht looks like."

The Captain's handshake was warm and firm, though his greeting smile seemed a bit forced. "I'd be glad to give you a tour, but it will have to be quick. The CEO and several board members are aboard. Big business stuff. And I would prefer that you not mention seeing us here. It's all hush hush."

Simone put on her best French accent. "*Non. Non. Je ne dirai rien.* One of my husbands he do business the same. Much hush hush."

"I don't even know the name of this yacht," Justine added.

Perkins led them through the main salon, galley, library and gym, working up to the bridge. Behind the bridge they gathered in the captain's office.

Justine closed the door while Simone positioned herself next to the Captain. She nodded to Marshall.

Marshall was not happy about what they were doing, but understood the necessity. "Dave, we have a favor to ask of you. We know why you're here, a clandestine meeting on *Night Watch*. *Dragon* and *Zerelda* are here for it, too."

"How do you know about that? It's top secret. What's going on here, Marshall?"

Marshall glanced at the two vampires, hoping they'd say to forget it. They didn't.

"Simone can tell you."

Using all the power of her glamour, she did.

While Simone and Justine convinced Captain Perkins to go along with their plan, Luney had sorted through the male crew members ready to chat up an attractive female to find out who was the pilot of *Atlas Flight's* launch. Without much effort on her part, Scott offered to show her his boat, a twenty foot speedboat with a canvas dodger and a small cabin forward. After inspecting the boat and finding it perfect for the plan, she looked him deep in the eyes and reinforced his responsibility to follow the captain's orders—strange as they may be.

Night Watch

Teresa lay on her bunk, legs stretched out, arms slack beside her. She'd worked her way through anger, frustration, dread, and despair. She'd tried magic. She'd tried kicking the door. She'd tried cussing at everyone and everything. Twenty four hours later, nothing had changed. Now, again, she waited, calm, mind blank, for something to happen.

A loud clank of the heavy lock roused her from contemplation of nothing. The scarred woman from the shadows entered. Eyebrows raised in question, she studied Teresa as if waiting for her reaction. Teresa lazily turned her head and studied her back, saying nothing, waiting. Her visitor closed the door, not locking it, then leaned casually against the bulkhead, arms and ankles crossed. Her thumb and middle finger casually rolled a strand of long, dark hair. She wore flowing dark blue linen pants and a yellow long-sleeved man's shirt with the sleeves rolled up. In the light, despite the scar, she was a striking woman whose dark eyes had nothing to do with vampires.

"I am Ahlam," she said, her voice gravelly and deep, suited to her exotic look.

Teresa shrugged and waited.

"My name means one who has pleasant dreams."

"How pleasant for you."

Ahlam's face became a dark mask. Unconsciously she raised a hand toward the scar, then stopped. "Not always."

More than once Teresa had seen a woman's face cut up. Victims sometimes relived that terror for years afterward.

"No, I don't imagine it is. You're an Oracle. That scar have anything to do with that?"

Ahlam stared into a corner, seeing much farther. "I was twelve. I would see what I thought were dreams, then they would happen. My mother tried to keep it quiet, but my father found out. He thought I had a devil's face and tried to cut it off." A finger touched the scar's end at her chin. "I managed to run away. My mother and aunt helped when they could, but I was on my own, did what I had to do to survive." Ahlam took a deep breath and shook herself out of the past. "Rubicon heard of me, saved me from…He saved my life."

"So you owe him."

"Yes."

Teresa drew her legs up and stretched her arms and shoulders. "Are you like the Queen of Oracles then?"

"No. But there are maybe twenty others who we work with when necessary." Ahlam's face took on a meaningful look. "Who tell *me* what they see."

Teresa didn't miss the look or the emphasis. "And you decide what to pass on to Rubicon. What do you see about my future?"

"Nothing. Even here, I cannot see anything for you."

"Maybe I don't have a future."

"Possible, but I think it is the magic."

"But it doesn't work here."

"You used the blocking spell before you appeared here, yes?"

"It's still working then?" Ahlam did not deny it. "What about others I might have been shielding?"

"Justine Kroft and Simone Gireaux. They are not shielded."

Teresa's gut tightened. She swung her legs off the bunk, leaning toward Ahlam. "What of them? Where are they?"

Ahlam darted a glance to the world outside the door, then sat on the toilet, leaning forward, elbows on knees, close enough that she could lower her voice. "I believe they are coming for you. You must be ready."

"When? Now?"

"Soon."

Teresa's thoughts raced. Where had they been? How were they coming? Why now? Why was she telling me? She glanced around her cell. "I'm as ready as I can be. Why are you telling me? If Tito and Rubicon know they're coming...?"

Ahlam dropped her eyes and pressed her lips tight.

"You haven't told them? Why?"

Ahlam glanced at the door. "There is a meeting onboard tonight. I do not want it to happen. If I do what is normal and expected, you're friends will be stopped, and the meeting will happen. If I say nothing, perhaps it won't."

"*Dios mio.* What is this meeting?"

The Oracle puffed out an exasperated breath. "I don't know, exactly. But I've seen glimpses of where it leads for the world. I have to try and prevent it."

Spreading her hands, Teresa asked, "What can I do from in here?"

"I don't know," Ahlam blurted. "I'll help if I can, but I will be at the meeting." She jumped up and moved to the door. "Please do two things for me. Don't let your friends kill me, and make sure you take Antonia with you. It is imperative."

"To take her is why I'm here. What have you seen about her?"

Again, her frustration came through. "Nothing. Something. It is all a muddle. Not good, I do not think. Like with you, her magic obscures what I see."

"Antonia's magic?"

"She is your daughter, is she not? Just make sure and get her off this boat." Ahlam turned to leave.

"Wait. If she has magic, she could use it to get away."

Standing in the doorway, Ahlam said, "Only Jang's magic works here. And they have not told her she has magic. They are afraid she will use it against them."

"Can you get me to her? I can explain to her—"

"I must go. Other Oracles watch me. Take her away."

"Wait!"

Ahlam slipped out the door and locked it.

Teresa sat still trying to make sense of it. Was that all real, or all bullshit? She knew Justine would come for her, why now? Did it have something to do with the meeting? Justine and Simone were good and clever, but there had to be at least twenty, twenty-five crew, half vamp, all tough. Even with Ahlam's help, what chance did they have? And what could Teresa do except sit on the bunk and wait?

Mover

Justine drew her knees up and rested her head on them as Scott smoothly piloted *Atlas Flight's* launch, nicknamed *Atlas Float*, away from the stern of the larger yacht. She had no illusions that their plan would unfold as smoothly as the launch cut through the darkening water toward *Night Watch*.

They had returned from their visit to *Atlas Flight* confident that the Captain and Scott were sufficiently glamoured to perform their part.

Since *Mover* had arrived Harry or one of the crew had been surveilling *Night Watch*. Deck plans for *Night Watch* were obtained from one of Simone's French contacts. As the meeting drew near Harry determined the crew's dress for the occasion. *Mover's* crew scrambled through their own clothes and a closet packed with clothes left by previous guests to come up with burgundy polo shirts and white pants for Justine and Simone. The shirts were a bit large, which was okay, they hid the knives strapped underneath. A large folding sailing knife and a small handgun hung from their belts. They also carried a thin bladed machete, almost a sword. It had no sheath. They had no plan to put it away until they returned or…

Harry wasn't thrilled with their plan, but under the circumstances had no other alternative. He had to bypass his cop ethic. Totally out of his jurisdiction, all he could do was support the main players.

At eight that evening Captain Perkins signaled they had half an hour until his people would board the launch, *Atlas Float*. Justine pulled her hair back into a short ponytail while Luney tightly braided Simone's longer hair.

Harry pulled Justine aside. Before he could speak, she placed a finger to his lips. "I know," she said. He sighed, tenderly caressing her face. "Do what you have to do, just come back to me." Then he pulled her to him and kissed her, putting all the passion of his feeling into it.

She placed her hands on his and kissed him back with equal passion. For those few moments they were totally alone with no past or future. Only that kiss.

"Justine." Simone's voice drew her back.

Justine touched his lips and turned away.

Simone kissed him on each cheek. "Do not worry, Harry. I will take care of her."

The last gasp of a blazing sunset lit the way as Luney ferried them through the red reflection on the glassy water to *Atlas Flight*. *"Comme le sang sur l'eau,"* Simone said to Justine. "Like blood on the water."

"Not a good sign," Justine said.

They stood with shoulders touching, watching the water pass. "For somebody," Simone said.

Only Scott waited for them when Luney brought her boat to a momentary stop beside Atlas Float tied sideways to the stern landing step. Before reaching the pool of light illuminating the whole aft section, Justine and Simone had concealed themselves below. When the two boats touched, the big light illuminating the stern went out for five seconds, plenty of time for them to jump the rails and vanish into the cabin of the larger launch. Luney then moved her boat to the port side, the side away from *Night Watch*, where Scott helped her tie up.

Five minutes later, *Atlas Flight*'s three passengers boarded the launch—CEO Richard Marking, just fifty, Talbot Albacent, chairman of the board of directors, close to sixty, and Karen Karso, forty-two, VP in charge of all mining operations. All were dressed in tropical business casual: polo shirts, light weight pants and light sports jackets. Karen carried a thin briefcase. None of them smiled or made eye contact, or paid attention to Luney as an extra crew.

Justine thought about the secret meeting. One of the world's largest mining companies meeting with the richest woman in India, Inda Sigu, with interests in shipbuilding, energy generation and distribution, pharmaceuticals, and transportation. Also Mita Chang Yum from Hong Kong with shipping, manufacturing and construction interests around the world. All meeting with a thousand year-old multi-billionaire vampire. She had no clue what they were cooking up, but figured it wasn't good for the rest of the world's population in general. At that time, she didn't care. Teresa, Antonia and Sinakov's head were Justine's interests.

As the launch slowed to dock with *Night Watch*, Justine heard Karen Karso mutter, "Are we really ready for this?" She received no reply. Ready or not, they boarded the large yacht.

A couple of seconds later *Atlas Floats'* engine coughed, and died. "Damn it." Scott tried to restart to no avail.

"What is wrong?" a heavily accented voice demanded.

"Ah, we got some crap in the fuel tank a while ago. I thought we had it cleaned out, but this is the second time it's clogged the filter. Can I tie up along side there? Take me about ten minutes to fix."

A long hesitation, then, "Sure. But quick. They won't like you staying here."

"No problem."

Justine felt the boat bump and swing.

"We have a new tank waiting at home. Just didn't have time to install it before we left. Where are you guys from?"

"Europe. Work quick."

Scott lifted up a deck hatch then jumped into the cabin.

"You ready?" he whispered.

"When it's clear," Simone whispered back.

Scott grabbed a bucket filled with rags and a new filter. He leaned into the hatch and pretended to do something. A couple minutes later he motioned them up. "Looks clear. He's gone around the portside. This side's clear. I probably can't hang here more than ten-fifteen minutes. Good luck."

In an eye blink Justine and Simone were over the rail and walking along the side deck as if they belonged there.

Night Watch

Waiting. She tried magic, again. Nothing happened. She tried pacing, but at the end of every three steps all she wanted to do was beat her fists against the wall. So she sat on the bunk and tried to empty her mind as before. A failure, though she did achieve a kind of blankness. All the questions, all the possible and impossible answers, bounced unconnected in her head creating a blur of white noise.

Real noise made her eyes pop open. The lock clicked and the door swung open to crash against the bulkhead.

Sinakov strode in, stopped and looked around as if unsure where he was, then spied Teresa.

"Teresa." Like they were old friends. "We had dinner together and you betrayed Justine, your best friend. We should do that again."

He jumped on the bunk, grabbed the front of her jacket and, though she had almost a foot in height and maybe forty pounds on him, lifted her and pinned her against the wall.

"*Ou est Justine, ma chere?* She cut off my head and I am going to cut off hers instead. Then I will toss it into the sea for the sharks. Tell me where she is and we will have dinner."

Rubicon and Tito, Teresa could handle, but Sinakov's instability scared her. From what Harry said he could easily kill her and forget about it a minute later—or just space out and walk away. He seemed to have shrunk since she last saw him after trying to kill Harry the first time. He had been thin before, but had some muscle and substance on his bones. Some even said he was handsome. Being decapitated and having your head reattached had to take a toll, even on a three hundred and some year old vampire.

"I don't know where she is." Exactly.

"Yes you do. You know." His tone grew conspiratorial. "She's close, isn't she? Coming to me. Where? When? She's going to give me her head. Isn't she?" His face turned mean, like someone flipped a switch. "Isn't she?" he ground out, and punched her high up in the ribs. No damage, but it hurt like a thrown sledge hammer. "Isn't she." Another punch. "Isn't she?" He let her go. As she sank to the bunk he pummeled her body, chest, head, face, punctuating each blow with "Isn'tshe? Isn'tshe? Isn'tshe?"

Each blow planted a seed of pain. Sinakov may have been a scrawny example of a vampire, but he still had some strength in him. Teresa lost her breath, tasted blood, and felt the sting of a split cheek. She wanted to fight back, kick his skinny vamp ass over the side. But breathing was too hard. On her knees she wrapped arms around her head, taking the blows on her hands and back. His skinny legs pinned her against the wall.

One blow, no different from any other, was one too many. Teresa uncoiled in a burst, knocking Sinakov off the bunk. Sprawled on the floor, he opened his mouth wide to show his fangs. In an instant, he was up, stretching her neck.

"Master!" The Girl grabbed him from behind and lifted him off Teresa.

He screamed his rage, a real horror film shriek, hands like claws grasping for their prey.

"Master, Rubicon will be angry if you feed on her. And we...you need him to—"

Sinakov froze in her arms, like a prop from that same horror show. She set him down and he stood loosely as his fangs retracted and mouth closed. Looking around with a bewildered expression, his gaze passed right over Teresa.

"I must talk to Rubicon about Teresa," he said. "She could be trouble."

"After the meeting, he will talk with you, I'm sure," the Girl said.

"No, now. She and her friends are...are...trouble." He squared his thin shoulders and marched out the door, where he stopped, paralyzed with indecision whether to go left or right.

The Girl shot Teresa a look of pure hate. Which Teresa returned. Then she went to guide her master to the left, slamming the door shut behind her.

Teresa waited for the click of the lock. When she didn't hear it she pushed the dull throbbing pain of her back and shoulders and head and arms aside and dragged herself to her feet.

The lever moved down easily. The door opened without effort. Nobody was there.

She shut the door and leaned her hands against the bulkhead. Blood dripped from her chin, forming several small spots that blended into one larger one. Teresa wondered if it was a trap, though why anybody would need to do that she couldn't think. Didn't matter, she wasn't staying.

In the sink she washed her face and wet her hair, finger combing it back. She winced as she patted her face dry. Red streaks stained the towel. In the mirror she studied her face. "You look like you've been beat with an ugly stick, witch." She laughed, then winced. "Fuck it." She stepped through the door.

The entrance to the cells went through the engine room. Most everything in the huge space was pristine white or polished stainless steel; some red equipment provided a bit of color. Neat bundles of wires and black hoses offered some contrast. A glassed in control room on the upper deck looked out over the massive engines, generators, watermakers, and other equipment.

An engineer sat in one of the chairs. Teresa had to wait. No way could she climb the metal steps without being seen. While waiting, she studied the engine room.

Her father had owned an old bus with a diesel engine that always had something he needed to fix. As a little girl she often helped him in the evenings or weekends. She wasn't so interested in the mechanics of the bus as spending time with her father. Nevertheless, some of the work stuck with her. She identified the fuel lines and the substantial filters and the lines running through a bulkhead to the tanks. She wondered where the right place to toss a match and start a fire would be. Her eyes followed thumb thick electrical cables and she wondered how big a spark would be necessary to light up a bilge full of diesel fuel.

The engineer turned his back to scan a wall full of gauges, readouts and multi-colored lights. Teresa raced up the steps and ducked into the corridor leading to crew cabin number four. Without knocking, she entered.

When she'd entered the cabin before, Teresa hadn't had time to examine the space. An enhanced sense of smell wasn't needed to know that Antonia lived there. She froze in the center of the cabin as the scent of Antonia's favorite citrus shampoo brought a rush of memories. She pressed hands to chest and breathed deep as her face bunched, fighting unwanted nostalgic tears. She had no time for this. She shook it off and inspected the approximately ten by ten foot cabin. Whatever else had changed, her daughter's lack of personal space organization hadn't. The bunk wasn't made up and a few pieces of clothing occupied corner floor space. Magazines, clothes, and a half eaten bowl of cereal covered a built-in table with two wooden straight back chairs. A narrow hanging closet held a few dressy tops and dresses, fashion suitable for a mega-yacht. The rest of the clothes were basic casual wear.

Monogrammed towels, a black eye over a globe, littered the floor. In the medicine cabinet over the sink Teresa found the shampoo and toothpaste Antonia liked. It seemed a bit odd that if the boat came from Europe she had those American products. A bit of indulgence on some-one's part. Shampoo became unimportant when she found a pill bottle among the other toiletries.

Primperan. Though the label was in French, she scrutinized it for the drug's use. She caught her breath when she saw metoclopramide. She knew that drug from working with nurses who had worked in Europe where it was used to treat nausea related to morning sickness. Thirty pills were indicated on the bottle; eight remained. "*Madre de Dios.*" Rage rose up in her, which she quickly tamped down, but didn't put out. "What have those bastards done to my little girl?"

Voices in the corridor reminded Teresa what she was about. She jammed the pills into her pocket. Letting her anger out, she tipped over a chair, stepped on one leg and, embracing the pain in her body, lifted up on another leg until the chair splintered apart.

Down the passage Teresa walked into the crew's dining area across from the galley. Seven people sat at a long table. A quick scan assured Teresa they were all mortals.

At the end, back to her, was Antonia. One by one they noticed the scowling Mexican woman with the bruised and bloody face, holding a broken chair leg, and fell silent. Antonia turned around.

"Mom? Mom." Her eyes bulged and her mouth formed an O of shock and apprehension. "Oh my God, what happened to you?"

"Later. Let's go, *mi hija*. Time to get off this boat."

"Mom, I can't. They won't—"

"—let you go. I know. So I won't ask."

Teresa grabbed Antonia's arm and yanked her out of the chair. "Time to go home."

"Leave her," a French accented voice said.

Teresa spun to look at a male vampire around thirty. He wore the burgundy uniform shirt and dark pants. He had a hand on the handle of his machete.

"Screw you." Teresa was not of a mind to waste any more time talking.

The new vamp drew his blade, but Teresa was already swinging. He yelped as the chair leg smacked his hand. Before the machete clattered to the floor Teresa struck his head. He staggered back. She closed in and delivered a blow with her knee where it always counts. He doubled over and she smashed him hard, twice, on the back of his head. The room was silent except for Teresa's heavy breathing.

She snatched up the machete and turned to the shocked group. "Vamps heal fast. He'll be okay." She took hold of Antonia's arm. "*Vamos.*"

Too shocked to protest, Antonia allowed her mother to drag her out of the room, through the galley, past the offices, into the formal dining room. There, Antonia jerked loose. Clutching the back of a chair, she glared at her mother.

"Don't you understand? I don't want to leave."

Teresa faced her daughter from the other end of the table.

"Why? Because you're pregnant?"

"How…how did you know…that?"

"I'm your mother. I know those things. You were kidnapped and raped and you want to stay? They glamoured the hell out of you, haven't they. Do you even know who the father is?"

Antonia's mouth worked a few seconds before she managed to say, "It wasn't like that. You don't understand. I…I'm…"

"What? You're in love? You're barely seventeen and you fall in love with somebody who rapes you. You're the one who doesn't understand. Who is the father?"

Eyes blazing, Teresa stalked through the room to Antonia and shook her by the shoulders. "Who?"

"You're hurting me."

"Not as much as they've already hurt you. Shit. We'll talk later. Come on."

"Teresa. Stop." Tito said from the door at the other end of the room.

"You can't leave with my baby."

"You're a damned vampire, you can't conceive a child."

"All it takes is a little magic."

Teresa's thoughts ran a thousand miles an hour. She understood. She had no words as she stared at her daughter.

"My baby will be special," Antonia said.

"Let us hope she's not a fool like you. Move."

She pushed Antonia through the door and down the narrow passage by the offices. Around the corner she flattened against the wall and held Antonia beside her with the arm holding the machete.

Tito rounded the corner after them. Teresa swung her blade at his neck. Only his extra-speedy reflexes allowed him to block with his own weapon. Teresa had learned a few moves from watching Justine do her martial arts workouts. She dropped down and kicked the legs out from under him. Tito fell flat on his face. Teresa rose up and stomped his head.

"Don't!" Antonia cried, grabbing her mother's raised arm.

"Shit. Move."

They sprinted down the passage to the wide cross corridor. Teresa turned to the port side. Two guards, one with gun drawn, blocked the open doorway. Teresa reversed and pushed Antonia toward the starboard exit. Biggs waited with a grin and a ready blade.

From behind, a machete blade took a diagonal slice out of his head. Before he could fall, hands pulled him to the rail and flipped him over.

Justine and Simone came through armed and ready to rumble.

"Hi, Tee. Got your bags packed."

They moved side by side along the starboard side deck. Full night had fallen quickly as it does in the tropics. A half moon illuminated cotton ball clouds. Lights on the other yachts were muted, as if trying not to call attention to themselves.

"I can smell her," Simone said.

"She needs a bath." Justine sniffed. "Antonia is here, too. Smells the same as when I knew her, but different somehow."

A shout came through the entrance ahead of them.

"Something going on." Justine's hand pulsed on her machete's handle.

"Tee."

A massive vampire wearing the uniform burgundy shirt emerged onto the deck farther forward. He strode swiftly toward them, weapon drawn. Justine felt his scrutiny, but no alarm. He reached the entrance ahead of them.

Peering around the corner, it only took a few seconds to size up the situation. The big vamp was in Teresa's way. He was so tall Simone couldn't take off his head cleanly. They pushed him over the rail. Simone kicked the head slice after him.

"Hi, Tee. Got your bags packed."

"Get me ten feet away from this bucket and we won't need a boat."

"This way."

But it wasn't that easy. Two crew stood in place of the one big one, armed and unhappy. Simone took them on, but they were experienced, too. They drove her and the others back.

One of the armed crewman from the port side fired.

"Do not fire." Tito shouted from the narrow passage entrance. "You might hit Antonia."

Justine stared at Tito. She wanted to go after him, but the fight went into overdrive and she got busy. Her martial arts training got a full-on test. Others knew a few moves, too. A hard front kick sent her flying at the two crew standing guard outside the old-world study where the meeting was going on. One guard jumped out of the way, the other cushioned her crash into the wall.

"Shoot her," a voice shouted. Probably Tito.

Justine jumped up in a second, and saw the shotgun aimed at her head. She pushed the door lever, ducked in and slammed the door a half second before the shotgun blast plowed a gouge in the outside of the door's fine finish.

Curses and apprehensive faces greeted her.

"Sorry, Gentlemen, whatever scheme you're cooking up won't work. Meeting's over."

A second later, she leaped out the door, rolled, drew her own gun and fired. The shotgun wielding crewman dropped with a bullet in his head.

Simone held two vamp guards at bay, though they blocked the starboard exit.

Antonia crouched against a wall behind Teresa who battled a mortal crewman, neither one giving an inch. Justine wanted Tito's head. Strangely, he did not join the fight. He stood inside the entrance to a narrow passage, his attention on Teresa—or was it Antonia?

Teresa was getting the better of the man. Then Antonia slid a foot along the floor and kicked her mother's foot forward a few inches—enough to knock her off balance and give her opponent an opening.

Justine whirled, aiming a backhand slice at his neck. At the last second she turned her blade to smack him with the flat hard enough to land him in a heap next to Antonia.

Teresa glanced at her feet, at her friend, then, eyes narrowed, weapon half raised, at Antonia, who cringed into a corner. That's when Tito started across the wide corridor. Justine moved to meet him.

"Justine Kroft," a voice rang out loud enough to freeze everybody in place. "Young Blood. I am going to give you *real death.*"

Sinakov's appearance shocked Justine. Six months ago, while wiry, he'd been young, muscled, and vital, even handsome, if one could overlook the fact that he was a monster. He seemed old now, stoop-shouldered, gaunt, as if his three hundred plus years had begun to catch up with him after she'd taken his head off.

She struggled to contain her loathing. She wanted to rush in and eviscerate him. She wanted to hack him to pieces then look into his eyes as she cut off his head and stomped it into a mush of bone, brain and blood. The three foot sword he held meant nothing to her.

Rage forced under control, all else pushed aside, she warily circled him. Though he didn't look like much now, he had been a formidable fighter, quick and experienced.

"Why are you here? The family you stole doesn't want you. You'd be better off dead."

His Girl lurked in the one shadowed corner.

Speaking through the sneer on his lips, Sinakov said, "I don't need them to want me. Soon I'll be Master of a larger, more powerful Family and the old Sinakovs will bow to me or be dust."

By the door to his study Rubicon raised an eyebrow even as his mouth formed a tight frown at Sinakov's statement.

"Nobody will bow to you, *Henri*. Not even your mother."

"Do not speak of my mother. She died centuries ago." His expression went blank for a moment, then he snarled, "Do not call me Henri. My name is Stephan Sinakov. She died when she tried to kill me. She does not exist."

Simone stepped toward him, machete twitching at her side. "But I do exist, Henri."

Sinakov spun to face her, sword held high ready to strike. "And I am disappointed in you. I had such hopes you would be a man like your father. Not the evil you have become."

"You…she…my mother meant to kill me when I was eight years old."

"Once before I said I would carry that guilt no more. Now, I say it again. It would have been best if I had been successful. No one will bow to you, Henri."

"You will bow. You all will bow. I will be Master of you all."

Grim faced, Simone stepped back. She nodded to Justine behind him. With both hands she readied to finish Stephan Sinakov.

"Master!" His Girl charged Justine. Warned by her anguished cry Justine spun and caught her with a foot in the gut. She slammed the Girl to the floor and held her with a knee on her chest. The pixie sized Girl struggled, screaming curses, but was no match for Justine.

Justine held her blade across the Girl's thin neck. "Stop it, girl. Don't make me take your head."

"He's my Master. Don't take him from me."

"You need a new Master."

Rubicon looked down on them. Before he said anything Simone shouted, "Henri. No."

Looking up over her shoulder, Justine saw Sinakov with his sword raised over her, and the tip of Simone's machete protruding from his chest. She met the sadness in Simone's eyes. Justine rose and swung her weapon so swiftly through Sinakov's neck his head didn't move until Simone yanked out her machete.

The Girl wailed.

Justine caught his head by the hair. She consulted silently with Simone, then stalked toward the starboard entrance. The crew blocking the exit stepped aside. Justine flipped the head over the side, then leaned on the rail and watched it fall. All heard the plunk as it hit the water.

Two muscled vampire crewmen escorted her to stand before Rubicon. The boss vampire held the Girl by her neck, like a worn out floppy doll. Justine felt a pang of sympathy at her devastated expression. She knew what it was like to lose the center of your life.

"I am taking this one," he said.

"You're welcome to her," Justine said. "We only want Teresa and Antonia. Then you'll never see us again."

Rubicon lifted the Girl off her feet and handed her back to one of his guards. Hands stuck casually in pockets, he stared down at her. As a mortal Justine had been no shrinking violet; she'd used that intense thoughtful stare herself. But it took all her willpower not to turn away.

Still thoughtful, he glanced at Antonia who stood behind Tito, one hand gripping his arm.

Oh shit. It took Justine two seconds to read the expressions on their faces and what that small hand meant. No wonder Teresa was so wired. She stood apart, body tense, face tight, hand twitchy on her weapon's handle, trying to watch Justine, Rubicon, Tito and Antonia simultaneously.

Rubicon faced Justine. "Antonia stays. Teresa is her mother, she's clever, and her magic has, I believe, wonderful potential. She will stay also. You and the always delightful Simone boarded my ship without permission, killed six or seven of my crew, executed an old friend and guest—"

"Which you could have stopped at any time."

He freed up a wry grin and tiny shrug. "You disrupted a very important meeting, and now stand in front of me and ask to be allowed to take my property and leave. I think I would like you both to work for me. So you will stay also. Your launch has already been sent on its way. Take them."

Justine jerked her machete into a defensive posture. Despite senses on full alert, she didn't see Rubicon move. In less than a blink he had the weapon out of her hand, his hand around her neck, and her feet off the floor.

His other hand squeezed her face. "If you try anything like that again I will tear off your head." His expression was one hundred per cent threat. He released her. "Teresa knows the way."

Justine stopped next to Tito and Antonia. She ignored him. "Antonia, your mother will never give up on you. These people are using you. When they're done they'll toss you overboard with the garbage."

"You know nothing," Tito said. "She will be with us for a long time."

"Better out with the garbage than with you," Justine spat.

Tito snarled, "Shut up, bitch," and punched her face.

"Smug bastard." As the two guards seized her arms she twisted a side kick that pinned him against the wall until she was dragged away. "People have died to rescue you, Antonia. Are you worth it?"

Mover

Harry watched through high-powered binoculars from *Mover's* uncovered aft deck. He saw *Atlas Float* tie up and the suits disembark. His index finger vibrated against the glasses while he waited for

Justine and Simone to board. He almost missed their leap over the rail. He followed them as they moved along the deck. His finger resumed tapping when he spied the big crewman. He gasped, held his breath and froze when Simone sliced the man's head and they dumped him over the side.

Night Watch swung on its anchor, giving Harry a partial view through the double doors. He saw—Teresa, wild dark hair, machete raised. Justine and Simone charge into the fray. Heard—A shot, the clang of blade against blade, cries and curses drifting over still, dark water.

Silence. Then—gunshots—shotgun and handgun. An anguished scream—the Girl. Two crewmen blocking the entrance stepping aside. Justine tossing a head over the rail. Sinakov. Damn. No reanimation for him. Harry gasped as the weight he'd been carrying for weeks lifted off his shoulders. Relief brought tears to his eyes.

Movement aft. A crewman, gun in hand, throwing lines off and pushing *Atlas Float* away. Luney asking what the hell's going on. Crewman not answering. Scott starting the engine and motoring into the darkness.

Not good. Binoculars trained on the entrance, Harry wiggled his fingers to relax his cramping grip. Crewmen exit, walk forward out of sight. *Night Watch* has swung away and all Harry can see are shadows moving. He waits. Waits for Justine and Simone and Teresa and Antonia to emerge, knowing they aren't going to.

The elation of a few moments ago dissipated, replaced by fear, doubt, indecision. César joined him. "Luney was told they would return the three executives when the meeting was over. No mention of the others."

"Shit. They've been taken. Think I could slip aboard?"

"Are you James Bond now? They'll be on full alert."

"Damn it. There must be something I…we can do."

"I have only known those ladies for a few days, but I think all we can do now is be ready and trust them."

Night Watch

Conveniently, they each had their own cell on the same side. It didn't take long to discover that the connecting air vents clearly carried their voices. In her familiar cell, Teresa sat on the bunk against the bulkhead with legs drawn up. The others inspected their new quarters, tried the doors, searched without success for anything to use as a weapon and washed the blood away.

Justine briefly wondered if she could ever wash the blood off her hands, but gave it up because she knew she wouldn't like the answer. She sat on her bunk next to Teresa, separated only by the steel bulkhead.

Simone lay down, hands behind her head, ankles crossed. "Hey, Tee. How is the food in this place?"

"Wonderful. They serve only the best grade of blood here."

"Well, that's something."

"So what do we do now?" Justine asked.

"Wait," Teresa said. "That's all you can do here."

Justine felt the slight heat of Teresa through the quarter-inch steel partition. "So Tee, what's happened since you've been here?"

"Waiting mostly," she said. Then she told them everything. Once they related what they did, she asked, "Do we have any idea what this meeting is about?"

Simone had said little, letting the two long time friends talk. She broke a long silence. "Teresa, I am sorry to say this, but Antonia being pregnant may have something to do with it."

"*No hay problema*. Tell me."

It *was* a problem. Justine could feel her friend's distress through the steel. She pressed a hand to the spot warmed by Tee.

Simone said, "I knew Rubicon maybe a hundred and twenty years ago. We crossed the Channel together. He was a brash, arrogant son of a bitch then. Maybe not so brash now. We were at a ball of some kind a month later. I heard him expound to a group of wealthy businessmen and government men on the dangers of vampires who could walk in the sun. 'What a magnificent army they would make,' he said. 'No one could stand before it.' He was looking for investors. There have been rumors ever since of experiments seeking to cross breed mortals and vampires."

"I didn't think that was possible," Justine said.

"It is not. Male vampire sperm overpower the mortal woman's egg, destroying it. And the vampire woman's eggs are too tough for mortal men."

"What about two vampires getting together?"

"The egg and sperm battle each other until one or both are destroyed."

"Just like real life."

Teresa said, "Tito said he was the father of the baby. And that Antonia had magic."

Simone was silent for thirty seconds. "If that is so, it is not good news. Can you imagine an army of vampire human soldiers, with magic power, able to walk in the sun? None would be safe. The world would be theirs."

Justine let her head rest against the steel. "I was going to ask if Rubicon was arrogant or bold enough to try something like that. But I think we know the answer to that."

"But what does this meeting have to do with vampire armies?" Teresa asked. "You said that that Atlas woman is in charge of mining."

"I don't know, Tee. Maybe nothing," Simone said. She lay with an arm over her eyes, visualizing possibilities. "Maybe they have discovered a cancer cure and are planning to gift it to the world." She got no reply to that.

"Let us say they are making soldiers. It would take generations to grow an army of any size. If they didn't want to take that long they'd need hundreds, thousands of women to bear the babies. There are many poor women in China and India. Much empty space in China for the breeding factories. They'd have access to construction, transportation, bio research, food production."

"Maybe they won't need the babies," Justine said. "All they'd need was one mortal-vampire hybrid. Use his DNA and figure out how to clone him. Or artificially change an already grown soldier."

"That would be quicker," Simone agreed. "Plenty of people in China, India, Bangladesh to recruit or abduct. Change them, ship them in floating laboratories to training bases in China."

"Or Africa. Plenty of off the grid space. And Atlas has huge holdings there."

"They would need large populations to feed all the vamp soldiers."

"In ten years they could have a hell of an army. Even mortals could wait that long."

"Rubicon was serious when I heard him before. Old vampires have long memories, and now he has the money and technology to do it."

Teresa said, "Are you saying all that could come from my Antonia?"

Neither Justine nor Simone spoke the answer they all knew. A minute later Justine heard Teresa quietly crying.

Once Justine was sure Teresa slept, she whispered into the vent, "Do you really think the baby is a vamp?"

Simone whispered back, "Unless some mortal nobody knows about snuck into her bed, then yes. And that's not good for many reasons."

"Then we need to get her away, one way or another."

"That's extreme."

"Do you want to go up against vampires that make you seem mortal?"

"You have a point. Let us save the extreme for last. Even you, Teresa would never forgive if you had to go there." Simone sat up, scrutinizing every inch of the cell for a weapon or a way out. "They will have to attack *Mover*. They do not want anybody to know of this meeting."

"I agree. Will Rubicon believe us if we say we will work for him?"

"Doubtful. He wants Tee and Antonia. We are expendable."

They both cocked their heads, listening.

Justine said, "The launch is leaving. Meeting's over. They will probably come for us soon."

"Then we'd better get out of here."

Simone inspected the floor, under the bowl, in the corners. A steel plate held up the foot of the bunk. Underneath, in the corner, Simone found what she needed. A large wire paperclip. *"Bon. Tres bon."*

"What?" Justine asked, not bothering to whisper.

"A way out, maybe."

Simone talked as she bent one end of the clip around her little finger, knelt by the door, worked her arm through the food slot, and began working on the lock.

"These locks are strong, but simple. It is a little tricky using one hand. Good for us, they are well oiled. It is only a matter of bending the paperclip in the correct way to simultaneously make turning pressure and put pressure on the pins." Eyes closed, lips tight with concentration, she gently found the correct combination. "Ah, like that. Now to apply enough pressure to move the bar." She winced at the effort. *"Merde."* A few seconds later she slammed the door with her free hand. Click. "Ah, like *that.*"

"Great. Are the top and bottom bolts closed?"

Simone pulled her arm out and rebent the clip with a hook at the end. "Alas, yes. However…" She pushed her arm through again, adjusting position for maximum reach. "I believe I am able to reach the low one, almost." She grunted as she pushed hard to gain an extra inch of reach. *"Ah, bon. Maintenant, si…?"* She kicked the bottom of the door several times. Clunk. "Yes! Yes. Almost free."

Arm withdrawn, she shook out the kinks then stepped back and gave the door a serious kick. *"Merde!* The latch is unlocked, but still caught."

"Can you hold it down and push?"

"Not enough." She kicked it again. She thought a moment. Quickly, she yanked the blanket off the bunk and folded it. Reaching through the slot, she pushed down the lever, then bumped the door with her butt several times. Each time she stuffed the blanket a bit farther in the gap until it held the door open enough so the latch would not catch. "Now we kick."

Simone stood back, stepped, leaped, and delivered a kick high up opposite the top bolt.

Justine felt the impact two cells away. "Are you out? I think we should hurry."

"You are not comfortable in your beautiful room?" Simone kicked again. A small gap opened at the top.

"I'd like to take a moonlight walk later."

"Madame, your desire," another kick, "is our only pleasure." Another blow. The gap widened. The next kick, the door flew open, slamming back against the bulkhead.

Wide awake, Teresa said, "Simone, you're my new best *amiga*. Sorry Justine."

"Better wait until she opens your door."

Within seconds Simone worked on Teresa's door. A few more seconds and it was open. "*Bon soir*, best friend."

Fifteen seconds later Justine joined them in the narrow passage. "We need to go. I think our time is limited."

Teresa led them to the engine room. She peeked up at the control center. "When they're not looking, we can go."

Justine gripped Teresa's hand. "Teresa, we have to get Antonia away from these people, no matter how."

Simone gripped Teresa's shoulder. "And you. They will want to use you."

"Because of the super vampire thing?" She absorbed their seriousness and looked each one in the eye. "I understand. But I will do whatever I have to to keep her alive. "*Vamos*." She darted up the steps past the control room.

They burst into Antonia's cabin. Empty.

"Probably with Tito," Justine said.

"We need weapons," Simone said.

"Let's find someone to ask." Justine grasped Teresa's arm. "Breathe, *amiga*."

A pretty mortal woman about twenty-five occupied the second room Simone entered. She wasted no time. She grabbed the woman's face and glamoured her hard. "Where is the girl Antonia. Where are the weapons?" The girl had no choice but to answer. "Sleep. You will not remember this."

They found the weapons locker past the galley and crew's dining room. Simone had it open in less than a minute. Inside they found rifles, shotguns, handguns and machetes of various sizes. They armed themselves with blades and bullets then moved on up a few steps to a passage with only four wooden doors. Justine pressed an ear to a door marked B-1 and listened while gently trying to depress the handle. She backed off, shook her head, then kicked it open. Simone went in first with a shotgun ready. Justine followed with a .45 semi-automatic.

The cabin was three times as large as Antonia's, with a queen bed, and a plush bench seat and matching armchairs. Antonia had been lying on the bed. By the time Justine entered she had fumbled in a nightstand drawer for a handgun which her trembling hands tried to aim at everyone simultaneously.

"Mrs. Kroft, Mom, you can't be in here. Can't you just leave me alone? I'm supposed to shoot anyone who comes in."

Simone stood by the door with the shotgun aimed at Antonia while Justine addressed the girl and Teresa hung back a little, frozen with fear, love, anger and ten other emotions.

"Antonia, you can't kill me, or Simone over there. The only one it will hurt if you shoot is your mother. Are you really going to shoot your mother who's gone through hell to find you and rescue you whether you think you need it or not?"

Antonia's hands shook as she swung the gun between the three women. Aiming at Simone, she said, "Put that gun down. I'll...I'll shoot her if you don't."

Simone said, "Foolish girl, I will if you will. If you shoot your mother I will shoot you in the belly." The hard glint of her eyes left no doubt she meant it.

Confusion bunched up the girl's face, squeezing out tears.

Teresa said, "*Mi hija*, you must come with me. These people are using you. No matter what they say, what Tito says, he does not love you."

"He only wants that baby," Justine said. "Is he really the father?"

Antonia's face contorted with uncertainty. "I...I..."

"Is he the only one who raped you?" her mother demanded.

Her mouth opened, but no words came out, only mascara stained tears from red eyes.

A rumble vibrated through the yacht as one of the main engines started.

"Grab her and let's go," Simone said from the door.

"Bitches!" Sinakov's Girl darted through the door past Simone. Knife raised, she headed for the closest body in sight, Teresa.

Simone took a half second to remember the Girl was a ghost, undetectable by other vampires. Then she moved.

The Girl had the knife an inch away from Teresa's neck when the butt of Simone's shotgun slammed into her head. Instead of severing the carotid artery, the tip struck her shoulder and raked a foot long gash down her back. Before the Girl hit the floor Simone kicked her hard, sending her flying into a corner.

"Mom?" Antonia lowered the gun when she saw the streak of blood down her back.

Justine took advantage of the distraction to snatch Antonia's gun and press her hard by the neck against the wall. "She okay?" she asked Simone.

Voice thick as she fought the lure of fresh blood, Simone said, "Only another scar for her collection." She held a towel against the wound. Her eyes never left the spreading crimson stain.

Teresa winced against the sting. She said over her shoulder, "You can taste it if you need to."

"*Merde.*" Teresa winced again when Simone lifted the towel, ran two fingers along the wound, and sucked the blood off. "I'm sorry."

"I think you saved my life. Least I can do."

The second engine added its throb to the first.

Another swipe. "Justine, we have to go. Now."

Justine held Antonia's wide-eyed gaze. "Do you really love Tito? What do you really feel, not what they tell you?"

Her mouth opened; her eyes opened even wider.

"Let go of her, Justine," Tito said from the door. He knew she wouldn't obey, so he marched toward her.

Simone spun to stop him. His blade slipped in six inches between her ribs as he passed. She grunted. Pain was pain, vampire or mortal. She grabbed Teresa's uninjured shoulder, pressed her forehead against her back.

Tito kept moving. "Release her. That baby is mine."

"How?" Justine asked. "Vampires and mortals cannot create a baby."

Tito grinned. "Have you no romance, Justine? All it takes is a little *magic* to make it work. Give her to me."

Justine pinned Antonia to the wall with an arm against her throat while holding a machete against her stomach. "Why don't I just cut the baby out and give it to you. That's all you care about anyway."

"No. The baby will not survive."

"Not to mention the mother."

"I don't want her hurt, either."

"So you have feelings for her?"

He wore an earpiece connected to a radio on his belt. All the vampires in the room heard the static pop and Rubicon's voice speaking Russian, "Tito, where are you?"

"In my cabin, sir."

"Our visitors?"

"In my cabin, sir."

"I see. Bring me the two witches, now. The others…a pity, dispose of them, permanently."

"Yes, sir."

Even as Tito said in English, "Sorry, I had hoped our time together would be more painful for you," he drew his handgun and aimed at Justine's head. "And you would not hurt her. You still think too much like a mortal."

His eyes glistened with the anticipation of killing. His finger tightened on the trigger.

A blur of steel. The gun and the hand holding it fell, landing on the carpet with a dull thud.

Teresa held the machete with both hands. Her nostrils flared with each deep breath. "I'd have told you to keep your hands off my daughter if I'd had a chance."

"God damn Mexican bitch witch. I'll feed on your magic." He swung at her, but the missing hand put him a little off. She blocked with her blade. "One handed I will slice you to shark bait."

She knew he was right. He still had speed and power. Simone was wounded, Antonia tried to hold Justine back. For the first time in a while, she felt real fear. She might be dead in seconds. Would her daughter be sad or relieved to see her dead? That it might be the latter was her greatest fear.

Tito swung.

Teresa managed to block him because Justine rammed her blade through his back and out his stomach—a major distraction even for a tough-guy vampire. In an instant Teresa's fear turned to unleashed anger. She sliced off his other arm at the elbow, hacked at his body and pulled back for the decapitating blow.

"Mom! No!"

Too late. Teresa screamed as she swung so hard she stumbled against the door to the bathroom.

Antonia screamed with her, falling to her knees, staring at the head glaring back from the floor.

"Ah, fuck." Justine yanked the blade out and guided Tito's body to fall out of Antonia's sight. "Simone, you okay?"

Dark blood marked Simone's clothes and hand. "As always with you, Justine, never better." She hefted the shotgun and pointed it at Sinakov's Girl who sat still in the corner, watching. "Stay."

Justine moved to Teresa and wiped her tears with thumbs. She turned her head away from the sobbing Antonia. "Tee, it's done. We have to go. We should have been out of here minutes ago."

"Justine," Simone said in her warning voice.

Simone held her shotgun on Rubicon who stood in the door, casual, hands in pockets, shoulder against the jamb. "She's right. You should have." He eyed Tito's headless body. "He was one of my best minions."

Justine lifted Antonia to her feet and handed her over to Teresa. "If you had let us take her and leave quietly, it would have saved a lot of trouble," Justine said.

"Indeed. I assume you'd like to do that now."

"Yes." Wary.

"A pity. All of you are most promising." A casual little shrug. "However, I am a patient man." He studied Antonia, who leaned against her mother, expression and body slack, unresponsive to the arm around her shoulders. "Now that I know what is possible, we can move on."

"Move on to where?"

"I am so sorry, Justine. That information is only for trusted associates. And you are not quite on that level, yet. What is more, you are leaving us." He moved back a step and swept his arm in the stern's direction. "We will notify *Mover* to send a boat."

The three women traded eye contact all around. There wasn't much to say. They had to go or stay.

Simone considered the Girl in the corner.

"I said before, I will keep that one," Rubicon said.

Simone shrugged. Shotgun leading, she led the others down the passage.

Tension surrounded them like a thick mist. Armed crew dotted the passage. Every one of them looked like they wanted nothing more than to open fire on the quartet.

Ahlam waited nervously by the galley. Catching Teresa's eye, she said low, "Don't go to the aft deck," then stepped back.

Teresa, guiding Antonia with a tight grip on her shoulder, said, also low, "Did you hear her?"

Justine, "Yes."

"We should go forward and jump. If I can get ten feet away I can take us to *Mover*. Simone, go out where you came in."

"Will they let us do that?"

"We should probably run when we get to the outside deck."

"*D'accord.*"

A vampire crew woman stood by the double exit doors to the starboard side deck.

All innocent, Simone asked her, "Which way to the, how do you say, aft end?"

The woman, about forty, attractive and buff when changed, glanced and pointed to the right. Simone took advantage of the short distraction to plunge a wooden stake into her heart. She grunted, her eyes rolled up, and she dropped straight down.

Simone caught her and swung her out to the deck. "Maybe gives us a few seconds. *Alons-y.*"

Mover

Harriet said, "Looks like the meeting's over."

Harry's eyes popped open. "What?" For a few seconds he wondered where he was. Why were there a zillion stars overhead? What meeting?

"The launches are collecting their people. No sign of our people."

Our people? "Shit." Justine.

He swung off the lounge chair he'd been lying on. César had insisted he lie down before he made himself crazy and did something foolish. César and Lucian joined them at the rail.

Harry said, "I thought Luney said they would deliver them?"

"Change of plan," Lucian said.

"Not a good sign," César said.

Harriet hadn't moved the binoculars off the *Night Watch*. "Did you see another boat there?"

"Lots of shadows with all the boats and lights."

"I guess," Harriet said with some uncertainty. "But—"

The muted rattle-rumble of a huge diesel engine starting interrupted whatever she was about to say.

"Those guys aren't sticking around," Harry said.

"Not a good sign."

"God damn it, aren't there any good fucking signs?"

A billow of exhaust puffed out of *Night Watch's* stack.

"Not yet."

"Can we follow them?"

"They will know. And not if they return to Europe. I don't have that much range. And if we did, in the middle of the ocean they could turn on us. I don't like our chances if they do."

"Christ, Mr. Sunshine."

César spoke into the radio on his belt. "Marshall, get ready to start engines. Luney, stand by the launch." He received affirmatives from them and spoke to Lucian. "Stand by the anchor. Harriet, you're on the bridge with me. Harry, keep an eye on them over there. Everybody, arm up. Just in case."

The crew went about their tasks. Harriet brought Harry a handgun with a clip-on holster and a rifle. Lucian worked the windlass to shorten up the anchor chain.

Dragon had already moved far enough offshore to turn and steam south to open water. *Zerelda* backed toward deeper water while *Atlas Flight* weighed anchor.

With the powerful binoculars Harry had a good view of *Night Watch* and the crewman at the side entrance. He scanned the rest of the boat, noticed activity on the bridge and at the bow. Toward the stern the launch was quickly raised and secured to it's deck cradle.

Movement at the side entrance drew his attention. A crewwoman faced in. Simone came into sight. She talked to the woman then staked her and drug her out on the deck. Teresa and a girl appeared, then Justine. Relief flooded him. He hadn't realized how scared he'd been she might be lost to him. And how helpless he was to do anything for her.

"They just exited amidships and are running forward. Three crew pursuing. They're going to need help."

Through the radio César ordered, "Marshall, start 'em up. Luney head over there. Lucian anchor up. Harry, what's happening?"

"They have the anchor up and are backing away from shore. Oh shit. Justine and Simone are on the rail. They're pulling Teresa and a girl up with them. They're jumping."

"We're being attacked," Harriet yelled over the radio. "Starboard side."

Night Watch

Justine figured they'd made it as far forward as they could when two crew raising the anchor spotted them. With three more crew closing fast from behind it was time to get off the boat. She leaped onto the wide teak rail cap. Simone jumped up beside her.

Antonia, teary-eyed and dazed, made a step toward the pursuing crew, then stopped. She looked at her mother and at the hand Justine held out. They had no time for her to make up her mind. Teresa raised her arm so Justine could lift her up to the rail. She then let Simone haul her up as well.

"Too many *pommes frites* for you, mortal." Though Teresa was as thin as she'd ever been.

"You need to drink more high calorie blood, skinny vamp."

Justine wrapped an arm around Antonia and yelled, "Jump."

They all jumped together—but never made it to the water.

Mover

Harry tore his eyes from *Night Watch* and glanced forward. A black inflatable with five black clad men was partially hidden under the bow flare. Already, the first invader climbed hand over hand up a line attached to a grappling hook over the rail. Harry knew Harriet had been right. They'd hidden behind the other launches then motored up close to the beach, knowing the *Mover* crew would focus attention on the big yacht.

He recognized the long shadows of guns. This was no social call. He drew his sidearm and snapped off a couple of shots. Immediately, a burst of automatic rifle fire answered him, ricocheting off the aluminum hull and tearing chunks from the teak rail he leaned on.

Forced back, he radioed, "Five of them boarding on starboard side at the bow. Fully armed."

Another quick peek.

"Two aboard. One going forward. Vamps I think."

Rifle in hand, Harry ran to the corner of the upper superstructure. A couple of quick breaths and he leaned around the corner, took two seconds to find his target in the dark, and fired. The head of the one attacker still in the small boat snapped back and he toppled over the side and vanished into the dark water. Vamp or mortal, a slug to the head will slow them down.

"Marshall. Lock down," César called into the radio.

Shots came from forward, automatic fire and the pop of small arms. Lucian radioed, "One more down, but I'm down, too. Be a bit before I can help nail the rest of the bastards."

"Bridge is locked down," César said. "Tracking two coming toward the bridge. Where the hell's the other? Harry?"

"I'm looking."

More shots, coming from inside, down low.

"Shit. Engine room." Harry ran down a couple of decks to the interior engine room entrance.

César ordered into his radio, "Marshall. Report."

No answer.

Harry reached the entrance door. It was open. Crouching, gun held two-handed, he moved down the short passage. He spied a smear of blood just inside. He stepped over it and glanced right.

Marshall sprawled in a pool of blood. The front of his shirt glistened crimson. He was still conscious. One bloody finger pointed between the two huge engines.

A figure in black looked down at a small package in his hands. Harry knew what it was and didn't waste any time telling him to stop. He shot him twice, once in the head. Then he went up and shot him again in the head, just to make sure.

He picked up the package. It was mostly C-4, with a timer counting down from two minutes. "Well, fuck." He headed for the door. "I'll be back," he yelled at Marshall over the engine roar. He sprinted through the boat searching for an exit to an outside deck.

To the right at the top of a narrow set of stairs he spied a door. Before the gunshot registered in his ears his left leg jerked out from under him. He stumbled sideways and landed hard against the wall as the bomb slid to a stop in a corner by the door—timer passing through thirty seconds.

Harry glanced back. Another black clad figure stalked down the passage, rifle aimed at Harry's face. He was a dead man, whether by bullet or bomb. A second of sadness passed through him, never to see

Justine again.

A second or two was all he had. Don't waste it. He scratched for his gun and managed a wild shot down the passage. *I tried.* He braced for the impact of the bullet entering his head. A gunshot filled the narrow passage. A second shot, a third, assaulted his ears. He felt nothing, then realized he still felt everything. Harriet strode down the passage and shot the attacking vampire in the head with a .45.

"Harry," she shouted, pointing at the ticking bomb.

"Shit." Pain and relief at being alive forgotten, he scrambled to his feet and snagged the bomb with one hand. 8 seconds. Wrenched down the door latch. 7 seconds. Slammed against the heavy door with his shoulder. 6 seconds. Stumbled through onto the deck. 5 seconds. Grunted with pain as he fell to the deck. 4 seconds. Scrambled to the rail. 3 seconds. Braced himself and flung the package out over the water. The bomb vanished into the dark. 2, 1.

Boom.

Night Watch

Twenty feet below the bow rail glassy water rippled with moonlight—safety down there, waiting for them. Five feet down Justine thought she'd landed on an invisible warm cloud. For a moment the four of them floated, able to move their limbs, but stuck in midair. Justine managed to flip over and look up at the grinning crew. Above them, on the outside bridge wing, a man faced them with eyes closed. Slowly his hands moved together, up and down, fingers working as if he guided a grand puppet.

"Jang, *Dios maldita sea!*," Teresa spat.

Justine felt herself float upward, and the temperature rise. Strength and speed meant nothing. They were helpless.

"Teresa, what the hell's happening?"

"Jang's fucking magic. Remind me to take his head off when he's not looking."

"Can't you—?"

"No, God damn it. As long as I'm under his magic fucking dome, I'm useless."

"You are never useless, Tee," Simone said, squeezing her hand.

"What planet are you living on?" Teresa said. But she squeezed back and attempted a smile, even as they rose slowly over the rail and hung just above the deck. Well-armed, burly crewmembers, men and women, surrounded them. Like shooting fish in a barrel, Justine thought.

Antonia was the first released.

"Antonia, *te quiero*," her mother cried out as the girl was led away. Looking over her shoulder, Antonia twisted her lips into a sneer, signaling pure hatred, yet her eyes did not match that sentiment.

One at a time Jang lowered them to the deck where their wrists were secured behind their backs with thick plastic tie-wraps. In addition, Justine and Simone's wrists were also tied with strong braided nylon line. The three were then escorted aft, each surrounded by three crew, to the stern landing platform. Rubicon lounged in the stainless steel and teak fishing chair.

Strong lights shone down from an upper deck, illuminating the aft end of *Night Watch* and the people gathered there by choice or by force.

In the distance *Dragon*, *Atlas Flight*, and *Zerelda* were spots of light quickly steaming in different directions toward their own horizons. *Night Watch* slowly backed away from shore toward deeper water.

Gunfire erupting from *Mover* almost a quarter mile away drew everyone's attention.

Right away Justine knew what was happening. She struggled to shake off her guards—they were no longer just crewmen—and attack the old vampire. "Leave them alone. They aren't part of this."

Rubicon pressed his fingertips together and appeared to consider her request. A huge explosion on the far side of *Mover* startled everyone, except Rubicon. "No," he said, followed by a smug grin. Then he turned severe. "They have seen too much. This meeting was, and will remain, private."

"Too late for that. How do you think we found out about it?"

Rubicon's eyes flared for a moment, glistening black obsidian, gazing deep into Justine's head. He sat back and nodded to a lanky black man with a long face, like a skull covered by tight black leather. The black man picked up a length of heavy chain attached to a rusty twenty pound anchor, locked the chain tight around one of Justine's ankles, then wrapped it around her legs, finishing by pushing the anchor between her legs so it drew the wraps tight.

Justine realized what was going to happen. She made a last full strength, yet futile, effort to free herself.

Rubicon grabbed her face, stopping her struggles. "You have caused me some damage, Justine Kroft. This meeting did not end as positively as I had hoped. It will take some time to repair the trust you broke. You will soon have much time to think about that."

Grim faced, Jang watched from behind the fishing chair. Hate and fury fueled Teresa's glare. With all her strength and determination she marshaled her magic against his suppression spells. She pushed.

He staggered a half step back, and turned his attention to her. His grim frown turned into a mocking grin. His head made tiny side to side movements—No, no, Teresa, I am too strong for you.

Simone followed the interplay between the two. They stood together, one guard with Teresa, one at Simone's side, one behind her, the guards' attention more on Justine than on their charges.

"That Rubicon's tame sorcerer?" Simone said quietly so as not to draw attention.

"Yes."

"His magic is what prevents you from using yours?"

Teresa nodded, raising a quizzical eyebrow.

"If he were to lose his head, the spell would end, and you could fly us away?"

Another nod.

"Be ready." Simone shuffled around so her back angled away from her guard and he couldn't see her hands.

"It is a pity," Rubicon said to Justine. "You and Simone would have been a great asset to me. But now, even if you swore yourselves to my service, I could never trust you. Think about that." With a regretful shake of his head, he pushed Justine into the water.

"No!" Teresa surged toward the spot where Justine disappeared. Her guard easily restrained her. "Bring her back. I will—"

"Tee, do not say it," Simone shouted.

"But Justine…"

"No, Tee. Magic. Like you said. Be ready."

Uncomprehending, Teresa stared after her friend.

"Tee!" Simone caught her eye, and Teresa comprehended.

Faster than Teresa's mortal eyes could follow, Simone's arms swung free. Gripping the small knife Sinakov's Girl had used she sliced the neck of the guard beside her, yanked his machete from its sheath and severed the head of her other guard.

"Down!"

Teresa bent her legs and bowed her head as Simone continued her beheading with Teresa's guard. A flick of the knife freed Teresa's hands.

"Tee. Come." It took Simone two leaps to jump up to Jang who raised his hands to put her down with some serious sorcerer power. But he wasn't fast enough. Without hesitation, Simone rammed the machete blade through his chest to the hilt.

Everyone on the yacht froze, then shivered as if an electric shock sparked through them. Most hunched shoulders as if a weight had been lifted off them. A few cried out. Stars seemed to gleam a bit brighter.

"Now, Tee. Now," Simone said.

"But Justine?"

"We can't help her if we're dead, which we will be if you don't get us out of here now."

"Shit, shit, shit." But she started the hand movements and mumbled the words she'd been practicing for days against the opportunity to use them. Now!

The surviving guards quickly shrugged off the change Jang's death had brought. Simone swung Jang, still skewered on the machete, around as a shield between Teresa and the weapons being drawn. Several bullets thunked into the body. A shotgun blast almost knocked her down; a few pellets stung her neck. She ignored them.

Simone gripped Teresa's arm. "*Vite,* Teresa. *Vite.*"

Then they, and Jang, vanished.

In the Water

The Turks Island Passage between Grand Turk Island and South Caicos Island reached depths of over seven thousand feet. As Justine and Rubicon spoke, and as she was wrapped in chains, *Night Watch* slowly moved away from shore toward deeper water. Because of the disturbance caused by their escape attempt, the mega-yacht was not as far offshore as it might have been. With the Passage only twenty-two miles wide the walls were very steep. Only a mile offshore, even wrapped in chain, one might take the better part of an hour to reach the bottom.

But *Night Watch* floated about a half mile off, not far past the famous reef wall, when Rubicon unceremoniously consigned Justine to the dark water.

Justine knew nothing of depths and distances when the water closed over her. She sucked in a deep breath, a mortal reflex, and struggled with all her vampire strength against her bonds. To no avail. Rubicon had chosen well. How many times had he done this? How many vampires languished at the ocean bottom, alive, but trapped forever?

That's when the real fear took over—fear of being trapped in the frigid water hundreds or thousands of feet down, never to see Teresa or Simone or Harry again. As the light from *Night Watch* faded, an instinctual fear of the dark gripped her. With the dark, fear of monsters. What might come out of the stygian darkness with teeth to rip her apart or tentacles to crush her?

She stopped struggling after a minute, hour, day. Time stopped, the only change the gradual drop in water temperature and rise in pressure. Her mind went blank; maybe she slept.

Something brushed her arm. Shark! Monster! She wanted to cry out, she wanted to cry, but there was no air and no tears. Her feet hit something, she tumbled over something else then came to a stop on an almost level sandy area.

Time passed. Justine worked through her panic, fear, loss, anger, and acceptance. This led her to determination. The determination that took her from a widow to a commercial real estate agent worth almost a million dollars when she talked Simone into changing her; that led her to Sinakov and the taking of his head; that took her to a small ledge on a big wall hundreds of feet underwater.

Inch by inch she squirmed or rolled or wiggled herself around on her tiny patch of sand. It seemed to be a long ten foot wide, slightly sloped shelf covered with fine sand that had drifted down through the years. It butted up to an irregular, sheer vertical wall. It was too deep for anything to grow there. She didn't try to explore the outside edge. She had no doubt it only offered more down.

Using her feet, she scooped out a small hollow in the sand next to the wall. Her little undersea nest. She did not want to slip over the edge.

Then she started to explore her bonds. How was the chain wrapped around her body and legs? What could she do with the tie wraps and the line about her wrists? If they were free, she was free.

Freeing her legs was relatively easy, though how long it took, she couldn't say. Lying on her side, using her feet, she dragged the anchor close, then squirmed around until she could grab the anchor's shank with her hands and maneuver it back between her legs. A few rollovers and her legs were free, though the chain was still locked around one ankle.

Elated at her small victory she gingerly slid a few steps along the wall, exploring the surface with her shoulders. She discovered deep grooves and protruding knobs of rock scoured smooth by millions of years of moving water.

She sat down against the wall and for the first time opened her eyes and really looked out into the pitch dark water. After some time—total darkness did not allow for meaningful estimates of time passage—lights appeared. Hallucinations maybe, manufactured by her mind desperate for something to focus on. Maybe the pressure affected her brain. She'd begun to feel its effects; the constant pressure on her whole body, compacting everything, bringing a constant dull pain and sapping her strength.

Focusing on the pale lights that occasionally floated past, Justine realized they were fish. She remembered her grade school reading about the deep sea fish with their own phosphorescent light. An image of a big-headed fish with a mouthful of needle teeth came to her. Instinctively, she drew her legs up. The more she looked, the more she saw, or thought she saw. A single glow, a group, or a string of undulating lights, whether real or imaginary, all beautiful, a welcome something to focus on.

Mesmerized by the lights, Justine sank into a stupor that might have kept her on her little ledge until her body dissolved into the passing water, leaving nothing but bones and chains. But a different form yanked her back to reality and would have sent her heart racing if it was capable of such a thing.

A pressure wave rocked her against the wall, almost knocking her over. Sand trickled down on her. Then she saw it. What the fuck? A huge shape glided through the dark. Too far away to discern its true shape, it was a pale, amorphous presence. A gigantic shark, she thought. A whale, a giant squid, a submarine. Could be a giant sea serpent, for all she knew. It wasn't that long ago she thought vampires didn't exist. Why not a freakin' sea serpent?

Whatever it was, it was no hallucination. It scared the hell out of her, and motivation back into her.

Once again Justine focused on the chain around her ankle. She thought the immense water pressure might have compressed her body enough to pull her foot through the encircling chain. It hadn't. Climbing up the wall with that weight dragging her down seemed an impossible task. One slip and she might end up deeper than she was now.

Another problem: Hunger. She felt a tightness in her gut, a slight quiver in her hands. Cold crept into her bones. She found it hard to concentrate on her task of freeing her hands. She had to keep reminding herself that to feed she needed to be free, though the urge to climb, swim, jump up the wall to warmth and blood persisted.

Justine knew what she needed to do. She stood up, and slid along the wall to an outcropping at the right height. She backed against it and positioned her hand just so. A few practice bumps to get the alignment right, then, with a mental deep breath, she arched her body forward, screamed a silent, "Chi!" and slammed her hand back against the rock. Pain shot up her arm. She dropped to her knees and shivered with pain that overwhelmed any Hunger or cold, but the maneuver worked. Time had ceased to mean anything; giving herself a minute or hour or day, Justine twisted and pulled her crushed hand through the tie wraps and line that bound her.

Free, except for that chain around her ankle; there's always something trying to hold you back. But Hunger could not be denied.

Justine sat in the sand on her little ledge, back against the wall, working her left hand. It had little grip, but the pain had gone. She worked at the chain. No matter what she tried that chain was not slipping off her foot. She had two options; crush her foot, or break the chain.

She pulled the anchor to her and inspected it with her fingers. Hope gave her a surge of energy. Rubicon should have had a sailor prepare the chain and anchor. No seizing wire secured the screw pin and once she had it situated right, she easily unscrewed it.

As easy as freeing her hands was, removing the chain was difficult. A movie vampire might have been able to break the chain with a bit of a grunt and grimace, not so in real life hundreds of feet underwater. She could find no way to slip the chain or break the lock no matter how hard she pounded them with the anchor.

She had to go up. Hunger balled in her gut like low blood sugar when she was mortal—insistent, demanding. It gripped her chest, like fear. She could afford no more time lying around feeling sorry for herself. With trembling hands and chain draped over her shoulder, she started to climb.

About twenty feet up she reached out with her injured hand and found a small jut of rock covered with sand. As she used the handhold to pull herself up, her hand slipped, and she fell back into the dark.

Mover

Ablast of water stung Harry's face like a hundred bees as the explosion threw him back through the door to land sliding on his back. The deck rocked violently, sloshing water around him. Double vision, dizziness and pain forced him to lie still.

Harriet knelt beside him, face slowly coming into focus. Her mouth moved, but he couldn't hear a thing.

"What?" He sounded to himself like somebody shouting from a great distance.

Harriet leaned close. "You okay?"

He nodded, then froze until the dizziness went away. He struggled to remember the last few minutes. "What happened?"

Harriet helped him sit up. "You tossed the bomb. Saved our asses."

"Wasn't there another bomb?"

"We have it. I tracked the guy with the CCTV, told César when to open the door. Boom. Took him down before he set it. Where's Marshall?"

Harry remembered more. "Engine room."

Harriet jumped up and headed down the corridor.

"Harriet," Harry shouted. She stopped. "It's bad."

Harry struggled to his feet and stumbled his way to the bridge, hearing slowly returning on the way. In César's quarters he found Lucian applying bandages to César's side.

"Harry," César greeted, wincing at Lucian's ministrations. "I assume that was you with the bomb."

"Thanks to Harriet."Lucian said, "Who'd have thought, Harriet, hero of the day."

"You okay?" Harry asked.

"Through and through my love handle. No big deal, *hombre*." His body vibrated as he sucked in a hissing breath and his skin had lost two shades of tan. "Marshall?"

Harry dropped onto the bunk and grunted with a sharp stab of pain.

"Let me look at that leg," Lucian said, not waiting for permission.

"He was bad when I ran out with the bomb. Way too much blood."

A long silence was broken by Harriet over the radio.

"César." They all heard the tears in her voice.

Harry handed César a radio. "I'm here."

"Marshall is dead."

"I'm so sorry. He was a good man."

"He was." The eyes of the three men glistened. "Tell me he…died well."

Harry took the radio. "He saved my life. If not for him that bomb would have gone off down there. He saved the boat, and all of us."

"Thank you, Harry. Can we get the bastards who sent the bastards that did this?"

Harry nodded. "I have an idea."

Night Watch

Teresa, Simone, and Jang's still skewered body appeared on the small platform at the bottom of the metal stairs from *Night Watch's* engine control room. Teresa staggered against the railing, head hanging, gasping for breath.

"What the hell are we doing here, Tee?" Simone shouted. Though the engines idled the noise necessitated shouting to be heard. She yanked her weapon out of Jang, letting his body crumple to the metal floor.

The set of Teresa's face answered her question. She pointed to the control room. "Can you keep them out of the way?"

"Don't hurt yourself."

Teresa faced into the main engine space, and concentrated on a gang of fuel filters. She didn't really know what she was doing. Balls of flame were beyond her. But the power rushed through her body, swirling faster and faster, eager to get out. Like a B movie wizard she pointed hands at the filters, willing the power to them.

Somewhat to her surprise two of them began to smoke. Fuel began to leak. A gasket melted and a thick spray of diesel fuel shot out ten feet soaking both engines.

Teresa gasped as her concentration slipped. The heavy odor of diesel permeated the air, choking her. Diesel is much harder to ignite than gasoline. The jump and melting the filters took a lot out of her. She'd have to rest and recharge before she could consider starting a fire.

Alarms buzzed. Red lights flashed.

A large red tank strapped to the hull off to the side was clearly marked for engine oil. A rubber hose hung from the bottom, running to the closest engine. She did have enough oomph to melt the hose, allowing a stream of oil to join the growing pool of diesel.

An engine coughed. Ran. Coughed again. Rattled, raced, kicked and bucked to a stop.

Teresa coughed and gagged at the fumes. A step up the stairway proved difficult. She stumbled. Anger, at nothing, at everything, surged. She directed it at a large generator. A fuel line burst, dumping more fuel into the bilge.

Simone lifted her to the top of the steps.

"Need some fire?" Simone asked.

"Por favor."

Simone raise an automatic rifle she'd acquired somewhere and fired at a steel box sprouting several wiring harnesses. Bullets ripped through the box, cutting wires. Some shorted out, sparking. In seconds, the spray of fuel turned into a spray of flame.

More alarms sounded. Flame engulfed one engine. Thick smoke from burning oil roiled up, filling the engine room.

"I disabled the fire suppression system," Simone said. "We should leave now." She glanced into the control room at the two engineers unconscious on the floor. She handed Teresa the gun. "Hold this." She grabbed the men by their collars and dragged them out. "Go. Up. Shoot anybody you see."

"I have to find Antonia."

"Of course you do."

They made their way down the passage to the steps leading up to the main deck. Two vampire crewmen raced down the steps heading for the engine room. They ignored the intruders. Simone dropped the two mortal engineers at the foot of the steps. Smoke boiled quickly into the passage. Nobody mortal would survive long there. *"Merde."* She dragged the unconscious engineers up and dropped them in the fresh air on the outside deck.

To the east, a gray band shading to blue outlined the horizon. Daylight was coming. Vampires needed to make some decisions.

Other crew ran past, ignoring them.

A low whomp shook the yacht. Smoke billowed through the passages and out the doors. Screams followed. More vampire crew headed toward the engine room. Most mortals ran toward the stern.

"Simone, where would she be?"

Another sound came from above.

"Double *merde*. This way."

They reached the upper deck just in time to see the helicopter lift off the pad, its blades swirling through black smoke. In the front seat Rubicon stared straight ahead. Behind him, Antonia peered out the window at her mother. Teresa, silhouetted by the pad lights, looked up at her. Tears glistened on Antonia's cheeks. Her expression was unreadable. Contempt? Sadness? Her small hand pressed against the window as if waving good-bye, the only clue.

Teresa tapped her chest, pointed at her eyes, pointed at her Antonia. She held up a hand, mirroring her daughter's gesture. The helicopter spun and flew North into the remaining night.

Simone put a supportive arm around Teresa's shoulders. "Tee, we have to get off this boat."

Teresa dragged her gaze from the sky and slumped against her friend. "I don't think I can."

"Yes you can, *mon amie*. And you don't need magic to do it."

She turned Teresa around and pointed at *Mover*, headed straight for them.

Mover

Night Watch drifted dead in the water a mile from shore. What was left of her crew were gathered at the stern with their two launches, all eyes on *Mover*. Lucian stood by on the lower stern deck, rifle held ready, handgun on his hip. Harriet manned the upper deck, similarly armed. Also armed, Harry stood on the bridge wing deck, eyes on Simone and Teresa, waiting amidships. Where the hell was Justine? He tried with little success to ignore the sinking feeling in his gut.

César maneuvered his yacht to approach *Night Watch* on a parallel course from the bow. Half the size of the big boat, *Mover's* wing deck came about even with Night Watch's main deck.

Simone had opened a boarding gate in the rail. César brought his boat to a stop less than a foot away. Harry and César helped an exhausted Teresa climb onboard. Simone jumped without help.

"Where's Justine?"

Simone sighed. Her shoulders drooped. "They wrapped her in chains and threw her overboard. I'm sorry, Harry. There was nothing we could do."

"Overboard? It's seven thousand fucking feet deep here."

"I don't know what it's like underwater, but it wasn't this far out. It was closer to the edge of dark water."

Harry gazed toward shore, as if hoping Justine would pop up and wave.

"She's not dead, Harry. She can't drown. She's tough and resourceful."

"Christ. Antonia? Was she even on there?"

"Oh yeah. Wait until you hear."

"Harry. You ready?" César called.

"Bastards. Hell yes."

Harry picked up a cloth grocery shopping bag tied to a long line. He lowered the bag until it hung at the water line. He tied it off on a *Night Watch* rail stanchion. Then he pulled it up and reached into the bag. "One minute!" He let it down. "Go!"

César hit the throttles. *Mover* surged forward. As they passed the watching crew, Harry yelled, "Better get on those launches."

One of the crew, a vamp, looked over the side, and knew what he was seeing. "Fuckers." He drew his sidearm and fired at *Mover's* bridge, until Lucian and Harriet shot him down.

Mover had cleared the yacht by two hundred feet when the bomb detonated with a bloom of smoke and water. Harry studied the site through binoculars. "About a three foot hole. Ought to take care of the sons-of-bitches. Now, let's figure out where Justine is."

In the Water

Justine felt the water rush past as the chain dragged her down. She kicked and clawed at the water. How much farther down could she go and have any hope of returning to the surface? In the few feet already climbed she had felt the stiffness of her joints and tightness of muscles and skin compressed by hundreds or thousands of feet of water.

During those seconds the chain dragged her down, Justine felt that she was floating down a thin column of light guiding her down and down to the deepest depths. She would lie flat on the bottom with her face looking up to a tiny sparkly spot of light she would eternally yearn for but never reach.

Her fingers slipped over the wall surface, unable to find a handhold. Her feet hit the ledge. The chain slid off her shoulder onto the sand, and snaked over the edge, dragging her feet with it. She scrabbled at the sand, seeking a solid handhold; feet and legs slipped over the edge and dangled over the abyss. Her injured hand found a crack, but couldn't stop her slide to oblivion. Hips and upper body slid over the edge, lubricated by centuries old sand. Her chest constricted, forcing out a small animal whimper of fear.

NO, No, no. She could not drift down through the deep again. She'd go mad, without even a way to find the real death. Her feet scratched for a foothold. Her hands clawed down through the sand for a crack or bump to grab hold of. Her chin scraped the edge. Her teeth ground with effort.

For a moment she considered letting go. Stop struggling. No more worries, no fear, no bad vamps and witches and Oracles watching her every move, no danger…no grief.

No love, no friends, no revenge.

Her fingers found a narrow crevice. Hope flushed all the fear and doubt and rage out of her. Forehead resting on the edge, Justine took a minute to gather herself before cautiously attempting to drag herself out of danger. Her good foot found a tentative toehold. With her left arm spread out on the sand, she managed to pull herself up enough to move her right-hand fingers a few precious inches along the crevice toward the wall. In this way, each move thought through, Justine climbed back onto her ledge.

She wasted no time congratulating herself. Back against the wall, the damned chain pulled up, she felt around until she found the anchor. Without thinking, without allowing any hesitation, she positioned her chained leg on solid rock, raised the anchor over her head, and smashed it down on her heel. And again, and again, again, again, screaming in her mind at the pain and terror and need and desperation that necessitated mutilating herself in cold, lonely darkness.

Slipping the chain off her leg produced one last stab of pain, quickly eased as a wave of relief surged through her body. Then, free, she curled into her shallow nest for a time, her body trembling with growing Hunger and residual fright.

Lying in her sandy depression, Justine gave herself a pep talk. I'm stronger, smarter, braver and more determined than this. If I want to see Harry, Simone, or Teresa again, all I have to do is climb, one step at a time, like climbing a mountain. It's just a damn wall. I can do it, rah rah, blah blah. Besides, Hunger insisted she'd have to feed soon, and the idea of fish blood was not appealing.

Protecting her mangled foot, she began climbing.

Now that she was able to move freely, the pressure on her body again took its toll—joints stiff and painful, strength barely more than mortal.

She climbed.

Once rid of the chain, she thought she might at least have neutral buoyancy. She'd thought that with an occasional push or pull she'd glide easily up the wall to the surface, however far that may be. She quickly realized that without something to hold on to, she drifted down, not up.

She climbed.

She climbed by feel alone. Super vamp vision was no help. She pulled or pushed using irregularities in grooves or cracks in the wall. Occasionally there was an outcropping, sometimes a cluster of them she could stand on, or sit on to rest. It had been a long time, even as a mortal, since she needed to sit and rest. She didn't rest long—she didn't think it was long, anyway.

A few times she dreamt. Like a commercial for the "fresh" feeling of a vaginal spray—her in a bright sundress bounding through a golden field toward Harry, his dazzling white shirt open to his navel, mounted on a brilliant white charger, gleaming in the sun by a lone stately oak tree at the top of a grassy hill rounded like a breast. Pure treacly romance, until she looks behind and her sappy smile turns to a fearful frown because a wall of darkness is behind her, overhanging, dark arms protruding, grabbing, pulling her back into the darkness of deep ocean.

Stilling the racing heart of her dream, Justine climbed on through the dark.

Time still had no meaning, until light arrived. She didn't notice it at first. Much of the climb passed with eyes closed, feeling her way like the blind men and the elephant. When her hand touched something soft instead of hard she jerked back, eyes opening. She saw, on a tiny ledge, a round pale spot in the dark. She saw her hand, just as pale, reach out and touch the spot. Only a thin layer of something, but alive. She looked up, and saw lightness.

New energy propelled her up. She noticed fish, and more and bigger growth, corals, anemones, plants and creatures she'd never seen before. Then she saw something else, and stopped. Divers.

The reef wall off Grand Turk Island was a scuba divers paradise. They came from around the world to dive the vast beauty and variety of the wall. She didn't think seeing a pale-faced woman dressed in black climbing up from the depths without a tank was what they were expecting. The questions that would raise were not ones she wanted to have to answer.

Though blue sky beckoned, Justine allowed herself to sink back. She found a small coral outcropping to sit on. What was she going to do when she did reach the surface? For that matter she didn't know how the sun underwater would affect her. Was the water enough of a filter to protect her? And where was she exactly? Where were Harry and Teresa? Was Simone thrown over, too? She might be a hundred feet away or a thousand.

Now near the surface with mortals in sight, Hunger returned in force. While waiting for the divers to go away she amused herself with different scenarios. She could find a lone diver and drag him down to her lair and feed. Maybe she could swim up to a boat and gorge on the divers as they returned. But she wasn't that kind of vampire.

She wondered if any divers saw her. If they did they probably had a video camera. Everybody seemed to have one. She'd be on YouTube by tonight — the mysterious Grand Turk Mermaid. Probably do wonders for the dive business. They should see the huge whatever it was she saw. That would scare them out of the water.

She didn't know the time of day, though she had the feeling of morning. A quick glance told her the divers were still there all along the top fifty feet of the wall.

Harry was an ever present question. Had he abandoned the search, assumed her lost? How long had she been down? A day, a week? Thinking about their relationship always raised questions, which could be brought down to one—did she really love him? Sitting two hundred feet under the surface with her legs drawn up and head resting on knees the answer, as always, was—yes, damn it. It would be so much better if she didn't, vampire-mortal relationships being as problematic as they were.

Justine dreamed again. She walked on a pristine white sand beach with Harry. She looked really hot all tanned in her bikini and Harry tanned and buff in his board shorts. Palm trees lined the beach, light-green tropical water lapped the sand at their feet. She was filled with that open, giddy feeling that only love can bring. The sun beamed down its warmth from a cotton cloud sky. All was right with the world until she looked at Harry and besides his lovely smile she saw smoke rising from his head, then his shoulders and body. The skin of his face blackened as it blistered and split, leaking flame from the cracks that zigzagged down his body. And all the while he smiled.

Justine jerked awake, mouth stretched open in a silent scream.

Fuck it. She was going up, divers or not.

Cockburn Town

It had been three days since *Night Watch* sank. Twenty three crew survived in the two launches and a large outboard powered inflatable. Mostly mortals, four vampires. There'd been no SOS calls. Only a small audience witnessed the thirty million dollar yacht vanish. The survivors anchored south of the cruise ship dock with the fishing boats and cruising sailboats. That night they went ashore and a plane came and took them away.

Mover's crew buried Marshall at sea and began searching and waiting for Justine to appear. Simone and Lucian had swum down two hundred feet or so, but once into the total blackness they gave it up. Enhanced sight still needs light.

On the third day *Mover* dropped anchor and César and Harriet went ashore into Cockburntown for fresh supplies and a short break from the search and the gloomy atmosphere.

They sat at a table on the patio of a beach bar overlooking Grand Turk Strait. Not speaking, they were alone with their own thoughts, though both thought of Marshall who had been a good guy and at least half the thoughts were of revenge. They sipped their beers and gazed out at the water.

Six tourists, three middle-aged couples, all scuba divers, drank at the next table.

"I'm telling you," one of the men said. "I saw a woman on the wall at least a hundred fifty feet down without a tank. She looked up, saw us, and sank down out of sight. I have a picture."

"Steve, I think you got some bad air."

Harriet and César looked at each other, eyebrows raised, interest piqued.

"Or you ate something bad."

"Come on you guys, look at the picture with an open mind, would ya?"

Steve handed the camera to one of the men.

"It's just a big crab. The shadows make it look like a woman, if that's what you want to see."

One of the women said to Steve's wife, "Now you know what to dress as on your next date night—a mermaid."

Steve took his camera back and stared at the little screen. "There was a woman down there, alive, climbing the damn wall. Laugh all you want, say what you want, I saw what I saw."

César leaned toward the table. "Excuse me, sir. I couldn't help but hear your conversation about the woman. Might I see your photo?"

Steve hesitated a few seconds, then said, "Sure. Maybe you have better eyesight than these old men."

"Thank you." He and Harriet studied the photograph. If one looked at it cold it was unlikely a woman could be picked out. But, if you were looking for a woman and knew what Justine looked like, the pale oval spot with dark shadows behind could easily be a woman climbing the wall.

"Where did you take this?" Harriet asked.

"On the wall, about a half mile south of here. They usually don't take divers down that far because of the currents."

"This morning?"

"Yep."

"What do you think?" César asked her.

Harriet made a face and shrugged.

"What?" Steve asked, eyes wide.

César handed back the camera. "There's a story, not very well known, from the Twenties. Two men were fighting over a woman on a yacht. The woman, Sarah, Sadie, Sally, something like that, was killed accidentally. These were upstanding men and couldn't have the scandal, so they threw the body overboard."

"That's awful," Steve's wife said.

"Sounds like a man thing," another woman commented.

Harriet continued. "Occasionally someone reports...ah, what you saw. A woman in the deep trying to climb out. My father knew a guy who swears he saw her. So..."

"Awesome, Sadie's underwater ghost. Now we have a story to tell."

"We should go back there tomorrow. Maybe she'll still be there."

"She's been there for eighty, ninety years. She probably is still there."

"You guys better be careful. She's probably lonely and will drag one of you down for company."

César and Harriet left as soon as they could.

Harriet slapped the captain on the back. "And a new legend is born."

"Do you think that was really her?" César asked.

"Don't you?"

They confirmed the location with the dive shop. The owner laughed. "I guess we'll have to start a special Sadie's Ghost Tour. Good for business, even if it's all bullshit."

A half hour later *Mover* raised anchor and cruised south with all hands who could live in the sunlight on deck.

In the Water

The wall had an abrupt edge. One second Justine moved easily straight up, the next she stood on a flat expanse of white sand. Her hand had healed by then, but her foot still had some pain if she put pressure on it. The need to feed drove her, though simultaneously sapping her strength.

The ocean surface rippled silver and blue ten feet above her head. An orange sun hung low over the horizon. Arms out, she soaked up the warmth of the surface water. Within minutes she felt the extra warmth of the sun, and relished it.

Now what? Slowly at first, getting the rhythm of it, she walked/swum a good fifty feet away from the edge then angled left toward where she thought the island was. In minutes—time now had meaning—a ten foot diameter coral head came into view, its top maybe five feet from the surface.

Suddenly, gaining the top of the coral and sticking her head above water was the most important task she'd ever had. One leap gained the top. She hesitated a moment, prepared for the full impact of the sun, though it was close to the horizon. Didn't matter. A minute to orient herself and smell air and see clearly was all she wanted.

It took a moment for her eyes to focus on the first pink tinged cloud bottoms and the cerulean sky. She coughed out the seawater that had permeated her lungs and inhaled the fresh salt air, raised her head to feel the breeze on her face and turned her head to hear a seagull's cry. A minute passed, head and arms raised, before she looked for land. Barely visible from her low point of view, a dark smudge on the horizon, the island lay waiting for her. If she wasn't so weak she could swim it before sunset. Maybe walk it just as fast. Then what?

Well, she'd figure that out when she got there. Justine knelt on the coral, thinking. Being underwater felt natural now. Dry land would take a bit of adjustment.

Where were the others? Did Simone survive? Did Teresa get Antonia back? If they were all reunited, then what? Where would they go? There were other girls missing they had information on. What of Rubicon's vamp-mortal breeding program to take over the world?

For more than a moment Justine considered disappearing—somehow making a new life someplace. No more evil vampires or tricky magicians or all-seeing Oracles. Get a second chance, meet some guy, start an internet business and live in a cute house with a fucking picket fence she could only see through a fucking window. Right. As if.

She gave up that pipe dream when she begged Simone to change her into a vampire. The four of them, Teresa, Simone, Harry and her were linked by blood now, an attachment not so casually broken.

One decision was easy, get the hell out of the water. Justine stood up and looked around. A lot of those other decisions were moot. A large yacht approached, cruising along the edge of dark and light water. About where her life was cruising, she thought.

A shake of the head. Focus. *Mover.* At least it survived. Though a large area seemed to be missing paint, and the rail was not as straight as it used to be. There were people on deck with binoculars. Looking for her. They hadn't left. And suddenly she was so very happy, and so very tired. Almost too tired to stand and hold her arms up, and fuck the sun.

They saw her. In minutes the launch headed toward her. A few more minutes and it slowly came right up to her. Simone pulled her straight up, into Harry's arms. He twitched when she hugged him back. He was hurt. Blood scent surrounded him. She pushed him away. Fists clenched, she said, "Harry, I…need to—" She willed her mouth to stay shut as tight as her fists.

Simone moved between them. She held up an open water bottle filled with dark red liquid. "Drink this, *cher.* I think you need it."

Hunger overwhelmed her. Turning away, supported by Harry and Simone, she drank.

"Teresa?" she asked.

"Waiting on board."

Justine had a thousand more questions, but those were for later. Right then, it was all good. Any thoughts of vanishing had disappeared. She thought of asking about Antonia, but had the feeling that subject was far from finished.

EPILOGUE

<u>Jasmine's House</u>

It had been a week since Justine came out of the water. All the stories had been told, what happened where, who did what to whom, what did it all mean? Three days after Justine came aboard *Mover* docked in Port Everglades.

There was a bill.

"It's been taken care of," César told them.

Justine's eyebrows lifted. "By who?"

"The Royal Council of Vampiric Families," César intoned with only a hint of sarcasm.

Simone started; her eyes narrowed and fixed on the captain. "Why would they do that for us?" Simone, and by extension, Justine, was not affiliated with any of the twenty-four vampire families. She liked it that way.

Being a member or associated with one of the families—and most vampires were in one way or another—provided you support and protection. In return, you played by their rules, did the family's work. If someone from another family fucked with you, they fucked with all of them. The Hatfields and McCoys had nothing on vampire feuds, which could last centuries.

Simone was an accidental vampire, made by Stephan Sinakov on a raid of her village in 1648. She should have been fully dead, but she survived on her own. She'd been friends with Darius Rubinio, master of the Rubinio Family, until they had stolen a bit too much of the other families' money and were wiped out. Darius, now Darwin, was one of the few to escape. Recruited or hunted, Simone had survived and remained free to live by her own rules. César shrugged. Vampire business was vampire business, though the idea of an army of vamp-mortals was a bit unsettling. "Seems the Council has some interest in Rubicon's ambitions."

Blair and Paula drove them north to Claire in Delray Beach. She'd fixed up Harry and Teresa with new stitches, pills and antibiotics. Only once did she ask who was doing something stupid. Claire thanked Justine and Simone for killing Sinakov, then asked if she could examine them, which she did with great enthusiasm. She also met Blair with great enthusiasm, them both being single and in on a strange secret.

"Good thing she's a nurse," Paula whispered to Simone. "She don't know the skanks he hangs with."

Now they had all, including Claire, congregated at Jasmine and Lenny's house by Fort Myers. Some stories were retold, new questions asked. Simone had had a long conversation with Darwin, who was pleased to hear of Sinakov's real death.

Justine and Harry had some time together. Cold had seeped into her bones and she couldn't get enough of his warmth. She hadn't realized how much she missed him until she lay safe and warm in his arms. She wished the trip back to Florida would never end, knowing it would.

On the yacht back Justine and Teresa had some time together. They didn't say much, just sat in the shade, sometimes holding hands as best friends do. Teresa cried. Justine wanted to cry with her. She felt the heat in her eyes and the heartbreak in her chest, but the tears never came. The vampire's burden.

On a cool night they all gathered in the living room, and the one question Justine, Simone, Teresa and Harry had avoided so far finally had to be asked—what now?

They had information on four other girls sold by the Sinakov family around the same time, the buyers and their preferences and locations. Harry had to go back to work, or quit. It was decided, reluctantly by Harry and Justine, that his access to information sources was too important to lose.

They discussed what Tito had meant by magic helping to produce a baby. They agreed that the power of magic protected Antonia's eggs from the power of the vampire sperm. They couldn't agree on what Rubicon had in mind, except that it would not be good.

Jasmine came in after taking a phone call in a sound proof room. She stood behind her son's chair and frowned at the floor. Simone and Justine traded glances. They didn't like that they couldn't hear the phone call—and they'd tried—and they didn't like that frown.

"What?" Justine asked.

"The Council of Families…Well, a group from within the Council, is sending a representative to discuss Rubicon. They want us to stay here until he or she arrives."

"Which will be...?"

Her frown deepened, followed by a shrug, "Tomorrow?"

Teresa spoke up, "So we wait while Antonia..."

"You need to rest. You all do. Honey, when we have some solid information on where your baby is, we'll let you know. Right now, none of you are in any condition to go after anybody."

Understandably, Teresa wanted to go after Antonia. Jasmine had made inquiries of the Vampire Families through her worldwide network. Rubicon and his entourage had gone to ground and nobody had any creditable information where. Until they had more information, Justine, Simone and, reluctantly, Teresa had agreed to go after the other girls. Maybe they could bring some joy to another girl's mother.

Simone studied Jasmine's bunched up expression. "You are bothered by this visit from the Council. Why?"

"It's...unusual."

Paula didn't care what the Council did and went outside for a cigarette. Not having to worry about lung cancer made smoking all the better, though she still had to go outside. The night was cool and quiet, with a moon and stars and a gentle breeze. Romantic, if you gave a crap about that stuff.

Half way through her cigarette a sound came to her. Faint yet, even when she concentrated on it. Low down, coming her way. Just a helicopter. There were plenty of them around, police, news, traffic, sightseeing, military. Something about it, though, raised the hairs on her neck. From the side of the house Paula stared in the direction of the sound. No lights, yet coming right at her. Shit. She ran for the back doors.

Inside, Teresa, who had said little, jumped up, eyes wide, searching for the source of the danger she felt was close. "Something's coming," she said a few seconds before Paula burst through the sliding glass doors and yelled, "Helicopter coming, and it ain't good."

Jasmine, too, jumped up. "Rubicon. Lenny, open the weapons closet. Everybody, grab something and get out."

Thirty seconds later the first missile ripped through the house, blasting the patio sliding door outward where spinning glass shrapnel instantly cut down Lenny and Jasmine. A large shard sliced through half of Paula's arm. Simone threw Teresa down and covered her with her body. Justine shielded Harry behind a palm tree. Flames erupted from the blown out middle of the house.

A second missile rode a trail of flame into the house.

A section of roof spun up crazily and crashed down to crush Blair's leg.

As a flaming wall with nothing left to hold it up toppled toward Teresa and Simone, Teresa raised a hand. A small dome of shimmering power spread from her fingertips.

Justine lifted the wall off them, allowing Simone to crawl out, dragging Teresa with her. Together they pulled Blair free.

The helicopter, a veteran Vietnam era HUEY, slid around the smoke to hover sideways beside the yard. Its downdraft fanned the fire and sent flaming debris skittering about the yard. Antique or not, the man behind the .50 caliber machine gun meant business.

Simone grabbed up a pump shotgun Lenny had said was loaded with deer shot, thumb-sized slugs that would knock a big vamp down for a long while. As fifty caliber rounds dug a divot trail through the grass she fired three times. A spider web hole appeared in the windshield.

Justine lifted a small machine gun—she didn't know or care what make it was—and sprayed the interior through the open side door. The gunner jerked as he caught his share of slugs and slumped on the floor.

Simone's remaining slugs penetrated the engine cowling. The engine sound changed slightly. A puff of black smoke shot out of the exhaust and the engine coughed. The chopper lurched, dropped, lifted, and disappeared from sight. About half a minute later the whup-whup of the rotors stopped and a distant crump was heard over the roar of the flames.

"We must leave here now," Simone insisted. "This will not have gone unnoticed."

"Absolutely," Harry said, struggling to stand. "Not more than five minutes." He tried to move but one leg wouldn't hold him.

Justine caught him. "You just can't help but get yourself hurt, can you?"

"You set a bad example."

Blood dripped from Claire's chin while she worked on Blair's leg. "Leg's gone," she answered the obvious question. "The rest is minor. I can stabilize him, but he really needs a hospital."

"There will be questions we don't want asked," Simone said.

Paula asked, "Will he make it back to Fort Lauderdale? I know people who don't ask questions."

Claire puffed out a deep breath. "He'll need blood, surgery."

"Gotcha covered."

"Jasmine and Lenny are dead. We have to go," Justine insisted. "Teresa, can you shield us from their Oracles?"

"Gotcha covered. *Vamos!*"

Two minutes later Jasmine's van sped away from the burning house. From the driver's seat Justine said, "Rubicon will really be looking for us now. Where the hell do we go?"

Teresa said, "I vote we go kick Rubicon's ass."

Nobody voted against her.

Simone said, "I vote we make sure this was not the visit from the Council we were waiting for."

Nobody voted against her, either.

The End